Praise for *New York Times* bestselling author

P.C. CAST

"Watch out for this author, she's sure to rise to the top
of the romantic fantasy genre."
—*Rendezvous*

"With heaps of conflict and well-developed drama,
Divine by Choice is a real treat."
—*Book Loons*

"Cast is a fabulous storyteller. Her narrative and ideas are
spot on. Shannon may be a smart and sassy heroine, quick with
the one-liners, but her heartache and conflict make her vulnerable
and sympathetic. Partholon is a fascinating world fully realized
with well-drawn characters."
—*Fresh Fiction* on *Divine by Choice*

"The seductive power of darkness is at the core of this
cautionary tale of mothers and daughters. This is a very
welcome addition to the series."
—*Romantic Times BOOKreviews* on *Divine by Blood*

"*Brighid's Quest* is an evocative and haunting tale of prejudice,
grief, courage and redemption. Cuchulainn and Brighid's acceptance
of their 'impossible' relationship will determine their destiny.
P.C. Cast's spellbinding saga of vengeance, madness,
forgiveness, and healing touches the soul."
—*Fallen Angel*

"Superlative world-building and a modern, sarcastic heroine
make this an accessible and delightful read. The first of this series,
Goddess by Mistake, earned a 4 ½-star rating; the updated reissue,
Divine by Mistake, is even better. While *Divine by Choice* can stand
on its own, pick up both of these treasures for your keeper shelf."
—*Romantic Times BOOKreviews* [Top Pick]

The Partholon series
by *New York Times* bestselling author

P.C. CAST

Divine by Mistake
Divine by Choice
Divine by Blood

And coming in 2010
from Harlequin Teen:

Elphame's Choice
Brighid's Quest

DIVINE BY MISTAKE

P.C. CAST

LUNA™

www.LUNA-Books.com

LUNA™

Recycling programs
for this product may
not exist in your area.

DIVINE BY MISTAKE

ISBN-13: 978-0-373-80316-3

Copyright © 2006 by P.C. Cast

Originally published as GODDESS BY MISTAKE
by Hawk Publishing Group in 2001

Copyright © 2001 by P.C. Cast

First mass-market printing: September 2006

First trade printing: August 2009

Author photo by Kim Donor

www.LUNA-Books.com

Printed in U.S.A.

Dear Fabulous Reader,

I love this book! It's a planned love. When I sat down to write *Divine by Mistake*—long before I wrote my House of Night series—I told myself I was going to write The Book I'd Most Want to Read, and that's exactly what I did. I created a heroine who made me laugh and sent her to a world straight out of my favorite daydreams, to live a fantasy filled with wine and sex, adventure and true love, and all of that is great fun.

But I have to be honest with you. The most important reason I love this book so much is that in it I created ClanFintan, who will eternally be my favorite hero. Of course he's strong and handsome and sexy—those qualities are part of the hero blueprint—but ClanFintan has two other things going for him that make him stand out from the hero pack. First, his sense of integrity is deeply moving. His word is more than his promise; his word is *who he is.* Second (and this might be what I like most about him) is the sense of fun and innocence that awakens within him when this otherwise very worldly and tough guy falls in love with my heroine. His joy at discovering love will always keep him close to my heart.

So curl up with a glass of your favorite wine and enter Partholon, but beware! Like me, you may never want to leave....

Happy reading,

P.C. Cast

ACKNOWLEDGMENTS

I want to warmly thank the very vocal, very enthusiastic fans of the original *Goddess by Mistake*. You made my career possible. Thank you thank you thank you.

I would also like to acknowledge the review staff at *Romantic Times BOOKreviews*. Y'all "discovered" me with a 4 ½ Stars Top Pick Gold review when this was just an obscure small-press book. Wow! I'll never forget the excitement of that very first review. Thank you.

Thank you to my friend and agent, Meredith Bernstein, who read this book overnight and knew we had something special.

And it's with gratitude that I acknowledge the fabulous Stacy Boyd, who really "gets" Partholon and Shannon, which made the editorial process totally unpainful.

DIVINE BY MISTAKE

This book is dedicated to my father, Dick L. Cast
The Old Coach.
Eternally my Mighty Mouse.

PART ONE

1

Finally, on my way. My Mustang felt sweet as it zipped down the nearly empty highway. Why is it that cars seem to drive best when they're freshly washed? Leaning down, I popped a CD into the player, skipped forward to track 6 and began singing at the top of my very tone-deaf lungs with Eponine about the futility of love. As the next song keyed up, I swung around a slow-moving Chevy and yelled, "God, I love being a teacher!"

It was the first day of June, and the summer stretched before me, pristine and virginal.

"All those days of sleeping in to go!"

Just saying it aloud made me happy. In my ten years of teaching I've noticed that teachers tend to have a bad habit of talking to themselves. I hypothesize that this is because we talk for a living, and we feel safe speaking our feelings aloud. Or it could be that most of us, especially the high school teacher variety, are just weird as shit.

Only the slightly insane would choose a career teaching teenagers. I can just see my best girlfriend Suzanna's face screw up and the involuntary shudder move down her spine as I relate the latest trials and tribulations of the high school English classroom.

"God, Sha, they're so…so…*hormone filled*. Eew!"

Suzanna is a typical college professor snob, but I love her anyway. She just doesn't appreciate the many and varied opportunities for humorous interludes that teenagers provide on a daily basis.

Jean Valjean's dynamic tenor interrupted my musings, bringing me back to Oklahoma I–44 East and June 1.

"Yep, this is it—the life of a high school English teacher with a sense of humor. Doomed to having no money but plenty of comedic fodder. Oh, crap, there's my exit!"

Luckily my little Mustang could take the hard, fast right onto US–412. The sign said Locust Grove 22 miles. I drove half with my knee and half with my hand while I fumbled to unfold the auction flyer that held my written directions. Somewhere about midway between Locust Grove (what an awful name for a town) and Siloam Springs there should be a big sign that pointed to a side road till another sign, another side road, and so forth, until I came to the Unique Estate Auction—Unusual Items—All Offers Considered—All Must Go.

"Well, I certainly like weird old stuff. And I really like weird old cheap stuff."

My students say my classroom is like a bizarre time warp. My walls and cabinets are filled with everything from prints by Waterhouse to posters of Mighty Mouse and hanging *Star Trek Enterprise* models, along with an almost scary number of wind chimes (they're good chi).

And that's just my classroom. They should see my condo. Guess they really wouldn't be surprised. Except at home I'm a neat freak. My classroom is always in a perpetual state of disarray. I can't seem to find anything if everything is found. Whatever the hell that means.

"I've got to stop cussing!" Saying it out loud would, hopefully, reinforce the idea. Kind of a twist on the Pavlov's dog theory. I keep saying it; it will begin to happen.

"I can't take you today, Javert." Flick! Off went *Les Misérables*. On goes the jazz station out of Tulsa. It's cool that I could pick it up way out in the boonies.

The sign read Locust Grove City Limits. So I slowed down, blinked, and the town was gone. Well, maybe it was nominally bigger than a blink. And I stayed slowed down. Time to stop and smell the green of Green Country. Oklahoma in early summer is an amazing display of color and texture. I went to college at the University of Illinois, and it always annoyed me that people talked about Oklahoma like it was a red dust bowl. Or some black-and-white scene of misery from *The Grapes of Wrath*. When I tried to tell the college gang that Oklahoma was really known as "Green Country" they would scoff and look at me as if they thought I'd eaten too many tumbleweeds or punched too many cows.

I passed through the tiny town of Leach (another unfortunate name) and topped a rise in the road. Oklahoma stretched before me, suddenly looking untamed in its beauty. I like to imagine a time when these roads were just paths, and civilization hadn't been so sure of itself. It must have been exciting to be alive then— not exciting like facing the principal after he has just heard from a parent who is upset about me calling Guinevere a slut—but exciting in a rugged, perhaps-we-won't-bathe-or-brush-our-teeth and we-kill-our-own-food-and-tote-our-own-water kind of way. Ugh. On second thought… It's delicious to dream about the days of cowboys or knights or dragons, and I will admit to an obsession with poets of the Romantic era and literature set, well, way back when (technical English teacher term). But reality reminds me that in actuality they did without penicillin and Crest. As my kids would say, "What's up with that?"

"There it is! Turnoff number one, as in a road sign, not to be confused with the blind date who comes to your door in navy blue double-knit trousers and a receding hairline."

UNIQUE ESTATE AUCTION AHEAD and an arrow, which pointed down a side road to my left.

This road was much less traveled (poetic pun intended). Kind of a sorry little two-laner with potholes and deep gravel shoulders. But it twisted and rolled in a pretty way, and "To Grandmother's house we go" hummed through my mind. I tried in vain to remember the rest of the song for the next several miles.

UNIQUE ESTATE AUCTION AHEAD and another arrow. Another side-side road. This one more gravel, less two lane, than the other. Well, maybe the out-of-the-wayness of the estate would serve to dissuade the antique dealers, whom I considered the bane of every broke auction-goer. The jazz station faded out, which was actually fine because the Grandmother's House song had also faded from my internal radio— and been replaced with the theme to *The Beverly Hillbillies* (these words I did remember all of, which I found vaguely disturbing).

Speaking of hillbillies, I hadn't seen many houses. Hmmm…maybe the "estate" was really an old ranch house, smack in the middle of what used to be a real ranch owned by some Bonanzaesque rich folks. Now they've all died off and the land would be subdivided into neat little housing divisions so upper-middle-class folks could commute to…well, wherever. I call that job security for me. Upper-middle-class folks always have the prerequisite 2.5 kids, plus an additional 1.5 kid (from a previous marriage). And those kids gotta pass English to graduate from high school. God bless America.

Over a crook and a rise in the "road" loomed what I had been imagining as an old ranch house. "Holy shit! It's the House of Usher!" (Summer was definitely not the time to work on the cussing thing.) I slowed. Yep—there was another sign: UNIQUE ESTATE AUCTION, planted next to the gravel trail leading to the estate. A few cars, but mostly trucks (it *is* Oklahoma) were parked on what at one time was obviously a beautifully maintained front…I don't know…what the hell do you call something like that…it stretched on and on…yard seemed too simple a word. Grounds. That sounded better. Lots of grass. The drive was lined with *big* trees, as in *Gone with the Wind,* minus the weeping moss.

I realized I was gawking because an old guy dressed in black slacks and a high-necked white cotton shirt was waving me in with one of those handheld orange flashlight things, and his face had an irritated "stop gawking and drive, lady" look on it. As I pulled up next to him, he motioned for me to roll my window down.

"Afternoon, miss." He bent slightly at the waist and peered into my window. A fetid rush of air brought his words into my air-conditioned interior and killed my initial joy at being called "miss," which is definitely younger sounding than "ma'am." He was taller than I first thought, and his face was heavily lined, as if he had worked outside in the elements most of his life, but his complexion was a sickly, sallow color.

Good God! It was the daddy from *Children of the Corn.*

"Afternoon. Sure is warm today." I tried to be pleasant.

"Yes, miss." Ugh—that *smell* again. "Please pull forward onto The Green. The auction will begin promptly at two."

"Uh, thanks." I tried to smile as I rolled the window up and moved to follow his pointed directions. What was that smell? Like something dead. Well, he was awfully pale; perhaps he wasn't well. That would account for the smell and the fact that he was wearing long sleeves in June, and I was a seriously hateful bitch to call the poor old guy *Children of the Corn's* daddy. And the front yard is called The Green. Learn something new every day! I said to myself with a grimace. Clichés are the bane of educated mankind.

Before I turned off the car, I took my required several minutes (a man once told me he could always tell how attractive a woman was by how long it took her to get out of a car—I try to take a longgg time) to reapply my lipstick. I also took a minute to scope out the house. Scratch that—mansion.

My first impression held. This place seriously conjured images of Poe and Hawthorne. It was humongous, in a sprawling, Victorian-type of way. I'm usually drawn to unusual old homes, but not so with this one. I tipped my sunglasses down my nose to get a better view. It looked odd. It took a moment to figure out why, then it hit me—it looked as if it had been built in several different parts. The basic building was roughly a huge square, but added on to this square were two different porches, one rectangular with steps leading up to the entrance in a grandiose, sweeping manner. Not twenty feet down from the first porch was a second, rounded gazebo-like structure just, well, stuck on to the front of the building, complete with latticework and gnarly-looking roses. A large turret room was attached to one side of the building, like a cancerous growth, and a slope-roofed wing emerged from the opposite end of the structure. The whole thing was painted an awful shade of gray, and it was cracked and crinkled, like an old smoker's skin.

"There should really be some *unique* items to be had here." Muttering to myself, I got ready to tear my eyes away from Usher's abode when a shiver tickled down my spine. A thick cloud passed in front of the sun and the "walking on my grave" feeling hit me like a bad dream. *Is it late? It seems to me that the light darkens.* My English teacher mind plucked the quote from *Medea.* Greek tragedy, replete with revenge, betrayal and death. Seemed, in an inopportune way, appropriate.

2

"Jeesh, get a grip, Parker!" Ridiculous—I needed to shake out of my gruesome mode, and get into my junk-shopping mode.

Oklahoma heat was waiting to embrace me with its humid arms as I stepped out of the car and clicked the lock on my keypad. Set up around the side of the house was a large table with a line of assorted auction-goers milling about it. I figured that was the sign-in table and headed that way, keeping part of my attention on the various piles of "stuff" that began stretching from the side yard around and disappearing into the rear of the grounds. My palms were already all atingle at the thought of digging through those heaped boxes. But first the sign-in.

"Whew! I should've put this hunk of hair up in a ponytail!" I was making neighborly small talk with the matron in front of me in line.

"Yup." She fanned herself with one of the UNIQUE AUCTION flyers, and her eyes slid from my already frizzing and sweaty hair, down past my white silk tank top, which slid just over the waist of my very hip (and short) khaki Gap skirt, to my long (and very bare) legs. "Ugf." She made a sound like a hen expelling an egg, and I guessed that was the end of my attempt at neighborly conversation.

"This place sure looks like it should have some interesting stuff for sale." I valiantly tried a second attempt at conversing, this time with the receding hairline behind me.

"Yes, I couldn't agree more." The hairline fidgeted, blinking sweat out of his eyes. "I heard that they will be auctioning several pieces of Depression Era glass, and just knew I had to make the trek. I find American glasswork fascinating, don't you?" By this time his squinty little eyes had found my cleavage, and it was obvious that glass wasn't all he found fascinating.

"Mmm, hmm, glass is cool." I stepped forward. It was the matron's turn to get her ticket, but she was so busy watching the hairline watch me that she could hardly give the registrar her info.

"Actually," he leaned way into my Personal Space, "I'm in the middle of editing a wonderfully informative coffee table book on the origins of Depression Era art and how to distinguish the difference between authentic pieces and facsimiles."

"Oh, that's, um, nice." He was still in my Personal Space and I tried inching forward, obviously crowding the matron, who was still standing in line pinning her auction number to her Depression Era bosom.

"I would be happy to offer you my expertise if you find any pieces you are interested in bidding on. I would hate to see such a *lovely* young lady taken advantage of...." His voice cracked and he nervously dabbed the sweat off his upper lip with a folded handkerchief. I noticed the yellowed stains shadowing his pits. Guess that button-down oxford was just a little too warm for this trek.

"I'll be sure to let you know if I need you." My turn, thank God.

"Name, please." I could sense hairline's ears growing to catch the answer.

"Shannon Parker."

"Ms. Parker, your number is 074. Please fill out your address next to the 074 slot. Keep the number with you at all times, the auctioneer will refer to your number if you purchase an item. When you have made all your purchases, simply give the cashier your number and she will present you with your bill."

Typical auction directions—I grabbed my number and fled before Hairline turned into a sticky booger. I will never understand why short men are attracted to me. I'm not an Amazon, but in flat feet I stand five foot seven, and I love high heels so I'm rarely in flat feet. My height aside, I am definitely not a small woman. Don't get me wrong, I'm not *big*. I work out like a fiend, but I always seem to carry around about five to ten pounds more than I wish I did. I'm not the lean, lanky, anorexic type that's so "in" today—I'm the voluptuous, chesty, hippy, leggy type. And I feel ridiculous around small men; I always imagine that I could probably beat them up, which makes me totally disinterested in anything else coming up. Give me a man the size of John Wayne and I melt like a Popsicle in a warm mouth. Unfortunately, my love life is as dead as the Duke.

The bulk of the auction was behind the house in what once must have been gorgeously landscaped gardens. Smack in the center stood a crumbling fountain complete with a naked nymph. The auction lots were in a rough semicircle around the fountain—the open end of the circle pointed toward several pieces of farm equipment. Billy Joe Bobs and Bubba Bo Bobs were clustered in groups amidst the equipment, obviously in a feeding frenzy. Carried on the wind, I could overhear the Oklahoma melodies of "y'all" and "yup." One of them had a piece of straw stuck in a gap between his front teeth. Really, I'm not making it up.

The other items were grouped in lots, and upon closer inspection it was obvious that someone had been meticulous in setting them out. Neatly arranged together were pieces of like furniture (bedroom sets, dinettes, ornate chairs, etc.) in one area, and tables filled with lamps, fixtures, sconces and crystal in another. (I noticed Mr. Receding Hairline making a beeline for that particular table.) Knickknacks in boxes marked with lot numbers were spaced so that customers could paw through them without maiming each other, and artwork was displayed tastefully on folding tables and easels.

The art was where I gravitated. I couldn't help sending a covetous glance in the direction of the furniture, but a glance was all it took for me to be fairly certain that a schoolteacher's salary wouldn't allow for any purchases in that area.

The soon-to-be ex-owner's tastes were certainly consistent. All of the paintings displayed on the easels had a like theme—mythology. I wandered from watercolor to acrylic to oil. Everything from Venus's birth to a great lithograph of Wotan's farewell to Brunhilde.

"Ohmygod, that's hilarious!" I couldn't help nudging the Garage Sale Queen standing next to me and pointing to a wonderful full-color print of a huge fiery dragon roaring flame at a blond female warrior on a plunging white horse. She was deflecting the fire with a shield and brandishing a sword. I couldn't make out the artist's name, but the title painted on the bottom of the print read, Stamp Out Forest Fires.

"I have to have this one." I was still chuckling.

"Well, it's kinda strange." The Garage Sale Queen's nasally twang interrupted my smile.

"Yep. But I like to think of it as not normal, versus simply strange." She gave me one of those sheepy, duh looks and started over to the household items section. I sighed and opened my little notebook to write, "Lot #12—dragon print."

A closer look at the frame made me wonder if I had a chance of affording it, but maybe everyone would think it was "kinda strange" and I would be the only bidder.

Many of the other paintings were interesting, but I had already decided to focus my financial energy on a single print, and maybe a small vase or sculpture or some such "strange" knickknack. Behind the paintings were the lots filled with artsy stuff. Tables held individual pieces, along with boxes of variously grouped odds and ends. Again, there seemed to be a theme. Sculptures were miniature reproductions of stuff that looked very Greek or Roman, and, well, very naked.

This would be fun.

Three male statuettes were placed on one table. They each stood about two feet high. I paused and gave each the respectful, proper attention they seemed to deserve, while trying not to ogle as I read the identification and lot tags: Lot #17 Statuette of Zeus, Thunderbolt at the Ready (very nude—actually naked, and he looked very, um, *ready*).

"Sorry, sweetie. Can't take you home—too kinky." I tweaked his thunderbolt.

Lot #18, Statuette of Hellenistic Ruler, possibly Demetrios I of Syria. Demetrios was a large, muscular, naked man. Very large.

"Oh, baby, wish you were Galatea and I was your enamored sculptor." I patted his cheeks and giggled, while I looked around to make sure I wasn't causing a stir.

Lot #19, Statuette of Etruscan Warrior. Too skinny for my tastes—only two things stuck out about the statuette: his weapon, and, um, his *weapon*.

"Bye-bye, boys. It's just so…well…hard to leave you." I chortled at my own pun and moved to the next table, which was filled with about half a dozen large vases. My gaze drifted over the elegant urns…

And the world stopped. Suddenly, and totally, the day stood still. The breeze died. Sounds ceased. I didn't feel the heat. My breath stopped. My vision tunneled until my awareness was completely filled by the vase.

"Oops, sorry. Didn't mean to bump ya." Breath rushed into my lungs and the world started again as a kind man grabbed my elbow to steady me.

"That's okay." I sucked air and attempted a smile.

"Guess I wasn't looking where I was going. Almost ran ya over."

"I'm fine now. No harm done."

He looked at me like he wasn't sure, but nodded and went on his way.

I brushed a trembling hand through my hair. What was going on? What happened? I was looking at the vases and...

My attention turned back to the pottery table, and my eyes were immediately drawn to the last of the vases. My feet were moving toward it before I told them to go. My trembling hand reached out to touch the lot identification tag. It read: Lot #25, Reproduction—Celtic vase, original stood over graves in Scottish cemetery—Scene in color represents supplications being made to the High Priestess of Epona, Celtic Horse Goddess.

My vision was blurred and my eyes felt strangely hot as I looked back at the vase. Blinking my vision clear, I studied it, attempting to ignore how strange I was feeling.

The vase was a couple of feet tall and shaped like the base of a lamp. A curved handle balanced off one side. The top was open with a gracefully ridged circumference. But it wasn't the shape or size that drew me; it was the scene painted into the pottery, stretching from one side all the way around. The background color was black, which made the scene seem to jump out with the other colors all highlighted in golds and creams.

A woman reclined on some type of cushioned lounge chair. Her back was to the viewer, so all that could be seen of her was the curve of her waist, one outstretched arm with which she motioned regally to the supplicants on their knees before her and the cascade of her hair.

"It's like my hair." I didn't realize I had spoken aloud until I heard the words. But her hair was like mine, only longer. The same red-gold, the same wavy semi-curls that never wanted to stay put. My finger crept forward of its own accord and I found myself touching the vase, transfixed.

"Oh!" It felt hot! I yanked my finger back where it belonged.

"I didn't know you were interested in pottery." Mr. Receding Hairline squinted up at me. "I am actually quite knowledgeable about several categories of Early American pottery." He licked his lips.

"Well, I'm not really interested in Early American pottery." Hairline's reappearance into my Personal Space had served to dash cold water on whatever weird feelings I had been experiencing. "It's way too Southwest for me. I'm more of a Greek/Roman-esque kind of girl."

"Oh, I see. What a fascinating little piece you were admiring." He reached his sweaty hands out, and in a jumpy, cockroach-like movement he lifted the vase, turning it upside down to peer at the bottom. I observed him for any signs of weirdness, but he just kept on being his normal, nerdy self.

"Um, you don't notice anything, well, *odd* about that vase, do you?"

"No. It's a rather well-made reproduction, but I don't detect anything odd about Epona or the urn. What do you mean?" He put the vase down and dabbed at his upper lip with a damp handkerchief.

"Well, it seemed to feel a little, I don't know, hot, when I touched it." I stared into his eyes, wondering if my neurotic breakdown was obvious.

"Might I suggest—" he leaned even farther into my Personal Space, practically resting his pointy nose on my cleavage "—that the warmth may have been generated by your own generous body heat?"

He was almost salivating. Ugh.

"You know, you might be right," I purred. He stopped breathing and licked his lips again. I whispered, "I think I have been running a low-grade fever. Just can't seem to get rid of this nasty yeast infection. And it sure is sticky in this heat." I smiled and squirmed a little.

"Goodness. Well, my goodness." Hairline quickly receded from my Personal Space. I smiled and followed. He continued backing up. "I feel that I had better go back to my Depression Era glass lots, I certainly want to be there to open the bidding. Good luck to you." He turned and scuttled away.

Guys are such a pain in the ass. But really easy to get rid of, just call into play the dreaded Female Problem card and watch them freak out. I like to think it's just one small way God lets us get even. I mean, we *do* have to give birth.

"Now what's up with this damn vase?" It was just too *Dark Shadows* for words. Blurred vision—loss of breath—hot pottery—same hair. Oh, please, I was probably just having a premature hot flash (twenty years early—okay, *fifteen* years early, at least). So, I decided I'd simply confront the source. The Dreaded Mystery Vase/Urn/Friggin Pot.

It sat innocently enough just where Receding had left it, vaguely moist spots glistening where his sweaty little fingers had smudged the glossy surface. I took a breath. A deep breath. It certainly was an intriguing-looking pot. I squinted and bent to get a closer look, careful not to touch it. The Priestess did have hair that looked like mine, only longer. Her right arm was draped in a creamy, gauzy white cloth, and there was a definite grace and beauty about the way it was stretched, palm held up and forward, slightly tilted. She seemed gracious in her acceptance of the offered gifts from the kneeling supplicants. A rich-looking gold armlet snaked around her bicep, and golden bracelets adorned her wrist. She wore no rings, but the back of her hand seemed to be decorated with a design—

"Oh, God!" My own hand flew to my mouth to stifle my screech. I felt a sinking in the pit of my stomach, and all of a sudden it was again difficult to catch my breath. Because it wasn't a tattoo or a jewel that decorated the back side of her hand. It was a scar. A scar from a third-degree burn. I knew because my right hand was "decorated" with the exact mark.

3

"Ladies and gentlemen, the auction will now begin. Please make your way to Lot #1, directly east of the fountain. We will open this afternoon with bedroom and living-room furnishings…"

I could hear the auctioneer droning in the background as opening bids were taken for Lot #1—Victorian reproduction oak six-piece bedroom set, but the pot captivated my attention. Along with other stragglers, I remained by the item of my choice, waiting for the auction to come to me. With a shaking hand I dug into the black depths of my purse and fished out a wadded-up, aged Kleenex. Slowly, I reached toward the pot and wiped off all the smudges left by the Receding Nerd. Maybe it was just a trick of sweat and the light. I blinked hard and looked back at the priestess's hand. Then I looked at my own.

The familiar burn scar was, indeed, there—and had been since I was a four-year-old and had precociously thought I could help Grandma boil water for macaroni faster by shaking the handle of the pot. Of course, boiling water had painfully poured onto my little hand, leaving a funny-looking scar that resembled a star. Thirty-one years later the raised tissue still evoked comments from friends and strangers. And the lady on the pot had the same scar tissue?

Impossible. Especially in a reproduction of an ancient Celtic urn.

Yet there it was, in all of its hair-looks-like-mine-hand-has-my-scar-and-makes-me-feel-like-I'm-having-a-nervous-break-down glory.

"I need a drink." Understatement of the year. A glance toward the auctioneer told me they were only on Lot #7 (reproduction of Louis XIV armoire—bidding was fast and furious). I had time to find the refreshment stand and get a grip on myself before they got near the artsy stuff. Needless to say, I wouldn't be bidding on Lot #25; the cool dragon print would have to go home with someone else. The pot was where my money and my energy had to be focused.

Strangely enough, I noticed that as soon as I got away from the pottery table I began feeling normal again. No hot flashes, no trouble breathing, definitely no "time is suddenly freezing" moments. The makeshift refreshment stand was situated near the farm equipment. They had cold drinks, coffee and evil-looking hot dogs for sale. I ordered a "diet anything" and took my time sipping, wandering slowly back toward the pottery.

I have always had a great imagination. I love fantasy and make-believe. Hell, I'm a friggin English teacher—I actually read. For pleasure, as shocking as that seems to be to some people. But I have always known the difference between fantasy and reality—even relished the difference.

So, what in the hell was going on with me today? What was up with the strange feelings? And why did the woman on that pot look like me?! I pinched myself, and it hurt. So I wasn't having one of my ultravivid weird dreams that seem real.

I meandered back to the pottery area, and instantly my stomach tightened. It was utterly bizarre. I should buy the damn dragon print, get in my car, go home and drink a medicinal bottle of Merlot. All this ran through my mind as my legs carried me straight back to the pot.

"Friggin thing still looks like me."

"It is rather odd, is it not, miss?" The skeletal guy from the entrance stood behind the pottery table. He reached out and let his hand slide slowly over the pot, pausing briefly on the priestess's hair, then tracing the line of her arm with his finger.

"So you noticed it, too." My eyes narrowed and he pulled his bony hand away from my pot.

"Yes, miss. I noticed your hair when you drove in. Quite a nice color to see today—too many young women seem to want to ruin their hair by dying it unnatural colors: burgundy, yellow, black. And cutting it short. So, yours stands out." His tone was harmless enough, but his eyes had an intensity that suddenly made me feel uncomfortable. And even across the table I could smell his nasty breath.

"Well, it's been a surprise for me, actually, kind of a shock." I watched him. His attention kept leaving me and refocusing on the pot with an almost sexual intensity. And he kept touching it. A lot.

"Probably Fate telling you that you must buy it." He turned that unnatural gaze back to me. "This urn must not go home with anyone else."

That made me laugh. "I hope Fate knows to keep the bidding within a teacher's price range."

"She does." With that cryptic remark he caressed the pot one last time and glided away.

Damn, that guy was strange. More like a talkative Lurch than *Children of the Corn*'s daddy, though.

The auction was moving quickly and the bidding was beginning for the statuettes. Seems several people were interested in "the boys." Can't say that I blamed them. I stepped into the group around the mobile auctioneer's platform as it was being wheeled into position behind the table. Bidding began at fifty dollars for Zeus, but five people quickly raised that fifty to one-fifty. Finally it sold to a solid-looking woman for one hundred seventy-five dollars. Not bad. The Syrian got more interest (must have been the muscles). Bidding quickly went from the opening bid of fifty dollars to three-fifty. I was beginning to worry about the price range.

The Syrian went for four hundred fifty dollars. A bad sign. I had budgeted two hundred dollars for my auction outing today. I could scrape together another fifty, but above that was beyond my limited means.

The skinny warrior went for four hundred dollars even.

My stomach clenched again as I drifted with the crowd over to the pottery table and listened to the auctioneer talk about what excellent museum-quality reproductions of Greco-Roman and Celtic pottery were exemplified in the next six lots. Couldn't he please just shut up? I pushed through the crowd, ignoring the disconcerting feeling that being so close to the pot gave me. The bidding on Lot #20 opened at seventy-five dollars.

There were only three people who were seriously bidding on the pottery. I noticed that all three had the look of dealers. They had the little handheld notebooks, the glasses perched on their noses and the look of professional intensity casual auction-goers never wore. It was a whole different look than just falling in love with an estate piece and wanting to take it home. The dealer has a clinical attitude about his or her pur-chases, an "Oh, boy, I can't wait to get this into my store and mark it up 150 percent" attitude. I was doomed.

Lot #20 went to the dealer with the frizzy blond hair (roots desperately needed a touch-up) for three hundred dollars.

Lot #21 went to the dealer who looked English. You know:

proper, prim, smart, well-bred, but in need of a bath and some orthodontic attention. He paid five hundred dollars (and, sure enough, he had an accent) for the beautiful second- to fourth-Century Roman pot which the auctioneer described as made in the Moselkeramik style, which meant (he explained to us ignorant lay-folks) that it was of the highest quality and exquisite. The English guy looked smug with his purchase.

Lots #22, #23 and #24 went to the third dealer. Believe it or not, it was the Depression Era matron I had offended with my legs earlier. Great. Ms. Matron paid three hundred, four twenty-five and two hundred seventy-five dollars, respectively, for the pots.

"Now the last of our beautiful pottery pieces is Lot #25—Reproduction—Celtic vase, original stood over graves in an ancient Scottish cemetery—Scene in color represents supplications being made to High Priestess of the Horse Goddess Epona. It is interesting to note that Epona was the only Celtic deity adopted by the invading Romans, and she became their personal Goddess, protectress of their legendary legions." His voice sounded stuck-up and proud, like *he* had created the pot and perhaps was a personal friend of Epona. I hated him. "Notice the exceptional use of color and contrast on the urn. Shall we open the bidding at seventy-five dollars?"

"Seventy-five." I raised my hand and caught his eye. It's important to telegraph to the auctioneer (via eye contact) serious buying intent—and I was Morse-coding him to death.

"I have seventy-five, do I hear one hundred?"

"One hundred." The Matron raised her fat hand.

"One-ten." I tried not to shout.

"One…ten." There was no mistaking the patronizing tone to His Majesty's voice. "I have a bid of one hundred and *ten* dollars. Do I hear one twenty-five?"

"One hundred and fifty dollars, please." It was the Brit. Figures.

"The gentleman bids one hundred and fifty dollars." Now his voice was ingratiating. What a little weasel. "One hundred and fifty, do I hear two hundred?"

"Two hundred," I said through clenched teeth.

"Ah, the lady bids two hundred dollars." Back in his good graces. "Do I hear two twenty-five?"

Silence—I was holding my breath.

"The last bid is two hundred dollars." Expectant pause. I wanted to throttle him. Say "once, twice, sold," my mind was screaming. "Do I hear two hundred and twenty-five dollars?"

"Two-fifty." The Matron again. Before I could raise my hand to spend more than my budget allowed, the Brit, in a flutter of long white fingers, softly raised the bid to two seventy-five.

Above the pounding in my ears I could make out the bidding war between the Matron and the Brit. It culminated at three hundred and fifty dollars. Beyond my budget—way beyond my budget. I backed away slowly as the crowd moved on to the next set of lots, and found myself sitting on the edge of the rotting fountain. I watched as the auction assistants began boxing up the pottery. The Brit and the frizzy-haired blonde were hanging around, obviously done bidding—they probably owned shops that specialized in works d'art. They were laughing and talking with the good-natured camaraderie of peers.

The pot wasn't going home with me. It looked like me. It made me feel neurotic, but it was going home with the Brit. My sigh came straight from my confused heart. I didn't know what the hell was wrong with me, but I felt, as I'm sure the Brit would say, buggered and bloody awful.

In Oklahoma we'd just say I felt like shit.

Maybe I should ask the Brit for his card, and save up enough money to...what? Put the damn thing in layaway? Maybe I could pick up a summer-school class and...

I noticed the Brit lifting my—I mean, *his* pot. He was examining it with a proprietor's smile as he waited for the assistant to pack the waiting box with enough tissue to keep it from breaking. Suddenly, his smile changed to an angry, distraught expression. Hmm—I stood up and moved closer.

"My God! What the bloody hell is this?" He was holding the pot up above his head, looking intently into the interior.

"Sir, is there a problem?" The assistant was as confused as I.

"I should say so! This pot is cracked! It is totally useless to me." He set it carelessly back on the table, and it rolled around on its bottom edge, coming precariously close to tipping over.

"Sir, let me take a look." The assistant grabbed the pot and held it up to the light, mimicking the Brit's actions. His expression blanched.

"Sir, you are correct. Please accept my apologies for this damaged merchandise. Your bill will be corrected immediately." As he spoke, another minion rushed off to the accounts payable tent.

"Excuse me..." I tried to sound nonchalant. "What will happen to the pot now?"

All three turned to stare at me.

"It will be reauctioned, *as is,* of course." And he handed the pot to yet another assistant, who hastened toward the auctioneer area. I followed on rubbery legs, feeling suddenly like the proverbial moth to a flame—or more appropriately Okie-like, the mosquito to the heavy-duty two-acre bug zapper.

"Oh, my. It seems we have an error in need of correcting." The auctioneer's voice was annoyed. "Before we continue to Lot #31, we need to reauction Lot #25. The reproduction pottery evidently has a hairline crack running the width of the base. Quite unfortunate."

I pushed my way through the crowd as he held up the pot,

open end to the audience, so that we could all peer into its imperfect depths. I squinted and looked…and the opening of the pot seemed to ripple, like the surface of a black lake. I felt dizzy and blinked hard several times, trying to clear my vision.

The auctioneer looked into the opening and shook his head, contorting his face into a grimace of disdain for such abominably damaged merchandise. Then he shrugged his shoulders and said, "Do I have an opening bid of twenty-five dollars?"

Silence.

I couldn't believe it—I wanted to shout, but contained my exuberance as he surveyed the mum crowd and quickly revised the bid downward. "Fifteen dollars? Do I hear fifteen dollars?"

Silence. Just ten minutes before, the bidding war had been on, and it had brought three hundred and fifty dollars. Now it wasn't perfect, and the guy couldn't get fifteen bucks. Fate whispered in my ear.

"Three dollars and fifty cents." I couldn't help myself. It was some kind of quirky justice.

"Sold! For three dollars and fifty cents. Madam, please give your number to my assistant." He grimaced. "You may collect your pot immediately."

4

"My number is 074. I'm here to settle my account." The accounts payable person appeared to be an hourly employee…she moved very slowly. I tried not to fidget. *I want my pot I want my pot I want my pot.* I was turning into a psycho.

"The total is $3.78…that's with tax." She even blinked slowly, reminding me of a calf.

"Here ya go. Keep the change." I handed her a five-dollar bill. She grinned at me like I was Santa.

"Thank you, ma'am. I'll have your merchandise brought right out." Over her shoulder, "Zack, bring out number 74's stuff."

Zack emerged from behind the building bearing a box like those I had observed the other pots being packed into. The lid was open and he held it so that I could see that it was *my* pot. But I didn't need to actually see it, that now-familiar yucky feeling was back in my stomach.

"Thank you, I'll take it from here." Before I could chicken out, I grabbed the box, slammed the lid shut and headed for my car. "I'm getting the hell outta Dodge."

Talking to myself kept my nerves at bay. Well, almost.

I double clicked the passenger's door unlocked, and gently set the box in the seat. On second thought, I decided I had better seat belt the thing in; I didn't want it flopping over, falling out and making me grab at it while I was driving. Gulp.

The air conditioner began its magic as soon as the engine rumbled to life. Trying not to peek sideways at my passenger, I threw the Mustang into gear and retraced my path out.

"What now!"

Children of the Corn's daddy, aka Lurch, was back at his post, again waving the orange wand in my direction. I rolled to a pause and tapped the window open—halfway.

"I see Fate was faithful." His eyes skittered back and forth from the closed lid of the box to me. God, his breath was awful.

"Yeah, there was a crack in the bottom of it, so I got a great deal." Letting up on the clutch I started to roll forward. Couldn't he take a hint?

"Yes, miss, you have no idea what an extraordinary deal you have purchased for so little." His eyes pierced me, then he glanced up at the sky. "The weather is changing. You be sure to drive—" pause "—*carefully.*" (What the hell was he implying?) "I'd hate to think of you having—" pause "—*an accident.*"

"Not a problem. I'm an excellent driver." I pressed the window up and let loose the clutch. Glancing in the rearview mirror I saw Corn Daddy take a few steps after me. "Freak." I shivered.

Turning onto the gravel road felt good, and I gunned the engine, enjoying the juvenile rush of pleasure that spewing gravel with my tires gave me. Glancing in the rearview mirror again, I could see that Corn Daddy was now standing in the middle of the road staring obsessively in my direction. The Freak's warning about the weather flashed through my mind. I looked up at the sky. "Oh, great, this is all I need." Puffy gray clouds towered, giving the blue horizon a bruised look. I was heading southwest, the way back to Tulsa, and apparently the way into a lovely example of an Oklahoma summer thunder-storm.

"Well, friends and sports fans, let's check what the local-yokel weather stations are predicting."

Flipping through my radio all I could tune in clearly was a country-music station, a farm show discussing how bad the ticks are for June (I'm not making that up) and a gospel preacher who seemed to be screaming about adultery (I didn't listen long enough to figure out for sure if he was for or against it). No weather—not even any jazz or the elusive "soft rock."

"What say we just pretend like we're Meatloaf and drive home like a bat outta hell?" I was talking to the damn box. Great. I was stuck in the middle of friggin nowhere, driving smack into (another look forward and a little to the left told me the bad news) a wall cloud, and I was talking to a box filled with a pot that made me feel as if I had taken several diet pills and chugged a large frappa-cappa-mocha-latte. "That's it—first town I come to I'm stopping at the bumpkin gas station. I'm going to get something chocolate to eat, and find out what the hell is going on with the weather." Suspiciously I glanced sideways at the box. "And get some fresh air."

For an instant I almost regretted my cell-phone phobia. I don't own even one cell phone. All of my friends do—usually multiple phones, like it's some contest to see how many they can have and how small they can be, kinda the opposite of the penis thing. My best girlfriend (the stuck-up college professor) has a special one installed in her car so she can blab on the phone without taking her hands off the wheel. She also has a cute little deceptively harmless-looking model that nests in her purse. I tolerate the ridicule of my peers because I've decided that when they are all dying of brain cancer I am going to tell them "I told you so." I continually explain to them that, no, I am not a

Neanderthal out of synch with the modern world. I simply do not need a phone in my car, my purse, my desk, my gym bag, etc., etc. And I will visit them as they are pitifully wasting away from basketball-size brain tumors caused by constant cell-phone radiation waves bombarding their skulls as they chatter about where to meet for lunch and whose stepkids are the most screwed up.

So I won't die from brain cancer, but the thunderstorm-wall-cloud-possible-tornado was making me just a little nervous. Studying the sky as I drove quickly down the road, I realized the incoming storm was definitely getting worse. Oklahoma storms have personalities, big mean personalities. It has always amazed me how the summer sky can change so quickly and completely. I remember one time I was lying out in the sun at the current flavor-of-the-month boyfriend's pool. As proper sunbathing etiquette requires, I was facing the sun and drifting in that wonderfully relaxing sunbathing la-la land (obviously the boyfriend wasn't home, you can't drift in la-la land while a male is telling you what great tits you have) when suddenly the wind shifted and cooled. I opened my eyes and glanced behind me to see puffy gray clouds forming. I grabbed my stuff, left a thank-you note for the boyfriend and took off. I only lived fifteen minutes away, but I didn't make it home before the skies opened. The gray puffy clouds had morphed into blacks and greens. The bizarrely cool wind bent trees. Sheets of rain made driving impossible. I was lucky that I made it to the little hospital in Broken Arrow. I just had time to run through the E.R. entrance and into the basement before a tornado blasted through the center of town.

Okay, maybe I was more than a little nervous. And the damn pot wasn't helping any.

The green-and-white road sign said Leach 10 miles, which turned out to be the last road sign I could make out, because at that moment the sky puked ropes of rain that began to beat up my Mustang.

Now, I love my car. Really. But the little sucker is truly not the car to drive in rainy weather. It loves to slide and hydroplane all over the road. So I downshifted to slow, turned my wipers on high and tried to keep to my side of the centerline.

The radio was static. The trees I could vaguely see on the side of the road were bent over at insane angles. I flipped the headlights on, trying vainly to help visibility. It felt as if the wind was slapping my car around; it was taking both of my sweaty hands to hold the wheel still.

Sweaty? "What the hell?"

The car felt warm. Why? There was cool air blowing from the vent, but I was still uncomfortably hot.

And then I noticed it. The heat was coming from the damn box. My eyes darted from the nearly invisible road to the box. I swear it was glowing, like it had a heat lamp inside it, and someone had just flipped on its switch.

I tore my eyes from the box and back to the—

"Oh, God!" Suddenly there was no road! I could feel the tires crunch in the shoulder gravel and, too quickly, I yanked the wheel to the left. My overcompensation began a spin and I tried desperately to correct back to the right. No good. The wind and rain completely disoriented me. I struggled, just trying to keep the wheel straight; my heart fell into my stomach as the spin carried me across the road, tires screeching. And then the world turned upside down.

At the same time I felt a slice of pain shoot through the side of my head, I realized that I smelled smoke. My eyes must have been closed, because I wrenched them open and it was like I was trapped in the middle of the sun. The pot had burst from its box. It was a ball of heat and light hurling, slow motion, in my direction. Time stalled and I seemed to be suspended on the outskirts of hell. Staring at the luminous globe, I got a bizarre glimpse of myself, like I was looking into a rippled pool of water that had been set afire, but was still able to show a reflection. My mirror image was rushing forward, naked, with arms outstretched and head flung back like a glorious pagan dancer being submerged into the fiery ball. Then fire and smoke enveloped me, too, and I knew I was going to die. My last thought wasn't a flashback of my life, or regret about leaving friends and family. It was simply, "Damnit, I should have quit cussing. What if God really is a Baptist?"

PART TWO

1

Consciousness didn't return easily; it was an elusive thing. It felt like a dream, like the kind of dream I have had during an especially yucky period, complete with awful cramps. In my dream I change the cramps to weird, sugar-laced labor pains and then I give birth to a Twinkie, which somehow makes me feel better. I know. I'm Freud's wet dream.

My head hurt. A lot. Worse than a sinus headache, even worse than an I-can't-believe-I-drank-all-that-tequila hangover. And my body felt like—no, I couldn't feel my body at all. Couldn't open my eyes. Oh, yeah, I'm dead. No wonder I felt…

Blackness closed softly, like a friend.

The next time I woke, my head still hurt—a lot. And I was sorry to realize that I now felt my body. Every joint ached, like the flu from hell. Oh, God, maybe this was hell (if someone started yelling math problems at me, I was in hell *for sure*). But I couldn't hear anything except a strange ringing that seemed to be inside my ears. I tried to open my eyes, but they wouldn't obey. That was probably because corpses don't have functioning eyelids. If it wasn't for the fact that I was dead, I think my heart would have pounded out of my chest. Can corpses panic?

Obviously, yes…this time blackness wasn't friendly, it was seductive, and I willingly spiraled into its waiting arms.

"Be still, my Lady, all will be well."

The voice was sweet and familiar, but it had a funny lilt to
it that I didn't recognize. My head was heavy, hot and sore. My
body felt beat up. Something that lay on my head focused my
disjointed attention to a sudden wet coolness. I touched a
thick compress, but someone gently brushed my hand away.

"All is well, my Lady. I am here." Again, that elusive famili-
arity.

"Wha—" God, my throat was raw and still on fire. Fire!
Memory hurled back, bringing fear and panic. This time when
I told my eyes to open they obeyed. Kind of. I tried to concentrate on seeing, but images and lights blurred together into
confusion. The large blur sitting next to me moved, and my
eyes began to focus on—

Thank God, it was Suzanna. If she was here then I couldn't
be dead, and maybe everything would be all right. I tried to
maintain my focus on her as the room pitched and I struggled
to blink my vision clear. She was already holding one of my
hands, but, strangely, she tried to pull away as she saw my eyes
open. I just grabbed on all the harder. It seemed she went pale,
but it also seemed like there were four of her, then two of her,
then four again as my vision wavered.

"My Lady, you must lie still. You have been through much
tonight, your body and soul are in need of rest. Do not worry,
you are safe and all is well."

I tried to say, *what the hell is wrong with you,* but the sound
my throat made was like a whispering snake—or one of those
horrible opossums caught in headlights. (No, they don't just
play dead, they hiss and scare the crap out of unsuspecting
women who have stopped the car on a dark country road just
because they're looking for some privacy so they can pee,

jeesh.) Anyway, I couldn't understand me, so I knew Suzanna couldn't, either.

She pulled her hand loose from mine and someone I couldn't focus on handed her a goblet. Goblet? A golden goblet? In a hospital?

"Drink, my Lady. It will soothe your throat and help you to rest." Her gentle hand lifted my head and she held the cup to my lips as I tried to gag down the sweet, thick liquid.

Lifting my head had set off waves of renewed pain in my temples. Before the world went black again, I tried to stay focused on my friend. She was taking the cloth off my head and exchanging it for a new, cool bandage handed to her by an incredibly young nurse wearing an odd, flowing uniform. The "nurse" looked like she was ready to frolic in the meadow, not go to work in the E.R., or ICU, or…

Blackness was tinged with the sweet, cough-syrupy taste of medicine.

The next time the blackness lifted suddenly. It was not a gentle awakening. Oh, no, I was going to—

"Here, my Lady. Let me aid you." Suzanna supported my back and held my hair out of the way as I puked my guts up over the side of the bed (she really is a good best girlfriend—I'm sorry I called her stuck-up before). When I finished barfing up my innards, she guided me back to my pillow and wiped my face clean.

I seriously hate puking. Always have. It makes me shake and feel out of control. I'm glad I don't do it very often, but when I do, I admit I'm a baby about it. So, true to form, I couldn't stop shaking. I was weak and disoriented, but I thought that might have been because I was dead, not just because of the puking.

"Wa…wa…ter." I managed to get an understandable squeak out of my throat, and Suzanna immediately motioned to a waiting nurse, and another goblet appeared. She held it for me and helped me to drink.

"Uuuckk!" I spewed most of it out—it wasn't water, it was weak wine. Now, I adore wine, but not after puking.

"Suz! Wa...t...er." I gave her the *girlfriend, I'm gonna kill you* look as I tried to get my point across.

"Yes, my Lady!" She paled again and turned to the nurse, handing her the goblet. (What kind of hospital was this, anyway?) "Bring Lady Rhiannon water immediately!" The nymphlike nurse rushed away. Suzanna turned back to me, but she wouldn't meet my eyes. "Forgive me, my Lady. I misunderstood. Blame me, not the maiden." She folded her hands together over her breast, like she was praying or something, and bowed her head, still not meeting my eyes.

Okay, what the hell was going on? I caught hold of one of her hands and tugged, trying to get her to look at me. And then I noticed her hair. It was her normal color—blondish, with pretty, natural highlights—but it had become tangled with my hand. *Because it was waist length and falling over her shoulders and breasts and was therefore entangled in our hands.*

"No. How..." I managed to sputter. Suzanna has always had a short, sexy haircut. I love to kid her about it looking mussed and naughty. She says, "Why, thank you!" like a cat that just lapped up cream. How could it possibly have grown down to her waist? Oh, great. Had I been in some kind of coma? Perhaps I'd been "out" for a gazillion years, and out of grief she'd descended into some unfortunate Lady Godiva phase while I was unconscious, and without my astute girlfriend-telling-her-what-looks-right fashion sense she had grown her hair down to her butt.

Nope, she didn't look any older. The bitch.

She still avoided my eyes as I studied her. It was definitely Suzanna. Same petite bone structure. Beautiful round face that somehow radiated goodness. Her long tresses were pulled behind her perfect little ears, just like when her hair was short. The same freckles dotted her nose and high cheekbones. If she'd smile (which didn't appear too likely) I bet I'd see familiar dimples on either side of her gentle lips.

"Suz..." I tugged on her hand, trying to get her to look at me. As she glanced up, my eyes met the same golden-brown eyes that have been peering back at me for years. "Wha..." I tried to rasp out a question while giving her the *what's up, girlfriend?* look. She seemed to soften, but the nurse ran in (really, the nymphet actually ran into the room) with a new goblet.

"Here, my Lady."

Thank God, real water. And it was even cool. I tried to suck as much down as I could, but my throat rebelled.

"Th...anks," I managed to rasp. Suzanna had to lean forward to hear me, but I knew she understood because she suddenly blushed, hastily grabbed a soft cloth and began wiping my face dry.

It amazed me to realize I was exhausted. All I'd done was puke my guts up, try to talk and drink a couple swallows of water. Suzanna stroked the hair back from my forehead, humming a tuneless song.

"Rest, my Lady. All is well."

And just what the hell was she wearing...?

My other friend, blackness, stealthily took me away again.

2

"**F**orgive me, my Lady. You must awaken."

No, I've called in a sub, let me sleep. This must be a horrible dream. Maybe if I screwed my eyes tightly shut and concentrated on conjuring up a dream image of Hugh Jackman enslaved to me by love, I would drift back into my Dreamland.

Then I made the mistake of swallowing.

Crap—my throat was killing…crap. Oh…that's right. I might be dead. And my eyes popped open.

Two nymphet/nurses flanked the long-haired Suzanna. One had a gauzy something-or-other draped over her shapely and very bare arms. The other was holding combs and brushes and a lovely little crownlike golden thing (I think they're called coronets). Hmm… Hell couldn't be all bad if it had jewelry.

"My Lady, your father's messenger has just arrived, and he announces that the banns have been posted and your betrothed will be meeting you here to finalize the handfast ceremony."

My what?

"Today. Please, we must make you ready."

All I could do was blink up at her. What was she talking about? My betrothed? I wasn't even *dating* anyone! I'd fired the last guy I'd gone out with halfway through our blind date (Note to self: never, ever go on another blind date).

Suzanna seemed to hesitate. "Mistress, are you still unable to speak?"

"Misssss—uhh." What was up with this "mistress" and "my Lady" crap?

Obviously, my rasping opossum-like whisper was answer enough. I noticed that the sound of my very messed-up voice sent the nymphets into an attractive state of panic. Suz acted pissed off; suddenly she was snatching the gauzy robe, combs and jewels from the nymphs.

"You are dismissed." (Boy, she sounded stern—which intensified the strange, almost musical lilt to her voice.) "I will care for our mistress." They scampered away, looking relieved. Guess they don't make nurses like they used to.

"Here, my Lady, lean on my arm and I will take you to the baths."

You'd think getting up and walking to take a (much-needed) bath wouldn't be a tough thing to do, and maybe it wouldn't have been if the damn room would quit moving.

"Uuuuhhh—" I felt like I was hobbling, like one of the old crones from Act I of Macbeth—God knows my hair felt scraggly enough that I must have looked the part.

"You are doing well, my Lady. Come, it is only a few more steps."

We were walking down a dimly lighted hall. Glancing up, I noticed the lighting was dim because, well, because (and this made me come to a total halt) there were live torches jutting out of wrought-iron holders. I have a college degree; you can't fool me. Live torches are not normal for a hospital! And, damnit! I most certainly am not engaged!

"My Lady, do you need to rest?"

What had happened to Suzanna? Did they stop making

Prozac while I was "out," and had that sent her into some kind of tragic medieval hysteria? One of my arms was already linked with hers, so grabbing her other hand was simple. I forced her to turn toward me and look directly at me. Taking my time, swallowing several times in an attempt to clear the opossum from my throat, I held her gaze with mine and said slowly and intently, *"What has happened?"*

Still, she tried to look away, but I gave her hands a quick shake and her eyes darted back to mine.

"My Lady…" She paused and glanced around her like she was afraid of being overheard, then she whispered in a serious-as-Oprah-in-a-shoe-store voice, "What is your name?"

Okay, I'd play. But if Sean Connery showed up around the next corner, I would know for sure that I was having the Mother of All Bizarre Dreams.

"Shannon." I rasped as clearly as I was able. She didn't even blink.

"And what is my name?"

Jeesh. Maybe she was drunk—the woman never could drink. One little sniff of tequila and she was off into some blonde la-la land. Deep breath—nope, I didn't smell any alcohol.

"Your name is Suzanna."

She leaned even closer to me and shook her head slowly from side to side. This time she seemed more able to force herself to meet my gaze. I couldn't help noticing that the fear that had been flickering through her eyes was now shadowed by pity.

"No, my Lady." Her gentle-sounding, strangely accented answer rocked me. "My name is not Suzanna, it is Alanna. And you are not Shannon, you are my mistress, Rhiannon, High Priestess of the Goddess Epona, daughter of The Mac-

Callan, betrothed to and soon to be handfasted with the High Shaman ClanFintan."

"Bullshit."

"I know this must be difficult for you, my Lady, but come with me. I will help you ready yourself and I will try and explain how this came about." She did sound concerned as she helped my numb body move forward down the hall and through a door which stood ajar to the right of us.

The room we entered conjured images of those PBS specials that first show current-day ruins, which look like a jumbled, confused mess of old stone and decaying columns—then they morph a computer image over the ruins so that the audience can see what the original supposedly looked like in all its glory. This room definitely looked like one of the computer-morphed images. The floor and ceiling were smooth marble. It was hard to tell if the gold color came from the stone or the many wall torches. The symmetry of the walls was interrupted often by cutout niches, which looked to be carved into the stone at varying heights. In the niches lighted candles nestled in odd-looking golden holders (gosh, I really appreciated a room accessorized with gold), giving the walls the appearance of being set ablaze by faceted jewels. Along one wall hung an enormous mirror in front of which sat an elaborate vanity. The mirror was softly fogged by steam wisping up from a deep, clear pool of water that bubbled up from the center of the floor, and overflowed out in a fast-running stream which emptied itself into another pool in an adjoining room. The air was so warm and moist it felt caressing. Just breathing it made me feel relaxed, and the smell reminded me of something…

"It's a mineral spring!" Even my voice responded to the room's healing aroma and Suz/Alanna didn't have to strain to understand me.

"Yes, my Lady." She seemed pleased that I had enough

sense to identify the metallic smell of the water and speak semiclearly (a little like walking and chewing gum). "Here, let me help you out of your robe." Which she did, quickly and expertly. Then she motioned for me to follow the rock steps down into the steaming water. It was deep, but there were several comfortably smoothed ledges conveniently placed all along the near side of the pool, and I sank gingerly onto one with the sigh of the truly dirty. I watched through half-lidded eyes as Suzanna/Alanna gathered sponges and small pots and bottles from the vanity, poured me a glass of dark red something from a waiting pitcher into yet another golden goblet, then knelt on the side of the pool near my ledge.

I gratefully accepted the goblet and sighed in pleasure at the taste of a wonderful cabernet. Then, as if she did it every day, she lifted my arm that was not holding the goblet, and began running a soapy sponge down it. I yelped and pulled away.

"My Lady, you need be readied to meet your betrothed."

"I can—" (swallow, take a breath) "—wash—" (swallow) "—my—" (breathe) "—self!" I slammed the goblet down next to her and whispered forcefully, "And don't think you can lull me into forgetting the bizarre crap you just laid on me in the hall. I want to know what's up—*now*, Suzanna Michelle." Girlfriends only use each other's middle names when a crisis exists or when deviant sex is being discussed, so she had to know I was serious.

"Forgive me, my Lady. I did not mean to offend or prevaricate." She bowed her head and clasped her hands over her breast, like she was waiting for discipline.

I didn't know what was going on; something was definitely wrong. But whatever it was, I was sure the lovely cabernet would help. Another sip felt soothing to my throat, almost as soothing as the warm water felt to my body. Another sip—deep breath.

Suzanna hadn't moved. Okay, if I only tried to whisper, maybe I could make my opossum voice last long enough to get this mess cleared up—or get snockered enough that I didn't care.

"Suz." Her chin moved up slowly at the sound of my whisper. "I'm not mad, you know better than that." Before she got her expression under control, I was sure I saw shock reflected on her face. "But I am confused." Another deep breath. I cleared my throat again. "Start over and tell me where we are." Seemed like an easy enough question.

"We are in your bathing chamber in the High Temple of Epona."

I mentally shook my head. Oh, sure—a hospital named after a pagan goddess deep in the Bible Belt? Maybe I hadn't been specific enough in my question.

"In what state?" Another goblet or two of wine and my opossum and I would be ready to take on the world.

"You appear to have been injured, my Lady, but you look to be recovering remarkably well." She blinked up at me with what I liked to think of as her soft little rabbit look.

"No, Suz, not my state of being, I mean what state am I in?" She was still giving me the rabbit look. Sigh. "Which of the fifty United States?" Man, I wished I could yell.

"You mean our location in the world?" The lightbulb clicked on.

"Yes, friend of mine." I was going to personally lace her favorite brownies with her new Prozac prescription.

"Epona's Temple controls all the lands around us. As High Priestess to Epona you are Mistress of Her lands."

Well, that was comforting. I was having a psychotic episode, my best friend was having a nervous breakdown, but, hey, at least I was Mistress here! As the King (I mean Elvis, not some medieval dreamworld phony) would say, "Thank you, thank you very much."

"Suzanna, I don't want to shock or upset you—and please don't cry (she always has been a crier), but I have no friggin clue what you're talking about."

"My Lady," she said tentatively, "perhaps that is because you are no longer in your own world."

Now, *that* got my attention.

"Suzanna, you just said *I* am *mistress* here, and *my* betrothed is on his way. Can you explain what the hell you are talking about? Oh, and please pour me some more wine, I have a feeling I'm going to need it." I think she was relieved to turn away from me—maybe she could collect her neurotic thoughts and I could get to the bottom of this. Actually, this could all be an elaborate plot to get back at me for forgetting her birthday last month. (Damnit, I knew she was still mad.)

"It is complicated, my Lady."

"Suz, you sound like Jeannie when you say that my Lady stuff." She ignored my comment—I hated it when she didn't get my jokes. "Just make it short and to the point, I'll try to figure it out from there." And we'll get you some professional help very soon.

"My original mistress, the Lady Rhiannon, has exchanged places with you. She said your world made magic with machines, and power with money made from those machines, and she longed to live there. So she sent her soul there during one of her Magic Sleeps and found you. She said you are her mirror, her shadow, and that she could trade herself for you, thus entering your world. She believed that she could leave enough of her consciousness here, as she does when she enters the sacred grove, to aid and guide you." Intently studying my face, her litany slowed, "But I do not think she is here with you. You appear to be her, but you do not have her…" Here she faltered, as if catching herself in the middle of a thought.

Then she continued, "…her manner. Now she has become you, and you must become her."

"This can't be. I don't believe it."

"The Lady Rhiannon directed me to ask a question of you if you did not seem to understand or believe."

I raised my eyebrow like Spock and waited.

"In your world do you know stories that tell tales of gods and goddess, myths and magic, spells and sorcery?" She paused, and looked expectantly at me. Obviously, she wouldn't take the eyebrow for an answer.

"Yes, of course, I'm a teacher, I teach those stories to kids."

"My Lady Rhiannon said to tell you that this world is where those stories came from. They leaked across The Divide like shadows and smoke, seeking their mirror images in your world. Thus have I learned of that world, in the form of smoke and shadows, and thus I found my mirror image—you."

"That's fantasy sci-fi crap, Suz. How can you expect me to believe it?"

"Lady Rhiannon told me that she would use her image that was already in your world, and a wall of fire to move through The Divide."

"That friggin pot." It couldn't be.

"Pardon me, my Lady?"

"The fire. How was she not harmed if she passed through a wall of fire? And why wasn't I burned up, too?"

Suzanna's face drained of color.

"More wine, my Lady."

"Yep. And you haven't answered my question."

Two quick taps on the door interrupted her. She had the good manners to look sheepish…and keep looking and looking at me. Wha—?

"You may enter," she finally called.

A new nymph bowed her way into the room.

Suzanna was still looking apologetically at me. Oops, I kept forgetting, *I* was the mistress, which (I guess) meant I should be ordering around the nymphs.

Okay, I'd give it a try. "What?" Even though I was still sounding like a whispering opossum, I tried to project that "don't interrupt my classroom" voice my students knew and loved so well.

The little nymph turned toward me and spoke in a charming lilt. "Mistress, your betrothed has arrived."

I looked quickly at Suzanna. She was no damn help; her eyes were squeezed shut and her lips were moving in what looked like some kind of silent prayer. Jeesh.

"Fine. Tell him (stall, think, think) tell him…um (at the "um" the nymph's eyes widened in surprise—oops—guess mistresses/my Ladys don't um) tell him I will greet him when I have finished dressing." So there. I'm female—no matter where the hell I was, men must be accustomed to waiting on women to get ready.

"Yes, my Lady." She bowed her way out. My ruse seemed to have worked. I almost felt like Penelope.

"How'd ya like that, girlfriend? Did I sound like The Mistress Here?"

"We are players in a dangerous game, my Lady."

"Oh, come on, Suz. This is all a dream or something!"

"Please, my Lady—" she grabbed my hands and squeezed "—if you bear any love for your Suzanna, please listen and heed my words. More than just your own life rests upon your actions today."

"Okay, okay, Suz. I'll listen."

"First, you must not call me by that name. You must only call me Alanna. You must meet with ClanFintan. Your betrothal period is over, it is time to enter into the formal handfast."

Something about her eyes caused me to bite back my refusal.

She really believed this. She was not pretending or kidding. She looked terrified.

"You know I will always help you, my girl—"

"Alanna! If you call me by name you must use that name. Do you understand?"

"Yes, Alanna." Whatever was wrong I couldn't fix it without more information, and Suz—oops—Alanna definitely needed fixing. "Okay, isn't a handfast a temporary marriage?"

"Yes, my Lady. It is a marriage that is arranged for only one year." She definitely wouldn't meet my eyes.

"Why was Rhiannon only marrying him for one year?"

"That was the agreement." She was suddenly oh so busy reaching for and then pouring something that smelled like honeysuckle into the water from one of the little bottles that sat on a marble ledge near the side of the pool. Yep, she was hiding something. Lots of something.

"So, how do you expect me to pull off a handfast with a man I have never met?"

"Lady Rhiannon has met him." By the look on her face I was beginning to think that might not be a good thing. "I will present you and explain that you had an accident during the last Moon Ritual, and your voice has left you. I will speak for you." Helping me from the warm pool she was totally businesslike, and I told myself that I would ignore the fact that she was matter-of-factly toweling me dry.

"Okay, but what about the…um…intimate details of this handfast thing? I don't even know this guy—I'm certainly not going to consummate anything with him!" And if he turned out to be the mirror image of my ex-husband, I was outta there.

"Simply remember *you* are Lady Rhiannon, High Priestess and Beloved of Epona. The Lady Rhiannon is only touched when she allows it."

"Even by the man she is handfasted to?"

"Yes, even him." She sounded pretty confident. I must be a real bitch. Smile.

The gauzy bit of nothing that she had carried into the room had somehow found its way into Alanna's hands. Man, it really was pretty. It was my color, a shimmery golden-red that seemed to move by itself.

"Please hold your arms out from your sides, my Lady."

Doing as she asked, I was a captive audience, entranced as she wrapped the diaphanous material around my body. Reaching behind her with one hand, she rescued two lovely woven circles of gold from the vanity, and expertly pinned one at my waist and one at my shoulder, much like a Highland kilt would wrap and hang (except that I didn't think kilts were semitransparent and silky, unless purchased from MacFrederick's of MacHollywood). Stepping back, she surveyed her work, making alterations and tucks here and there. She always had been good at crafts.

"My God, it's see-through!" And it was—not in a slutty, stand on the corner of Eleventh and Peoria Streets at midnight kind of way, but in a sultry Elizabeth Taylor as Cleopatra kind of way.

"Oh, forgive me for forgetting." She lifted a small triangle of the same gauze from the vanity (I thought it was a hankie) and held it for me to step into. Seriously, it was a teeny thong. Gosh, I felt so much better, so much more "covered." Jeesh.

"Please be seated, my Lady, and I will dress your hair." Fine. I might as well have some part of me dressed.

Frowning over my damp locks, she began attempting to work a wide-toothed comb through them.

"Your hair is shorter than hers. The same, but shorter. I will arrange it up until it grows longer." Seemed like she was talking to the hair, not me. Relaxing into her ministrations, I thought I'd enjoy my coiffure.

I don't know about you, but having my hair brushed is a borderline sexual experience, secondary only to getting a really great foot rub. Yum. Only Alanna reaching for a piece of jewelry could snap me out of my hairbrush trance (proving that jewelry can combat apathy as well as accessorize).

She settled a thin gold band around my forehead, artistically arranging my swept-up hair to complement it. I turned my head from side to side to get a better look. The candlelight reflected off the polished gold and caught a diamond-shaped stone set in the center of the circle, making its facets flash. I leaned closer.

"Garnet?"

"Yes, my Lady. Your favorite stone."

"*My* favorite stone?" My eyebrows crept up in suppressed amusement.

She actually smiled at me, almost like my Suzanna. "Well, Rhiannon's favorite stone."

"Mine is a diamond, but garnets are nice." Smiling back at her felt good—almost normal.

"But, my Lady, you must remember you *are* Rhiannon." Back to serious Alanna.

"Okay, not a problem." She looked relieved and continued to pull tendrils of reddish curls out of the cool updo to frame my face and hang down my back.

"Now I will work on that face." I guess a closer look at "that face" was pretty sobering, because she gave me the stubborn Suzanna look and went to work, stroking on creams and powders from beautiful glass jars scattered in disarray on the vanity.

"Uh, I don't care what you do, but my one request is for lots of golden-brown lip color."

"Exactly as Rhiannon would have chosen."

"That's pretty weird."

"She said you would be of one soul." She glanced nervously at me, only briefly meeting my eyes.

We needed to get this crap straight right now. For good.

"She lied."

"Pardon, my Lady?" Alanna looked like she had just received an electrical shock.

"I said she lied, Alanna. I am not her—I am Shannon Parker, a high-school English teacher from Broken Arrow, Oklahoma, who has been caught up in something even more bizarre than the World of the Teenage, which takes some damn doing. I'll help you. But I know who I am, and I am not her." My gaze never left hers. "Understand?"

"Yes, my Lady. But it is difficult."

"No shit." She smiled again.

"You have a very odd way of speaking."

"So do you. It's something like a cross between a Scottish burr and Deanna Troi's Star Trek accent." Now she looked really confused. "Never mind. It's not important."

She smiled again and returned to making me up. My eyes strayed around the unusual room. I felt relaxed and warm but not sleepy (guess a semi-death/coma experience replaces a good eight hours of sleep). My eyes kept being drawn back to the myriad candles set within the smooth, creamy walls. It was like my eyes *wanted* to look at them—a weird but not exactly unpleasant feeling.

"Those sconces are really unusual. They remind me of— *eeuew!* Are they skulls?"

"Yes, of course, my Lady." She sounded surprised at my screech. "Skulls form an intricate part of your devotion to Epona." Now she gave me a schoolmarmish look. "Surely, even in your world you understand that all things powerful and mystical come from the Fire in the Head, the Seat of Learning and Knowledge?" I swear she made a very Suzanna-ish hmmph noise when I didn't respond. "You have always surrounded yourself with the power of the mind. It is only right."

"But they're skulls dipped in gold!"

"Of course, my Lady, the High Priestess and Beloved of Epona has only the best." She sounded as if I had just tried to choose a Days Inn over the Hyatt.

Well, looks like I had finally found something I didn't like in gold. Amazing.

"So, tell me something about my betrothed. What was his name?" She continued to work on my very tired-looking face, attempting a transformation from yuck to non-yuck.

"His name is ClanFintan. He is a powerful and well-respected High Shaman." That was it. Hmm… good thing I'm not Hamlet, 'cause something sure stinks here in Denmark.

"So, uh, I'm in love with him?"

"No, my Lady." She was looking nervous again. "It was a marriage arranged by your father."

"Hey, I thought I was mistress here!"

"You are, my Lady, but sometimes the greater good of the people must overshadow the desires of the one."

Who was she, Spock?

"Okay, admit it. I can take it. He's hideous, isn't he?"

"No, my Lady." She actually looked like she was telling the truth. She was a good little actress when she wanted to be.

"Then what's wrong with him?" Herpes? Balding? Tiny penis? Or worse—was he a tightwad?

"Nothing that I know of, my Lady."

Okay, she wasn't going to tell. Guess I'd have to find out for myself.

"Your toilette is complete." She looped through my pierced ears two waterfalls of garnet beads and slid a golden garnet-encrusted armband up to encircle my bicep as I stood. "Beautiful, as always." Did she sound smug?

She was right, though. For a woman who thought she was in hell just hours before, I was looking damn good if I did say so myself—scantly clad, but good.

"Showtime."

"What shall I show you, my Lady?"

"Never mind. Let's just get this over with—I'm starting to remember I haven't eaten in days, or whatever."

"Follow me, my Lady." I followed—she chattered in a low conspirator's voice. "Normally, you would, of course, lead the way. But today I will walk somewhat in front of you." She observed my progress as I followed her out of the room. "Good, my Lady. You are recovering. Remember, the Lady Rhiannon never hurries unless she desires to get somewhere quickly. Walk slowly, languidly, as if you rule all you see."

"Do I?" I teased.

"Of course."

Huh! I do? Not the response I expected.

I rule all I see. So I gawked/looked around as I languidly made my way to meet some guy I didn't know but to whom I was engaged. We were in a hall much like the one that led to the bath, only we were walking in the opposite direction from which we had come (I think). We kept moving forward. Alanna had straightened her spine. Actually, she was walking like she had something stuck way up her butt, so I did the same. We rounded a corner in the hall and ran into a huge set of double doors. They were carved with intricate looping designs, interweaving like Celtic circles. I blinked and could have sworn some of the circles looked like skulls (yeesh). But my attention didn't stay with the carvings long, because decorating either side of the doors were two adorable men, scantly clad.

At my approach they snapped to very attractive attention, banging hateful-looking swords against their firm, muscular chests (God bless them). One jumped forward to open the doors for me (now, *that's* what's missing in America today—guys don't think they have to open doors anymore). Unfortunately, I wasn't able to give them the attention they so obviously deserved. Alanna was nudging me into a huge room.

High ceilings, carved pillars (I swear I saw more of those stupid skulls everywhere) and exquisite frescoes, complete with frolicking nymphs and…oh, jeesh…*me!* also scantily clad, astride a gorgeous white horse, very obviously leading the frolicking. (Does the weather never turn cold here?) In the middle of the room, on a clichéd raised dais, was a lovely gilded throne. A couple of the prerequisite nymphets were lounging on the dais steps, but at my entrance they leaped to their bare little feet and bowed their cute little heads.

I should have been nominated for some kind of Greco-Celtic Academy Award for Best Voluptuous Ascent to a Throne. God, it felt good to sit down.

Before the dead airtime grew, Alanna, who had situated herself directly to my right, jumped in with, "Inform Shaman ClanFintan that Lady Rhiannon will see him now." One of the nymphets scampered out another enormous arched doorway, and I wondered briefly if the men guarding it were proportional.

My eyes met Alanna's briefly and she gave me a tight smile of encouragement. I dropped one eyelid in a quick wink as the doors reopened and the nymphet returned in a cloud of transparent wisp masquerading as clothing.

"He comes, my Lady." She seemed flushed and excited (maybe he really wasn't hideous) as she melted her way back to the dais steps. With all that skin showing she probably couldn't help being high-strung.

Everyone was looking expectantly at the arched doorway. I noticed a distinctive sound beginning to roll from the open doors, building as it came closer. It reminded me of…hmm…

of…I know! Horses! My betrothed was riding a horse into my throne-room-chamber-place? Okay, I realize Epona was some kind of horse goddess, but he and I were going to have a talk about proper palace etiquette. Soon. I mean, as my grandma would have said, that certainly couldn't be mannerly behavior.

The hoof sounds were now quite loud. There must be several of them. Oafs!

That's it. He was probably the mirror image of an Oklahoma bubba. I could see it now, he would want to call me his sweet thang and slap me on the butt.

I could see my door guards (yes, they *did* appear proportional) snap crisp sword salutes as the horses reached the doorway and entered the ro—

And the breath caught in my throat. Just like in the movies. I felt like I couldn't breathe and I had to struggle not to make the Universal Choking Sign as I swallowed my heart.

Two abreast they entered the chamber. I quickly counted— amazed I could still think well enough to count—ten of them.

"Centaurs." My voice, already strained from whispering too much, barely squeaked the word, but Alanna's expression said she heard me. So I closed my mouth (which was flopping open like a wind sock) and shut up. No, Toto, we were damn sure not in Kansas anymore.

The two lead centaurs kept coming toward the dais, while the other eight spread out in a neat flanking motion. As the leaders got close to the steps, one of them stayed a little behind, while the other approached the stairs and made a graceful, sweeping flourish with his arm.

"Well met, Lady Rhiannon." His voice was surprising, deep and smooth, like dark chocolate, with the same musical accent as Alanna's.

At least it was damn obvious that he wasn't my ex-husband.

Before I could attempt a reply, Alanna executed a neat little curtsy and began to address him.

"Lord ClanFintan, my Lady Rhiannon regrets that she has temporarily lost the use of her voice." His eyes narrowed at her words, but he didn't interrupt. "Lady Rhiannon has directed me to greet you and to say she is ready to finalize the handfast."

"What a most—" pause "—*inopportune* time for you to lose your voice, my Lady."

Was that sarcasm? Sure sounded like it to me. Guess I wasn't the only one disconcerted by this arrangement.

"Yes, my Lord, Lady Rhiannon has been most distressed by it." Alanna didn't lose a beat.

"How did it happen?" He didn't even glance at Alanna, but kept looking at me, like the words were really coming out of my mouth. I thought I'd better just keep looking into his eyes; if I allowed my gaze to travel I was certain my mouth would probably flop open again.

"During the Moon Ritual she became ill, but my Lady's dedication to Epona would not allow her to withdraw. After the ceremony was completed, she retired to her bed for several days, and has just today emerged. Her health is returning, but, as yet, her voice has not." I could hear the reassuring smile in her voice. "Do not worry, my Lord, it is only temporary and will heal quickly as long as she rests and gives herself time to recuperate."

"I understand your situation, Lady Rhiannon." He didn't sound understanding, he sounded pissed. "But I trust this—" another pause "—unfortunate malady will not delay our business today."

Business! What an odd way of describing a marriage, albeit a temporary one. And I really didn't like the tone of Mr. Ed's voice. I couldn't say what Rhiannon would have done, but I sure as hell knew what Shannon Parker was going to do. As

Alanna took a breath to answer for me, I reached out and put a restraining hand on her arm. My eyes locked with Mr. Grumpy. Slowly and distinctly I raised my chin (in a stuck-up, bitchy way) and shook my head from one side to the other. Once.

"Good. I am pleased. Your father sends his blessing, and his regrets that he has been detained and cannot join us for the ceremony."

Oh, goodie.

"Will you come to me, or shall I join you on your—" another rude pause "—*pedestal,* my Lady?"

I could feel my jaw setting, but before I could respond, Alanna stepped in. Gracefully, she took my hand and helped me to my feet.

"Lady Rhiannon will continue, as is customary." Alanna and I descended the dais steps until we were standing on the floor. ClanFintan backed one step to allow me a little room, but he really was very close. And very tall. He seemed to fill the space above me. His scent came to me then, a little horsey, but not unpleasant, like a mixture of sweet grass and warm man.

Reaching down he grasped my right hand in his. I jumped and Alanna covered my squeaky yelp by saying, "My Lady is ready to proceed."

The hell she is.

His hand felt hard and warm—almost hot. I looked down at it and saw that it engulfed mine. It was a burnished tan color, like the rest of the human part of his body. At the sound of his voice, my eyes shot back up to meet his.

"I, The ClanFintan, do take you, Rhiannon MacCallan, in handfast this day. I agree to protect you from fire even if the sun should fall, from water even if the sea should rage and from earth even if it should shake in tumult. And I will honor your name as if it were my own."

His voice was no longer bordering on sarcasm. It was deep and hypnotic, as if his words painted fantastic images of our covenant in the air between us.

Then Alanna's soft voice spoke for me. "I, Rhiannon Mac-Callan, High Priestess of Partholon and Beloved of Epona, do take you, The ClanFintan, in handfast this day. I agree that no fire or flame shall part us, no lake or seas shall drown us and no earthly mountains shall separate us. And I will honor your name as if it were my own."

"Do you agree to this, Lady Rhiannon?"

With the question his hand tightened until his grip bordered on painful.

"My Lord, she cannot recite the oath." Alanna sounded worried.

"Not an oath then, but a single word either agreeing or disagreeing with it." He squeezed my hand even tighter. "Do you agree to abide by this oath, Lady Rhiannon?"

"*Yesssss.*" Purposefully I let my abused voice drag the word out.

He didn't blink. Instead, he loosened his vise grip on my hand, and turned it in his so that it rested there, palm up.

"Then it is settled. For the length of a single year we belong to one another." Without moving his gaze from mine, he lifted my palm to his mouth. Gently, taking the meaty, muscular area below my thumb between his teeth he bit down. The bite was quick, and, quite frankly, more surprising than unpleasant.

My eyes must have been huge as I pulled my hand out of his intimate grasp.

I've married a friggin horse.

And he bites.

Okay, I'm from Oklahoma and I like big horses, and I'm a John Wayne fan, so I like big men, but this was more than a little ridiculous.

And, well, shit, he bites!

3

"My Lord, please allow me to show you to the Great Hall so that you and your warriors can partake of the feast we have provided to honor your handfast." Alanna smiled and gracefully led the way from the throne room.

ClanFintan bowed his head slightly to me and offered his arm. With my hand placed lightly atop his, we followed. I could hear his men (horses?) in turn following us.

"I know how distasteful this is to you, but I am glad to see that you have finally managed to set aside your own desires and do your duty."

He didn't look at me and spoke low, for my ears alone. Glancing up at him, I saw his face was an unreadable mask.

What the hell had I stumbled into?

"Because we have sworn to honor each other for the next year, I will forgive the dishonor you have shown me by refusing to meet with me during our betrothal, returning my gifts and forcing me to follow you here to finalize our contract." His low voice sounded strained.

Horse or no horse, I wasn't going to let him bully me.

"And I will forgive the disrespect you're showing me now

by criticizing me in the temple of my goddess on the day of our handfast." Ha!

He had to tilt his head down to hear my whispery voice. His expression registered instant surprise, and he came to an abrupt halt.

"You are correct, Lady Rhiannon. I dishonor our vows and myself when I disrespect you. Forgive me for my rude behavior." His dark eyes held mine.

I had to clear my abused throat before I could squeak out an "I forgive you."

He still looked pissed, but now he seemed more pissed at himself than me. At least for the moment he appeared satisfied with my answer, because he began following Alanna again, with me in tow.

Alanna had just reached another arched doorway (yes, flanked by two more bewitching guards—Rhiannon certainly had an eye for muscles) and we entered a large banquet hall. Man, this was truly weird.

Okay. This has to be a dream, but even for me it was one wicked weird dream.

The room held at least two dozen large, flat couches. Each had one side that was raised with a kind of reclining armrest, a little like old-fashioned chaise lounges. Next to the raised end of the lounges stood squatty marble pillars with flattened tops. On each flattened pillar sat a golden goblet. Endless supplies of beautiful, nymphlike young women were scurrying from chaise to chaise, filling the goblets with yummy-looking red wine. I tried not to drool.

Make that one wicked *cool* dream.

Alanna motioned us toward two of the strange-looking couches situated head-to-head near the center of the room. They shared one pillar. The rest of the couches were placed in an oblong circle surrounding ours.

"Shall we to dinner, my Lady?"

Guess I had no choice. And I was suddenly starving to death. So I nodded and approached the deceptively comfortable-looking dinner torture device. I mean, come on. It reeked of Ancient Rome. Please. All those Romans and their "He who controls Rome controls the world," blah, blah, lie down to eat, eat too much, go puke. They couldn't even figure out a dining room table. Get serious.

Well, at least reclining would make me look thin....

The instant my butt touched the couch everyone looked flustered, like I'd emerged from the potty with toilet paper attached to the heel of my pump. Please, God, let Alanna know what the hell was up. I gracefully arose and snatched a piece of her sleeve, pulling her toward me so that I could whisper.

"What am I not doing?"

She smiled and curtsied to me like I'd said the right thing, which I knew I hadn't.

"Lady Rhiannon wishes you to forgive her lost voice. She is dismayed that she cannot bless the feast of her own handfast, but she cannot make her much-abused voice carry." Smiling, she began to help me re-recline (was that a word?).

"Can she not whisper to you her blessing, and you could speak her words, as you did earlier?"

My new husband's voice held a very apparent challenge. Mr. Ed was turning out to be a real pain in the ass. (And he was a biter.) Perhaps he thought he was dealing with some kind of slow-witted, cobwebby priestess.

May I just say, he was so wrong. I felt a smile begin to spread over my face.

Again my hand stayed Alanna's intercession as I whispered close to her ear, "Repeat what I say."

"My Lady!" Her response was filled with concern that

edged on panic. She obviously didn't realize she was dealing with a high school teacher—we make a living handling weirdness on a daily (or hourly, depending on who has or hasn't been suspended recently) basis, and we manage to stamp out ignorance *and* touch the future in the midst of chaos. This was small potatoes. Thinking on my feet is the norm for me—it's even what I consider fun.

"Trust me." I winked quickly at her and she nodded, albeit reluctantly.

"You are correct to remind me of my place, Lord Clan-Fintan. Forgive me, I will repeat my Lady's blessing on this happy occasion."

Showtime—again. I knew all those semesters of European Lit would come in handy some day—I just thought it'd be on *Jeopardy.* Leaning dramatically (and showing a nice amount of cleavage), I whispered to Alanna lines from an ancient Irish blessing I had memorized for some useless college class. This just had to be appropriate:

"Wishing you always—"

"Wishing you always," Alanna's sweet voice echoed mine as I spoke the ancient blessing, smiling at my rapt audience, loving their respectful silence.

"Walls for the wind—"

"Walls for the wind—"

"And a roof for the rain—"

"And a roof for the rain—"

"And tea beside the fire—" (I felt a moment of panic as I hoped they drank tea.)

"And tea beside the fire—" (smiles all around, I guessed they did.)

"Laughter to cheer you—"

"Laughter to cheer you—"

And now the coup de grâce. Turning to my new and temporary husband, I looked directly at him as I whispered the final line, and then enjoyed seeing his eyes widen in surprise as Alanna repeated the closing of the blessing.

"And those you love near you, as well as all that your heart might desire!"

Her words echoed mine, and were met by the centaurs' shouts of "Salute!" I swear I saw ClanFintan's cynically twisted lips form the word *checkmate.*

As my favorite college prof once sagely said, "Don't fuck with an English major. They keep lots of useless crap trapped in their heads. Once in a while they let some of it out and it bites you square on the ass."

Alanna's shining face was further evidence of my victory, and the smells emanating from trays being carried in by the…well…thicker-looking employees (I guess nymphs can't be expected to hold up all that transparent gauze *and* dinner, too) were going to my head. I felt dizzy. Wonder how long it had really been since I'd last eaten?

"My Lady, please be seated." Alanna saved me again with her well-timed intervention.

My temp husband's herd of friends followed suit, and the kitchen help began setting lovely plates before us. But the supposed object of my affection executed a neat bow in my general direction and stepped aside to put his head together with a guy who must be his friend/assistant/whatever. Sipping my wine, another excellent red, this time more like a rich, smooth Merlot than a Cabernet, I used the fact that his attention was elsewhere as an opportunity to sneak a peak at him.

If I had to play the Describe Him In One Word game, the word would be Power. He was huge and muscular—very muscular, which in no way counts against him. I'm an equal-opportunity kind of a girl. I try not to penalize skinny wimps *and* try not to obsess over muscular Swarzenegger types. (Please note I said *try*.) He seemed engrossed in his conversation, so I took my time and got a good long look. Yes, I managed to allow my mouth to flop open only wide enough to catch the wine I was pouring into it.

The hair on his head was thick and black, with an errant-looking wave. It was long, but he had it tied back in some kind of a leather thong (almost bigger than the one I had on). His face was ruggedly masculine—high cheekbones, a straight, well-formed nose and a deep cleft in his chin (a little reminiscent of Cary Grant, God bless him). His neck was thick without being steroidesque and it tapered nicely to wide shoulders and—yes, I'll just admit it—an absolutely wonderful chest smattered with just the right amount of tightly curled dark hair. His skin was a deep bronze, gilding him with a statue-like perfection. He was wearing a vest made of dark leather, which was open, giving me a lovely view of sleek, well-defined pectorals (I did very well in my college anatomy and physiology elective) tapering down to my personal favorite of all clichés: the six-pack abs. And a smooth, yummy waist. In short, the human part of him, which ended low on his abs, about where a man's hips would start, looked like a pretty damn handsome guy in the prime of his life—eighteen—no, just kidding, he was probably thirty-something. Whatever that was in horse years.

The horse part of his body was a maple-bay color, like ripe acorns or the leather binding of old books, shading down to mirror the black of the hair on his head from knees to hooves. He shifted his stance, still deep in conversation, and his coat rippled and caught the light from the sconces. He might be a grump, but he must groom himself regularly. Like I said before, he was large, and would probably measure fifteen or sixteen hands high at the withers. He was shaped more like a Quarter Horse than a Thoroughbred, heavily muscled and built for bursts of speed.

Studying him, I realized that I was not revolted or horrified by this merging of horse and man. And I didn't have to waste too many brain bytes pondering my acceptance. I grew up horse crazy, which definitely was the norm for an Oklahoma girl, and had my own horse until I left home for college. Actually, my dad liked to joke that I could ride before I could walk. (Wonder if being an experienced equestrian was a prerequisite for this kind of marriage? It certainly couldn't hurt.) And, truthfully, if he wasn't Mr. Frown Face I would say that he was actually attractive in a bizarre I've-lost-all-touch-with-reality kind of way.

Their discussion appeared to be over. His friend saluted him and headed toward the door, pausing only long enough to bow quickly to me. ClanFintan settled himself into the chaise next to mine. He really did move gracefully for such a big guy/horse/whatever.

In a formal, stilted voice he said, "Please excuse the interruption, my Lieutenant had matters of great import to discuss with me."

He truly sounded like he had a cob up his big ol horsey butt.

"Not a problem. Join me in a glass of this excellent wine," I whispered. Ignoring my abused throat I beamed him a big, gosh-I'm-such-a-nice-girl smile.

"Thank you."

Maybe if he had a drink he'd loosen up and act human (or whatever).

Servants were spilling out of a distant doorway with platters so laden with food that they reminded me of scuttling crabs. Smells engulfed me, and my tummy suddenly rumbled so loudly that I swear ClanFintan had to fight back a smile. I would have whispered an explanation about being "just a tad" hungry, but I didn't think my voice would carry over the ladylike roar of my stomach.

Several wonderful servants (sorry I thought of them as crabs) began offering first me, then ClanFintan, choice portions from platters steaming with delicious-smelling fish in creamy sauce, tender mouthwatering poultry (well, it tasted like chicken) sprinkled liberally with what appeared to be lemon pepper, grains that had a distinctly garlicky smell and veggies that looked like a nice mixture of pea pods, whole mushrooms and baby onions. Being a dainty and ladylike eater, I snagged helpings of everything while motioning for more wine. Yes, I realized I was drinking perhaps a tiny bit too much wine, but it was medicinal. I had, after all, recently been dead.

The meal decided it. I couldn't be in hell; the food was too wonderful. Between bites I did manage to glance at my dinner companion, and I was interested to note that he was also eating with gusto, and not just the grains and veggies. It looked like centaurs were omnivorous. (Note to self: be careful, he likes meat and he's a biter.)

I guess he noticed my lingering glances, because his mouth twisted in a sardonic smile as he announced, "A good appetite is a sign of returning health."

"Well, thank you, Dr. ClanFintan."

You'd think I sprayed milk out of my nose the way his eyes opened at my whispered retort. His look made me worry that I had a big piece of food stuck in my tooth or a big booger stuck in my nose.

"You know that I am not a physical doctor. I am spiritual High Shaman."

I had to swallow a piece of chicken before I could whisper an answer. "I'm just kidding you."

"Oh. I. Oh." Now his eyes narrowed at me, and I swear he gave a very horselike snort before he returned to chowing down.

I was starting to believe Rhiannon didn't have any sense of humor at all.

"My Lady, my Lord and honored guests. To demonstrate the Muses' approval of your handfast, Terpsichore, incarnate Muse of the Dance, will perform."

The centaurs' ears all pricked up (figuratively speaking) as Alanna clapped her hands twice and music began. I hadn't noticed the three women sitting in the far corner of the room, but the silky sounds of harp and flute and some kind of heart-beat-like drum were enchanting. Then, from the arched doorway nearest the musicians, in floated the dancer. She moved with a ballerina's grace, head down, arms beautifully rounded, to the center of the room, which was, of course, directly in front of my chaise. Being High Priestess obviously meant having the best seat in the house. There she seemed to melt into a deep curtsy, head still lowered, while the music paused. As the music began again, and she raised her head in time to the beginning tempo, I was caught swallowing and I did (delicately) spew wine out my nostrils. Thankfully, everyone was watching her and not me, so I had time to wipe my nose and regain my composure.

Holy shit! The dancer was Michelle, a girlfriend I'd been teaching with for ten years! And here she was, Goddess Incarnate Muse of the Dance—that friggin figures. Michelle and I love to laugh about the paradox of two of the three passions in her life. Passion number one is dance, passion number two is science (and she really likes reptiles, which has always worried me, especially because my classroom is next door to hers and at least two or three times each school year some kind of snake escapes from its cage and gets "lost"). So she combined her first two passions by attending Northeastern Oklahoma University as a chemistry major on a dance scholarship. At our high school she combines them by teaching honors chemistry and choreographing the school musicals. Strange girl.

Watching her move languidly in time with the sensual beat,

I took another gulp of wine and smiled gratefully at the little servant who darted obediently in to replenish it. There was no doubt—it was certainly Michelle, or rather, as I'm sure Alanna would have clarified, Michelle's mirror image. Same thick, dark hair and, as in Alanna's case, her shoulder-length chic modern cut had been replaced by waist-length tresses that rippled and glistened with her every movement. And covered her petite dancer's body more than the totally transparent shimmery pieces of gauze she was dressed in. As she danced, the slips of fabric floated around her, exposing enticing glimpses of her tight little body with every change in movement. Her body has always been sleek and gorgeous though she eats like a sparrow—ten times her body weight per day. She's the only person I've ever known who can eat a full school lunch off the Main Line, complete with every fat and carbohydrate known to man, every day, and not get violently ill or gain weight. The bitch.

The music was increasing in tempo, and Michelle/Terpsichore increased her seductive movements as she wove between the chaises. The centaurs sure were having a good ol' time— they'd stopped chewing because they were so busy gawking. She really was a great dancer. Right now she was performing an amazing dance—sex and grace all rolled up together into one delectable ball. Kind of like Bob Fosse Does Swan Lake. Her sexy little hips were moving rhythmically and seemed to be calling every bit of erotic energy in the room to attention. She was making eye contact with each male audience member, and the nasty girl just touched herself!

Which brings to mind the third of her three life passions— men. She adores men. Tall men, short men, hairy men, slick men, muscular men, lean men…etc., etc. She likes them all, as long as one part of their anatomy is big (no, I'm not talking about their wallets). Yes, she truly enjoys a big, hard penis more than any woman I know. With her it's a veritable art form. She's not exactly a slut—let's just say that men are her hobby and, well, she stays incredibly busy.

Her dance was climaxing, and she was working her way back toward center stage. There was no doubt about it—she was a sexy woman. Glancing at Mr. Ed I saw that he agreed with me; his rapt attention was centered on Michelle. She locked eyes with him as each pulse of the music drew her hips (and her scantily clad crotch) nearer and nearer his chaise.

Because I wasn't romantically attached to him, it was easy for me to watch the spell she wove around his hormones. With clinical detachment I realized this must be how Salome got Herod to chop off the Baptist's head. At the closing chord she collapsed into a satiated heap in front of us as her audience erupted into thunderous cheers. She raised herself liquidly and took her bows. I was smiling, waiting to catch her eye. But the "attagirl" look I intended to telegraph to her froze on my face when she finally looked at me. The hostility in her gaze was no less obvious because it was quickly replaced with cold propriety.

"Blessings to you at your handfast, Beloved of Epona." Her voice was an odd mirror of Michelle's. It sounded the same, but the words were hard and flat, totally devoid of the familiar warmth we share in another world. "I hope this mating brings you all the joy you so richly deserve." With a visual caress to the mate she was wishing me joy with, she turned and floated back out of the room.

Well, spank me and call me bad—I think I had just been insulted. And more and more I was wondering what Rhiannon had been up to. A little bird was telling me she might not be a nice girl. I glanced over at ClanFintan and noted he was still gazing, or should I say leering, at Michelle's departing form.

"She dances well, don't you think?" Noting his guilty start, I smiled knowingly up into his eyes.

"Yes, my Lady, she evokes Terpsichore's presence well." His voice had taken on a decidedly husky tint. He was almost purring. As we would say in Oklahoma, *Sheeet boy, settle down!*

But instead of looking away from those eyes, which were still glazed with passion, and instead of being annoyed by that purring, husky voice, I found myself becoming intrigued. Under the pretense of leaning closer so that he could hear my whisper, I got all into his Personal Space.

"Her dance was a blessing to our occasion." Man, he was warm. I wasn't even touching him and I could feel heat radiating from his body. Which, for some reason, made me want to giggle.

Reciprocating, he leaned toward me, which did make me giggle. (Quick note to self: yellow light—wine alert!) Oh, well, a yellow light was just a warning.

"The handfast dance is meant as more than a blessing." He paused—my eyebrows raised, inviting him to continue. "It is typically used as an *incentive*." On the last word his velvety voice dropped to match my whisper. "But as an Incarnate Goddess yourself, I am sure you are very aware of that."

Yipes.

My eyes broke from his heated gaze to trace the length of his body as his did the same to mine.

Had I forgotten that he was…well…a *horse?*

As if by a will of its own, my body stiffened and sat straight up—definitely out of his Personal Space. My abrupt movement brought on a wave of dizziness, a blur to my vision and a throb to my head. The Yellow Wine Alert changed to Red.

"Uh…" Trying to set my wine down, I totally missed the tabletop. Wine spilled all over. The goblet clattered and clanged. All attention was suddenly centered on moi.

"My Lady, are you well?" God bless Alanna's concerned sober little self.

"Too much to drink…" I wished she would quit dividing into several Alannas. Blinking hard, I got her image to settle back into one person. As I rubbed my forehead I risked a look at ClanFintan. He was watching me closely.

"You have overexerted yourself, Lady Rhiannon." His attempt at concern felt more like a challenge. "For one so recently ill, today has been overtaxing."

Now, *that* was the understatement of the decade.

"Perhaps it is time we retire." Did he just smirk?

"Uhhh!" The noise I made was somewhere between a shriek and a gasp. Retire? As in go to bed with him? In the Biblical sense? Where in the hell had my head been? Suddenly I realized I hadn't really considered all of the ramifications of this handfast. Yes, I had discussed the consummation thing with Alanna—she had reassured me—but I didn't know then that my intended was a horse! I had been worried about sex with a stranger, not bestiality! My stomach clenched. Please don't let me barf up this delicious meal all over my chaise.

"Uhhh…" And why the hell hadn't I been thinking about the sex issue? On my last wedding day when I married my stupid ex (who I like to think of as my starter husband), getting into bed with him was *all* I thought about. It wasn't like I was an innocent virgin and not aware of what happened on a wedding night!

"Uhhh…" Guess almost dying and changing worlds could truly screw up a normal thought process. Not to mention drinking too much wine. Medicinal or not.

Well, I'd better think about it now.

Consummation.

With a horse.

Who bites.

4

"I think I'm going to be sick."

"My Lady, shall I escort you to your chamber?" At least Alanna's concern was real. Her hands felt soft and cool as they pushed sticky tendrils of hair off my visibly moist forehead.

"Yes, please." Standing was suddenly a nautical experience. Pitching…rolling…ohh, feeling sick…eyes shutting tightly.

"Whoa—" Just as my butt was getting ready to slap the lovely marble floor, I felt myself being lifted into a firm burrow of heat.

"Allow me, Lady Rhiannon."

Holy shit the horse had just picked me up! Peeking one eye open, I saw his face at close view. He wasn't paying any attention to me, though, he just nodded at Alanna, who beamed some kind of thank-you smile at him and led us out the way she and I had come in. Looking at her retreating form from above reminded me of just how big ClanFintan really was— and how far above the ground I must have been and—

"Ugh." Maybe I should just keep my eyes closed.

"You will feel better after you sleep." His wide chest vibrated with his words. With my eyes shut he kinda reminded me of a large, warm vibrator, and I had to stifle a silly giggle.

"I didn't realize I drank so much wine."

He made a deep hrmmph noise in his throat, which only heightened the vibrator effect.

"You did."

"You vibrate when you talk."

"What?"

"It's okay. I like vibrators." I realized I was sounding tipsy, which was okay because I was definitely feeling tipsy. And for some reason my head was very heavy, like my hair weighed a lot. With a sigh I felt it plop down on ClanFintan/Mr. Ed's shoulder. Yes, I was most certainly deeply entrenched in The Land of the Lush.

"You smell good." Yes, I realized I was speaking my thoughts out loud. And, yes, I realized I was going to have a serious wine headache in the morning. But, no, there wasn't a lot I could do about it just then. Giggle.

"You have had too much to drink."

"No way!"

Another snort from him, which rumbled his chest and made me giggle again. Then I noticed that the snort had stopped but the rumble hadn't, and my eyes popped open.

He was laughing. At me, but he was laughing. And it was a nice laugh, which suddenly turned his face from a handsome cold face to a handsome nice face.

Of course, about this time my giggles gave me the hiccups, which *really* cracked him up.

Alanna stopped in front of the door I vaguely remember as the one to Rhiannon's room, and she seemed to be having a hard time containing her own laughter as she watched us. She saw me watching her through my semi-hysterical wine-hiccup giggles and her face flushed a bright pink right before she turned hastily to open the door and usher us through. Yep, Rhiannon obviously had no damn sense of humor.

"Dang," hic! "I have a seriously," hic! *"big,"* hic! "bed!"

Setting me down on the seriously big bed he studied me through his lingering smile.

"Thank you," hic! " for the," hic! "ride." Convulsing in wine-soaked giggles against my smooth pillows, I couldn't help but crack myself up. Thanking him for the "ride"—now, *that* was funny!

"You are different from the last time we met." His smile was still in place, but his deep voice had a contemplative quality to it that, even wine-soaked, I recognized. Glancing at Alanna, I saw the cheerful pink of her cheeks suddenly drain to white.

I felt myself struggling to sober up.

My hiccups evaporated.

"I'm, uh, me. As usual."

"Nothing is ever usual with you, Lady Rhiannon." His smile faded then, and for an instant I was sorry to see it go. Then I remembered that he was a horse and this was supposed to be our wedding night—and, according to Alanna's fearful face, there was lots of stuff going on around here about which I was clueless.

I closed my eyes and let myself slur a whispered reply, "Whatever…" and took a deep snorey breath. As if on cue, Alanna piped in.

"My Lord, perhaps you would like me to show you to your chamber." The silence that answered her made me want to open my eyes, but I could feel his gaze, so instead I took another deep breath and let it out in a decidedly unladylike snore.

"Your chamber adjoins this one, my Lord." Alanna's voice was insistent.

"Yes, I am definitely ready to retire." His voice was back to cold formality. His retreat from the room was loud and abrupt.

So loud it almost drowned out Alanna's musical lilt.

"My Lord, she has been through much recently." The

softness in her voice mirrored Suzanna's sweetness so completely that I felt an unexpected rush of homesickness.

"So have we all." And the door closed with a grim finality.

"He is gone, my Lady."

As was my giggly, tipsy feeling. Nothing like a little personal intrigue in an alternative mirror world to sober you up.

Returning, she stopped at the basin of water on the nightstand at the foot of the bed. Her hands shook as she made fluttery movements wringing out a small cloth.

"He knows I'm not Rhiannon."

Her hands still shook as she wiped my clammy forehead with the cool cloth.

"No, my Lady, he just knows you are different than he expected."

"Tell me about Rhiannon." Her hands stilled.

"She is my mistress and High Priestess, Goddess Incarnate of Epona."

"I know all of that. Tell me what kind of person she is."

"She is a powerful person."

Sigh.

"Alanna, I don't mean that. I mean her personality. You say she isn't like me, so I want to know what she is like."

Silence.

"Don't you know enough about me already to know you don't need to be afraid to tell me the truth?"

"It is difficult, my Lady."

"Okay, I'll help. Tell me why ClanFintan doesn't like her."

"She did not want to handfast with him, so she avoided him when she could. When she could not, she treated him coldly." Alanna's eyes shifted away from mine.

"Why didn't she just break off the betrothal?"

"Duty—the Incarnate of Epona has always mated with a High Shaman of the centaurs. If she wanted to remain High

Priestess, she must handfast for at least the required year with ClanFintan. Most matings between Epona's Beloved and the centaurs' Shaman last for life, though."

She certainly looked uncomfortable talking about it.

As she should!

"I know I'm not from here—but I really can't blame her for not wanting to have sex with a horse!" Alanna blinked in surprise at me. "I mean, please! It's freaking me out, too." Alanna tried to interrupt but I put a hand up and shushed her. I was sobering up, and I was on a roll. "And I don't appreciate you not warning me. He's nice-looking, and seems okay when he loosens up, but what the hell are you people thinking? How am I supposed to, well, *do it?* The logistics alone are mind boggling!"

"My Lady, it is not what you think." Her cheeks certainly were pink. "He is a High Shaman." She said it like that should clear everything right up.

"Yes, and he's a friggin horse!"

"What is 'friggin'?"

"Just an expression. I'm trying to quit cussing. Never mind." Sigh. "Are you saying that he and I are not expected to consummate the handfast?"

"No, of course not." She looked shocked.

"No, we're not to consummate—or no, we are to consummate." My headache was back.

"Yes, you are to consummate the handfast."

"Please explain how. Is he not a horse *from the waist down?*" God, my throat hurt.

"Well, yes, my Lady. In his present form." Now she was downright red around the cheeks.

"Alanna, I don't know what the hell you're talking about! What other form does he have?"

"He is a High Shaman, which means he can shapeshift into many different forms. A human is only one of them."

"That's impossible." Wasn't it?

"Not for ClanFintan." She said it all matter-of-factly, like water running downhill or wine inducing giggles and hiccups.

"So, I don't have to have sex with a horse?"

"No, my Lady."

"Well, that's a relief."

"Yes, my Lady. Here, let me help you get more comfortable." And she promptly started puttering around, removing my crown-thing, jewelry, makeup…

"You still haven't told me about Rhiannon."

Now it was her turn to sigh.

"Did she know ClanFintan could turn into a human?"

"Of course, my Lady."

"Stop puttering! I'm fine. Sit here and talk to me." She reluctantly sat next to me, looking prim and uncomfortable.

"It was not ClanFintan she abhorred. It was the idea of being mated to any male."

"Why?" Oh, great. Was I a lesbian? Not that I was homophobic or anything stupid like that, but being gay would seriously complicate an already difficult situation.

"Lady Rhiannon has made it exceedingly clear to him that she would not be happy limited to one man." She sounded embarrassed and sad. "Not even for one year."

"No wonder he doesn't like me." It all made sense now.

"Yes, my Lady."

"You didn't approve of her behavior, did you?"

"It is not my place to approve or disapprove of Lady Rhiannon's behavior." Her voice was flat and impersonal.

"Why not, aren't you her assistant or something like that?"

"Assistant?"

"Yeah, like an executive secretary or the person in charge of her schedule? You know, her employee."

"My Lady, I am her servant."

"Sounds like she didn't appreciate you or give you a decent job title. I'll bet the pay is crap, too. Couldn't you just quit?"

"You do not understand, my Lady. She owns me. I am her property."

Ohmygod.

"You're her slave?"

"Yes. And now I'm your slave, my Lady."

"No! I can't have a slave! I'll set you free. Give me the papers, or whatever. This is absolutely ridiculous."

"You must not, my Lady." Her face had paled once again and her voice sounded panicky. "Being Rhiannon's slave is my life. The MacCallan purchased me for his daughter when I was just a child. It is the way of our world."

"It isn't my world."

"It is now, my Lady."

A wave of exhaustion overwhelmed me. What was I doing here? How could this be real?

"Sleep, my Lady. Everything will be more clear in the morning."

"Everything will still be screwed up and bizarre." But sleep tugged at me. Wine and the stress of the day combined to make an excellent Tylenol PM. My closing eyes were leaden, my strength and desire to open them gone. Blackness was a welcome respite.

Besides Diana Gabaldon's Scotland and Anne McCaffrey's Pern, DreamLand is my favorite land to visit. My dreams have always been in color (and 3-D, of course) and wonderful. The Land of My Dreams is populated with flying heroes who fall in love with the heroine (me, of course), save the world (which has a sky that is a lovely shade of lilac violet) and then grind faceted diamonds out of raw coal with their strong (yet gentle) hands. My favorite suitor always begs the privilege of being allowed to pay off my enormous Ann Taylor credit card debt to prove his worthiness. In between scenes of being wooed by Pierce Brosnan (who can also fly), I laze about the lilac sky on clouds of golden cotton candy (the nonsticky kind) tickling the tummies of fluffy fat black-and-white cats, drinking fifty-year-old single-malt scotch and blowing the little white things off of old dandelions, which turn into snowflakes.

So, you can understand how drifting into my Land of Dreams would be something that I would look forward to after several days of stress and a change of worlds. Curled up on my side, breathing deeply, I fell willingly into a deep sleep, happily anticipating the newest dream in my fantasy land.

Which is also why you can understand I wouldn't be alarmed at first when I began to experience a floating sensation and I opened my eyes to see my soul detaching from my sleeping body as I drifted up and through the roof of my room.

And, yes, I did have a big bed—even from an overhead view.

Flying or floating is a cool side effect of visiting my Dream-Land. Granted, in my dreams I usually have to take a running start and hold my arms in front of me before I can leap off the ground and become airborne, but what the heck, it's Dream-Land, and not exactly steeped in reality—so just about anything goes…

…Back to floating through my ceiling. As I drifted up and out of the confines of Epona's temple I had an unusual moment of vertigo. Flying is always a pleasant dream experience, consequently the dizzy, gut-clenching feeling surprised me, but the vertigo was fleeting and I soon forgot the momentary oddity. Floating in the night air I was relaxed, breathing deeply and enjoying the beauty of the high, puffy clouds passing in front of an almost full moon. I noticed that they weren't the usual golden cotton-candy clouds of my dreams, which also was a little odd. And, yes, I realized that in tonight's dream I did seem to be able to actually smell the night air, but my dreams are normally very graphic and realistic, so I was curious, but not overly concerned with the vague fluctuations from the norm. After all, I was in another world. Maybe my DreamLand had been affected, too.

Looking below me, I was interested to see that my dream had totally made up a whole set of lovely buildings that pin-wheeled around the stately temple. Movement in a corral just outside of a rich-looking building which must be a stable piqued my interest. The stable was actually attached to the side of the temple, but that figured because it was the temple of a horse goddess and, of course, my dream layout would give horses extra privileges. Besides, I really do like horses—I've dreamed about riding/flying Pegasus several times. The movement caught my eye again, and my dream body floated down toward the corral until I was hovering just above the stone fence. A soft gust of wind pushed the puffy clouds away from the moon, and the sudden brightness illuminated the interior of the corral. I smiled and cooed in awe at the per-fection of a silver-white mare. At the sound, the mare stopped grazing and lifted her dainty head in my direction, blowing softly at the surrounding air.

"Hi there, you gorgeous girl." The mare's neck arched at the sound of my voice. I was delighted that instead of being afraid of my floating body, she seemed to recognize me (well, it was *my* dream) and pranced toward me. I held out my hands to her and she stretched her muzzle in my direction.

She was an amazing-looking animal. She reminded me of one of the Royal Lipizzaner stallions I had seen several years ago when their tour stopped in Tulsa. She was a nice-size mare, probably almost fifteen hands high. From a distance her coat appeared to be all one glistening silver color, but as she got closer to me I could see that her muzzle was dark, like black velvet, and her silver coat faded to darkness around her expressive eyes and her well-shaped hocks. I had never seen a horse like her before, and I smiled at my dream imagination. She continued her contented grazing and I gave her a last look as I floated back up into the night. Maybe I would return before my dream was over and we could go for a lovely ride in the sky.

The puffy clouds seemed to have cleared for good, and from my aerial view I could turn my floating body slowly in a circle and see for miles in all directions. The elaborate temple buildings were surrounded by a huge marble wall. The land outside the temple proper was sweet and rolling, reminding me of the Umbria region of Italy. (I took ten high-school kids on an "educational" trip to Italy a couple of years ago. They did just fine chaperoning me.) The gentle hills looked to be covered with grapevines. Which figures because, of course, my dream would have to touch on wine somehow. Hopefully, a floating waiter who looked like Pierce Brosnan would soon appear to serve me my favorite Merlot.

But I guess I'd had enough wine for one night, because Pierce didn't show. Yet.

Exploring my newest DreamLand seemed like a fun idea, so I kept floating and gawking. In the distance, probably to the north of the temple (don't quote me on that, though; I am directionally impaired) I could make out what appeared to be a large mountain range. While I was beginning to float toward the mountains, I noticed, again, the breeze which, again, struck me as an odd addition to my DreamLand because it had a scent. The breeze was coming from the west and I turned my head into its softness. I took a deep breath and recognized the smell of…hmm…I think salt in the air. An ocean? My shifting of attention also changed the direction of my

airborne body, and I felt myself float into the wind. By squinting my eyes I could barely make out some flickering lights and,
maybe, the reflection of the moon on water. Smiling in anticipation of the dream possibilities, I decided to head in that
direction—and was shocked by how quickly my dream self responded.

The land passing quickly beneath me was populated with
sleepy little villages that were scattered between vineyard-
covered rolling hills. A shimmering river connected them and
I noticed several small, flat boats moored at each village site.
The scent of salt was stronger, and I could make out a large
body of water in the quickly decreasing distance directly in my
flight path. Its shoreline looked imposing—rugged and green,
which suddenly reminded me of Ireland's Cliffs of Moher. (I
took students to Ireland one summer. We called it the Educational Pub Tour.) The shoreline stretched on in the distance
as far as I could see in the moonlit night, and as the dark liquid
horizon met the night sky, I could see silhouetted the western
edge of the mountain range I'd noticed earlier.

My body was still racing forward and I could see that I was
headed toward some type of large structure situated solidly near
the edge of one of the most dramatic-looking cliffs. (Kind of
like Edinburgh Castle—yes, I took a group of high-school
students to Scotland, too. I didn't cause them too much
trouble…no matter what they say.) Drifting closer, I felt myself
slowing down and I took a good look at what I could now see
much more clearly.

It was a wonderful, enormous old castle, and I was floating
directly above the entrance that faced away from the sea. Unlike
most of the castles I've toured in Europe, this one looked like
it was in perfect condition, complete with four massive towers
over which flew flags decorated with a rearing silver mare.
Huh. Looked just like the cool horse back at the temple.

The rear side of the castle was situated near the edge of the nasty-looking cliff; the inhabitants must love the amazing view. The front of the castle, above which I was floating, looked out on a tree-covered plateau, which gradually dipped down to a valley where a neat-looking village nestled. A well-worn road ran from the village through the forested plateau up to the castle, giving evidence of a congenial relationship between castle and town. The typical walled ramparts surrounded the castle itself and were joined at an enormous gated entrance, but rather than looking menacing and cold, the castle was well lighted and its entrance was open and welcoming. A castle used as a military fortress would be closed and guarded. The lovely forest of old trees would be shorn so that an advancing enemy couldn't sneak up. My dream castle obviously wasn't war friendly, and it was probably "guarded" by (who else?) Pierce Brosnan! It was more than likely that he was waiting inside for me to quit my floating tour so that he could rub edible pink coconut oil all over my body. Then lick it slowly off. Yummy… Which is why it was odd that my body was still floating over the castle. Okay, I was definitely ready to stop flying now and get to the more "personal" part of my dream.

Anticipatory smile.

Nothing.

Still floating.

Okay, I was ready to stop flying now!

Nothing. What in the hell was up with this? DreamLand was *my* fabrication. It obeyed me. I remember when I first realized not everyone had the ability to control their dreams. I was in third grade and a friend of mine was looking pale and upset one Monday morning. At recess I asked her what was wrong and she said an amazing thing—she said she'd had a horrible nightmare the night before. I told her she should have just told the dream to change, and she looked at me as if I was crazy (or scary), and told me that that was impossible. Dreams did what they wanted to do. Until then it hadn't occurred to me that everyone couldn't control his or her dreams. If my dreams ever began to get uncomfortable or frightening, I just told them to change. And they accommodated my request. In thirty-five years I have never had a dream that wouldn't obey me. My girlfriends think it's way cool, my boyfriends think I'm making it up. So my dreams have always been mine to control.

Until tonight.

Hovering over the castle, my feeling of confusion was compounded by my rising frustration level. I wouldn't really classify this as a "bad" dream; it was more like an annoying dream. And I really wanted it to stop—

Then everything changed. Fear enveloped me. It was like nothing I had ever known. More terrifying to me than my car wreck. More horrible than my snake phobia. It was the raw fear that comes with the certainty of being in the presence of evil. Living evil, like the kind that inspires pedophiles or rapists or terrorists.

Trying not to panic, I took deep breaths and reminded myself that this was only a dream…only a dream…only a dream. But the feeling persisted. Gazing beneath me, I studied the castle for some hint that could explain my terror. The castle looked sleepy and innocent. In a room built on the wall near the open front gates, I could see two men dressed in uniforms who might be guards or night watchmen. They were sitting at a wooden table playing what appeared to be some kind of dice game. No evil there; slacking employees, perhaps, but nothing overtly villainous. Various other rooms in the castle were still lighted, and once in a while I could glimpse figures moving in front of windows. No one seemed to be committing any murders, no raping or pillaging was going on. At the side of the castle that overlooked the ocean I could see a man standing on an observation ledge, but he wasn't cutting up any babies or raping any grandmas; he was just looking. No evil there, either.

But it was here. I could feel it. I could almost touch and smell it. It was like after you drive your car over an animal that has been lying dead in the road for a very long time. The stench seems to cling to your car's wheels and to your throat even after you've left it miles behind.

My body turned gently as I continued my search, and I found myself looking out over the forest—

That was it. No question about it, the evil was there, coming from the forest. It emanated from the northern edge, the part that eventually met the distant mountains. It was so strong that I found it difficult to keep my eyes focused on that area; my vision kept shifting, like I was trying to concentrate on one of those 3-D pictures but couldn't quite get the hidden image right.

It was as my gaze slid over the trees, not quite focused, that I saw it. A ripple in the darkness of the night-shadowed trees. Blinking, I focused above the tree line and, again, the forest rippled. It was like ink seeping down a naked page—crawling shadows, oily and thick. A mass of something was moving through the trees, singular in intention and demeanor. The forward line of it was swift and silent.

I gasped in realization. Its destination was obvious—it was converging on the sleeping castle.

5

There was nothing I could do to help. I tried to scream at the dice-playing guards, and my ghostly voice was carried away by the wind. My body still wouldn't descend, and, for a moment, I felt shamefully thankful as I realized that the thought of being in the castle as the darkness drew closer and closer terrified me. And I couldn't wake up. Glancing back to the edge of the northern tree line, I was horrified by how quickly the darkness had advanced. And as they got closer, the evil radiating from them felt thicker. How could anyone in the castle sleep or play cards or hang out? How could they not feel it, too?

And suddenly it wasn't a dream to me anymore. Here and now the unfolding horror had become my reality.

As if responding to my thoughts, my floating body moved closer to the dark line. I was afraid, but curious and committed to understanding what was happening. I watched the front of the line break out of the trees. I drifted closer.

At first I thought they were tall men wearing dark, flapping cloaks. They appeared to be running with amazingly long strides, and then leaping, like a long jumper at a track meet, only not landing on two feet and falling, but landing on still-running legs.

This odd manner of movement ate up the land beneath them and gave them the appearance of gliding more than of running.

Like instead of being living beings they were really specters or shades of the dead.

As they got closer, my attention was riveted on their long, loose cloaks. I watched them move against the wind currents caused by the gliding run, until in horror I realized that the movement was voluntary. More and more of them poured out of the forest, and I understood what the cloaks really were— wings, enormous dark wings that spread and trapped the wind, aiding the leaping run and enabling the glide.

A shiver of revulsion shuddered through my floating body. There must have been hundreds of them. They were like huge predatory humanoid bats, or gigantic humanoid roaches. I began to be able to make out individuals and their features. It was only their wings that were dark, and because they were so large and outstretched, they lent the line the appearance of being dark. In truth, under the wings, their bodies were so white they almost seemed translucent. They were naked except for loincloths, and their thin torsos looked skeletal. Their hair was light colored, ranging from blond to silver and white. Their arms and legs were abnormally long, like what would result if a human was mated with a spider. But they were most definitely humanoid. They had the faces of men—cruel, determined men.

And a short Bobby Burns poem flashed through my mind:

Many and sharp the numerous ills
Inwoven with our frame;
More pointed still, we make ourselves
Regret, remorse and shame;
And man, whose heaven-erected face
The smiles of love adorn,

Man's inhumanity to man,
Makes countless thousands mourn.

I was unable to look away from them as they spread to the unguarded castle doors beneath me like a virulent strain of a terrorist's plague, and then they were there. They poured into the castle, silent and deadly. The dice players didn't notice. No new doors closed or windows opened. Silence. Silence. Silence.

But I could feel them. Somehow, I could feel what they were bringing. I couldn't see what was happening inside the many rooms below me, but I could sense the terror and pain rustling through the castle like a silent cancer spreading throughout a diseased body.

Frantically, I searched for some way to warn them. Some way I could help them. And my errant body began floating in a different direction. This time it was taking me toward the solitary man still standing on the observatory ledge. Getting closer, his shadowed shape took on familiar lines.

Oh, my God. My breath rushed out of me in one word. *"Dad!"*

He turned at the sound of my voice, and as he glanced around, presumably looking for me, I saw him clearly in the moonlight. It was my father. Damn the mirror-image crap; damn the alternative-world garbage. This man was my dad.

In his mid-fifties his football player's body was still powerful. One of my cousins once told me that as a child he thought my father was the strongest man he had ever known—and now that he's an adult he's sure of it. And he's probably right. Not that Dad's a huge guy, he's not. Probably only five foot ten, graduating from a small country high school he was told he wasn't big enough to play football at a major university like the University of Illinois. But they didn't figure on his tenacity.

Like a mean little bulldog, he was just too damn tough to be benched. After a successful college-football career, he passed his strengths on to the players he coached, was recruited by the biggest high school in Oklahoma and become the coach who took his team to the state championship seven years in a row. And won all seven times.

I have always been a Daddy's Girl. I grew up trusting in his strength. As a child I knew that there was no dragon he wouldn't slay for me, no demon he couldn't banish.

I saw all of this reflected in the man below me.

"Dad!"

His head shot up at the sound of my disembodied voice, but his brow was wrinkled with confusion. How well could he really hear me?

"Rhiannon? Are you here, daughter?"

Perhaps he could only hear the echo of my soul. Summoning all of my concentration into one word like a prayer, I cried.

"Danger!" The word ended on my sob.

"Yes, lass, I sensed danger in the night!"

His brow suddenly cleared and he began striding purposefully off the ledge. Leaping to the wooden catwalk that ran the length of the inside wall of the castle, he broke into a run. My hovering body was right behind him as he rushed toward the watchtower, booming in a voice very like Dad's except it was thick with an almost Scottish-sounding brogue.

"Get yerselves armed and awake the castle! Epona has warned me of danger! Hurry, lads, I feel a crawling in me skin that says we donna have much time." Through the window I observed the shock on the faces of the guards as they followed the man who looked so much like my dad into action. Arming themselves, they rushed down into the bowels of the tower, and I could hear them waking other men. The night was now filled with the sounds of shouting men and clanging weapons.

And screams, which originated from the interior rooms of the castle.

Led by my dad, half dressed in hastily tied kilts, men scrambled to arm themselves as they rushed out of the towered barracks toward the heart of the castle, only to find the enemy already there. Helplessly, I watched as the creatures leaked out of the inner castle to meet the guards. The blood of their early victims had dimmed the white of their skin. They were not creatures of nightmare—they were *the* nightmare. I could not make out any weapons in their hands, yet as the guards began battling them, their swords and shields did little good against the man-creatures' bared teeth and claws. The sheer number and ferocity of them overwhelmed the castle guards. Many of the man-creatures had time to stop and feed at the necks and warm entrails of still-living men, as others stepped around them to resume the slaughter. The ripping and tearing of flesh is a sound like no other, and as I watched I felt my soul begin to shake.

I had lost sight of Dad, and I tried to get my body to float closer to the battle. It wouldn't obey me. And then there was no need—I saw him. Man-creatures surrounded him. Blood poured from open wounds that had been torn in his arms and chest, but his huge sword was still swinging in an arch around him. At his feet were two headless things, victims of his strength. The man-creatures circled him, being careful to stay out of the reach of his blade.

"Come to me, ye bloody cowards!"

His voice reached me, and I recognized the challenge it carried. I had only heard it once before. It was at football practice. Dad had benched the star linebacker because he'd been caught shoplifting at a local store. The smart-ass kid was telling Dad his behavior off the field didn't matter, that he should still play because he was the best they had. Dad took him (and his ego) to the middle of the field, and while the team looked on as witness he said to the kid, "You can play tomorrow night if you can knock me off my feet." The kid was almost six inches taller than Dad, more than thirty years younger, and outweighed him by at least forty pounds, but he couldn't knock my father off his feet, and he damn sure didn't play in another game that season.

I heard the echo of that challenge in the man's voice below me. His stance was the same, and his strength was the same. Again he was in the right, but this time I knew that wouldn't matter. He had caught the attention of more of them. One by one the ring grew until at least twenty man-creatures, their wings taut, surrounded my father, their bloody mouths snarling in expectation.

I'll never forget how he stood there. He didn't panic. He was calm and sure. As one being, they began to converge. I saw his sword flash and heard it slice through the first and second and third, until it could no longer keep up. Then their fangs and teeth reached him. He fought with his fists, which were slick with his own blood. Even as he dropped to his knees, he didn't cry out.

And he didn't quit.

But I could take no more. My soul felt like it was shattering with his body and I shrieked my agony to the night—

And I was wrenched abruptly awake.

"No! Dad, no!" My body was shaking and my cheeks were wet with tears.

Alanna and ClanFintan burst through different doors into my room at almost the same instant.

"My Lady! Oh, my Lady, what has happened?"

Alanna rushed to me. Not caring that she wasn't really Suzanna, I wrapped my arms around her and wept into her embrace.

"It was horrible." Around sobs my broken words came out. "They killed my father. There was nothing I could do but watch."

Alanna was making wordless, soothing noises as she stroked my back.

"Is there danger? Shall I summon the guards?" ClanFintan's voice was a warrior's, and I had a sudden feeling that he would be courageous in battle, and like my dream premonition of evil, I knew this, too, was true.

"No." My sobs had begun to quiet to whimpers, but the tears still flowed freely down my face. "It happened in my dream, not here."

Abruptly I felt Alanna still. She gently moved my body back from hers far enough so that she could look into my eyes.

"You must tell us what you saw, my Lady." Her voice was calm, but I could hear the fear in her words.

"It was a dream."

Over her shoulder I saw ClanFintan move restlessly, his eyes dark with some emotion I could not identify.

"What did Epona reveal to you, Rhiannon?" His voice beckoned to me, and I closed my eyes tightly, feeling confused.

"*It was no dream.*" Alanna's whisper was for my ears alone, and it sent more shivers of shock through my already abused body.

Oh, God, what had happened?

Forcing myself to square my shoulders and still my body's quaking, my eyes lifted to meet ClanFintan's steady gaze.

"I need a moment to get myself together, please. Then I'll tell you everything I saw in my dream."

The compassion that flashed through his eyes gave me a glimpse of his kindness. Little wonder he was spiritual leader of his people.

"Of course, my Lady. Have your servant send for me when you are ready."

Not caring about the consequences, I said, "She is not my servant. She is my best friend." I could feel Alanna's shocked intake of breath.

"My mistake, Lady Rhiannon. Have your *friend* send for me." His smile looked sincere and unexpectedly it comforted me.

As the door clicked softly shut my shaking resumed.

"My Lady, I am not your friend. I cannot be your friend." Alanna's voice sounded frightened.

"No, Alanna. What you are not is Rhiannon's friend. You were her slave, her servant. I am not her." I wiped my eyes and smiled my thanks to her as she handed me a cloth so I could blow my nose. "I realize you are not Suzanna, but I can't help but see her in you—and she is my best friend. I hope that you will humor me and maybe eventually you will come to feel that friendship for me, too. And, Alanna, I really need a friend right now." And I promptly started to cry. Again.

"What you say is true, my Lady, you certainly are not Rhiannon." Her eyes filled with sympathetic tears as she brushed the hair back from my face and gave me a sweet, impromptu hug. "And your voice seems to be recovered."

"Yeah, it does, doesn't it?" My smile felt awkward and strained, as if my face had forgotten how.

"Shall I get you something soothing to drink so that you do not cause it to relapse?"

"How about some hot tea? I want to stay away from wine for now."

Alanna clapped her hands twice and a sleepy nymph appeared to fetch and carry for me. (Oh, jeesh, is that another of my slaves?) Despair felt easy to slip into and I was disgusted when my tears began anew.

"Alanna, help me understand what has happened." Wiping my eyes again, I gained control over my hovering depression. "You said that what I saw was real? How can that be?"

"You experienced the Magic Sleep. It is one of the gifts you have that makes you High Priestess and Beloved of Epona. Even as a small child you were able to send your sleeping soul away from your body and observe events, and sometimes even communicate with people. You were not able to do this in your old world?"

"No, not exactly, but my dreams have always been mine to control, which is unusual in my world. I visited made-up places and had fun things happen to me." And now that innocence was gone. DreamLand would never again be a place of pure happiness. Not after tonight. I shivered again.

"That must have been how your gift manifested itself in a world devoid of Epona." After what I had observed tonight it was hard for me to understand why Alanna's voice sounded sad.

"But why tonight? I definitely didn't 'send' my soul anywhere. Remember, Alanna, I am not Rhiannon. Why would it happen without me even understanding what is going on?" My eyes filled with more tears. "It was horrible. Why was I forced to watch it?"

"Perhaps Epona touched you tonight because she required you to serve as witness."

"Is your Goddess so cruel?"

"No, my Lady. Great evil can only be combated by great good."

The nymph was back with a tray holding an exquisite tea set. I smiled my appreciation at her, which she shyly returned. But as she turned to leave I noticed she had brought only one teacup. "Excuse me." The nymph froze. "Please bring Alanna a cup, she will be joining me."

"Y-y-yes, my Lady."

"Thank you." She looked confused, but she scampered off to do my bidding. Alanna was studying me with what was becoming her familiar What Are You Doing Now face. "Don't start. I'm under too much stress to deal with this slave crap. You're going to have to get used to me treating you like you're my friend. Like they say, damn the torpedoes and full speed ahead!"

"Wha—"

"Just another expression." The tea was spreading comforting warmth through me and I was starting to feel a little less shaky. "It means let's try and forget all that is working against us and forge ahead." The little nymph-maid came back with another cup, which she handed to Alanna. She still looked confused, but she was enthusiastically returning my smile as she bowed her way out of the door. Alanna awkwardly poured herself a cup of tea. "Okay, so what you're telling me is that what I observed wasn't a dream or a vision. It was real, happening as my soul or essence or whatever floated above it all?"

"Yes, my Lady," she said sadly.

"So—" I took several deep breaths "—he's dead?"

"I am so very sorry, my Lady."

The teacup clattered against the delicate china as my shaking hand set it back on its saucer.

A sudden thought made my breath stop.

"My mother. What about my mother?" I felt a constriction in my chest. Not her, too. "I didn't see her, but wouldn't she be there, with him?"

"My Lady, your mother died shortly after your birth." Her voice was soft and she set her teacup down on its saucer and reached for my hand.

"Oh…" My voice trailed away thoughtfully. "Oh, that's good."

Alanna's eyes widened. "My Lady?"

"No, I didn't mean I was glad she is dead." Alanna looked relieved. "I'm just glad she wasn't killed by those creatures. In my world she divorced my father when I was a child." Alanna looked shocked. "It was a good thing, really. They both re-married and are very happy."

"If you say so, my Lady." She sounded doubtful.

"You don't have divorce here?" Oh, please.

"Yes. But it is considered dishonorable."

"Whatever your customs, I'm glad my mother didn't have to go through what happened tonight." Somehow it was easier to think that she had died thirty-five years ago, and not have to picture her being murdered tonight. Like Dad had been. I took a deep breath.

Still feeling shaky, I asked the question that suddenly mattered very much to me. "Was Rhiannon close to her father?"

"I think he was the only man Rhiannon has ever been able to truly love. He never remarried and he raised her alone, not sending her away from him, like many Chieftains would have done." She smiled sadly at me. "The MacCallan was so very proud of her. He doted on her. I believe he saw a side of her she never allowed anyone else to see. Rhiannon was always on her very best behavior around him."

My throat felt tight and hot. "Then we do have one simi-larity—the love we feel for our fathers."

"You must explain what has happened tonight to ClanFin-tan. He can help you. Trust him, my Lady. He could be a powerful ally." She grasped my hands and spoke earnestly. "Except for The MacCallan, Rhiannon did not care for anything that did not bring her pleasure, or anyone she could not manipulate and use to her advantage." Her soft brown eyes searched mine. "You look like her. You have her fire, her humor and her passion, but because of your strange world, and the different choices you made as you grew to adulthood there, you have developed into a very different woman. I do not believe you are as she was. You have a caring heart. Please, my

Lady, have more wisdom, too. Remember, your father approved of your mating with him. ClanFintan is strong and wise, he will know how to right this horrible wrong."

"Send for him." I gave her hands a quick squeeze. She smiled at me and touched my cheek before clapping her hands again and informing the answering nymph that I would like to see ClanFintan. Abruptly I realized how disheveled I must look, and with my fingers I began to try to comb my wild hair into some semblance of submission. Alanna's skillful hands stilled mine as she grabbed a brush off my nightstand and quickly fashioned my hair into a beautiful French braid.

"Thank you, friend."

Her warm smile was answer enough.

ClanFintan entered the room, closing the door softly behind him. Without hesitation he moved to the side of my bed and reached out to grasp my hand in his.

"I would like to offer you my deepest sympathies. The MacCallan was a great Chieftain and friend." His grip was warm and firm. "All of Partholon knows of your love for him." He squeezed my hand before letting it loose.

"T-t-thank you." My hand felt suddenly cold without the warmth of his touch.

"Are you ready to tell what you have witnessed?" His deep voice was filled with concern.

"Yes." I squared my shoulders. "My dream began here. I went up through the ceiling and visited the beautiful mare." Alanna and ClanFintan both smiled in acknowledgment, so I guessed she was real, too. "Then I flew up, loving the brilliance of the moon and the night."

"Yes, the moon does call." His voice sounded wistful.

"Yeah, um…" His eyes were warm and kind as they looked at me. Jeesh, now was *not* the time to be getting confused by a pretty face, or whatever. "Well, I found myself drawn toward the sea. And there was the castle on the cliff overlooking the shore." He nodded understanding. "Almost from the beginning I knew something was wrong. No, not just wrong. I knew there was evil present. I couldn't see anything, I just felt it." He nodded again, encouraging me to continue. "As I tried to find the source of my premonition, I looked out at the forest. That's where they came from." I stopped and shuddered. Alanna, who was still standing next to me, put her hand on my shoulder in reassurance. "They were horrible. At first I thought the forest was actually alive, some kind of nightmare creature. It rippled and surged. Then I saw that it wasn't the forest itself, but that there were awful things passing through it. And then I really saw them. They had wings, but they looked human."

"Fomorians," ClanFintan's voice hissed, incredulous.

Before I could question him, Alanna's hand tightened on my shoulder in warning. I glanced up at her and saw her nodding her head, agreeing with ClanFintan's naming of the abominations.

"When I understood what was happening, I screamed a warning to him, and he even heard me. But it was too late. They overran the castle. They killed all of the guards, and all of the people." I put my face in my hands. "I watched as they killed my father."

"Lady Rhiannon." His voice brought me back to the present. "Could you tell how many of them there were?"

"Lots. They were like a ravenous swarm of insects. They devoured everyone."

"I am sorry to ask this of you, Lady Rhiannon, but I need you to describe them to me—in detail." His kind eyes were gentle and apologetic.

I cleared my throat and took another drink of tea before beginning. "They seemed to be taller than most of the men from the castle." Pausing, I blinked away scenes of winged demons flinging themselves on the courageous guards. "They all had enormous, dark wings that grew out of their backs. They didn't fly with them, but they used them to help them run and glide. They moved amazingly fast. Faster than a man can run. Their arms and legs appeared to be very long and thin, their skin milky white, their hair was long and mostly light colored." I paused again, remembering. "What was most horrible about them was that they looked like men. Take the wings off, dress them in regular clothes, and they could pass for human men." I shivered.

"Did they use weapons?" He broke into my thoughts.

"Just teeth and claws." Then I forced myself to add, "They were stopping to eat the guards before the castle was completely taken—and before the men were even dead." My flat, empty-sounding voice could not begin to reflect the horror I felt at the cruelty I had witnessed.

"I did not believe it true until now." He paced back and forth in front of the foot of the bed, running his fingers through the thickness of his loosened hair. "I thought the stories told from our past about the Fomorians were myths, tales used to frighten children into good behavior."

"I don't understand." This is probably something I should already know, or rather, something Rhiannon knew, but now was not the time for me to play Ms. Silent (as if I ever could).

"You've heard the stories." He seemed too engrossed in his own thoughts to notice my lack of knowledge. "Partholonian mothers have frightened children who strayed too far from home with tales of winged demons who would swoop them up and devour them."

"Oh, yeah." I tried to sound nonchalant. "I don't remember the whole story. Where were they supposed to have come from?"

"They came from the other side of the Trier Mountains. I do not think any of the legends ever specified their origin."

"What happened to them?"

"Bards sing that generations ago Partholon rose against them. Although they possessed great evil, their numbers were small. They were defeated and the surviving few were banished back over the mountains. Which, according to legend, is why Guardian Castle was erected at the mouth of the pass, and how it got its name." He looked at me intently. "But, being Epona's Beloved, I would think that you would know this already."

"Epona does not traffic with evil." As soon as it escaped from my mouth, I had an intuitive feeling that it was the truth. But my intuition was haphazard and I didn't feel I could trust it. Great. Back to tap dancing. "And why would I concern myself with legends used to frighten children?" Grasping at straws, I glanced up at Alanna for help. "Epona is much too busy to bother with such foolishness." I was totally lost—completely clueless. Fomorians? Partholonians? Trier Mountains?

"Perhaps that is why she sent you to witness the horror of tonight, my Lady. So that you could realize what has been loosed upon Partholon." Alanna's voice was kind, and she reached down to take my hand. "Could Epona not have been warning you of a danger for which you have been unprepared?" Her words had special meaning for the two of us; she knew I was unprepared for *all* of this. Her smile was sad, and then she glanced at ClanFintan. "Perhaps that is why she has united the two of you. Epona knew her Beloved was unprepared for this evil, as she knew that as High Shaman you have been better informed about these legends, and would be more prepared to combat this evil."

"Of course. Thank you, Alanna." She saved my butt. Again.

"Yes, that does make sense." Thank God ClanFintan seemed too preoccupied to think too hard. And after all, horse or no horse, he *was* a guy. And, well, they just don't multitask very well.

"Which means Epona was warning me that this evil is coming." Like a big lightbulb going on, I abruptly sat up and shook off any lingering tears. "The damn things aren't going to be happy with just attacking my father's castle." I looked back and forth between the two of them. "I think what Epona is telling us is that we're not safe." And, as weird as it sounded, I knew it was true. Maybe Rhiannon was experiencing the same kind of thing in Oklahoma—a bizarre ability to intuitively feel things she didn't know before.

"Yes, Lady Rhiannon, this is a portent warning us of impending danger." ClanFintan's manner was suddenly brusque and professional. "With your permission I will send for the Fintan warriors so they can aid your Palace Guard in evacuating the people who live between here and MacCallan Castle. They can come here. As you know, Epona meant this site to be easily defended, and they will be safer here. I assume you have provisions stored in case of emergencies?"

Alanna's nod of assent helped me to breathe easier.

"Good. MacCallan Castle is two days hard ride from here." ClanFintan was pacing again, totally engrossed in his thought process. "Let us hope that the Fomorians will pause to enjoy their victory and not immediately begin their next attack. That should give us time to send for reinforcements from the herd, gather the villagers and warn Partholon."

"Wait…"

"Forgive me, Lady Rhiannon. I did not mean to take charge of your duties. As your mate, I only wish to aid you in preparing for that which Epona has warned you."

His voice was sincere. But he was a guy, and as usual he was missing the point.

"What about my dad?"

"I am sorry, Lady Rhiannon, but he is dead." Again, his voice was kind—his honest concern obvious, but he still didn't get it.

"I remember what I saw." My voice felt strained and I took a quick drink of tea. "But I didn't actually see him die." Clan-Fintan and Alanna exchanged worried looks. "What if he's still alive? Suffering…" I took another drink of tea. I was not going to cry. Again.

"Rhiannon—" his deep voice was comforting. "You must realize he could not have survived."

"I…I understand that. I know he must be dead. But, well, I can't leave him and those men just lying out there." I looked into his eyes, as close to pleading as I wanted to come. "You didn't see how brave they were."

"Of course, Lady Rhiannon. They were valiant warriors." He sounded confused. God, he was such a guy.

"Yeah, and I need to bury them." It was pretty simple. My dad and his men were not going to be crow bait.

Alanna's hand squeezed my shoulder again. "My Lady, you cannot go to MacCallan Castle."

"Of course I can. He just said it's only two days away, and—" here I faltered. She knew I had only been there in spirit. "Well…I've been there before." I was sounding like an idiot.

Alanna and ClanFintan exchanged worried glances.

"Lady Rhiannon, you cannot put yourself in such danger." He held up his hand to still my protest. "The people look to you for guidance. You are the Beloved of Epona. Especially now, no harm must come to you. At a time when evil is loose upon the world, the people will be looking to Epona for stability and guidance."

"And the warriors, my Lady, human and centaur alike, will look to you." Alanna's worried voice interrupted ClanFintan. "You are Goddess Incarnate of the warriors, too. It will be a hard blow when they realize The MacCallan is dead. If the Beloved of Epona is in danger, it would severely damage the spirits of the warriors."

Wonderful. I was in charge of the esprit de corps and I wasn't even Marilyn Monroe. Somehow it didn't seem fair.

"Think of what it would do to your people if you were injured or captured." ClanFintan took my hand.

His hand was warm. His grip was firm.

God, he was a big guy/horse. He'd be hell on a football field.

Dad would really like him. The thought almost made me smile.

"Listen to him, my Lady. What if the Fomorians are still at MacCallan Castle? Your father would not want you to put yourself in danger, not even for him."

"But I can't just leave him out there." I felt tears forming in my eyes again as my frustration overwhelmed me.

"Lady Rhiannon…" ClanFintan's deep voice penetrated my swirling emotions. "Ask yourself what The MacCallan would have you do."

I shut my eyes. Of course Dad wouldn't want me to get hurt. If only it were that simple.

My mind could tell me that the man I watched die was not really my dad. He was not Richard Parker, high-school biology teacher in Broken Arrow, Oklahoma, football coach, horse trainer, amateur artist (he liked to work with charcoal sketches of animals—which now seems vaguely ironic), excellent cook and a darn handy plumber. He was my dad.

No, not just my dad. My favorite man in the world. Yes, *my* world, and I knew rationally that my old world was not this one. But my heart said something else. It said that it somehow didn't matter. He looked like Dad. He sounded like Dad. And, no matter how bizarre and screwed up things had become since I'd awakened in this weird world, Rhiannon loved this man, too.

She might be a bitch. She was definitely a slut. She wasn't even a very good person. But she, too, was a Daddy's Girl. She loved her dad. Before now I hadn't thought too much about home. I'd been a little busy. But if something happened to my dad, I knew, somehow I just knew, no matter how crazy her new world seemed to her, Rhiannon wouldn't desert him.

And I wouldn't desert her dad, either. I felt the responsibility of a devoted daughter. I couldn't escape it and I was pretty sure that I wouldn't want to even if I could.

But Alanna and ClanFintan wouldn't understand.

I opened my eyes. Seeing clearly—finally.

"What you're saying makes sense." I gave them my best accommodating smile.

They relaxed.

And I pretended dizziness. "Oh, I'm so tired. Is it morning yet?"

They looked concerned, and I felt a momentary twinge of guilt. Alanna answered first, but ClanFintan squeezed my hand, looking worried.

"My Lady, it is not yet daylight."

"Rest, Rhiannon, I will see to sending the warriors to begin bringing the villagers to the temple." His free hand touched my cheek in a brief caress. He really was cute, in a horsey way.

"I'm just so tired." I played Lana Turner, falling back on my pillows, my free hand touching my forehead. The other one still clutched at ClanFintan's. (Well, it felt good!)

"Rest, my Lady." Alanna was clucking and arranging pillows.

"I will see to the warriors." ClanFintan bowed over my hand and turned it, palm up. My eyes shot open, and for a second

I was scared he was going to bite me again. Instead, his gaze caught mine and held it while he kissed the middle of my palm. I mean really kissed it. Man, his lips were warm.

Yep—it felt good, too. I'm telling you—Dad would like this guy. Dad always liked a guy who could keep me on my toes.

Then he dropped my hand and moved quickly toward the door. I could hear him yelling orders for his centaurs to be awakened and sent to him, then the door closed and I was left with the lingering warmth of his lips on my palm.

Alanna was still plumping my pillows and looking worried, kind of like a sweet little mother hen.

"Are you well, my Lady?"

"Yes, Alanna, thank you. I think I just need to rest for a while. So much has happened." I snuggled down into my comfortable bed. "You need to get some sleep, too. I'll be okay, go ahead and rest."

She gave me a doubtful look. "Can I not get you some warm mulled wine, or perhaps brush your hair until you sleep?"

Damn, she sure knew what I liked.

"No, honey. Thank you, though. I just need some sleep."

"Then I will leave you to your rest." She brushed the hair back from my forehead in a familiar gesture, and just before my eyes closed I felt her lips touch my forehead as she whispered, "Good night, Shannon."

As she turned to leave I couldn't help but ask the question that kept popping into my mind. "Alanna, did Rhiannon ever mention how she was going to get back here—and get me back there?" My eyes were still shut, but I could hear her feet stop, and I knew she had turned to look at me.

"She said it was not possible to return. It is only possible to pass through The Divide once and live." Her voice sounded sad. "I am sorry, Shannon. I know this must be difficult for you."

"Don't worry about it. It's not your fault." I wondered if she could hear my heartbeat all the way over there. Never go back home? I kept my eyes shut tightly.

Suddenly I understood Scarlett O'Hara. I couldn't think about this today. I'd think about it tomorrow.

I heard Alanna's footsteps fade away, and my eyes peeked open at the soft sound of the door closing. Then I sat up and downed the rest of the tea (caffeine is good for the soul). I had places to go and people to…well…inter. And this "stay safe and be good" crap might be okay for Ms. Rhiannon, but I'm a different kind of girl.

And my dad was not going to be abandoned.

6

Damn, I wish I had my Mustang. Mobility is the modern woman's emancipation. Who can keep a woman down when she can jump her ass into a car and drive to a different town/state/man/job?

I tried to figure out how to get myself to a castle somewhere northwest of here. In the middle of the night. With some kind of vampire-looking monsters loose upon a bizarre world. Without a car. Well, to be fair, no one here had a car.

So, with my theme song—"I Am Woman"—playing over and over in my mind, I tried to fend off a nervous breakdown. Okay, when in doubt, fix your wardrobe. First order of business—change these clothes. There was no way I could travel in pieces of filmy silk. And even here it must get cool at night. I'd catch my death dressed (or rather, undressed) as I was. Plus, if I couldn't have my Mustang—I could feel the big lightbulb clicking on in my mind again—the next best thing was, well, a *real* mustang. Alanna said my dream was truth. So that gorgeous silver mare must really belong to me. Bet she wouldn't mind a midnight ride. And this outfit was absolutely not made for horseback riding. (Ouch.)

Looking around my spacious room, I noticed several carved

wardrobes, like giant armoires. A little snooping yielded not just clothes but *lots* of clothes. No kidding, I felt like I was Barbie. Not just plain Barbie, but Prom Barbie, Summer Barbie, Cocktail Entertaining Barbie, Dating a Doctor/Lawyer/Corporate Executive Barbie…on and on. Rhiannon seriously had a lot of clothes, something I in no way held against her.

Trying not to get sidetracked (or hypnotized; I could see we had something else besides love for our dads in common), I covetously ratted through yards and yards of clothes until I finally stumbled upon what must be the Sportswear Armoire. It was filled to bursting with soft leather leggings and tops. All the pants were one style, the same buttery-yellow color, each with its own intricately tooled decorations. I recognized a very Celtic-looking knot woven down the sides of many of them. And I swear I could see more of those gross skulls hidden in the decorative leatherwork. They all had narrow legs, and weird ties that laced up high on the left hip (I guessed they were clueless about zippers in this world). I eyed them askance, hoping I hadn't put on any water weight lately. Deciding on one pair that seemed to have the least skull-like pattern, I started to pull them on, and couldn't help but gasp at the supple smoothness of the leather. They felt as if someone had fastened a baby's butt onto my legs. They didn't just fit, they molded their softness to my ass and thighs. Yep. Rhiannon was one spoiled girl.

She'd have a surprise coming when she checked out the price of clothes in my world, and the finite state of my closet.

I unwound myself from my silky top and grabbed one of the matching pieces of leather. This, too, laced up the back (which I had one hell of a time tying—I could see why I needed Alanna to help me dress). But I wasn't about to wake her and answer a gazillion questions, so I struggled all by myself (all the while maniacally humming "I Am Woman"...) and finally had the top tied securely. Actually, I was pleased to notice that besides being flattering, the outfit was obviously built for riding. The clothes moved with my body, yet they afforded support that Victoria's Secret would be proud of. (Let's be totally serious here, I'm thirty-five—my generous C-cup "girls" are old, and gravity is an evil thing. Know what I mean?) So I was pleased to note that I was wearing the Celtic equivalent of a sports bra. I could probably climb trees or slay dragons (I briefly but fervently hoped *that* wouldn't be necessary) in it.

Rummaging around in the bottom of the armoire, I found several pairs of very, very cool boots. They were made of the same buttery-colored leather, supple and pliant. They had thick soles, kind of like moccasins. As I grabbed a pair I noticed something on the sole and was delighted to see that into the bottom of each boot was carved a thick, five-sided star.

I would leave footprints of stars everywhere I walked. Barbie doesn't even do that.

Well, I was all dressed, but—

Remembering back to my dream vision, I could still envision the temple from above. If my iffy sense of direction was correct, the temple faced the west. The mountain range was to the north, spreading as far as I could see to the east and west. On the west edge it met the sea. Further down the coast was Dad's castle. I clearly remembered there was a wide river that wrapped behind the temple, and from there stretched roughly to the west. The northwest end of the river ended (or began, whatever) at the sea. All I had to do was follow the river away from the temple to the sea, and then turn right. I would eventually come to Dad's castle.

At least that was the theory.

I knew the stable was attached to the northern part of the temple, and that was where I would find the mare.

But how the hell did I find the area of the temple that held the stables? It wasn't like I could just wander around, unnoticed, until I stumbled into horse poopie. I had lifted up out of this ceiling. But I had no idea where I was located in the castle.

Great.

Then I got an idea. Remembering the adorable door decorations I had ogled earlier, I suddenly thought of one of my favorite mottoes: when in doubt, sucker a guy into helping you out.

I patted my hair, which was really staying in place for a change (thanks to Alanna's expertise), and gulped the rest of my tea. Then I proceeded to the door—the one I was sure led to the hall, as opposed to Alanna's or ClanFintan's room. I opened it quickly and surprised "the boys."

Yes, Lord, they were yummy.

Flat tummies. Bare chests. Strong chins. Tiny little coverings, and…(staying in character of Rhiannon the Slut I couldn't help but sneak a peek) large packages. And I'm not talking UPS.

They banged their muscley chests in some kind of adorable salute. I drew myself up to as haughty an attitude as I'm capable (while trying not to drool), and looked the taller of the two in the eye.

"I would like to ride my horse."

He blinked.

"Now."

He blinked again. Why do I always assume tall guys are smarter? (Note to self: tall guys are not smarter, they're just more attractive.)

"Well, inform the stable…um…servants that they need to saddle her for me." Nice save, but I knew I was reaching. (God, I hoped Rhiannon rode with some kind of a saddle.) I took a big breath and tried to act all sure of myself and bitchy—which, for some annoying reason, was suddenly more difficult than usual.

"Mistress, shall I have your escort awakened?" Mr. Muscles still looked confused.

"No!" I realized my voice sounded shrill and I got it under control. "I want privacy. Do *not* wake up any of my guards. Just have the stable servants saddle her for me."

"As you command, my Lady."

And I was right on his heels as he turned and headed for what had to be the exit to the stables. I did see him turn his head once, and caught his startled glance as he noticed me right behind him, but I figured he must be used to Rhiannon acting like a raving bitch—this was probably small potatoes compared to her screwing everyone in sight and God knows what else.

The cute guard led me down a corridor that wound in the opposite direction of the one that led me to my handfast and feast. After a short walk we came to a set of carved double doors. Mr. Muscles spoke to the guards standing before the doors, and they hustled them open before rushing off to wake the stable hands. I entered the stable and my little Oklahoma horse-girl heart went all a-pitter-patter.

It was a stable fit for a queen. Or better. The stalls were carved out of the same milky-colored marble from which the temple and its surrounding wall were made. They stretched down a wide hall on either side of me. There were probably twenty spacious stalls on either side, and as I walked down the hall I couldn't help pausing at each stall and cooing to the beautiful horses they held. They were the breeding stock of royalty. All mares, they ranged from dainty bays with an Arabian look, to long-legged sorrel Thoroughbreds. As I made my way down the hall, I was touched by how each mare seemed to recognize me. At each stall the enclosed mare would raise her soft muzzle and blow in my direction, looking forward to my caress and my whispered f lattery.

"Hey there, beautiful girl."

"Hi, sweet thing."

"Look at you, what a pretty lady."

The mares whickered back at me, vying for attention. It was familiar horsey talk to a girl raised around horses. Each mare's head reached out over the half door of her stall, waiting for my touch. Whatever else Rhiannon was, she certainly loved her horses. And they certainly reciprocated the feeling. Add another to the column of ways Shannon IS similar to Rhiannon. (I'd try to make sure that column didn't get too large.)

As I came to the end of the row of stalls, the chamber turned to my left, then widened into a gigantic stall attached to a private corral outside the stable. I recognized it as being the one my spirit body had visited earlier. Inside the spacious stall (which somehow reminded me of Rhiannon's bedroom— as strange as that may sound) three lovely (but sleepy and rumpled-looking) nymphs were readying the silver mare for me. I entered the stall and the nymphs paused long enough to curtsy to me, then returned to grooming the mare.

I stopped and breathed a sigh of happiness at the sight of such an exquisite horse. She really was magnificent, even more exceptional than she had appeared in my dream. She noticed my presence and I was delighted to see her twist her perfect head around so that she could see me. She telegraphed her greeting in a wonderful, full-throated neigh that made me laugh out loud with joy.

"Well, hello to you, too, gorgeous!" I moved eagerly toward her, taking a currycomb from one of the servants and enjoying the feel of her sleek coat under the soft brush.

I love grooming horses. I always have. Too many horse

owners think that grooming a horse or mucking a stall is mundane. They despise the ordinary tasks of caring for their animals. I never have. From the time I was a little girl, I have adored the smell of the stables and the feel of cleaning my horse's coat and stall. It's a labor of love. It's like lying in the sun—or weeding roses—soul- and mind-clearing work. Good for what ails ya.

The silver mare nuzzled my face and lipped my shoulder as I combed her already perfectly groomed neck.

"You are a sweet, beautiful lady." I clucked and cooed at her, feeling like I was a girl again, soaking in her scent and the feel of her warm breath.

Her head swung obediently forward when one of the servants approached with a dainty-looking hackamore (you gotta figure this mare wouldn't need a bit). I stepped out of the way as two more servants lifted onto her back a saddle blanket that looked like a 1970s sheepskin bucket-seat cover with stirrups and a girth.

The servant tightened the girth and stepped back. Then they all stood there. Just looking at me.

I looked at those high stirrups. And the tall mare. And considered my thirty-five-year-old body.

Great. Now I have to pretend to be Ms. Athletic.

Wait—no, all I have to pretend to be is Ms. Bitch. And some people would say that was not much of a pretense.

"Well, someone help me mount!" Damn, I sounded hateful. Smile. Without hesitating, I strode forward (relishing a true John Wayne moment), grabbed a fistful of silver mane and lifted my foot (hoping a nymph would catch it and give me a boost up). Thank God one did, and I scrambled aboard, sticking my other foot in the empty stirrup and squaring my shoulders.

But now I didn't know which way was out.

"Well, open the gate for me!" I seemed to be catching on to this pretend-to-be-a-bitch stuff pretty easily.

One of the nymphs scampered toward a door at the far side of the mare's stall, and another nymph scrambled to open a seamless exit in the outer wall of the temple. I clucked twice with my tongue on the side of my teeth (in what I hoped was the universal horse noise for giddyup) and the wonderful mare moved forward. Just before I went through the last opened door, I pulled her to a halt and spoke over my shoulder to the servants.

"Thank you. You may go back to your beds now. Sleep late, I will care for the mare myself when I return." I squeezed my thighs against the soft saddle blanket and leaned forward. The mare broke into a rolling canter.

We were out of the castle and on our way. The moon was still high and bright, so visibility was pretty darn good. I pulled the mare up so that I could look around and attempt to figure out just where the hell I was, and then I would theoretically know where the hell I should be going. The first thing I noticed was that the temple had been built strategically on the top of a hilly rise, and the grounds around it, although lush and green, were clear of trees. The temple itself was a huge circle, stately and rich-looking with marbled columns and a rushing fountain situated square in the foreground (some kind of giant horse rising from a fake ocean with what looked like hot mineral water spewing from several orifices—very Trevi Fountain–like).

I tried to look at the building with a soldier's eye, and I could see what ClanFintan had meant by it being built for defense. The biggest clue to that was the huge wall that encircled it. The wall looked thick and impenetrable, and the top of it had the stereotypical toothlike balustrades, complete with a battlement that would be a great place to situate archers (or sunbathers, whichever the current conditions of war or not-war called for). And the wall wasn't just solid, I noticed with a start of surprise, it was beautiful. It looked as if it had been built of one solid slab of enormous cream-colored marble. In the moonlight it gave off an otherworldly glow. I realized that if you took away the outer wall, the temple itself would have reminded me of the Pantheon in Rome, only the top didn't have a hole in it.

The reflection of the moon on water drew my attention to the river, which looped around and behind the temple—not so close it would flood, but close enough that barges could dock nearby. It was a convenient setup. If it weren't for those horrible flesh-eating man-creature things, this would be a very nice place to live.

Which reminded me that instead of sitting there all slack-jawed like a Japanese tourist at the Vatican, I should be following that river to the sea. I had more important things to do than gawk at a pretty temple. And I damn sure didn't have a camera with me. I mean, please, where would I get the film developed?

I headed the mare toward the river, glad that the night was so clear and quiet. I knew that somewhere inside the temple ClanFintan was rousing the centaurs and giving them instructions to start bringing the people to safety, so I leaned forward and squeezed my knees, urging the mare into a smooth gallop. It wouldn't do to be caught out here in the open and have to go through some horribly embarrassing public power play about what I've been up to. Plus, I might very well lose. Rhiannon's power seemed impressive, but I wondered how far it would extend if my desires were at odds with what was considered safe for Epona's Beloved.

Soon, the mare's gallop brought us to the riverbank, and I turned her to the west. The river itself was impressive. I had no way of telling how deep it was, but it was wide and the current was swift. It had a nice smell, not fishy and muddy like the Mississippi, but clear and rocky like the Colorado River. Trees lined the banks and I was relieved to see that the mare had picked out a small path, probably some kind of deer trail, which ran parallel with the bank. There wasn't so much under-brush that she couldn't have made her way without the path, but this made things quicker and easier. And I sure didn't want to ride down the road that I had glimpsed from the temple. It seemed to head in the general direction I wanted to go, but it looked like it was pretty well used. Not that it was a four-lane highway, but I was fairly sure that at first light it would be crowded with centaurs and people—and, please. Like they wouldn't notice Epona's Beloved trotting along on her shimmery silver mare?

Speaking of my beautiful mare, I pulled her up from a gallop. She looked like she was in great shape, but we had two hard days of traveling, and no horse could keep up a gallop for two days. Patting her silky neck I relaxed and found my seat as she settled into a smooth, ground-eating trot.

"Hey, sweet girl, what does Rhiannon call you?" Her delicate ears cocked back attentively at the sound of my voice. "I can't keep calling you The Mare, it's rude. It's like someone calling me The Woman, or considering my attitude lately, The Bitch." She tossed her head in obvious agreement. And in this world, you never knew, maybe she could understand my words. "Clearly, everyone calls you Epona, but that sounds too formal and stuffy for me." I reached forward and mussed her mane. "How about if I call you Epi? It might not be as dignified, but in my world dignified is usually synonymous with what politicians try to appear to be." I didn't think she'd be interested in a depressing lecture on the downslide of modern American politics, but it might be a long two days and

I filed the story away to tell her about later—if I got *really* desperate for topics.

Her sassy snort and a little prance to the side were answer enough for me. "Epi it is."

I let my fingers trail through her soft mane and settled back for a long ride. It was clear from the start that Epi was not one of those horses who need a lot of her rider's attention. She was smart and well able to trot forward along the path without me guiding and coaxing. So I settled back and took in the scenery. It certainly was pretty country. Between the trees I caught glimpses of homes dotting the scenic land. They looked well kept and adorably thatched, although thinking about all the bugs that lived in the thatching dispelled some of my romanticizing.

Between cottages stretched acres of vineyards and fields filled with crops, I think I recognized corn and beans, but I couldn't be sure in the moonlight. Once in a while I'd notice some sleepy animals, mostly cows and sheep with an occasional horse thrown in—and I was impressed and appreciative that Epi didn't neigh like a common mare. Every so often I could see the moonlight reflect off the road as it snaked between homesteads, keeping in a generally northwesterly direction, but it was pretty far away and I felt well concealed by the trees.

All in all it was a nice night. I guess some people (sissies) would be scared at the thought of being alone out in the middle of who-knows-where, but I have never been afraid of the dark and never been scared of being alone. True, my destination was daunting, and I wasn't even entirely sure what the hell I was actually going to do when (if) I got there, but I was Scarlett O'Hara–ing that, so it wasn't hard, with me deeply entrenched in denial, to find joy in a clear, lovely night ride.

Gradually it became lighter. At about the same time the trees started to become more dense and the path less defined. Epi didn't seem worried about it, so I let her pick her own path, and we gravitated toward the rocky riverbank. That horse-sense thing can really come in handy. Also, about this time I realized that I had ridden off, all Bitchy and In Charge, without giving one tiny thought to things like breakfast, lunch, dinner, water or toilet paper. Who knew what time it was, but by the time the sun was peeping over the top of the trees my butt and my stomach were both telling me that we had been riding "a while."

In Okie slang, "a while" ranges from five hours to five days. My mind said I had probably been riding about five hours. My butt and stomach said they were sure it had been five days. And let's face it, my butt and stomach are bigger than my mind, so they won.

Well, at least I knew where I could get some water. I could lithely dismount, lead Epi down to the sparkling river and (much like John Wayne) get a cool, refreshing drink. Maybe I'd even walk for a while and let Epi take a break.

Easier thought than done.

Have you ever ridden for "a while?" And I don't mean round and round in a little corral while a riding instructor beams encouragement. And I don't mean paying fifty bucks an hour to sit on a horse that could probably be declared clinically dead, following fifteen other Nags of the Walking Dead on an Authentic Trail Ride. Which lasts exactly thirty-five and one-half minutes.

I mean riding a horse (one that's actually alive) for several hours. Alternating between trot, canter, walk, back to trot. On a thirty-five-year-old butt. Without breakfast.

Well, it's not as easy as it appears in the movies, although I'm sure John Wayne really did ride a lot. His butt was probably made of iron. God bless him.

Sliding down the side of Epi I couldn't seem to find my

feet—or my legs. My butt was where I had last left it, except it felt like it had grown broader and flatter. What a lovely thought. So I stood there and attempted to restore circulation to my extremities, glad that Epi was the only one who witnessed my appalling lack of gluteal competence.

Eventually (almost "a while" later) I felt able to hobble— yes, I mean literally limping and cussing my way in the true tradition of the authentic Old West Hobble—down the bank to the edge of the river.

"Well, at least it's not muddy." I grumbled and patted Epi, letting her drink first. Slowly, I straightened up, listening to the musical cracking of my spine. Epi lipped the water and took several noisy gulps, saying "tastes good" in horsey language. I gimped upstream a couple of steps and crouched (amidst much creaking of knees), bending forward to wash my hands.

"Oh, baby, that's cold!" I was expecting the river to be a nice room temp, because the climate was so warm, but the river was icy, which told me it had to originate in the distant mountains. Hey—I'm a college graduate; you can't slip anything by me. Cupping my hands, I sucked the cold, clean water into my mouth.

It was like Grandma's well water. Nothing quenches a thirst as completely as cold water straight from the well. As a child I used to think that my grandma's well water was the Fountain of Youth. I'd pump like mad and then run around to the front of the spigot and slurp handfuls of the clear liquid. My creaky knees proved my Fountain of Youth theory wrong, but the taste still quenched and refreshed like a spring rain. And I was suddenly not quite as hungry as I had been.

"Well, old girl. How about I walk and give you a little break?" I smoothed her forelock and rubbed her broad forehead while she explored the front of my shirt and lipped my chin with her wet muzzle. God, horses are incredible animals. Being alone with her made me realize how much I'd missed owning one. Their smell, their equine beauty and intelligent kindness are things unique to them, not replaceable by a dog or even a thinking-it-has-no-owner cat (although cats are cooler than dogs—they're the haughty bitches of the animal world, and I can't help but appreciate that in them). But I've always adored horses. They are truly noble animals. Remember the scene in *True Grit* when Little Blacky allows John Wayne (Rooster Cogburn) to run him to death so that Baby Sister can be saved? Sob. What (sniffle) other animal would (blow my nose) do that (wipe my eyes)?

No wonder I thought ClanFintan was so damn cute—I was in need of a pet and a man. Apparently with him I killed two birds with one stone.

Except he was going to be really pissed when I got back to the temple.

And he thought I was a bitch.

After one more pat to Epi's neck, I turned reluctantly away from the riverbank, looped the reins over my shoulder and started back to find our scraggly, fading trail. Epi followed me like the polite girl she was, occasionally grabbing a mouthful of grass and chewing contentedly.

I started to whistle the "Hi-Ho" tune from *Snow White*. Epi blew through her nose at me, which I took as a commentary on my whistling ability, and I laughed over my shoulder at her, still whistling. Yeah, we were having fun now.

The trees were decidedly more dense, and I could glimpse fewer and fewer homes between the thick foliage. I tried to remember the layout of the land from my dream, but my spirit body had been moving so quickly that I hadn't gotten any landmarks more clearly defined than the river, the lush lands around it and the fact that it flowed from somewhere northeast of the castle and ran all the way down past my temple. I felt like Maid Marion lost in Sherwood Forest. Except I was pretty damn sure Robin Hood wasn't going to come rescue me (and, quite frankly, I'm no maid).

I hated to be a whiner, but I really was hungry. It wasn't too long before the whistling and the laughing stopped, and the Search For Any Kind of Edible Friggin Berry started.

"Here we are, surrounded by all of this damn nature." Epi's ears cocked forward, listening to me mutter. "You'd think there would be some wild strawberries. Or blueberries. Or mulberries. Even in Oz they had apple trees." Epi grabbed another mouthful of grass. "Is that stuff good?" It'd probably give me the runs, and I didn't even have any damn toilet paper. The visual picture that conjured was enough to keep me from trying Epi's dinner.

I truly hate camping. My parents used to make me camp with them (before they got divorced—I think it was their idea of quality family time, which sure as hell didn't work), and I began hating it then. Not that I don't like The Great Outdoors. I think nature is very inspirational and lovely. I like to hike, and I'm even willing to lie out in the sun and read a book while whatever man I happen to be with fishes. I just want to appreciate it during the day, and go somewhere with a comfortable bed, running water and a four star restaurant at night. I really don't like roughing it.

"So, what the hell am I doing out here?" Epi lipped the back of my French braid, and I swatted at her muzzle. "Stop—there's no way I can carve a comb out of a tree and rebraid this stuff." And my feet were starting to hurt. Rhiannon had broken the boots in, but they must have been made to be worn with socks, and, well, I had forgotten to look for the sock drawer before I left. Kind of like I'd forgotten to look for the kitchen.

"Epi, I think I have a blister the size of Rhode Island." Stopping, I rested my head against her warm neck and spoke into her softness. "And I think I need to ride again. Hope that's okay with you." I took her sweet nuzzle as an okay, and gave her a quick squeeze. "Let's get another drink first. Shall I buy this time, or would you like to treat?" She snorted at me. "I like my margaritas on the rocks, with lots of salt." I translated her look as horse language telling me how much more amusing I was than Rhiannon.

Turning toward the river, I noticed we had wandered several yards from the bank, probably because it was very rocky and suddenly looked a little steep. Carefully, I led the way back to the river, scrambling down the bank in a shower of loose rocks. After all the trouble it took to get back down to it, I was relieved to see the water was as clear and cold as ever, especially because as the day progressed it had become noticeably warmer. Not that it was too uncomfortable under the shading cover of the trees, but the cool water was a nice relief. To keep the heat in perspective, I reminded myself that it was nothing compared to a typical Oklahoma summer day when the humidity registered at about a zillion percent plus the normal one hundred–plus degrees. Almost enough to make Wonder Woman's bra melt.

The change in worlds had hurt my reputation, but it had definitely improved the weather. So I guess I should count my blessings.

Epi's nudge interrupted my thoughts. "Ready to go, gorgeous?" Her look said yes, so I led her to a rock large enough to use as a mounting block. The mare tilted her head and gave me an odd look.

"I guess you've already figured out that I'm not Rhiannon. She could probably leap up on you without any help." Epi's knowing gaze didn't falter, and I felt the need to stand up for myself. "No offense, but that could be because she's so used to thrusting herself up and down." Epi arched her neck and blinked her beautiful dark eyes at me. "Don't get me wrong. I'm not against some thrusting, but I like to think I choose quality over quantity." The mare tossed her head and made a very human-like squeal. Really, it sounded like a little horsy laugh, and as I heaved myself off the rock and scrambled aboard I found myself giggling, too. "So we understand one another?" Epi reached back and nudged my foot, which was dangling awkwardly out of the stirrup. "I'll take that as a yes." I smiled and put my foot where it belonged before giving the incredible horse the "let's go" cluck (as if she needed it).

I reached down and patted her neck fondly. There are some things about this world that were just plain cool.

Epi and I angled up toward the bank, and I was surprised to see how steep and rocky it looked from this direction. It hadn't seemed so bad coming down. Well, it was probably just the difference between seeing it from my feet and seeing it from horseback. Leaning forward, I urged Epi up toward our soft, green path—

Suddenly the rocks shifted, causing Epi to scramble and lunge awkwardly to keep her footing. I was jolted forward hard and had to grab her around the neck to keep from being thrown off. I could feel her struggling to regain solid footing. It was like she was trying to swim through rocky quicksand that kept sucking at her feet. She seemed to be unable to gain any ground as rocks and dirt tumbled around us. All I could do was hold tight and try not to let my weight shift too far to either side so that I wouldn't cause her to lose her already precarious balance.

All at once we broke free and lurched up over the bank and onto solid ground. Ignoring my quivering stomach, I slid off Epi and began running my hands down her muscular legs. She was breathing hard and shaking all over. Any other horse would have been white-eyed and panicked, but Epi stood quietly, letting me complete my frantic examination.

"Good girl. There's my sweet girl." I kept talking to her, trying to calm my nerves as much as hers. "You were so brave. I am so proud of you." I finished feeling all of her legs. No broken bones. No lacerations. She seemed okay.

But I knew from having grown up around horses the deceptive fragility of their legs. Once you witness one horse race where they come around the corner and a horse places a foot at just the wrong angle, and it snaps, you never forget it. I was ten years old the first time I saw a horse break a leg. It broke clean, between the knee and the hoof, and that horse kept on trying to finish the race with the bone of his leg jutting through the skin.

It just takes a single misstep.

I let Epi press her forehead into my chest and I rubbed her beautiful head, straightening her mussed mane. "You're okay, you're okay. Such a good girl." I kept murmuring inane endearments as we brought our breathing and heart rate under some semblance of control.

Eventually she lifted her head and nuzzled my cheeks, which were wet with tears. I wiped my face and stepped back from her, looking her over again with a critical eye.

"I think you're okay." I walked a circle around her while she lowered her head and blew at a tuft of lush grass. I smiled. "You're hungry. You must be okay." She chewed a mouthful and blew a sigh at me. "Let's not do that again. Okay?" She tossed her head. "Well, big girl, now I have to get back on you with no damn help at all." Epi stopped chewing, and I swear she made a very female sounding "hmmph" noise through her nose. "Just hold still and don't laugh."

She held still, but as I groaned and struggled my way aboard,

I can't swear she didn't laugh. We started forward and she seemed fine. Sighing in relief, I clucked her into a smooth trot. My hair, of course, had begun escaping from its braid of steel, and I began trying to poke curling red tendrils back into submission while humming the theme song from *Bonanza*.

"I give up." Epi's ears cocked back to listen to me. "No matter how tragically unfashionable, I seriously need a scrunchie." About half of my hair was curling around my head like I was Medusa's crazy redheaded sister. The other half was still clinging to the French braid. "Maybe I'll start a new fashion trend." Epi made no comment. I think she was just being nice.

Time for a new theme song.

I was halfway through humming the theme from *I Dream of Jeannie* when Epi's trot faltered and slowed to a strange-feeling walk. It felt like she was trying to stay on her tiptoes, or rather her tiphooves. I pulled her to a stop and slid quickly off.

"What's wrong, Epi?" I patted her neck and she tossed her head restlessly. "Let's check it out." Rule number one of horse troubleshooting: when in doubt, check the hooves. Grasping her left front leg low, I clucked at her and said, "Give, girl." Wonderful, obedient animal that she was, she lifted her hoof. It looked normal. With my fingers I picked a couple of small stones out of the hoof base and pulled free a small dirt clod. Carefully and firmly I pressed my thumbs down on the frog part of her foot.

Yes, horses have frogs. Don't try and figure it out, just take my word for it. Lift a horse's hoof sometime. Look at the part that Vs and is soft. That's the frog. And don't bitch about the name, some ancient frog probably martyred itself for the betterment of horsekind. Show some respect.

Well, this frog sure seemed okay. Working my way around Epi, everything was just fine until I got to her right front hoof.

When I pressed down on her frog she flinched and gave an equine groan of pain. I patted her neck to reassure her, and brushed away some clinging dirt and grass from the hoof. Moving my thumbs up higher on the soft V, I pressed again. This time the groan was louder and I could feel an abnormal warmth and mushiness under my thumbs. Gingerly, I set her foot down.

"Don't quote me on this, I'm not a vet, but I think you've bruised your frog." I was trying to keep my voice light and not let this unusually smart horse know that I was very damn worried about this turn of events. I looked down at the offending appendage. It was obvious she wasn't putting much weight on it. "Correct me if I'm wrong, but I think your hoof hurts."

She butted me with her nose.

"I thought so." I rubbed her jawline and she leaned her head into my caress. "So I probably shouldn't ride you. How about if we find a nice little clearing, maybe somewhere upstream where the bank isn't so steep, and we rest for a while?"

Walking slowly, I led the way with Epi hobbling painfully behind me. I kept up a chattering monologue, and she walked with her forehead resting against my back in the space between my shoulder blades. I was glad she couldn't see my eyes frantically scanning the land ahead of us, trying to find an easy place to descend. I knew I had to get her close to the river, and not just so that she could have water to drink. That hoof needed attention. My mind was rummaging through old horse-care-rules information I had filed away somewhere in my brain back in my youth. I just hoped they weren't filed in the cells that my affinity for red wine had killed off. I seemed to remember that Epi's kind of symptoms were telling me that the bruised area of her hoof should be iced. If I could get her to stand in the river for ten minutes or so, it seemed logical that it would stop some of the swelling and help the pain. Then she could rest and I'd figure out what the hell we were going to do next.

For a fleeting moment I wished ClanFintan would show up with the rescue posse. But reality intruded on my moment. The centaur was busy rounding up people and dealing with the creature crisis—one AWOL reluctant bride was not a big deal. And anyway, I've never been the kind of woman who lived her life pining after a knight in shining armor, praying that he would come charging in on a white horse to rescue me. In my particular case the whole horse/guy thing was causing me to unintentionally mix my metaphors. Which was giving me an English-teacher headache.

But luck was with me, and we hadn't walked too far when we came to an abrupt right bend in the river. There were fewer trees here, so there was more erosion, and the grassy incline sloped gracefully down to meet the tumbling river. Picking our way carefully, I led Epi to the water.

Without any major mishap we made our way slowly to the river's edge. Balancing myself with one hand against her flank, I pulled off my boots and rolled up my soft leather pant legs. Epi was done drinking and she nuzzled me with her wet muzzle.

"What we really need, old girl, is a couple of pedicures. But where the hell is a beautician when you need one, anyway?" I gave her a pat, then led her forward into the icy water. "How about we do the next best thing and soak our aching feet?" Epi seemed willing, gingerly following me as I picked my way between the largest of the slick rocks out a little way into the fast-moving current.

Ohmygod it was cold.

"Hey, Epi, have you ever heard the very sad, very Scottish love song 'Loch Lomond'?" She lifted her right hoof fretfully and I leaned my weight against her left side so that she was forced to put it back in the cold water. She looked at me doubtfully but kept her hoof submerged. "It's the story of two of Bonnie Prince Charlie's men who were captured in the revolt. One of them was executed and one was set free. Rumor has it the song was written by the doomed soldier as a final love letter to his sweetheart."

Epi looked clueless.

"Haven't heard it, huh?" Cold, cold, cold. "Well, you're in luck—not because I can sing, because as you already know, I can't, but I do know all the words to all the verses. And, yes, I'm willing to teach you." She sighed and I think she might have rolled her eyes. As I launched energetically into the first verse, I noticed that my aching feet were going numb. Clearing my throat I put on my best bad Scottish accent,

> By yon bonnie banks and by yon bonnie braes,
> Where the sun shines bright on Loch Lomond.
> Where me and my true love were ever wont to gae
> On the bonnie, bonnie banks o' Loch Lomond...

As I worked my way through a pitiful rendition of one of my favorite ballads, I noticed that Epi's attention was waning.

"Okay! Let's sing that chorus one more time!"

> ...O ye'll tak' the high road and I'll tak' the low road,
> An I'll be in Scotland afore ye,
> But me and my true love will never meet again
> On the bonnie, bonnie banks o' Loch Lomond!

I sighed melodramatically and gave a big pretend sob while I wiped pretend tears from my eyes.

"Beautiful, isn't it." She blew at me then lipped the water, shifting her weight fretfully. "I can see you're not impressed with tragic and depressing love songs sung with a tragic and depressing lack of understanding of even the basics of musical pitch. Okay, okay—how about I give you a little taste of something I am actually fairly decent at." She glanced at me, obviously gun-shy from the demonstration of my singing talent, or rather my lack thereof.

"Hey, smartie, I do remember a description of a horse from an essay I've taught to sophomores." Her ears pricked at me. "The author wrote, 'A duck is a long low animal covered with feathers. Similarly, a horse is a long high animal covered with confusion.'" She blinked at me and looked a little huffy. "Well, it seemed funny then. Guess you had to have been there." She was fidgeting again, and I figured I would only be able to get her to stay in the water for a couple more minutes. Groping around in my brain, trying to keep my mind off my freezing feet, the lightbulb of inspired thought suddenly clicked on in my head.

"Hey! I know what you'd like." She wasn't paying much attention to me, and I had to keep leaning on her left side, forcing her right hoof to stay submerged. Her back legs were starting to move restlessly.

"Yeah, I know this isn't any fun. Just listen to one more, and then we'll blow this freezing pop stand."

Clearing my mind, I delved back into my memory. My Bible as Literature professor had been an eccentric woman—a truly fine representative of a long succession of bad-clothes-wearing college English instructors. For part of our semester final she made each of us memorize and present aloud sections of the Old Testament that dealt with animals. My third year of college was a longgggg time ago. But as I started my hesitant recitation of the ancient verses, they began tumbling from my mouth as if they were happy to be set free of the cobwebs in my brain:

Hast thou given the horse strength?

Um…something—something…um…oh yeah.

The glory of his nostrils is terrible.
He paweth in the valley, and rejoiceth in his strength,
He goeth on to meet the armed men.
He mocketh at fear and is not affrighted;
Neither turneth he back from the sword.
The quiver rattleth against him,
The glittering spear and the shield.
He swalloweth the ground with fierceness and rage:
Neither believeth he that it is the sound of the trum-
pet.
He saith among the trumpets, Ha, ha,
And he smelleth the battle afar off,
The thunder of the captains, and the shouting.

At least this time I kept her attention.

"The Book of Job, Chapter something-or-other, Verse I-don't-remember."

Her ears were pricked in my direction and she tossed her head briefly, giving me a snort of what I hoped was horsey appreciation. And, more importantly, she had stood still with her hoof fully submerged in the healing water.

"Thank you, thank you. No, no, you're too kind." I bowed as gracefully as one can bow with frozen feet. "I think that about covers our literary moment for the day. Tune in tomorrow, same time, for another twisted version of my own personal PBS. Come on, old girl. It's damn cold out here." Leading Epi back to shore we moved slowly. Feet are odd appendixes when they're frozen. I felt a little like

Quasimodo hobbling out of the water to find sanctuary on dry ground.

Because of the erosion, the rocky ground was mingled with the ferny green carpet of the upper forest. It was actually a nice resting place. There was plenty of grass within Epi's reach, which was perfect because she really needed to rest. Pulling the saddle from her back, I tried to keep a close eye on how she was acting, without being obvious.

"Wish I had some currycombs. You sure look nappy." Improvising, I pried a piece of bark from a nearby log and rubbed it back and forth over her tired body, giving her a nice scratching. She sighed and closed her eyes. "Kind of like a foot rub, huh." I patted her rump. "Why don't you graze for a while and rest, then I'll take another look at that hoof." She stood with her right front leg cocked to take the weight off it and settled down to the business of eating.

And I realized that I really needed to, well, tend to The Call of Nature. Ugh.

"Epi, I'm going to take a little walk." She gave me a quick glance before returning her attention to her three-legged grazing. "Be right back."

Scrambling up the bank, I kept my eyes peeled for a nice-size bush and a soft-leafed plant. I hate camping. Wading off the path and into the indigenous foliage, I began testing plant leaves, grading them on texture and durability, like an insane Mrs. Whipple.

And, shazam! I bumble into a little slice of heaven. Grapes! Big, dark, ripe grapes! Rushing through my toilette (Note to self: remember to wash your hands), I (delicately) crammed several of the wonderful pieces of fruit into my salivating mouth. Yummy.

Yanking as many of the clusters off their vines as I could carry, I hurried back to where I left Epi.

"Hey, Epi! Look what I found." She looked unimpressed, but at least she wasn't restless or pawing. She went back to grazing. I put my stash of grapes down by the saddle blanket, went to the river to reclaim my discarded boots and wash my hands. Then, finally, I plopped my tired and f lattened behind down, resting my back against the saddle, and I set to work feasting upon nature's aphrodisiac. (Michelle told me once that grapes are nature's aphrodisiac. And she should know.)

The grapes were delicious, and I don't think it was just because I was starving. It sure felt nice to have a full tummy. And I didn't notice any unusual side effects from dining entirely on an aphrodisiac. At least not yet. But I did notice my eyelids felt verrrry heavvvvy.

Dragging my tired and sore behind up—God, my thighs felt like I'd been riding the entire Dallas Cowboy defensive line—I gimped my way over to the sleepy mare.

"Let me see this hoof." She roused herself long enough for me to take a look at the bruised frog. It didn't look any worse, and it didn't feel quite as hot as before, which must be a good sign. I patted her neck and gave her a tired hug. "To quote John Wayne as Rooster Cogburn—'Here. We camp here.' Forgive me if I don't make that quote more realistic by falling off you and onto the ground." She didn't even blink at my attempt at humor. Guess she was getting used to me. "Let's just take a little nap. Wake me if I sleep past time for school."

Gingerly, I returned to the saddle and let my body slowly come back in contact with the ground. How a rocky shore and a horsey saddle blanket could feel so good I didn't know, but I was grateful for whatever I could get. Not grateful enough to reconsider my aversion to camping, but grateful. As my eyes closed I mentally set the alarm clock in my mind to go off in "a while."

7

The first time I woke up it was dusk. It was like the setting sun had called open my eyes. The warmth of the day had been replaced by a pleasantly cool breeze scented with the clean, watery fragrance of the river. I stretched and shifted a little, reaching under my left butt cheek to remove a particularly uncomfortable rock. And heaved the sigh of the disgruntled. I had to pee. Getting to my feet was no fun. I was stiff and groggy and sleep clung to me like an annoying two-year-old.

Not too far from my makeshift bed, Epi was sleeping, horse-style, on her feet—which is an ability I've always coveted. I tried it once, on a particularly long flight overseas when my leg cramps just wouldn't go away. Leaning near the emergency exit situated over one wing, I had tried to doze, with little success. Every time I began to relax, my head would flop around, and to complete the failed experiment, I found that standing sleep woke in me an unfortunate propensity to drool. But Epi sure seemed comfortable. Her right front leg was still cocked, but she wasn't fretful and I decided she didn't need me obsessively checking her hoof. When she woke up I'd try and get her to soak it in the river again, but right now I was too tired to come up with any more poetry or depressing ballads.

I just wanted to pee and then go back to sleep.

Waking up was sudden and unpleasant the next time. I flailed around, trying to find my alarm-clock button. Despite the darkness I was sure I'd overslept for school. You know the feeling—that heart-pounding knowledge that you're late. And then the disorientation hit. Even my groggy brain recognized that I wasn't in my antique oak bed curled up under my down comforter. Sitting up, I blinked hard, trying to accustom my vision to such absolute darkness.

And the sound of water rippling on rock brought me totally into the present.

"Epi?" Relief helped my heart to slow as her muzzle brushed the side of my face. Gradually, I began to distinguish the mare as a light blob in the darkness. She was lying close to my left side. Her sleepy breath smelled sweet and grassy as she explored my face and hair.

"Feeling better, pretty girl?" Not wanting to stand yet, I scooted over to her and ran my hands down her neck and over her back. He legs were tucked up under her body, so I couldn't reach the sore hoof, but she didn't feel overly hot, and she sure wasn't acting like she was in pain.

"Wonder if the moon will come up soon." I leaned against her soft body, very aware that the cool of the night had not helped my sore, overused muscles. "Man, I could use a hot, soaking bath."

My stomach rumbled.

"Guess we can't do anything until it gets lighter." Epi's light, horsey snore answered me.

And what the hell did I think we were going to do, anyway? I had no idea how badly Epi had been bruised, but she couldn't be ridden, that much was obvious. Now what? Using my crappy sense of time and distance, I estimated that we had traveled for ten, maybe twelve hours. We'd been asleep for, I don't know, maybe eight hours. So, if we were lucky, we were at about the halfway point. And hungry. And tired. And hurt.

I closed my eyes and tried to relax, think, forget about my stomach and keep warm.

Taking Epi back to the temple was the only reasonable solution. It would be slow going. Maybe one of those little cottages would be willing to feed Epona and Her Chosen. Goddess Incarnate–hood ought to be good for something. Several days of eating just grapes was bound to do something to my system—the visual images coming to mind weren't pretty. I could see it now—I'd turn into some kind of pathetic nymphomaniac with violent diarrhea. And no toilet paper.

So, we'd get started at first light. I'd try and get Epi to soak her hoof again, then we'd head back the way we came. Until then I'd better follow Epi's example and get some sleep—it would be a long next several days. Snuggling as close to the mare as I could get, I shared her body heat. Feeling warmer and sleepy again, I imagined her as a big, silver horsey heater...

At first I didn't notice the sound. Almost. It was a vague rustling. Not like the too-cool breeze through the tree leaves. And not like the water over rocks. Different.

A twig cracked. I froze and tried to stay still so that I didn't draw attention to us. But, swallowing around the dryness in my mouth, I was sure the sound of my pounding heart telegraphed "Here they are!" out into the night.

Another twig cracked. This time I felt Epi stir. I could feel her head raise and turn to face the forest.

And I remembered the things. Man-creature things. And how they had made the forest seem to breathe and pulse with their movements. How could I have forgotten?

This wasn't my world. There were forces loose here that I

didn't begin to understand. While I had been busy Scarlett O'Hara—ing, I had totally overlooked the entire damn reason behind why I had to go to MacCallan Castle. Man-creatures had slaughtered a castle full of people. Strong, courageous men hadn't been able to stop them. And here I was, meandering around the countryside with my silly modern woman head all in the clouds and my ridiculous modern woman "you go, girl!" attitude.

Burying Dad was a good idea. Making sure he was dead was even better. But getting this mare and myself killed while attempting to be The Good Daughter was decidedly Too Stupid To Breathe. And Dad would be the first in line to tell me so.

The brush crackled again. Something heavy was heading this way. In my mind I could see the creatures, wings spread and taut with air, running with their fluid gliding strides. The moments between noises became prophetic. The pauses in sound were simply time between one hovering stride and another. God I was a moron. Not only was I not going to get to bury my dad, but I might very well be coming to a tragic end that would make those gross bodies on *CSI* look tame.

Clearly I should have thought this whole thing out.

Epi shivered and surged to her feet. I stood close to her, stroking her neck and murmuring shushing sounds. My mind struggled to come up with A Plan. Neither college nor past experience had prepared me for this kind of numbing fear. So, as Epi and I watched dark shapes detach from the forest and descend down the eroded bank toward us, I did what I always hoped I wouldn't do in time of emergency. I froze. Like a deer waiting for an eighteen-wheeler to smush it across the highway, I stood there overwhelmed by my fate. I was proud of Epi's courage. She faced the intruders, ears pricked forward, blowing softly through her muzzle. She showed no fear. Horses are just damn brave animals. I was honored to have her by my side as our death approached us and—

"Lady Rhiannon?" The voice was deep and familiar. For a moment I was surprised into not responding. The gross creature things had voices like ClanFintan?

Epi's soft nicker of recognition broke my spell of stupidity. At least for the moment.

"ClanFintan?"

"She is here!" he called over his shoulder, and suddenly the rocky bank was alive with dark shapes that looked vaguely horsey. "Get a fire built, it is black as the Underworld this night."

I could hear brush and rocks being moved, and perhaps even flint striking. All sight was blocked not just by the night, but by a large horse shape directly in front of Epi and me. It spoke. And it sounded pissed.

"Are you injured, Rhiannon?"

"No, I'm fine. It's Epi, she's bruised her hoof."

"Epi?"

"Oh, um, I mean Epona's mare." At least I hoped that was what I meant.

Fire flared to life a few yards downstream, and as the centaurs fed it to flame my vision returned. ClanFintan was standing in front of us, arms on his waist (his, uh, human waist), forehead furrowed into a frown.

"Which hoof?" He sounded brisk and businesslike.

"Right front." I stepped under Epi's neck, squatted and ran my hands down her leg. "It doesn't feel swollen or hot, so I think it's just a bruised frog." (I peeked up at him—he seemed to understand. Oh, yeah, he should. He's part horse.) "Take a look." Epi obediently lifted her hoof and he bent to study it. His strong hands prodded the same spots my smaller ones had examined hours before. Epi gave a soft grunt when he hit the sore spot, and he immediately stopped pressing and stroked her neck, speaking soothing words to her that I couldn't understand, which sounded musical and lilting, a little like Gaelic. Epi relaxed and sighed as I set her hoof down.

"A bad bruise." He sounded accusatory. "How did it happen?"

I straightened and took a step closer to Epi, hating the guilt he made me feel.

"Downriver the bank gave way as we were climbing it. Her hoof must have come down too hard on a pointed rock."

"She could have broken her leg."

"I know that! I feel bad enough. I don't need you blaming me, too." I felt stupidly close to tears. Epi bumped me with her muzzle and I turned my face into her neck.

"She will recover." His voice had gentled.

"I know!" Well, I did now.

"Come over by the fire. You look chilled."

He took my elbow and spoke softly to Epi. We walked with him toward the fire like errant children. Propelling me to a semi-comfortable rock (at least it was warm from the newly made fire) he began issuing orders to his men/horses/whatever. And out of seemingly nowhere a blanket was draped over my shoulders. A couple of the centaurs were busy rubbing down Epi, and she stood quietly, obviously enjoying the attention. Another centaur was busy building a fire a few yards from this first one, and I was excited to see him unloading saddlebags filled with—be still my heart—food. ClanFintan handed me a floppy sacklike thing, and when I stared stupidly at it he uncapped it for me.

"Drink, my Lady. It will help to restore your strength." Something in his tone made me think what he really meant was it might help to restore my common sense, but I was too close to agreeing with him to argue the point.

The wine was rich, red and scrumptious.

Glancing over to where Epi stood, I was delighted to see that one of the centaurs had attached a feed bag over her head and she was munching contentedly. The frying scent of something wonderful made my mouth fill with water, and as I took another swig of wine my stomach let out a roar that couldn't have been much more embarrassing.

"You did not think to bring provisions with you?" Clan-Fintan looked down at me with an expression that could be only described as incredulous. Trust me on this one—English teachers know incredulous when it looks them in the face.

"No. I, well, uh. No, I did not." Now I sounded as stupid as I felt.

"Hmmph." He turned and walked away from me and made like he was oh so busy at the other fire.

Feeling miserably stupid and inept, I hunkered down under my blanket, clutching my wineskin (trying not to think about what kind of skin my wine was in—yuck).

He returned shortly with a hunk of hard bread, kind of like a big dinner roll, that had a piece of wonderful-smelling meat stuck in the middle of it. And a slice of fragrant yellow cheese. I had never smelled anything so delicious in my life.

"Here. You must be hungry."

"Thanks." I tried not to take off any of his fingers as I snatched at the food.

Chewing enthusiastically I watched as he settled across the fire from me. I noticed that the other centaurs—I counted ten of them—were grouped around the other campfire, and their good-natured conversation was a comfortable accompaniment to the whispered noise of the river.

"Why did you leave?" His voice brought my attention back to my own campfire.

I swallowed a piece of cheese and took a quick drink of wine. "I had to see about my dad."

"Then why did you not ask me to escort you?"

"I—well, I—"

"I have understood from the beginning that you did not want our union." He raised a hand to stop me when I tried again to speak. "And I know you do not have a mate's feelings for me, but I swore to protect and respect you. To honor you above all others." He looked away from me and out toward the river. "Running from me was an insult I did not deserve."

Uh-oh, I hadn't even thought about that. Guys and their egos. Jeesh.

"I wasn't running from you."

"Then what name do you give it?" He still wouldn't look at me.

"I was doing what I thought I had to do. I didn't think you would take me." His eyes swung back to mine. He looked shocked.

"You are Epona's Beloved and my mate. Of course I would escort you."

"Well, you didn't want me to go. Neither did Alanna." I added for good measure.

"Rhiannon, of course we did not wish for you to undertake such a painful and dangerous journey, but you are Epona's High Priestess. Has anything ever been denied you?" He sounded puzzled, and I realized what a faux pas I had made.

I lowered my eyes and plucked at a loose thread on my blanket. "I wasn't thinking straight. I just wanted to take care of my dad." Looking up at him I saw the lines around his mouth relax a little. "I'm sorry. I should have come to you."

He blinked in surprise. Rhiannon the Great obviously didn't apologize very often.

"You are forgiven. I am pleased that we found you and that you are safe."

My eyes were drawn to Epi, who was munching happily on her grain a little way to my right. "Is she really going to be okay?"

"Yes, my Lady. She needs rest and soon she will be able to carry you on any escape you can plan."

"But, I didn—" He was smiling. Oh, that was his idea of a joke. I'll give him this one. "I didn't really plan anything. At least not very well."

"Exactly." He looked smug. But it was a cute kind of smug.

"I am sorry for the trouble I caused."

"It is forgotten." His eyes glistened in the firelight and the flickering flames did delicious things to the glimpses of his chest I could manage to see whenever he moved a little and that wonderfully skimpy leather vest fell open.

Damn, I must be hungry for more than food. Maybe Rhiannon was rubbing off on me. I busied myself eating my sandwich, trying to pretend that ClanFintan wasn't studying me from across the fire. No, I was pretty sure I didn't feel like leaping up and humping the first guy (or horse) that happened to cross my path. It was *this* guy (or horse) in particular that I was feeling, well, sluttish about. Or maybe it was all those damn grapes.

When in doubt, change the subject.

"Are the people being brought to the temple?" Oh, good, ClanFintan stopped the visual caress and became Mr. Business-like again.

"Yes. I have sent some of your guards, as well as my centaurs out to spread word of what has happened and to gather the people to Epona's temple."

"Has there been any sign of the creatures?"

"No. Carrier pigeons were released with warnings to all of the Clan Chieftains asking the Clans to respond with any news of Fomorians. All have replied—" he paused "—except for the MacCallan and Guardian Castle."

"Do you think they're still at MacCallan Castle?"

"I do not know, my Lady."

I looked down at my half-eaten sandwich. "Are you still willing to take me there, knowing the creatures might be there?"

"For the space of one year I will take you anywhere you wish. All you need do is ask." His eyes locked with mine.

"Out of duty." Returning his unblinking gaze I realized I wanted more than duty from him.

"I gave my oath to you." His voice was mesmerizing.

"Then I am asking you. Please, will you take me to bury my father?" My voice was almost a whisper, rough with emotions I was just beginning to feel.

"Yes, Lady Rhiannon. I will take you and protect you."

"And keep me close to you?" I couldn't stop myself from adding.

"I will keep you as close to me as you wish to be."

Oh, jeesh, what a loaded comment that was! I wondered about the etiquette of asking him to shift into man-form. Is it kind of like excusing yourself to put in a diaphragm? Or get a condom?

The clattering noise of pots being cleared snapped my thoughts out of the bedroom, and I was mortified to feel my face blushing—until ClanFintan's gaze registered the redness of my cheeks. And then the soft smile he gave me made me ridiculously glad I've always been a blusher. God, I felt like a goofy teenager (although that's redundant, teenagers are all goofy).

"You must be tired."

Well, I had been thinking about bed, if that counts. He smiled as if he could read my thoughts. I'm pretty sure I blushed again.

"Rest while I tell the centaurs of our plans." He started to move toward the other campfire, but turned back at the sound of my voice.

"Um, what are our plans?" Damn, he looked good in the firelight.

"We will escort you to MacCallan Castle." That was easy.

"What about Epi, uh, Epona?" She pricked her ears in my direction at the sound of her name, and I blew quick kisses at her.

"I will delegate two centaurs to stay here with her and await our return. By the time we come back, she will be ready to travel, although she probably will not be able to bear your weight."

"Then how am I going to get to the castle and back home? Did you bring a horse with you?" Well, I meant, besides his friends.

"No." His smile had broadened.

"Am I supposed to walk?" Like that wouldn't take forever.

"No." Now he looked like the damn Cheshire cat.

"Well, then how?" What the heck was he thinking?

"You will ride me." He gave a little mock bow, then spun around (like any good cutting horse) and headed to the other campfire.

For once I was rendered speechless—utterly devoid of speech.

Ride him? Well, I already knew he was a biter.

I just hoped he didn't buck, too.

Wonder how the hell the Duke would handle this one?

8

Wine, food and warmth worked their magic, and by the time ClanFintan set Epi's soft saddle next to me for a pillow and nudged me off the rock, I was barely able to mumble a thanks before I fell into a deep, dreamless slumber.

It seemed as if I had only just closed them when the wonderful fragrance of frying meat forced open my undoubtedly bloodshot eyes. I stretched and was immediately sorry I'd done so. How was it possible for every single muscle in my body to be sore? I think my hair even hurt.

"Ahhh." Getting to my feet was a noisy affair. In the middle of trying to straighten my old, abused body, I made the mistake of glancing up, and saw eleven pairs of centaur eyes and one pair of Epi eyes watching me. Eleven of the twelve looked amused. Epi's eyes, I was pleased to notice, showed only her usual horsey adoration.

"What?!"

"Nothing, my Lady…" At least they had enough sense to look semi-embarrassed.

"Damn men." Mumbling under my breath I gave Epi a pat before heading down to the river's edge. I really, really wished I had a toothbrush. Bending over was decidedly not fun, but I did feel better after washing off my face and swishing water around my mouth (and using my finger as a toothbrush—yuck). Now, to top off an already lovely morning, I had to pee. Again.

I started marching purposefully downstream (but it's hard to march purposefully, or any other way, when your thighs are screaming like Richard Simmons in a candy store—good God, stop the madness). I came to an abrupt halt. And turned to see twelve pairs of eyes staring at me—and one centaur, decidedly the most handsome of the group, and just coincidentally my mate, obviously getting ready to follow me. Oh, no. No toilet paper is bad enough. Mr. Ed could just keep his hairy butt there, no matter how cute he was.

"I'm just going to—you know..." And I nodded toward the forest edge.

"Call if you have need of anything." ClanFintan and the rest of them tried unsuccessfully to hide smiles.

"Not in this damn lifetime," I muttered as I hobbled toward the bushes, scratching at various bug bites.

Have I mentioned how much I loathe camping?

Exercise is supposed to loosen sore muscles and as I climbed down the bank and made my gimpy way back to camp, I waited for my thighs and butt to uncramp. Of course, *my* muscles didn't know the loosening rule. They were screaming things like *Are you crazy? Do you know we're thirty-five years old? Sit down and feed us a Twinkie!*

It was going to be a long day.

The centaurs had put out the fire I had slept by, and as I walked up to the group surrounding the remaining fire, they made way for me, and one of them (an adorable palomino) handed me another hard bread and meat sandwich.

"Thanks." I smiled my appreciation and he gave me a sweet little bow. These guys were awfully cute.

ClanFintan joined us, and his centaurs made room for him next to me.

"How are you feeling this morning, my Lady?" ClanFintan asked sociably.

"My butt hurts like hell."

I thought the palomino was going to gag on his sandwich, and several other centaurs had sudden coughing fits. I smiled at them. They seemed relieved, and I could feel them studying me with new eyes. I kept forgetting what a bitch Rhiannon must have been.

ClanFintan's eyes were sparkling at me.

"Anything I can do to help you?"

A good, firm ass rub would be nice, but I didn't want to mention that in front of the herd.

"I don't think so." I glanced pointedly at his broad back, where shortly I was going to have to sit my sore butt. "Unless you can shapeshift into my bed and your friends here can drag us to MacCallan Castle." I looked inquiringly at his men, including them in my joke.

They repaid me with outright laughter and several of them slapped ClanFintan on the back saying, "She has you there." ClanFintan took their good-natured teasing well. Their laughter included me and made me feel part of them. I began to realize what Rhiannon had missed out on by being such a bitch.

"Forgive me, my Lady, but I cannot shift into a being that does not have the breath of life within it," he said.

"You are forgiven, my Lord," I teased. "Just be gentle with me."

"Always." His hand reached out and brushed an errant curl from my face. Over his shoulder I saw the centaurs smile knowingly at each other.

And I found myself feeling very glad that Rhiannon hadn't

done irreparable damage here. I really wanted them to like me. Okay, I'll be honest. I wanted their High Shaman to *more* than like me. But these were good guys/horses/whatever and their friendship was something I would like to earn.

"Can you finish breaking your fast as we ride? We need to get started."

"Yes." I hesitated.

"Is something wrong?"

I looked over his shoulder at my mare. "I'm just worried about Epi."

"She will rest comfortably while we are gone."

"She'll be safe?" A picture of the creature-things sprang into my mind.

"Any of us would give our lives for her, or for you." He certainly sounded serious. I didn't want anyone to die for my mare or for me, but his declaration was giving me goose bumps and causing me to have a John-Wayne-leading-his-marines-through-danger moment.

I didn't know what to say. Again. My students would be thrilled at me being rendered speechless twice in such a short period of time (of course, they wouldn't know what the word *rendered* meant, but you get my drift).

"Perhaps you would like a moment to say goodbye to her and to tell her you will return soon?" He was just so dang considerate.

I mumbled some kind of thanks, and took my sore-butted sandwich-eating self over to my mare, who was grazing contentedly. She pricked her ears and gave me a soft nicker of welcome.

"Hi there, sweet girl." I rubbed her jawline and cooed wordless love noises at her as she nuzzled me. Resting my forehead against her neck I spoke softly so that she had to cock her ears back to hear me.

"I have to leave for a couple of days. ClanFintan is going to take me to the castle." She craned her head around so that she could look into my eyes. "Don't worry, he's leaving a couple centaurs here to take care of you. And he won't let anything happen to me." She seemed okay with that. I continued, lowering my voice even further, "I have to tell you, I'm a little nervous about this riding-him stuff. I mean, please, how am I supposed to keep my hormones in control with him between my legs all day?"

She gave a deep, horsey sigh that seemed to say, *Well, don't then.*

"Some help you are." I gave her soft muzzle a quick kiss. "Behave yourself while I'm gone." She lipped my hair briefly then went back to grazing.

I felt a little like a mother whose four-year-old had just toddled happily off to preschool without her.

"Lady Rhiannon?" ClanFintan's voice held an edge of impatience.

"Coming," ready or not. Mostly, not.

The centaurs had been busy while I was snoozing. The eight who were going with us were loaded and ready to move out. I guess it had been too dark last night for me to notice that each of them had a couple sets of saddlebags draped over their horse backs, as well as dangerous-looking long swords, a lot like claymores, strapped over their chests and resting across their human backs. How confusing. Anyway, the saddle packs were obviously where the food and blankets had materialized from. Wonder what other goodies they were hiding. ClanFintan was standing apart from the rest of the group, his torso twisted around as he strapped my saddle blanket to his back. I finished my breakfast in one fast gulp.

Well, I might as well take the bull by the horns. So to speak.

At the sound of my approach he finished cinching the girth and flopped the stirrup down.

"Ready?"

"Sure." I stood there—staring. He was bigger than Epi, and I had had problems getting aboard her without help.

"Do you need help mounting?" He seemed to be enjoying himself. I glanced at the rest of the centaurs, but they were suddenly oh so busy studying the local flora and fauna.

"Yes." I paused and smiled teasingly, hoping I didn't have a big hunk of biscuit between my teeth. "This one time."

He grinned back at me as he reached down with his left arm and grabbed me firmly under my left elbow.

"On three... One...two...three!"

Up I went—actually up and almost over the other side. He was a lot stronger than I had anticipated, or maybe I was lighter than he thought I was, because I had to grab his shoulders to keep myself from being tossed all the way off his back.

"Ooof," I said gracefully.

"Oh, I am sorry." He sounded anything but sorry.

"Hey, don't worry about it. Not all horses can be as easy to mount as Epi."

"You might be surprised." I was pleased to notice he had his own teasing tone in his voice.

I busied myself putting my feet in the stirrups and acted as if I hadn't heard him. I thought I felt his chest rumble briefly with a chuckle.

"So, do I nudge you or cluck or something to get you to go?"

"Just hold tightly to me, I will see that we move from here."

I gave Epi a quick wave goodbye as he started forward. The rest of the centaurs fell in behind us. Maneuvering up the bank made me grab for a nonexistent saddle horn. Which brought to mind the first Riding My Husband Dilemma.

"Um, what exactly should I hang tightly on to?"

He smiled back over his shoulder at me. He was having way too good of a time with this.

"Put your hands on my shoulders, or grasp my waist. Basically, do what feels most comfortable."

I yanked on his thick ponytail (no pun intended). "How about here?"

I heard muffled snorts of laughter from the centaurs closest to us.

"I would rather you did not."

"Not a problem." Score one for me.

Once clear of the bank, he broke into a quick canter. I rested my hands on his shoulders, appreciating the feel of his muscles beneath my hands (and, quite frankly, my thighs). His gait was smooth and easy to sit, and I found myself relaxing and enjoying the speed at which we moved through the forest.

I leaned forward and spoke into his ear.

"How long can you keep up this pace?" It was a little like talking to someone while they were driving a motorcycle—except there was no engine noise.

"Quite a while."

I leaned closer to his ear, liking the way his back felt against the tips of my breasts. (Give me a break, he's my husband!)

"This would have exhausted Epi in less than an hour." I was delighted to see his bare arms break out in goose bumps as my breath tickled his ear. Or perhaps it was because my nipples tickled his back. My, he certainly was sensitive.

"Centaurs have more stamina than a horse—" pause for effect "—or a man." His voice had deepened and I felt a rush of pleasure, a little like electricity, pass down my spine, and for a moment I thought I was trapped in a steamy romance novel. Not that I'd mind.

"Glad to hear it." I breathed into his ear and squeezed his firm shoulders.

And decided once and for all—Rhiannon was a fool.

9

We didn't stay on the small path I'd been following. Instead, ClanFintan led us away from the river and through the trees until we came to a well-defined road (obviously the one I had been avoiding). Shortly we came to a fork in the road, and we took the northwest branch, decidedly away from the river. I searched through my memory of my floating trip and decided that this must be a quicker route than meandering along the river road. Incredibly enough, the centaurs picked up the pace. ClanFintan and his buds seemed tireless as their gallop ate up the distance to the castle. Tracking me had obviously slowed them down.

Traffic on the roadway was fairly brisk, but all were heading back the way we had come. The groups of travelers were mostly made up of large families, where the women rode in flatbed wagons and the men either walked or rode horses alongside, usually accompanied by a small selection of farm animals. I did notice that the people looked prosperous and well kept, not like I'd imagined peasants would look. They weren't scraggly with rotten teeth and matted, parasite-infested hair. Honestly, they were uncommonly attractive people—

almost as nice-looking as their horses. This land must really like fine horseflesh. All that day I didn't see one nag.

I couldn't help but feel a little smug at the fact that my Epi was outstanding even among these great-looking horses. Actually, so was ClanFintan, but he didn't fall in the strictly horse category, so I guess it was unfair of me to be smug about that.

I wondered, before we had crossed paths with any of the locals, if I would be recognized. My answer was quick in coming. The first family we passed began politely greeting the centaurs, but stopped as soon as they noticed me. Their polite greeting changed abruptly into exuberance.

"It is Epona!" The mother, who was driving the wagon filled with several adorable children and bags of supplies, noticed me first. Her children took up her cry and began waving enthusiastically.

"Epona!"

"Blessings to you, Lady Rhiannon!"

"May your journey be safe!"

I smiled and waved and felt foolishly like Miss America on a runway. But I've never been accused of being shy or timid, so I realized quickly that it was a feeling I could get used to. They were just all so nice! Guess Rhiannon's people weren't aware of what a bitch she was. Good thing for me. And that was pretty much how it went all morning. The centaurs kept up an amazing pace, and travelers headed in the direction of the temple kept trickling by.

We didn't talk much. I wasn't convinced that this pace was quite as easily kept up as ClanFintan had boasted, and I didn't want to bother him. I spent the time taking in the local scenery, waving to my adoring minions and trying my best to maintain a comfortable, well-balanced seat.

The land was beautiful, lush and obviously prosperous. The

countryside was covered with rolling vineyards interspersed with crops and cottages. Wildflowers decorated the meadows with splashes of orange and violet and yellow. We had to cross several clear, tinkling little streams that irrigated the green land. From the air and through the cover of night it had reminded me of the Umbria region of Italy. From up close it was more like England's Lake District, except the hills were more tamed. And it was warmer. And it hadn't rained. And, well, there weren't any Brits. But all in all it was a land anyone would be proud to call his or her own.

It was midmorning when I spied some lovely brush cover (and some soft-leafed plants) next to another stream that bisected our roadway.

"Could we please take a pit stop here?" I admitted to myself, almost unashamedly, that I sincerely enjoyed any excuse I could find to lean against his body.

"What type of stop is a pit stop?" ClanFintan's arms were covered with a thin layer of sweat, but his breathing sounded normal. He was in seriously good shape. (Note to self: yum.)

"It's a stop that we use to recharge our energy and, well, to take care of necessary things." Subjects like going to the bathroom get easier the longer you're married. The fact that we hadn't been married very long, coupled with the absence of even a nasty state-run rest stop, was awkwardness waiting to happen. No wonder I felt myself blushing again. "And I'm thirsty."

"Oh, of course. I should have thought of that earlier." His pace slowed to a trot as we drew closer to the stream. He spoke over his shoulder to the centaurs. "We will take a short—" he smiled at me "—*pit* stop."

To their credit the centaurs tried not to look too confused.

ClanFintan twisted at the waist and slid his arm around my waist, easily lifting me off the saddle. As my feet touched the ground, I was humiliated to feel them crumple under me and I grabbed for his strong arm. He was quick to understand the problem, and I found myself facing him, securely wrapped in his arms, my feet barely touching the ground.

"I'm sorry. I think my feet have gone to sleep." I looked up, waiting to see if he would make fun of my weakness.

"You need not apologize. You did not complain, so I kept pushing the pace." His handsome face reflected only concern. "I should have been more considerate of your needs. Here, sit on this felled tree and let me get the circulation moving in your feet again."

He helped me over to the skeleton of a fallen tree and lifted me to a seat near the broken trunk. My legs dangled down without touching the ground, and I grabbed at the dry branches to keep my balance. Thus seated I was almost level with his waist, which allowed him to easily pull my boots off one at a time. Then, starting with my right foot, he began firmly kneading and rubbing everything from my numbed pad all the way up my calf and back to my toes.

I felt suddenly all Marilyn Monroe–like as my eyes went to half-mast and a moan escaped my lips.

"Too hard?" He looked up from his work.

"Shh, don't talk. My leg is having a deep and meaningful experience with your hands. Let's not interrupt them."

He chuckled deep in his throat.

"Is the feeling coming back to your foot?"

"All sorts of feelings are coming back to me. Which in particular are you asking about?"

He just smiled and switched to my other foot.

"Mmm. You're very good at that." I've always had the sneaking suspicion that a man is much like a puppy—he needs to be praised and rewarded when he does well. "Thank you."

Having filled the praise square, my mind was happily contemplating the reward category, when he gave my calf a firm slap—which snapped me out of my decidedly R-rated daydream.

"I think you will have better luck walking now." He lifted me off my branch and stood me next to him. He was right; my feet did work better now. But for an instant I considered pretending otherwise.

"Right you are. But before I put those boots back on, do we have time for me to soak my feet in the stream?"

"Just a short time, Rhiannon. I want to be certain we are within sight of MacCallan Castle before the sun sets today."

"Will we be there that soon?" Knowledge of what we would find at the castle settled heavily in the pit of my stomach.

"You could stay here and let me take care of what needs to be done at the castle." His voice was gentle.

"Thank you, but no. He is my father. It's my responsibility, and I have to see for myself what happened to him."

"I understand and I will be there with you." He reached out slowly, almost reluctantly, and took my hand.

I realized suddenly that he probably didn't want to like me. For all he knew, any second I was going to turn back into a bitchy slut who didn't have any intention of caring anything about him, and who never wanted this marriage—temporary or not. The kindness he continued to show me was a testament to the depth of integrity he must possess. His reaching out to me must have been an amazingly difficult thing for him to do.

So I gave him my best "good boy! good boy!" smile and squeezed his hand.

"I'm glad you'll be with me. But now I need some privacy to, well, you know."

He smiled and squeezed my hand in return before dropping

it and heading to the stream to join the rest of the centaurs. "I will be close by if you need me."

"I'm so sure I'd rather die first…" I muttered as I tramped delicately off to find a nearby bush, being careful not to step my bare feet in any stickers. At least the hunk of cheese seemed to have stopped me up—which was truly a blessing.

Joining the boys back at the stream, I crouched and drank deeply of the clear, icy water, washing my face and running wet fingers through my hair in an attempt to tame my wild curls. Plopping my butt on the dry bank, I let the water run over and around my feet while I tried to do something with my hair.

"Allow me, my Lady." I looked over my shoulder to see ClanFintan kneeling behind me with a piece of leather in one hand and a wide-toothed comb in another. I recognized the leather as one like the thong that held his thick mane (well, what would you call it?) of hair back out of the way. Before I could respond, he had pulled free what remained of Alanna's French braid and was working the comb through my wild red tangles. I sighed happily and closed my eyes. In far too short a time he had it tied neatly back. "That should stay out of your way."

I managed to moan some semblance of thanks.

"You had better let your feet dry before trying to get those boots back on. We will need to get moving again soon." His voice was apologetic and his hands rested briefly on my shoulders before he stood.

"Okay. I'll be ready." I moved away from the stream, drying my feet in the tall grass surrounding the road.

One of the centaurs, an attractive young strawberry roan, approached me, and with a shy smile offered me something that looked and smelled like beef jerky.

"Thank you." I beamed my appreciation for his not being a herbivore.

"You are welcome, my Lady." He blushed sweetly before joining his buddies, who were forming up and getting ready to head out again.

I stuck the end of the jerky in my mouth and pulled on my boots, then hobbled over to where ClanFintan stood waiting. He, too, was munching on a piece of jerky while he tightened the cinch and made sure the saddle was ready for my butt.

"Okay, I'm ready." I reached out for him and we clasped arms. I was up and seated in less time than it takes to spell *equestrian*.

"Make it so." I pointed forward, giving my best Picard impression. I giggled at my own joke. ClanFintan snorted and shook his head at me before he accelerated into his smooth, distance-covering gallop. I guess my humor loses something in translation.

The rest of the day followed much of the same schedule. We would travel until I felt as if my feet were no longer attached to my body and/or I had to pee again. I would clue in ClanFintan to my desire to take a break. We would halt for what seemed like ten seconds, but was probably about ten minutes. I'd get a brief foot rub so that my legs would function, then we would take off again, chewing on a seemingly inexhaustible supply of jerky.

Other than a thin sheen of sweat, the centaurs didn't show any signs of tiring. My own exhaustion made me feel like a sissy, and I struggled against the desire to whine. But I figured whining was something that Rhiannon probably would have done—which helped me keep my mouth shut.

By the time I realized we hadn't seen any other travelers in quite a while, I also noticed the sun was beginning to dip toward the horizon. Taking a deep breath of the cooling air, I smelled the distinct scent of salt and water. To our right I could see that in the distance the vineyards had given way to forested land and realized that we must be approaching the castle from the eastern edge.

"We're almost there." My voice sounded a lot calmer than I felt.

"Yes." His pace slowed to a gentle trot. "You said the creatures came through the northeastern part of the forest?"

"Yes." My voice was a whisper as memory replayed the forest scene in my mind.

"Then we will circle around and enter from the southwest. If they are still in the castle, perhaps the glare of the setting sun will help to hide our approach."

Sounded like bull to me, but since English teachers aren't traditionally known for their great battle strategies, I decided to keep my comments to myself.

ClanFintan made a motion to the centaurs and they followed him off the trail as we began moving into the setting sun. I could feel his muscles bunching and working and I realized the gradual incline of the land had increased and was now rising noticeably as we climbed up toward the edge of the southern tree line. The smell of salt was heavy in the afternoon air and I could hear the sea rushing against the rocky shore. The centaurs' hooves made crackling noises as they galloped over needle-covered ground. The silent oaks and maples gave way to whispering pines, and I was surprised to recognize the tart scent of Christmas trees mixed with the salty breeze, and something else. It was a smell I couldn't place. An odd fragrance, indistinct and sticky. And then we slid to a halt as the trees changed to rocks, which led to an abrupt drop to the ocean. This was one thing I definitely hadn't exaggerated from my dream vision—it still reminded me of Ireland's imposing Cliffs of Moher. The coast stretched before us as far as we could see, and in the north the castle perched like a stone guardian, perilously close to the deep drop.

The sun lit up the western façade of the castle, turning the gray stone to bright, gleaming silver. My breath caught in my throat and I felt a sudden, unexpected rush of emotion. If I had been born into this world this amazing castle would have been where I had grown up. I blinked my eyes hard and told myself it was the briskness of the wind that caused them to fill with water.

"My Lord, look there on the grounds surrounding the wall." The palomino's voice was grim and he pointed to the area surrounding the western gate. I squinted and followed the line of his finger. There were clumps of debris scattered around the outside of the castle, as if field hands had piled sacks of grain or maybe bales of hay or—

"Oh, God. They're bodies." My voice shook and I understood what the nameless smell was.

"Dougal, check for any movement." The palomino nodded and melted back into the trees.

"Connor, join him." The strawberry roan backed into the pines and was gone.

Then ClanFintan addressed me over his shoulder. "Rhiannon, you said that that night you felt you were in the presence of evil before you actually saw the creatures. Are you sensing any evil now?"

I stared at the castle and tried to still the pounding of my heart.

"No, I don't feel anything like I did that night."

"Are you certain, my Lady?"

I closed my eyes and concentrated, forcing myself to remember that night, to remember the tangible evil that had seeped out of the forest and slithered into the castle like a poisonous mist.

"I'm certain. The feeling is unmistakable, and it is definitely not here now." My hands were still resting on his shoulders and he reached up and gave one of them a quick squeeze.

"Good." Then he turned to face Dougal and Connor as they rejoined us. "Report."

"Except for the carrion birds, there is no movement. And we could detect no sign or scent of fire." Dougal's voice was businesslike and calm.

"Lady Rhiannon can sense nothing of the creatures' presence. I believe it is safe to enter the castle." Then he addressed me again. "My Lady, you do not have to come into the castle. If you wait here, I will bring you word of your father. You can trust me to care for his remains with the honor he deserves."

"I do trust you, it's not that. I just…I just have to do this." My mouth felt incredibly dry. "It won't be real for me until I see for myself."

He nodded slowly and I felt him sigh. "Very well, we go. All of us. Centaurs, stay close. Be alert."

ClanFintan began trotting toward the castle, four centaurs on either side of him. I held his shoulders tightly and kept playing the words *you can do this you can do this you can do this* over and over in my mind.

As we approached the castle, the wind began to carry more of the sticky smell to us. At first it was just a teasing sourness, like when you open the door to the refrigerator and something doesn't smell quite right. Then the teasing changed. The smell hung in the air and surrounded us. I gagged and suddenly my dry mouth was flooded with bile.

"Try to breathe through your mouth. It helps." ClanFintan's voice was sympathetic. I wondered how he knew so much about the way death smelled. "Where did you say you last saw your father in your vision?"

"At the foot of the stairs that led to the barracks."

He stopped and his guard halted with us. "Rhiannon, let me look at the corpses. I will recognize your father and tell you when we have found him. You just hold tight. Close your eyes if you need to."

"I'll be okay. Let's get this over with." I tried to sound brave, but my voice was weak and shaky.

We started forward again. Soon we came to the first of the bodies. As we approached, dark birds lifted in a flurry of wings. I made myself look away from what they held in their pointed beaks. The bodies were clumped together, several in one area, then a few yards away several more. Amidst the horror it was somehow comforting that they weren't alone. I tried not to look at them, but my eyes wouldn't obey my mind—or maybe they obeyed my heart instead. It ached for these brave men and I felt that if I looked at them, acknowledged their sacrifice by keeping a visual reckoning rather than looking away, maybe their lingering souls would feel my respect and appreciation for their heroism and be comforted.

I glanced at the centaurs that walked at our side. Their faces were set in expressionless masks I tried to emulate. They checked each man, meticulously making sure none lived. We moved slowly around the southern wall to the front entrance of the castle. The huge iron doors were open; silent bodies and feeding birds littered the entryway.

"To the barracks." ClanFintan's emotionless voice echoed eerily off the dead walls as we walked through the gates, then passed through a smaller, arched inner-wall entrance, which led into a huge courtyard.

It was like a scene from a Dali nightmare painting. Men lay in dark, congealed pools, their bodies twisted and frozen at grotesque angles. But in spite of the carnage, I glimpsed snatches of lingering beauty in the thick, graceful columns that lined the courtyard and the fountain that still bubbled musically with oily reddened water. Something about that fountain held my gaze, and I realized with a sense of detached shock that the marble girl who was pouring water from a beautifully painted urn was a young version of myself. And the urn. That damn pot. It depicted a familiar scene, now tinged pink by the scarlet of the water. The seated priestess had her back to me, with her red-gold hair and her outstretched arm visible as she accepted homage from her supplicants. I knew if I looked closer I would see a scar on her hand, the same scar that suddenly blurred as I looked down at my own hand...

"Rhiannon!" ClanFintan swiveled at the waist and caught me before I could fall.

"I can do this I can do this I can do this." My body was shaking.

"Shall I take you out of here?"

"No! I can't quit now. Just give me a second." I recovered my balance and straightened my spine. ClanFintan hesitantly let loose his grip on my arm. "Let's find him."

He grunted a wordless reply and moved off to the left. The other centaurs slowly followed us, meticulously completing their gruesome task of checking each body. We walked between pillars and through a wide, breezy hallway lined with doors and large floor-to-ceiling windows. The centaurs' hooves clicked on the stone floor. That and the birds were the only sounds I could hear over the beating of my heart. Clan-Fintan moved purposefully through the hallway past a room that was furnished with long wooden tables and the bodies of men, turned to his left again and walked through another door, which led to a much smaller interior courtyard. This courtyard had several entrances, one of which was a steep flight of stone stairs that led up to a large, low room connected to the roof of the castle and its balustraded walls. The barracks the men had poured from that dreadful night.

Even if I hadn't recognized it from my midnight visit, the half-dressed bodies that littered the stairs and the yard before us gave testament to where we were. And in the far corner, near the bottom of the stairs, was a single body. This man was not joined in death by a comrade who died protecting his back. He slept alone in a bed of his own blood. The circled area around him was empty.

"He's over there." I pointed to the lone body and was surprised that my hand did not shake.

ClanFintan nodded in acknowledgment and walked to where I pointed.

It was my father. He lay on his back with his torso twisted toward the ground. His left arm was beneath him, his right one was shredded and his wrist bone jutted through the dangling skin, but it still clutched his sword. His kilt was black and stiff with the blood that pooled beneath and around him. His kilt was torn and it did nothing to hide the deep gouges in his back and chest. I could see that he had been disemboweled. I tore my eyes away from his gaping wounds and my gaze found his face. It rested on the ground, half turned away from me. His eyes were closed and already death had sunken them and heightened the ridge of his cheekbones. His skin was rigid-looking and had the pale grayness of death, but his lips weren't contorted and tortured. Instead, his shadowed face looked at peace, restful, as if he had finished a difficult job and lay down for a well-earned sleep.

"Why did he die here alone?" ClanFintan's voice mirrored my sorrow.

"He wasn't alone. The men fought all around him, but he was still fighting after they had been killed." I remembered his heroism as he challenged the creatures. "He took many of those things with him—that's why he's over here with a ring around him empty of everything except blood—their blood. They must have carried off their dead."

"Can I take you out of here now?"

"Yes." And suddenly I knew what must be done. "Burn them." ClanFintan looked over his shoulder at me. "Build a giant pyre in the courtyard and burn them all. Cleanse this place with fire." I smiled sadly at what remained of the man who had been a mirror image of my father and whispered, "Set them free."

"It will be as you say, Rhiannon."

ClanFintan bowed once to my father's still form, then turned and headed quickly for the front of the castle. I kept him in view for as long as I was able. I barely heard the commands ClanFintan gave the centaurs that would carry out my wishes. I was looking for a last time at the men around me—acknowledging each death in my mind, wanting to remember each act of bravery…

Then the thought hit me and the breath rushed from my body. ClanFintan twisted around, thinking I was falling again. I clasped his arm and looked intently into his eyes.

"The women! Where are the bodies of the women?" I thought I was yelling, but my voice sounded like a choked whisper.

He froze.

"Dougal!" The palomino centaur appeared quickly, his face pale—his eyes shadowed.

"Have you found any women's bodies?"

Dougal blinked in confusion, then his eyes widened in understanding.

"No. I have seen no women or girls. Only men and boy children."

"Call the others. Search for them. I am going to take Lady Rhiannon out of here. Come report to me at the place where we first left the pines."

Dougal spun away and began calling for the other centaurs.

"Hold tightly to me."

I reached forward and wrapped my arms around his body, burying my face in the back of his shoulder and breathing deeply, letting his warm, heady scent block out the cloying smell of death. I shut my eyes and felt his muscles bunch and release, bunch and release. The wind whistled past us and I knew each long stride was taking us farther away from the dead. When we reached the forest's edge he came to a smooth halt. He put his arms over mine where they crossed his chest. Neither of us spoke.

Finally, I was able to loosen my grip and he removed his arms from mine. He turned and gently lifted me. This time he didn't let go when my feet touched the ground, which was just as well because I couldn't make myself step out of the comfort of his embrace. The top of my head came only to his lower chest, and I lay the side of my cheek against him, letting his warmth seep into me. I realized I was shaking and my teeth were chattering, and I wondered suddenly if I would ever feel really warm again.

"You were brave. The MacCallan would have been proud of you." His voice rumbled low in his chest.

"I was scared shitless. I almost fainted."

"But you did not faint."

"No, but in the middle of all that I almost fell off you." My body shuddered at the thought.

"I would have caught you."

"Thank you." I tightened my arms around his waist and felt him lean slowly down until his lips rested, for just a moment, against the top of my head.

I tilted my head back and looked into his dark eyes. I didn't know what to make of this man-horse to whom I was committed for a year of marriage. That he interested me was obvious. He was, after all, like no one else I had ever met. Let's face it, there aren't a lot of centaurs running around Oklahoma—at least not in Tulsa (you never know what goes on in the Panhandle). One thing I did suddenly have to admit to myself was that I simply felt better whenever I was touching him. And that had never happened to me before.

Without stopping to contemplate the consequences or my motives, I reached one hand up until it rested on the front of his soft vest. Then I hooked my fingers over the open edge of it and tugged once. He was no dummy and didn't need any further prompting. I was surprised by the feel of his lips as they met mine—they were warmer than a man's lips would have been. And, damn, he was big. His arms circled me and I felt the world around us dissolve into his kiss. For a moment I forgot everything except his arms and his lips and the heat of his mouth as his tongue found mine.

And then the beating hooves of a quickly approaching centaur broke our trance. ClanFintan released me—reluctantly, I like to think—as we turned to hear Dougal's report.

"We could find the remains of none of the women, my Lord." The young centaur looked as if he had aged a decade in one evening. "But we found tracks leading into the northern forest. Amidst the creatures' footprints were smaller ones—soft, smoothed-toed sandals like those worn by—" His voice broke.

"Women and girl children," ClanFintan finished for him.

"Yes, my Lord. They made no attempt to hide their trail. It is as if they wanted all to know what they had done and where they could be found."

"They are through hiding." He spoke with such surety that I glanced up at him in surprise.

"How do you know that?"

He looked at me and smiled an apology. "I will explain later."

He sure as hell would.

Turning back to Dougal, he continued, "Stay here with Lady Rhiannon while I return and we finish what must be done at the castle." I started to protest, but his finger on my lips silenced me. "We will be able to move more quickly if you wait here. I do not want to be here after dark."

I had to agree with him on that.

"Watch over her," he ordered Dougal, gave my hand a quick kiss, then spun around and headed back to the castle. I didn't envy the task before him.

"My Lady…" Dougal's young voice sounded shy and hesitant. "May I offer you some wine?" He held out a wineskin that had been strapped to his back.

"Yes, thank you." I took a deep drink and stared back toward the castle. I could see the centaurs dragging corpses inside the walls. They had disrupted the feeding of the dark birds, which were now circling the castle fretfully. Their greedy cawing carried on the wind. Crows have always made my skin crawl— now I knew why. I took another drink and let the wine wash away the taste of death. Blinking, I forced my eyes away from the gruesome scene and let my vision focus instead on the whitecapped sea. Craggy rocks jutted dramatically up near the edge of the cliff and I had a sudden desire to climb up and let the salty breeze wash the smell of death from my clothes.

I had only taken a couple steps when I heard Dougal's hooves thud behind me. I spoke over my shoulder to him.

"I'm just going to sit on one of those rocks."

His expression looked as if he doubted my intentions.

"I promise not to hurl myself over the edge." He still looked doubtful. "I'll stay where you can see me."

The rocks were a lot smoother than they looked from a distance and I had trouble finding toe and handholds. I settled for perching on top of one of the smaller boulders. Facing the water, I loosened my hair from the leather binding, shook it free and closed my eyes. The ocean breeze whipped my hair, lifting it off my shoulders. I ran my fingers through it, willing the clinging scent away from me. I took another deep drink and sent a sincere prayer of thanks to God or Epona or who-the-hell-ever had filled this world with grapes.

I opened my eyes slowly, squinting against the insistent breeze. The shore far below me was wild and dangerous. Waves broke violently against jagged rocks. There was no beach. The sun had drifted down in the sky and, as I watched it kissed the water, making it blush violet and pink. The soft beauty of the sunset was unexpected and I felt my breath catch with pleasure.

Closing my eyes again, I concentrated on things in life that were lovely, not horrifying and unfathomable in their capacity for evil. Like sunsets over the ocean…tall men…red wine. Suddenly an image played across my closed eyelids like a video across a screen. It was a vision of the last time I'd visited Dad. We'd sat on the old wrought-iron chairs that were perpetually rusted because Dad always left them out on the front patio. Our feet rested on the flat top of an old Oklahoma sandstone rock that served as a footstool but was actually just too damn big to be moved out of the way. It was Sunday evening before the last week of school, and already hot for May—I remember the Coors was icy and tasted like spring rain. The warm breeze had covered us with the sweet scent of the butterfly bushes that Dad had planted all around the perimeter of the patio two years before. I told him I couldn't figure out why mine never did as well as his—he was succinctly explaining to me that his did better than mine because I didn't shovel enough horse crap on mine.

Which made me laugh then, as it did now. See, some part of my heart told my mind, he's still alive.

In another world, he's still alive.

My cheeks felt cold and I realized they were wet with tears. I opened my eyes and looked toward the castle.

The sunset that had earlier colored the ocean so beautifully had now darkened to deeper shades that were more reflective of the end of evening. Oranges and reds painted the uppermost walls of the castle an all-too-familiar bloody tint while casting the rest of the stones into shadow. Through my tears the building took on the blurred appearance of a crouching beast, still red from the kill. I knew all the rules of metaphor and the power of figurative language, but this image wasn't typed neatly on paper and I wasn't curled up with a favorite book and a glass of wine, getting a little too lost in an author's make-believe world. I shook myself and wiped my eyes. This world was my reality, but the malevolent image before me didn't have to define my new life. Turning my back on the castle, I concentrated on the sea and the sunset, breathing in deep, cleansing breaths of the evening air.

The sun had almost disappeared when I finally climbed down to the nervously waiting centaur who looked relieved as I approached.

"Don't ever worry about me doing something stupid like that. I'm not a quitter."

"Of course, my Lady." He looked slightly ashamed of himself. He really was a cute young guy/horse/whatever.

"Thank you for caring, though." I smiled at him and he blushed back at me. I glanced at the castle. The sinking sun had left a glow in the sky and it was getting hard to see, but I thought all the bodies had been moved inside the castle walls.

"How much longer do you think they'll be?" ClanFintan had been right; I didn't want to be here after dark.

"Soon, my Lady. They will be finished soon." He, too, was looking at the castle. "Most of the bodies were near the court-yard and outside the front gate."

As he quit speaking I thought I noticed rising from the castle a wisp of darkness against the graying. "Is that smoke?"

"Yes, my Lady. Look, they return." I could see the centaurs, illuminated now by torches they carried, just outside the walls of the castle. As I watched, they threw the torches within the castle and the yellow and orange of catching fire reflected off their coats. I saw all seven of them back slowly away from the castle, bow their heads in unison and salute the dead. Then they turned as one and galloped to where I waited.

I felt my heart perform a funny little leap as ClanFintan drew near me. His face was set and serious, as were the rest of the centaurs' faces, but his eyes sought mine and I swear I could feel the warmth of his gaze as he closed the distance between us.

"Rhiannon, let us leave this place." He held out his arm for me to grasp, and the centaurs barely paused as I was swept up to his back and we headed through the forest of pines. I craned my head around and looked at the castle. Smoke billowed from it and flames were already licking its walls.

"We will rest in the storage barn near that last stream." His voice brought my head back around and I gripped his shoulders as he picked up the pace. I vaguely remembered some kind of barnlike structure that we had passed just before we left the road and cut through the forest.

I hated to complain, but I couldn't help asking. "Can't we stay in, well, a house or something in the town that's just south of the castle?" A real bed and a bath sounded like a wonderful idea.

"Rhiannon, Loth Tor was the first town evacuated to the temple."

"I'm sure the people wouldn't mind if we borrowed a place to stay for the night." Was that me whining?

"Of course they would not mind." He glanced over his shoulder at me as if I had turned into a moron. "They would be honored to succor you, but firing the castle will draw attention to the area." He paused and seemed to consider his words before continuing. "If the creatures were to return, the village would be the first place they would raid."

"Oh—I didn't think of that. Never mind, I'm sure the barn will be fine."

"I think you will be quite comfortable, my Lady."

Well, of course he would consider a barn "quite comfortable." He was half horse. I scratched my hair and thought longingly of the huge mineral bath at the temple. I didn't even want to consider the possibility of any kind of parasites, but I started searching my memory to see if I could recall ever hearing about a case of horselice.

It wasn't full dark yet when we broke from the cover of the trees and crossed a fairly deep stream that bubbled and gurgled its way into the forest not too far from where a barnlike structure stood. ClanFintan set me gently on the ground and Dougal slid open the door. Peeking inside, I could just make out mounds of stuff that smelled like freshly cut hay—which was actually a very pleasant smell. But I knew from Oklahoma experience that snakes like the smell of hay, too (as do mice and rats), so I hung around nonchalantly while the centaur named Connor built a nice-size fire. I watched the other centaurs set up camp and noticed that they were much quieter tonight. And, something else…

"ClanFintan!" He turned quickly from unloading his packs and approached me with worry outlining his handsome face. "You're missing two of your centaurs." I hated to be the one to tell him, but he had to know. Were the creatures following us, picking us off one at a time?

The lines of worry softened and he smiled. "They are hunting our dinner. They will return shortly."

The other centaurs mirrored his smile, which helped to ease my feeling of embarrassed stupidity. At least they could still smile.

"Oh, uh, I knew that." I breathed deeply of the night air and was rewarded with a decidedly stinky smell. I sniffed again.

It was me—I sniffed in ClanFintan's direction—and him. "Sheuw!" It was the horrible stink of my sweat mixed with the lingering scent of death, oil (must be the lamp oil they used to light the pyre) and, let's face it, funky horse smell.

"I smell bad!"

ClanFintan shot me a shocked look and I heard several guffaws from the busy horsies.

"I think the water forms a pool a short distance downstream. If you can stand the cold, you can freshen up."

"Freshen, hell, I need a serious bath." I sniffed knowingly in his direction, "and I'm not the only one." This time Dougal laughed out loud. "I didn't mean just him, either," I said pointedly to the young, now blushing, centaur. That made ClanFintan laugh. Which decided me.

"Grab a spare blanket and come on then." I walked purposefully past him and headed toward the stream. I didn't hear him following, so I stopped and turned to face him. "You don't expect me to go out there alone in the dark and take a bath, do you?"

He still stood there, looking confused and helpless. Very much like a guy.

"Didn't you swear to protect me?" That seemed to get through to him, and he yanked a blanket from the hands of one of the eavesdropping centaurs and started after me. I decided suddenly to use a little of Rhiannon's bitchiness and turned to address the rest of the herd. "It would really be nice if I had a hot meal waiting for me when I finish my bath." Then I winked and grinned at them. "Something tells me I'm going to need it." I marched toward the stream, loving the sound of their laughter as it floated in the night.

"Where was that pool?" As usual, I had no idea where I was going.

"A little farther downstream. I noticed a small beaver dam

right over there." He pointed to a mound of tree parts that covered most of the stream.

And he was right. There was a round, basinlike area that made a nice catch pool of water just on the other side of the dam. We walked to the water's edge and stopped. Darkness had begun to thicken and the light from the centaurs' campfires threw an eerie glow around the barn. The light didn't actually reach us, but it reflected off the water upstream and helped to cut through some of the darkness. I could see the pool clearly. It looked about waist deep, fed slowly as the dammed water escaped from an open place amidst the limbs and collected in the basin. The excess ran off in a tiny tumbling waterfall.

"Uh-um." I succinctly cleared my throat. I felt him looking at me. "That water's going to be cold."

"Yes, it is." He definitely sounded amused.

"Don't be so smug—you smell bad, too. I have to ride you, which means you get a bath, too."

"Oh."

And we were silent again. Jeesh, this was ridiculous. This guy/horse/whatever was, after all, my husband. And it wasn't as if I hadn't done my share of skinny-dipping. I glanced over at him and found he was looking at me. Again. I took a deep breath—reminding myself firmly that I've never been shy (my mind whispered that I've also never had sex with a horse). Another deep breath and I reached out, resting one hand on his withers to balance, and began taking off my boots.

"Might as well get this over with. It's sure not going to get any warmer." I shook my hair loose, handing him the leather tie, then unlaced my pants and slid them off and lay them across a large, flat rock, trying to decide if I should leave my thong on or not. I opted for not (there are better reasons for having a wet crotch than bathing in your panties) and stepped daintily out of the small triangle of material. Without looking at Clan-

Fintan, I reached around and started trying to worry the knot out of the lacing in the back of my shirt—and I heard him move behind me.

"Let me do that." His voice was deep and had that velvety, sensual tone to it that I was already beginning to look forward to hearing. His fingers replaced my own and I could feel his unique warmth through the soft leather. Far too soon the tie was loosened and I could draw the shirt over my head.

As I walked into the water, I worried briefly about what my butt looked like to him (and hoped fervently that it didn't jiggle too much), but the second my feet stepped into the water thoughts of butt flub fled my mind and were replaced by—

"Ohmygod! That's freezing!"

I heard a snort of laughter from behind me.

Not allowing myself to hesitate (because I'd chicken out), I made my way out into the pool. The bottom was rocky, but the rocks were mostly small, smooth pebbles, which was a blessing. I would hate to add sharp, cutting rocks to my freezing feet. Before I could stop myself (and keeping in mind how rank I smelled), I took a deep breath and sank down in the water until I was covered to my shoulders.

"Oh, brrrr!" Actually, I was finding out it wasn't so bad once I was under the water. It especially wasn't so bad since the water was now blanketing the view of my naked body from him. I turned to face the centaur, kind of resting half on my butt and half crouching, but definitely under the water and covered to my shoulders.

His face was in shadow, but I saw the white of his teeth flash as he smiled at me.

"I wish I had some soap. My hair could use a good scrubbing."

He walked toward the edge of the water and I could see he was searching the ground near his hooves. Did he think someone had dropped a bar of Zest on the bank? Suddenly he raised a hoof and stomped several times on a dark, flat stone.

I thought that perhaps lust for me had driven him out of his horsey mind.

"Will this do?" He gestured to the ground, which was now covered with sandlike pieces of rock and lots of soapy bubbles.

I didn't move. As far as I was aware, Oklahoma doesn't have any rocks that doubled as soap. I was confused. Again.

"I know it is not perfumed and processed, but sand soap works well, even in its natural form."

Silly me.

"Um, of course. But, well, I'm going to freeze if I stand up. Do you think you could bring me a handful?" Somehow it was better to have him wade out here and join me while I was covered with water than for me to stand up, all naked and nippley, and parade to him. Maybe.

He started to bend to scoop up the soapy sand.

"Hey, you better take off that vest." I looked at him and couldn't help adding a teasing smile. "You're going to get wet."

I don't think I've ever seen a guy get out of a shirt or vest so quickly. *Eager* was too slow a word. In moments he was causing the pool to slosh and spill over as he waded to me, hands filled with bubbles and sand. As he joined me he offered me the sand soap and I gratefully scooped out a handful (which was, by the way, warm from his touch) and started soaping up my arms, pits, and well, other places. I had to rise a little out of the water to get to some of the other places. I tried to stay turned away from him because he just stood there, watching me, slowly rubbing some sand around his own chest. Which was now very bare—and very muscular—and very broad. Good thing the water was cold; I was suddenly beginning to feel warm. Imagine that.

To take my mind off his chest, I dunked myself all the way

under the water, shaking my head until my hair was good and soaked. Emerging back above water (and trying not to sputter unattractively), I reached for more of the sand soap from my very handsome soap holder. The sand felt wonderful as I rubbed it furiously into my hair, and I liked the unusual, sweet scent that drifted down my shoulders with the bubbles. It smelled a little like vanilla, or maybe honey, mixed with some kind of nut.

"I can do that." His hands replaced my own and he took over for me, massaging the soap into my scalp with warm, firm fingers. "You will be warmer if you stay covered by the water."

I crouched back down and felt him kneeling behind me. His hands worked through my hair, rubbing and pulling, being careful to keep the soapy bubbles from falling down into my eyes. His body was only a few inches away from me—I could feel the heat of him radiating through the water.

"That feels wonderful." I meant it as a comradely compliment, but it came out of my mouth as a breathy moan. His hands drifted from my head to my neck, gliding with slick, hot fingers down to my shoulders and back to the base of my neck then up through my scalp again. I leaned until I felt my back touch the heat of his chest. His hands stilled on my shoulders. I placed my hands over his and then glided them up his soapy forearms, loving the hard feel of his tense muscles.

"Don't stop," I whispered. Through my back I felt his heartbeat increase as his hands moved forward and down under the water, taking the heaviness of my breasts, one in each of his hands, and squeezing them gently while he drew me more firmly against his body.

This time I didn't even attempt to make my moan sound comradely. The cold of the water combined with his heat and the slickness of the soap. I felt everything inside of me liquefy. Turning in his arms, I rose just far enough out of the water so that our faces were almost even with each other. His hands dropped to cradle my waist and I reached up, ringing the excess soap from my hair into my hands and piling my sudsy hair in a ball on top of my head. Not taking my eyes from his (which was difficult because I *really* wanted to gawk at his gorgeous chest), I began rubbing the soap over his torso.

"I can do that," I purred.

He smiled as my words echoed his. I lathered his chest, working the sandy soap up to his shoulders and down his wonderfully muscular arms. Then I swiped the extra soap, cupping the bubbles in my hands and reaching under his arms to rub them around his back. The tips of my breasts worked seductively against his chest, moving to the rhythm of my hands.

I think his breathing had increased, but I couldn't be sure because my heart was hammering so loudly in my chest it seemed to be drowning out all sound—except his deep moan as he bent down and covered my mouth with his. His hands slid from my waist to cup my ass, and my breasts flattened against his chest as I wrapped my arms around his shoulders and pressed into him.

Naturally, my hair had to choose that precise moment to fall down out of the soapy ball on top of my head and flop directly into the space between our eyes and noses.

We split apart—sputtering and wiping soap from our eyes and mouths.

"Maybe I should rinse now." The sexy, throaty tone of voice I was going for was pretty much ruined when I spit a big blob of sandy bubbles out of my mouth and onto his chest. "Oops, sorry."

"Urmph." He was busy cupping handfuls of water up to wash the sand and soap out of his eyes.

I dunked myself under the water, rinsing and rinsing until

I seemed to have the soap and my hair under control. I ended up crouched back under the water, watching him try to get the soap out of his eyes.

There he was, this big, strong man/horse kneeling down in the water with about half of the horse part of him submerged, splashing water in his face, which really only caused more and more bubbles. He looked like someone who was being forced to take a bubble bath and was pissed off because of it. A giggle escaped my mouth.

He squinted at me, trying to blink the remainder of the soap from his eyes.

I giggled again.

"What is so fun—" As his lips formed the beginning of the word *funny* a bubble popped out of his mouth, just like he'd blown it from a big ol' wad of Bazooka.

I couldn't stand it—at the sight of that bubble popping from his serious, soapy face, my giggles convulsed into laughter.

At first he just stared at me, but when my laughter made me snort he joined me. Pretty soon I was clutching one of his arms to keep myself from drowning. Eventually our laughter quieted and left us smiling at each other. I shivered suddenly and wondered how I could feel so warm inside and actually be freezing on the outside.

"You look cold." He reached out and tucked a stray tendril of wet hair behind my ear.

"I am. I guess we should get dried off."

"Yes."

Neither of us moved. We kept smiling at each other like our brains were as frozen as our feet (well, my feet, his hooves). Standing so that the water covered me only to below my rib cage, I stepped slowly toward him, liking the way his eyes traveled over my wet body. I sucked in my tummy and knew the distant firelight was reflecting softly off my curves, flattering my voluptuous body. His dark eyes told me he liked what he saw, and I sent up a silent prayer of thanks that I had never been one of those women who felt it necessary to starve or puke away their bodies.

I reached forward and kissed him lightly, whispering into his lips, "You'd better rinse off—that soap will itch your fur if it dries." Then I turned and headed to where we'd left our clothes and the blanket. Behind me I could hear a lot of splashing and grunting as one very large horse-guy tried to get himself unsoaped.

I wrapped myself in the blanket and vigorously began drying with one end of it. Now I was really cold and my hands shivered and shook so hard I almost dropped the blanket. Clan-Fintan plodded noisily out of the water and joined me on the bank.

"If-f-f-f you s-s-shake water on m-m-me I'm going to p-pull your t-t-tail."

He snorted a laugh at me and grabbed the blanket from my frozen hands. Before I could complain, I found myself in the middle of his vigorous toweling. I sucked in my breath as the rough blanket brought the blood rushing back to my extremities.

"You take a lot of care." His voice sounded very business-like. He had part of the blanket draped over my head and he was kneeling to the side of me, drying my back and front at the same time. I felt a little like a piece of silver that was being polished.

"Don't complain—it's not attractive." I had to yell through the blanket to make myself heard. Suddenly the blanket was removed and draped over his shoulders and he began handing me articles of my clothing.

"It was not a complaint." His voice was gruff but his eyes sparkled mischievously at me.

"Well, okay then." I held my damp hair out of the way and offered my back to him. His warm fingers deftly retied the leather. After I slipped on my boots, I took the blanket from around his shoulders.

"My turn." As he put on his vest, I busied myself toweling off his wet fur. There really was a lot of him. I mean, he was a seriously big guy/horse/whatever. By the time I had him fairly well dried I wasn't so cold anymore. Folding the blanket and tossing it over his back, I slipped my hand in his.

I sniffed the air.

"Do we smell better?" He grinned down at me.

"Yes." I wrinkled my nose back at him. "And I think I smell something cooking. Something yummy."

His nostrils flared. "Pheasant." He took a step forward. Instead of moving with him, I tugged at his hand to hold him back. He gave me a questioning look. "I thought you were hungry."

"I am, but, well, I want to ask you something." I held his right hand in my left, and with my other hand I plucked nervously at my lip.

"What is it you wish to ask?" His voice was friendly and curious.

"It's, uh, about this shape-shifting thing." I tried to meet his eyes, but I kept glancing away like a kid asking about the friggin birds and bees.

"You may ask me anything you wish."

"Can you really do it?" My voice was a whisper he had to lean toward me to hear.

"Of course I can." I was looking at his chest, but I could hear the smile in his voice.

"Tonight?"

He paused for a moment. Then his hand touched my chin. Gently he lifted it so my eyes met his. "There is nothing I would like more. But I cannot shape-shift tonight."

"Why not?"

His thumb brushed across my lips. "Shape-shifting requires an enormous amount of energy. I can only maintain another form for a limited time, and when I regain my normal shape I am in a weakened state." His smile was bittersweet. "As much as I desire otherwise, we cannot afford that weakness tomorrow."

"Oh, I understand." I let my disappointment show and was rewarded by his warm hand traveling down to caress my neck. I shivered, this time not with cold.

"I am sorry." He lifted my hand and, as he had done on our wedding day, turned it over and took the meaty part of my palm gently between his teeth.

I swear, a rush of electricity shot from his teeth straight to my crotch.

"Be careful," I purred at him. "I may just bite back."

"I am counting on it." His nip turned into a kiss and I loved the way his hot breath felt against my palm.

We walked back to the camp hand in hand. I was cleaner, but decidedly colder—at least some parts of me were colder. I glanced up, enjoying his strong profile and liking the fact that he slowed his pace to mine. Some of my parts were warmer, too. Not that I minded.

The guys had been busy while we were gone. They had two large fires going a few yards in front of the barn entrance, and over both were spitted several chicken-looking things, already sizzling and popping with juices. More bread and cheese appeared. My mouth was watering, and I thanked Dougal with a big grin when he handed me a wineskin and a hunk of bread. The sweet horsies had pulled a fallen log near enough to one of the fires for me to sit comfortably. I took my seat and started running my fingers through my wild hair, attempting to calm it while it dried in the warmth of the fire (between bites of bread and gulps of wine).

"Try this." ClanFintan offered me the comb he had used earlier on my hair.

"Thank you." Purposely I let my fingers linger on his. I couldn't help it—he was just so damn nice to touch. Probably something to do with the horse/guy mixture. It made me want to pet him. A lot.

I worked the comb through my wild hair while the guys cooked and talked. ClanFintan moved between the two camp-fires, talking to his men and doing guy stuff (like wiping the already spotless blade of his claymore and scratching his privates—no, I'm just kidding, I didn't actually see him scratch). I felt his gaze continually find me. Every so often I would meet his eyes and a *look* would pass between the two of us. You know the look—when you first fall in love and you can feel his caress in a gaze. It was nice but a little disconcert-ing. My powers of concentration (such as they are) felt befud-dled and I was glad that I wasn't going to have to solve any math problems. Well, I mean even more glad than usual.

It seemed that very little time had passed when the centaurs began dividing up the cooked birds. They were so hot the skin was split and sizzling, making me blow on the leg I was trying to eat as well as on my fingers. But it was delicious—and I didn't hesitate to accept a second piece when it was offered.

After dinner we sat around the fires, digesting and talking. ClanFintan stayed near me. Dougal and Connor shared our fire. Three other centaurs clustered around the other campfire. Dougal explained to me before I could worry (he said with a shy smile) that this time the two "missing" centaurs were taking their turn watching our perimeter.

If I had given it much thought before tonight I would have probably found it bizarre that a creature who was half man and half horse could sit and converse after dinner. But I suppose you wouldn't really call it "sitting." Their horse bodies reclined with legs folded under them—which gave their human torsos the appearance of, well, sitting. It sounded strange, but I was beginning to understand that just about everything centaurs did was with an otherworldly grace. Which makes sense because, well, this was another world.

Anyway, we were relaxing and I was beginning to feel warm and dry and maybe a little sleepy. Dougal started humming a tune that sounded very much like one of my favorite Enya melodies, but I couldn't really place it. It was just vaguely Celtic. Suddenly he stopped humming and smiled expectantly at me.

"I was just wishing our bard was with us—then I remembered we have someone even better." He had raised his voice and all the centaurs were looking his way. "We have been blessed with the presence of Epona's Beloved! The best storyteller in Partholon!"

As I blanched, all of the horsies grinned and shouted something that sounded like, "Hear! Hear!" I looked at ClanFintan for rescue, only to find he was beaming proudly and leading the salute.

I know it was unusual, but I didn't know what to say.

The jubilation slowly died down, leaving Dougal looking at me as if I'd just told him he couldn't have dessert.

"Forgive me, my Lady. Perhaps you are not in the mood for storytelling after today's events." He looked at me pitifully with those big, brown eyes. Like a humongous puppy.

Jeesh.

"No, I, uh, just need a moment to, uh—" pause and stall for time "—think of which story I would like to tell."

Oh, God. Which story which story which story which story? I have almost the entire *Cat in the Hat* memorized, but somehow I didn't think it was particularly appropriate.

My little teacher brain started rifling through my mental file entitled "Nearly Worthless Stuff You've Memorized." And, bam! Sophomore English came to my rescue!

I smiled at Dougal and saw him practically squirm with pleasure. If he had had a puppy's tail, I'm sure it would've wagged vigorously—and he probably would've wet himself. He really was cute.

For years I have been attempting to hammer into sixteen-year-olds the *beauty of the poetic ballad*. I'm pretty sure to no avail. But my effort to enlighten the masses has had one side effect—I can recite *The Highwayman* and *The Lady of Shallot* backward, forward, in my sleep and standing on my head (which I've never actually tried in class—yet). I like them both, but I'm a little partial to *The Highwayman,* especially the version put to music by Loreena McKennitt. Alfred Noyes had written a very cool ballad, but Loreena had sprinkled it with Irish magic. Very tragic—very Celtic. And easier to recite than the original.

I played at straightening my hair (a futile attempt) and my clothes (another futile...well, you get the idea) as my mind raced through the stanzas, substituting appropriate phrasing for awkward words, such as *claymore* for *musket, blade* for *trigger, shattering the night with a scream* instead of the *blast of a musket*...etc., etc. I hadn't noticed any guns since I'd been here, and I figured that if this world had them then it was a pretty good bet that the centaurs would own some.

I stood up and threw back my shoulders, giving them all my best "pay attention to me I'm the teacher and I love to be the center of attention" look. They appeared to be an attentive class. I cleared my throat and began:

The wind was a torrent of darkness among the gusty trees,
The moon was a ghostly galleon tossed upon cloudy seas,

The road was a ribbon of moonlight over the purple moor,
And the Highwayman came riding—
riding—riding—
The Highwayman came riding, up to the old inn-
door.

Now, I know I can't sing, but I also know that even in my
own world I am a pretty darn good storyteller. My students
love it when I read or recite to them. I do all the voices. According to them, "it's cool." So, I may not be Loreena McKennitt with her hauntingly beautiful pitch and tone, but I wasn't
trying to be. I didn't sing the ballad; I recited it with passion
and expression.

By the second stanza I had them.

He'd a French cocked-hat on his forehead, a bunch of
lace at his chin,
A coat of the claret velvet, and breeches of brown doe-
skin;
They fitted with never a wrinkle; his boots were up
to the thigh!
And he rode with a jewelled twinkle,
His rapier hilt a-twinkle, under the jeweled sky.

I walked around the campfires as I spun the tragic and beautiful story of *The Highwayman,* working my audience. They
smiled their pleasure as Bess (the landlord's daughter) plaited
"a dark red love-knot into her long black hair." I gravitated to
ClanFintan as I told of how Bess's Highwayman kissed the
waves of her hair and swore to return to her by the moonlight, "though hell should bar the way."

Then I stiffened my spine and threw up my chin—and I

became Bess as the Redcoats gagged her and bound her to her bed, attempting to use her as the means to trap her beloved. I let my eyes fill with tears as Bess gallantly ran a sword through her breast and screamed a warning (which I substituted for the musket shot—I didn't think Noyes would mind, him being a dead Englishman, stiff upper lip and all) so that her Highwayman wasn't captured.

Then the centaurs' eyes widened when the Highwayman found out it was his love who was killed warning him.

Back, he spurred like a madman, shrieking a curse to the sky,
with the white road smoking behind him and his rapier brandished high!
Blood-red were the spurs in the golden noon; wine-red was his velvet coat,
when they cut him down on the highway,
down like a dog on the highway,
and he lay in his blood on the highway,
with a bunch of lace at his throat.

I began the last stanza standing in the shadows between the two fires, hands tracing the patterns of the words like a magician performing illusions in the shade-filled air of the night.

Still of a winter's night, they say, when the wind is in the trees,
When the moon is a ghostly galleon tossed upon the cloudy seas,
When the road is a ribbon of moonlight over the purple moor,
A Highwayman comes riding—

Riding—riding—
A Highwayman comes riding, up to the old inn-door.

I ended by clasping my hands before me and looking over my shoulder off into the distance—like I was sure the friggin Highwayman's ghost was riding up behind us. The guys were quiet for a second, then (thank God) they broke into riotous applause, all talking at once about the bad-assed Redcoats and wondering where they could find a Bess of their own.

I made my way back to ClanFintan, amidst the congrats of the troops, and reperched on my log.

"I liked your story." ClanFintan handed me the wineskin and I took a grateful swig.

"Thanks. It's one of my favorites."

"I have never heard it before." His voice sounded different—more contemplative than curious.

"Oh, well, I'm not surprised. I made it up." I had my fingers crossed behind my back. I truly didn't mean to plagiarize, and I sent up a silent apology to the dead Mr. Noyes.

"Who are the Redcoats?"

"The bad guys. It's a clothing metaphor for evil." He didn't look convinced, so I switched on and went into teacher mode. "Red is for blood. Blood has a negative connotation. There-fore, a red coat would be a figurative allusion for an evil person or peoples. As would a sun rising to a red sky in the morning be a portent of disaster to come. Or a red look would be a negative or bad look."

"And King George is who?"

At least he uses correct grammar.

"A made-up guy." My fingers were recrossing themselves.

"And a highwayman is…" He paused, waiting for me to fill in the correct answer.

"A thief who uses a road that winds its way like a ribbon

up a mountain. Hence the 'high' part of the word." I tried to meet his eyes, but didn't do a great job selling my fibs. I'm really not a very good liar. A good exaggerator, yes—a good liar, no.

"Hrumph."

I translated that as centaur for "You're full of crap." But I acted as if I didn't speak the lingo.

"Gosh, it's been a long day." Big yawn and stretch. "I think I'd better turn in."

For a moment he didn't react, he just looked at me oddly. Like he was trying to put the pieces of a puzzle together. And suddenly I remembered how adamant Alanna had been about me not letting anyone know I wasn't me. However confusing that might sound.

She had seemed kind of stressed and neurotic (even more than what was the norm for Suzanna), but her distress had been real. And let's face it, she knew a lot more about what was going on in this world than I did. I had to assume she had good reasons to be paranoid. Yet she had told me that I could trust ClanFintan. At the very least I better keep my mouth shut about my origin until I had a chance to question Alanna.

So I did my best to blink innocently up at my too-curious, handsome, petable husband. Then I glanced behind us at the entrance to the barn. "Hey, could you please go in there first and make sure there's nothing creeping or crawling around before I make up a pallet?"

His distracted look of concentration changed into a smile. "Of course." He found Dougal, who had migrated over to the other fire, probably to give us some privacy. "Dougal, Lady Rhiannon needs two blankets."

Dougal snapped to like a good boy.

"Come." He stood, holding out a hand to help me up. "I will not let anything creep or crawl on you."

I took his hand and we went into the shadowy interior of the barn. It wasn't very big, and it was packed with hay bales. They were bound together in clumps with twine, which was stacked on top of one another. ClanFintan busied himself tossing around some clumps and untying others. By the time Dougal handed him a couple of blankets, he had made a nice little nest near the front of the barn. He lay one of the blankets on top of the nest and motioned for me to join him.

"There is nothing in here that can harm you."

"Thanks. I don't like things that slither or dart." I sat in the middle of the nest and began pulling off my boots. He bent down and took over for me.

I really liked that about him.

The barn was dark and cozy and smelled like a newly cut field.

"Where are you guys sleeping?"

"We will take turns at watch. Between our turns at watch we will rest by the fires."

"I'm the only one who will be sleeping in here?"

"Yes." He cocked his head and I could see the white gleam of his teeth.

"So it wouldn't be indecent of me if I slipped out of my pants?" I hate sleeping in pants.

"No, I believe that would be fine." His voice had turned into liquid velvet again.

I took off my pants, folding them neatly and bending (using my best Marilyn Monroe imitation) at the waist to set them on a convenient clump of hay. I knew his eyes were on me, and I liked it. Curling up on my blanket-covered hay nest, I lay back and smiled up at him.

He covered me with the other blanket.

"Good night. Sleep well, Rhiannon." He didn't turn to leave.

"When is your turn to watch?" What the hell, he was my husband.

"Not until well after moonrise."

"Then would you stay with me until I fall asleep?"

"If you like."

"I like."

I sat up and scooted over, making room for his considerable bulk. He stepped into the nest and reclined. It was like he was sitting behind me—the human part of his torso was tall, but not so large that it was awkward. I gave him a chance to get situated, and then I leaned back so that the top part of my body rested comfortably against his chest and in his arms. I shifted position so that I was facing him, still resting in his arms.

My hair was acting crazy, as usual. Drying by the fire had made it curl like Medusa's. He brushed some of it back out of my face.

"Sorry. It gets in the way a lot. I should cut it short." I blew a stray strand out of my mouth.

He blinked at me in surprise. "Women do not cut their hair."

Oops. "It might be easier if we did." Crap. Wonder if he'd noticed that my hair was shorter than Rhiannon's? Hastily I added, "When Alanna trimmed it the other day I should have told her to take a little more off."

"Short hair might be easier, but less attractive." He sounded like a typical guy. They love long hair. And, quite frankly, I wouldn't have it any other way.

"You may have a point."

"Yes." His stray hand caressed my hair, getting tangled in the mass of it. He lifted his hand, still enclosed in my hair, leaned down and buried his face in the middle of it. His movement sandwiched me against his chest and I felt, more than heard, his breathy moan.

He lifted his face out of my hair and our eyes met. Our faces were very close to one another.

"So, you like my hair?" His eyes traveled to my mouth as I whispered the question.

"I am finding that I like many things about you."

I smiled softly at him. "You sound surprised."

His gaze shifted back to my eyes. "I am."

"Don't be. What you see is really who I am." Before he could get me backed into a conversation Alanna would not approve of, I reached up and pulled his mouth down to mine.

I wondered if I would ever get used to the feel of him. He was like liquid heat and as he explored my mouth, my mind wandered to other places on my body I'd like him to explore. I felt goose bumps rise all the way down my spine and I moaned against his lips.

And he pulled away from me. Just a little, but I felt the absence of his warmth like a cold wind.

"Why did you stop?" I sounded hungry.

"You need to sleep." He sighed and tapped my nose with one of his fingertips. "And I need to stop this before I forget that I cannot allow myself to shape-shift."

His finger had moved from my nose and was now tracing the line of my lips. That was giving me goose bumps, too.

"Oh yeah." I caught his finger between my teeth and bit down, gently. I was gratified to feel the sharp intake of his breath. I let his finger go with a kiss. "That's a bummer."

"What is a bummer?"

"A bummer is you not being able to allow yourself to shape-shift tonight."

"A bummer is a bad thing."

"Very bad." We smiled at each other like teenagers.

I curled my body around him and snuggled against his warmth.

"Try to sleep," he whispered into my hair.

"I can think of other things I'd rather be doing."

"Relax and think about sleep." His voice sounded strained—which made me smile against his chest.

One of his hands began rubbing the tight muscles of my back. I sighed with pleasure.

"That feels really good."

He grunted a response that sounded like a muffled order to be quiet. His kneading hand worked the muscles of my back and began moving its way down to my very sore and very bare buttocks.

"Uhhhh, that's sore."

"I know. Be still."

Now he sounded like my grandma.

But I hushed. The combination of my exhaustion and his warm, insistent massage was better than a Tylenol PM. I felt the stress drain out of my muscles. Sleep came suddenly, carrying me away on a tide of relaxation.

At first my dreams were disjointed snippets—scenes of being in a hot tub with the Lone Ranger and his horse, Silver. Which is odd enough, because I've never dreamed of the Lone Ranger before (if I'm going to dream of a masked guy, it's usually Batman—his good/bad boy stuff really does it for me), but add to that oddity the fact that my dream persona was coming on to Silver, and kept trying to tell the Lone Ranger to take a hike, and you *really* have a weird dream. Even for me.

Anyway, that didn't last long. Unlike Mr. Ed, Silver couldn't talk, so I lost interest. My dream faded out from the hot-tub fiasco and I found myself plunked down in the middle of a large Saks Fifth Avenue store with a big wad of money in my fist and several salesladies salivating to help me. I was just making my way toward the blush-colored cashmere sweater set (price marked $529.00—it was on sale), when my body was suddenly sucked through the ceiling of…

…Oh, great. The barn.

I was floating above the two campfires and the sleepy centaurs. The moon had risen and was a sliver of light against the star-filled sky. This time I steeled myself against the feeling of vertigo as, against my will, my body lifted higher and began floating toward the northeast.

I looked off to my left and I could see the glow from the smoldering castle. I closed my eyes and pleaded with who or whatever was in control to please not make me go there. Instantly I was filled with a sense of reassurance and comfort. I relaxed a little and opened my eyes.

Sure enough, I wasn't traveling toward the castle. Instead, I was heading in the direction of the distant mountains. I tried to will myself to the east so that I could check on Epi and maybe even float over the temple and snoop around and see what was going on there, but as I had discovered before, I had no real control over this type of dream experience.

But I told myself this time was different. Before, I didn't realize that what I was seeing was reality and not a dream. This time I knew better.

My floating body traveled over the dark settlements. I peered down, trying to make sure that there were no people left who had disregarded the evacuation warnings, but I had little time to look for signs of life because as I reached the edge of the forest, my speed increased so that the trees below me became a dark blur. My body hurled ahead as if it had been shot from a sling.

Then I slowed and stopped before a structure perched at the base of a rugged mountain pass. The castle was large, almost as large as my father's, but as I became accustomed to the darkness of my surroundings I realized it was not at all like MacCallan

Castle. Where MacCallan Castle had been graceful and picturesque, this building was stark and imposing.

And then I felt it. If I had been standing, I would have
doubled over at the waist. It was the same feeling I had had
the night I witnessed MacCallan's destruction. From the castle
before me evil emanated, thick and cloying like honey dripping
from a comb. The echoes of that night's horror reverberated
from the walls beneath me—not in the form of sound, but of
feeling. I blinked as I tried to focus on the castle and see it ob-
jectively—but the shadows of MacCallan stayed with me;
death colored my perception. I could not shake the ghosts of
those men from my soul.

The castle looked as if it had been carved from the mountains. It was a perfect square with thick walls and barred doors.
The walls themselves were built of a rough gray stone, which
gave its exterior the appearance of age, like gnarled wood that
had withstood many storms. As I studied the castle the setting
of one of Edgar Allan Poe's more obscure short stores, "Ligea,"
flashed into my mind. The main action takes place in an
ancient monastery, walled by thick, old stone. Within the walls
Poe's character subsequently watches his second wife killed by
the specter of his first—who then revives and consumes the
second wife as the narrator plunges into madness. Somehow
the comparison felt appropriate.

My hovering body moved forward until I hung directly over
the middle of the building. The castle was not asleep. I could see
many open fires burning in the large, square courtyard. Although
my dream body could not feel temperature, I realized it must be
cold here because the shapes that tended the fires were covered
with heavy blankets and capes with cowls. I shuddered, and for
a moment I was afraid I had mistaken blankets and capes for wings
as I had once before. But one of the figures shrugged off a
blanket as it added another log to a fire, and I saw that it was def-

initely human. A human female. Of its own accord my body moved closer. All of the figures were women, but they moved methodically and didn't speak to one another, like they were automatons.

"The women from MacCallan Castle."

I spoke aloud and saw one head turn in my direction. She was young, probably only thirteen or fourteen. Her cheekbones were high and promised a striking profile to come, but now they were still sweetly rounded with cherubic youth. Her eyes were large and thickly lashed—they swept like butterfly wings as she tried to blink away the vestiges of a numbness in which the other women looked to be deeply entwined. She stared in my direction, straining to see something that had no real substance. Her hair was a mass of curls that caught the light of the fire and gleamed like faceted stones.

I felt a surge of sadness at the sight of this lovely girl. Something terrible was happening. I knew it with a surety that was fueled by more than the clinging horror of what I had witnessed the last time the dream magic had overtaken me. I didn't understand it yet, but I knew what I was spiritually eavesdropping upon went beyond kidnapped slaves or abused concubines.

And then a horrible shriek split the night and the girl who had been straining to bring herself to see and feel retreated to the rest of the cowering females. Her eyes were once more glazed and empty. The women milled together like sheep whose shepherd had betrayed them to the wolves. They plucked nervously at their clothes and fretfully held their wraps tightly around their trembling bodies. Their attention was focused in one direction. They were staring at a closed entrance. The door was large enough to suggest it might lead to a main hall or chamber.

The shriek repeated. A couple of the women started to

move forward toward the door, but several of the others fretfully called them back.

Again the shriek sounded—almost inhuman in its raw pain. I couldn't stand it. With everything inside of me I wished I knew what was happening—and I wished I knew how to stop it.

As if answering my plea, my body flashed forward and was sucked through the ominous door like a gerbil through a vacuum cleaner. I was spit out into the air, hovering near the ceiling of an immense room. My first impression was that the room reminded me, in a vague, shadowy way, of the dining hall at Epona's temple. Fireplaces, big enough for several people to stand in, were blazing in each corner of the room. Flaming tapers were lit. But none of this dispelled the gloom of the chamber. Crude tables like ancient picnic benches had been pushed near the walls of the room, and in the flickering light I could see people seated all along the benches. Many of them had their heads lying on their arms and appeared to be asleep. None of them were talking.

Then another shriek, followed by a panting moan, drew my attention to the middle of the room. A group of people clustered around a single picnic bench. My body drifted toward the group and as I got closer I began to feel inundated by waves of evil followed by what I could best describe as a misting of despair. As on the night of the attack on MacCallan Castle, my premonition was almost palpable. I didn't want to look—I didn't want to see what was on that table, but my eyes refused to close.

Everyone in the group of people surrounding the bench had something in common other than their concentration on the table. They all had wings. Wings that rustled and stirred even though their bodies remained very still. I took a deep breath and braced myself as my spirit floated into position over the table.

I had found the source of the shrieking. It was a woman—she was naked but it was impossible to tell how young or old she was. She was lying on top of a table that glistened red with her blood. Her arms had been stretched over her head and tied down. Her legs were spread and her knees were up and bent. Her feet had been pulled back to her body and tied down, too. She looked like she was being prepared for some kind of obscene Pap test. Her distended belly rippled and writhed with a life of its own and she shrieked again—her neck muscles straining and her body quivering.

The watching creatures didn't touch her or move to comfort or help her. They stood silently watching. Their restless wings the only outward sign of their tension.

Then the laboring woman's screaming began anew with the raw terror of the doomed. As I watched, her pubis bulged outward—stretching…stretching…I had never imagined the human body could expand that much. Suddenly her groin exploded in a shower of blood that rained red droplets on the quivering wings of the waiting audience. Out of the gaping hole in the woman's twitching body protruded a cylinder-shaped thing that seemed to be wrapped in thick wrinkled skin dyed the brilliant scarlet of new blood. My mind rebelled with shock and horror at the scene playing out below me, but my eyes refused to obey my command to close, just as my body refused to take me away. In the cavity of the woman's ruined body the thing quivered. Something glinted amidst the hideous tube of flesh. Unwillingly, my eyes were drawn to that glinting; it sparkled wetly like light glistening off the sharpened blade of a freshly used knife.

My body floated down until I was only a few feet above the heads of the creatures.

Time seemed to slow. The creatures under me were frozen, as if an invisible hand had pressed a lifelike pause button. As I got closer, my eyes focused more clearly on the lump of deformed flesh still trapped in the woman's body, and I realized that I was looking at a newborn creature. What I had mistaken for wrinkled flesh was really a pair of immature wings, which totally encased the embryonic body within—much like a cocoon would encase a caterpillar. The light of the tapers flickered off two appendages at the topmost point of the joined wings. They looked like talons and they were shiny with amniotic fluid and blood.

"Oh, my God!"

My exclamation ended the freeze-frame. A head snapped up in my direction and the creature's eyes searched the air above the table.

"Take it to the incubating cavern!" His voice had a rough, breathy quality. His words sounded as if they had to fight to escape his throat.

A female winged creature rushed forward and plunged her hands into the open wound, carefully extracting the cocooned fetus. Before I could glimpse any more of it, the adult's wings folded forward, completely covering the newborn. She quickly exited the room, followed by almost half of the other creatures who had observed the obscene spectacle. I watched them scurry away and my gaze was drawn to the benches that lined the walls. The figures sitting on the benches cowered back as the entourage rushed past them to the exit—I gasped with renewed horror, realizing that those people were women, human women, all in varying stages of pregnancy.

A hissing sound near the table caused my attention to be pulled away from them.

The male who had spoken was still looking up, and I felt my spirit body tremble. I tried to remain very still.

"Nuada, what is it?" one of the creatures asked tentatively.

"I do not know." His rough voice spat the answer. "I can feel something here. I have felt this presence before, at Mac-Callan Castle just as we were defeating that lone warrior." His wings stirred aggressively as his hot gaze raked the air around me. "I can almost see it…"

In one fluid stride he leaped up on the table, legs straddling the bloody body of the dead woman. He was now directly under me.

"Perhaps I can touch it." He began to reach up toward me with one long arm, taloned fingers extended.

I felt a scream building in my chest and—

11

"*Aaaahhhhh!*" The scream shot from my mouth with the force of an exploded land mine. I panicked in the darkness even though my frayed senses whispered to me that it smelled like springtime and horse, not blood and horror. But my mind was numb with terror and I struggled violently, kicking and biting against the bonds that had me trapped.

"Rhiannon! Stop, you are safe!" ClanFintan's voice broke through the ice of my fear. I realized that I was back in the barn and I quit struggling, but adrenaline still coursed through my body. I was shaking uncontrollably.

"Oh, God. It was horrible." His arms tightened around me.

"It was the Magic Sleep?"

I nodded my yes against his chest.

"The creatures again?"

"ClanFintan, I found the women." He loosened his arms and I pulled back to look into his eyes. "They are in the castle by the mountain pass."

"Guardian Castle," he prompted.

"Yes, it has to be."

"Have you never been there?"

"No, of course not." I didn't take time to wonder if

Rhiannon had been. "But it's large and square and situated at the base of a narrow pass."

"That is Guardian Castle."

"That's where they are. They have the women, and, oh, God, they must be mating with them—" Here I had to stop and cover my face with trembling hands.

In one smooth motion ClanFintan stood and scooped me, still wrapped in the blanket, into his arms. He strode out into the comforting light of the campfires and deposited me gently back on my log.

"Throw me that wineskin," he ordered a surprised, sleepy-looking Dougal, who tossed him the wine and blinked at me with worried eyes. "Drink." He held the skin to my lips and I gratefully swallowed several gulps of the red liquid.

"Thank you." I wiped my mouth and tried to control my trembling.

"Now tell me." His voice was strong and reassuring. He reclined next to me and took my hand in his, squeezing gently. The other centaurs were all awake and listening. Their presence fortified me—I was safe with them.

I took a deep breath. "The women were there. At first I only noticed that they acted like zombies or like they were in shock. Then I heard the screaming and I followed the sound into a large room. A pregnant woman was tied to the top of a table. She was in labor. She was surrounded by a group of the creatures. While I watched, a…a…thing, a newborn creature, clawed its way out of her body. It was one of them." My voice sounded raw to my own ears. I tightened my grip on ClanFintan's warm hand. "And there were more pregnant women in the room. Many more. I saw them just sitting there, like their souls were already gone. Then one of the creatures sensed me and tried to grab me and I screamed and woke up back here." I ended in a rush of breath, lifting the wineskin once more to my lips.

"One of them sensed you?" ClanFintan's voice shot out the question.

"Yes, he said he could almost see me. He mentioned the night my father was killed. He said he had sensed me then, too."

ClanFintan stood abruptly and began to pace back and forth in front of the fire.

"I did not think they could break through Epona's protection, too."

"Too—what do you mean by 'too'?"

I watched him look pointedly at the listening centaurs. Then he turned slowly to face me. His face looked hard and remote, like it had the first time I met him. A shiver of foreboding fingered its way down my spine and I remembered his words outside MacCallan Castle: *"They are through hiding."* Like he had known more about them than he had let on.

"ClanFintan, what is it?"

"Centaurs have known the Fomorian evil was loose upon Partholon for some time now."

"You knew? But—"

Dougal stepped forward, his voice full of familiar concern. "My Lady, some of us knew and believed. Others would not believe the signs."

I looked from Dougal to ClanFintan.

"What signs? What are you talking about?" My voice had an angry edge to it.

ClanFintan answered my anger with calm detachment. "You know that I have recently, just before we were betrothed, become head of the Fintan Herd. As you also know, my father was Herdsmaster before me." I nodded like I knew what the hell he was talking about. He continued. "Almost one year ago my father began to behave oddly. At first there were only small changes. He developed new habits. For instance, he woke and slept at strange times. He changed some of his habits, just small things, which were only apparent to his family and close advisers. Then his trouble sleeping became more pronounced. He seemed uncharacteristically quiet, almost as if he was constantly preoccupied or deep in thought. Slowly, his problems became more obvious. Time progressed and he became more and more withdrawn. It was as if he was living in a dark world of his own making, where evil lurked behind every tree. Where old friends became objects of suspicion." ClanFintan paused; the thought of his father's degeneration was obviously painful, but he steadied himself and continued. "As you probably know, the Fintan Herd chooses their Herdsmaster as we choose our Shamans, not by blood but by a consensus and a spiritual calling. There is no dishonor to a centaur when, following a long term of rule, he steps aside to live out his remaining years as an honored adviser, allowing his younger and more capable replacement to assume his position. But if a centaur is forcibly removed because of..." ClanFintan's eyes were haunted and he could not make himself finish the sentence. "There can be no greater dishonor."

The centaur's face hardened back into his mask of detachment. "The Herd was losing faith in their leader and he knew it, but it seemed he had lost the ability to control what was engulfing him. The situation became intolerable. It was only because of the great love and respect he had commanded for so many years that none moved against him. Then, the ghost of his former self, he called a Council of Warriors, which brought the heads of all the families together. He addressed them with only a shadow of his old dignity. He told of dreams and visions, which had followed him from his bed until they had absorbed him into their evil. Horrible twisted visions of blood and death. They centered around Guardian Castle, then reached out to engulf Partholon and the Centaur Plains, sucking us all into their darkness." The centaur's voice faded, his memories of that painful council meeting taking him far away.

"ClanFintan," I spoke his name gently, empathizing with his grief over a fallen father.

His face softened for a moment, then he squared his shoulders and finished his story. "The rest tells itself easily. Half of the Council thought him mad and called for him to step down as Herdsmaster. The other half believed him and demanded action be taken to find the source of the evil. The vote was split exactly in half. They were deadlocked until they decided upon a compromise." His full lips twisted in a sardonic smile. "They appointed me as Herdsmaster, replacing him. They were all in agreement on one thing—a Herdsmaster who was also High Shaman should be able to discover the truth."

He stopped there, but intuition whispered to me that there was more I needed to know.

"So with all of this going on why were you so set on hand-fasting with me?"

"My father spoke to me in private after the Council appointed me in his stead. He was difficult to understand, but he kept insisting that I had to have Epona's help to fight the evil. I had to be allied with Epona's Beloved, following the ancient tradition of a centaur High Shaman being mated with Epona's Chosen." ClanFintan's gaze never left mine. "Even though you had made it obvious that you had broken with tradition. He told me to go to your father and explain everything, that if I did the MacCallan would give his permission to wed you, even if you remained firm in your desire not to be bound to me, and that, out of your love and respect for your father, you would consent to our mating. You knew, of course, that they were comrades. My father had great respect for your father. I told him I would do as he wished, and then he spoke a single word—Fomorians. When that word left his lips it was as if he had been rendered speechless. The next morning he was found dead."

"I'm sorry, ClanFintan. Your father was a great centaur." Even though I hadn't known him, I was sure it was true.

"Thank you." His face softened for a moment. "Now we are both fatherless."

"So that's why you married me." His sadness touched me, but I couldn't help the feeling of loss his words had evoked. I knew it was ridiculous, but I felt betrayed. "Why didn't you tell me what was going on?"

His look darkened. "If you will remember our first betrothal meeting, you can answer that question for yourself. You gave me no opportunity to explain my reasons to you. You refused my suit, insulted me and left."

I wanted to scream that it hadn't been me, but I didn't want to try to explain the whole mirror-dimension thing to him right now. Especially not in front of all of those frowning, sorrowful-looking centaurs. My common sense told me that I didn't have any right to be angry and hurt. Rhiannon had been a raving bitch to ClanFintan. He had been right not to trust me/her. But my heart said something else. It felt bruised.

So I didn't know what to say. We just looked at each other like two children who had had a fight and didn't know how to make up.

I felt exhausted and sickened by what I had witnessed. I just wanted to sleep—and I meant really sleep. I sent a silent plea to Epona to please not send me on any more of those dream things tonight.

"I need to get some sleep."

I stood up, keeping the blanket wrapped around my waist. I didn't look at the centaurs, but I could hear them salute me formally as I left and their sweet "Good night, my Lady" followed me into the barn like a soft breeze. I snuggled back into my hay nest, squelching thoughts of how comfortable (and happy) I had been only a little earlier that night. I closed my eyes.

I had already known he had married me out of some sense of duty. Why was I so upset to hear him say it? And, I reminded myself, he hadn't married me anyway. He had married Rhiannon, Goddess Incarnate and Beloved of Epona. I was just Shannon Parker, underpaid English teacher from Broken Arrow, Oklahoma. I didn't belong here and I didn't belong with him.

"Rhiannon?"

I hadn't heard him approach and his voice made me jump. My eyes flashed open.

"I did not mean to startle you." He sounded concerned. Probably worried about causing me to have a heart attack before I could fulfill my duty to him. And I didn't mean that in the Biblical sense. I meant it in some obscure Epona sense. Sigh.

I didn't say anything. I just looked at him and shrugged.

"You left before I could finish."

I sighed again. "What else is there to say?"

"I wanted you to know that I do not think of you as I did before our handfast. I do not understand it, but you are different now." His eyes were soft as they reflected the distant firelight. "There is one bit of good that this evil has caused. It has caused me to join with you. Good night, my Lady. I will be close by if you have need of me."

Before I could answer, he turned and left the barn. I tried not to think too much about the rush of pleasure his words had given me. I thought instead that it would take me hours to fall asleep, but my eyes couldn't have been closed more than a few minutes when I blissfully entered my DreamLand. This time I (thankfully) passed the rest of the night dreaming that I was spending a wonderful afternoon visiting a Godiva chocolate factory that doubled as a vineyard. Superman and Pierce were bickering over who was going to rub my feet and who was going to…

Well, you get the idea. (This time Superman won—and may I just share that he's called super for more than just his ability to fly.)

12

The tantalizing aroma of frying fish woke me. I yawned and stretched, rubbing sleep out of my eyes. Yanking on my pants, I shook out the blankets, slung my boots over my arm and made my way blearily out to find the source of the yummy smell.

"Good morning, my Lady." ClanFintan looked bright eyed and bushy tailed (literally).

"Mornin'," I muttered as I handed the shyly smiling Dougal my blanket mess and moved zombie-like to the edge of the nearest campfire. I'm not a morning person. Actually, I'm slightly suspicious of morning people. It's exhausting to be perky before 9:00 a.m. There's only a certain amount of perky that one individual can have over the course of one day. Morning people use up their perky too early and end up being just plain grumpy.

I didn't see any fish frying. But I still smelled cooking food.

Trying to run my fingers through my out-of-control hair while I picked out pieces of hay, I raised my brows at Clan-Fintan. "Don't I smell breakfast?"

"Yes, fish rolls." He pointed to big rolled-up leaves that were stuck amidst the hot coals of the only campfire still smoldering.

Well, that sure cleared everything up.

He's probably a morning person/horse/whatever.

Sigh. I pulled on my boots and headed toward the stream. Without looking over my shoulder, I said, "No, I don't need any damn help."

After finishing my morning necessaries, which included washing my face and rinsing my mouth out with cold water, and brushing vigorously with my finger (man, I sure missed my mint-flavored waxed dental floss—who'd have ever figured?), I felt semi-alive and awake.

The horsies were chomping contentedly on the fish that had been inside the rolled-up leaves. They were using the leaves as plates and picking flaky fish from the bone. I sat on my log seat next to where ClanFintan was reclining, and Connor handed me my own leaf plate of fish. It was wonderful. The fish's head had been cut off (thank God—I don't like it when my food looks at me) and its body had been stuffed with garlic.

"This is really great."

"Thank you, my Lady." Dougal and Connor spoke together.

"Are the rest of the guys hunting or something?"

"No. I sent them ahead to inform the warriors of your latest dream vision. They can travel more quickly than I can while I carry you." He smiled at me, so I guessed my slowing him down didn't piss him off. "They will notify the others who stayed with Epona and we will meet with all of them at your temple."

"Those creatures have to be stopped." Mentioning my dream vision had sobered me, and I almost choked on the fish.

"Our combined forces will stop them." His voice mirrored the conviction in mine.

We finished our breakfast in silence. The three of them broke camp quickly, burying the fire coals and reloading their packs like good little Boy Scouts. ClanFintan saddled himself and offered me a hand up. I tried not to feel pleased that he obviously let his hand linger on my arm.

"Hang on. We will be traveling hard today."

I rested my hands on his broad shoulders as he stepped out at a brisk gallop. Again I was grateful he had such a smooth gait. It would be embarrassing to have to tell my husband his gallop rattled my teeth.

We found the road that cut down to the southeast, and the centaurs stepped up the pace considerably. This time prosperous families didn't greet us as we traveled. The road was deserted. It gave the day an eerie, *Twilight Zone* feel—or, maybe more appropriately, an *Omega Man* aura. Like the norm had been turned inside out. As if to mirror the creepy feeling, the day was cloudy and dreary. The sky hung low and gray, and a misty fog crept over the gullies on either side of us and drifted in patches across the road.

The centaurs were working harder today; ClanFintan's torso glistened with sweat, although his breathing stayed deep and unlabored. His stamina amazed me, and my thoughts dwelled on that interesting fact without any type of sexual connotation (well, almost without any). I just tried to sit quietly and hang on—and not be a nuisance. I kept my potty stops to a minimum and chewed jerky in the saddle.

As the day progressed a light drizzle began and the fog turned thicker and more insistent. The world narrowed to a few yards around us; it gave the illusion that we were endlessly galloping in the same place and never getting anywhere. Time lost meaning. I began to fantasize that in this altered dimension the world could just stop and I would be caught forever in this moment—eternally travelling but never getting anywhere. I felt myself totter to one side and I jerked upright, hoping ClanFintan didn't notice.

At least my movement had allowed time to begin unraveling again.

"Slide your arms around me and lay your head down. I will

not let you fall." His voice didn't even sound strained as he spoke over his shoulder at me. He would be damn good in an aerobics class. But I couldn't imagine him in the workout tights.

Stifling a giggle, I realized I was getting goofy with exhaustion, which made me feel bad because, after all, he was doing all the work.

"Go ahead. Try to rest. You could not have had enough sleep last night." His voice was deep and hypnotic. I slid forward until I was very close to his back and gratefully wrapped my arms around him, somewhere midway on his chest, and lay my head against the strong valley between his shoulder blades. Maybe if I was close enough to him, he would help dispel the bizarre notions that kept trying to creep up on me. I sighed and closed my eyes, breathing deeply and loving the smell and the feel of him. His leather vest was soft next to my cheek. His warmth burned through the cool dampness of the rainy day, and I felt myself quickly lulled into a sleepy half-dream state by his movement, which was a little like how a train's *clack-clack* hypnotizes its overnight passengers.

I opened my eyes once some time later and it was fully dark. The centaurs were still traveling. I could feel ClanFintan's steady breathing had deepened, and as I shifted my weight and snuggled back into him, he squeezed my arm reassuringly.

"Rest."

That single word was like a drug, and I relaxed back into my strange half sleep.

When I next became fully conscious, it was because I could feel his gait changing from the never-ending gallop to a trot, and finally slowing to a walk. I pushed myself up and rubbed my face. It was still wet and cool, but the darkness was beginning to lighten to the gray of premorning. Teresa, an Irish-

American girlfriend from my last, and favorite, college writing class liked to call it "morning's gloaming."

I never really understood it until now.

"Where are we?" I blinked at the magic of the misty dawn and busied myself retying my wild hair back into some semblance of a braid. I noticed ClanFintan's had come loose, too, so I reached forward and began loosening it so I could replait it more neatly.

"We are only a short way from your temple." I was concerned to notice his words were punctuated by labored breathing. I could even hear Dougal and Connor breathing heavily as they walked beside us.

My hands stilled on his hair. I forgot about the pretty morning and shifted my gaze from Dougal to Connor. "Are you guys okay? Should we stop and rest?" Then I tried to peek around at ClanFintan, pulling his hair back to get a better look at his face, and asked, "Do you want me to walk for a while?"

The three centaurs let out horselike snorts. Dougal and Connor stepped a little closer to their Herdsmaster and gave him what I thought were concerned looks…until they spoke.

"Aye, Dougal, ClanFintan does look a bit rough." Connor threw a pointed glance at Dougal and I noticed their musical lilt was more pronounced as they struggled to catch their breath. I also noticed their apparent fatigue didn't do much to squelch their goofy grins.

"I must agree, Connor." They clucked under their breath sadly, looking at ClanFintan, who had been turning his head from side to side, watching their exchange.

"My Lord, if your Lady's weight has become too much for you I would like to volunteer to serve as your relief." Dougal's voice was the ultimate in gentlemanly politeness, but his smile was definitely smart-assed.

I frowned at him and started to open my mouth.

"And, my Lord, when Dougal grows weary from bearing such a slight, pleasant weight, I volunteer to take up his burden." He swept his arm forward in a flourish and bowed toward me as he executed a neat sidestep.

I frowned at him, too.

"Well! I just thought—" And they both exploded into laughter, interrupting my tirade. I glared at them. Damn silly horsies.

"Just save your breath for trying to keep up with me." Clan-Fintan sounded amused. "Impudent colts." He broke back into his road-eating gallop, leaving the chortling centaurs scrambling to catch up. I could feel his torso vibrating—it took a second for me to realize he was laughing.

I yanked on his thick braid as I retied the thong. He threw a smile over his shoulder at me. "Rhiannon, you say the strangest things."

"I was just trying to be nice." I grumped. "I don't want to weigh you down or anything."

He reached back and squeezed my calf, sending little chills up my leg.

"That you could never do."

"Don't be so sure. I may get old and fat. How would you feel about hauling me around if my butt was twice this size and it took both Dougal and Connor to lift me into the saddle?"

"Rhiannon—" his voice was rich with laughter "—you are far too vain to ever get fat."

I expelled air through my nose, imitating a centaur snort. Guess he might know me a little after all. Dougal and Connor caught up with us and I tried to frown at them, but their silly grins were too much and I smiled back at them.

"Disrespectful imps," I muttered into ClanFintan's shoulder. He must have heard me (and agreed) because his vibrating laugh rumbled through both of us.

I tried to relax and fade back into my semi-sleep state, but as the mist cleared so did my weariness. My mind didn't seem to be able to shut itself off. Images of batlike vampiric creatures haunted my thoughts. How in the hell could they be stopped? The futility and danger of the situation weighed on my mind. And suddenly I wondered why I should be so worried about it. This wasn't my damn world. Why wasn't I concentrating my energy on getting my sore butt home?

"Hold tight, my Lady. The trail gets steep here." ClanFintan's arms covered mine, which were laced loosely around the middle of his torso.

The strength and heat of his forearms melted into me, making me feel protected and cherished—a feeling that was totally alien to Shannon Parker's life.

And, damnit, that was it. It was this damn man/horse/what-the-hell-ever. And it was Alanna. And Dougal. And Connor. And my/her dad who had died before he was supposed to.

This screwed-up place was becoming home to me. I closed my eyes and buried my face into my husband's shoulder, and I realized that part of me was already attached to this world.

Damn Rhiannon and her meddling and scheming. Damnit, why couldn't I have married a nice lawyer and raised 2.5 maladjusted children in the suburbs and paid a fortune to a handsome shrink named something vaguely Italian who I could fantasize about, but never be literally unfaithful with?

Instead, I get this bizarre mirror world filled with a horse/guy who I have the serious hots for, creatures who are terrorizing civilization, my ass which is extremely sore, complete with saddle sores beginning on my inner thighs and deodorantless armpits that probably stink and no toilet paper.

As my students would succinctly say, *This sucks.*

13

The centaurs paused only for water over the next several hours. My burst of strength was gone and I had to fight to stay upright. Thankfully, I could see snatches of the setting sun reflecting off the river, which was pretty close to us on the right. That should mean the temple was near. Then ClanFintan raised his arm in some kind of salute to something off one side of the road.

"What's that?" My voice sounded scratchy.

"Another sentry." He sounded matter-of-fact.

"Oh, there, uh, have been more?"

"Yes, of course, for the past several hours we have been hailed periodically by those sent to keep watch."

"That's a good idea."

He made a snorting sound and I shut my mouth. If memory served me even a little bit correctly, I seemed to recall that Epona had been Goddess of the Roman Legions, as well as the Celts, and was hailed as a warrior's deity. I wondered if Rhiannon had been trained in the ways of warfare.

It might help her in my high school classroom. Maybe.

I felt ClanFintan's powerful muscles bunch as the road began a gradual climb and we turned sharply to the left. And there was the temple. ClanFintan pulled abruptly to a halt and he, Dougal and Connor paused, obviously trying to catch their labored breath. My eyes drank in the temple and grounds before me like a thirsty horse drinks in water. Now that I got a good look at it from the road and during the light of day, I realized just how amazing a structure it really was.

As I had noticed when Epi and I had snuck out, it was built on the crest of a gentle incline. Unlike MacCallan Castle the grounds around the temple for about the length of a football field were clear of trees or anything else that might serve to hide an enemy. The beautiful marble wall that encircled the temple looked creamy and even more impressive in the daylight. The river wrapped around the southeast side of the temple grounds, and the land surrounding the cleared area adjacent to it was covered with grapevines, which were heavily laden with dark fruit. Sprinkled amidst the fields were several attractive homes, reminiscent of Anne Hathaway's thatched-roof cottage in Stratford-Upon-Avon. Most of them had neat-looking barns with corrals beside them, although I didn't notice any animals. All very upper-middle-class peasant.

But there was one huge difference between the scenery before me now and the scenery that I had studied as I was riding away. People had been added—humans and centaurs. Lots of people were camped all around the temple walls. The tents they had pitched were blowing in the gentle breeze. They seemed to be efficiently going about their busy lives— herding animals and children, talking, cooking—it was like I had stumbled into a bustling medieval faire.

Then a shout was heard from very near us, and repeated and repeated again. All heads turned in our direction and the shout intensified to a series of cries as the people and centaurs raised their hands, waving and welcoming us home.

"Shall we forward?" ClanFintan glanced at his two comrades, and then all three looked to me.

It took a moment for me to realize they were waiting for my permission.

"Oh! Yeah, let's go."

ClanFintan broke into what can only be described as a perky canter, totally belying the fact that just moments before he and the boys had been struggling to catch their breath. I smiled. Men—they sure can be cute. Even though their butts looked like horses, they certainly acted one hundred percent like guys.

Belatedly I tried to retie my wild hair but decided I'd better go for the windblown look (like I had any choice). As we neared the throng of people who were rushing forward to greet us, I reminded myself firmly that I was used to (and was typically delighted by) being the center of attention. I mean, I admit that I've done ridiculous things during pep assemblies in front of hundreds of partially grown human beings. Goddess Incarnate should be a relatively unembarrassing part to play. So I did what I do in front of teenagers—I threw my shoulders back, held my head high and grinned at the masses like I'm cool (or insane—the children are never positive which).

"Epona!"

"Hail the Beloved of Epona!"

"Welcome home, Goddess Incarnate!"

"Epona's Beloved, bless us!"

I even managed to wave. Thank God I've watched a lot of PBS specials about The Royal Family.

As we passed within the temple wall, I noticed something else I couldn't have seen well enough to understand the night I left. The temple must be built on or around the site of a mineral springs. In the daylight I could now see eruptions of sparkling, steamy water amidst the moss and crags that I had thought before was just a huge, artificial fountain. My eyes widened at the imagination and the craftsmanship that had fashioned the beauty of a huge plunging horse out of natural rock. It was as if the fountain burst out of the side of the hill. I remembered (with relish) the wonderful bath Alanna had led me to, and I understood that the architects and builders of the temple must have somehow harnessed the mineral springs. Pretty smart of them—and they didn't even have TV, Japanese-made parts or the Internet to help them. Imagine that.

Speaking of Alanna—man, I was happy to see her. She stood in the shadow of the entrance, dressed in a very flatter-ing buttercup-yellow flowy thing, hands folded demurely before her. My impatience to get down must have telegraphed itself through my thighs (and I wondered briefly what other "telegraphs" he had picked up through my thighs), and Clan-Fintan reached around and helped me to exit his back. I nodded and smiled at my adoring crowd as I made my way quickly toward Alanna. I could feel that ClanFintan and the guys had turned and were facing out to the crowd, blocking them from adoring me so much that they cut off my exit. He was assuring the masses that I was fine, just tired, that I'd be back to bless them first thing in the morning…blah…blah….

Forgetting her unSuzanna-like reticence, I threw my arms around Alanna and hugged her hard. "I'm so glad to see you!"

"I am pleased to see that you are well, my Lady." Her voice was subservient, and I could feel the tension in her body.

I dropped my arms from around her and she bowed to me, then ushered me through the entrance. Instead of entering the lovely gardened courtyard in front of us (which was, inciden-tally, full of more adoring people), she turned abruptly to our left and opened a small, undecorated door. Inside stood two of the scantily clad guards I remembered so well.

Before following her, I paused and turned to face ClanFintan.

He smiled at me. "Rest and refresh yourself. I will have my warriors brief me on what has transpired since we have been gone, then I will join you later—" he paused, probably for effect "—in your chambers." His voice had deepened and become husky. I think I blushed. "If that is as you wish, my Lady?" Now I knew I was blushing.

Our eyes met and I was suddenly having trouble breathing. I forgot how tired I was. I forgot how mussed and just down-right stinky I was. All I could think about was his hot, slick chest and how his mouth felt against mine.

"My Lady?" Alanna's voice broke the spell.

"Oh, uh, coming," I told her, and blinked up at ClanFin-tan. "Yes, that's exactly as I wish." His sexy smile shot through me and I grinned back at him. Then I hurried after Alanna before I did something foolish like bite my husband in public.

The guard closed the secret door and I followed Alanna down a hall that looked vaguely familiar.

"Just around this corner, my Lady."

We turned the corner, and I spied the door to my chambers, flanked by two more yummy guards. I smiled at them as they saluted me, and in my best Mae West voice I said, "Thanks, boys" before they closed the heavy door behind me.

"Ohmygod! I can't wait to tell you everything!" I gushed and followed Alanna around as she rummaged through my wardrobe, pulling out gauzy this and scanty that.

"Yes, my Lady."

"Well, it was awful—" I took a breath "—and wonderful." I grinned at her and was momentarily disconcerted that she didn't return my grin. "Anyway, I found my/her dad—ugh—that was horrible. All those men dead. I've never seen anything like it. We burned them. I hope it's what Dad would have wanted."

"I'm sure his spirit understands, my Lady." For a second her voice was tinged with familiar tenderness as she paused to meet my gaze.

"Do you really think so?"

"Yes, my Lady." The moment was broken and she returned to rummaging through my wardrobe.

"Are you getting my clean things so I can take a bath?" My voice sounded almost as eager as I felt.

"Yes, my Lady. Please follow me to the bathing room." She turned and breezed to the door.

Bathing room! Complete with toilet paper! I'm not ashamed to admit that I was looking forward to savoring the experience. I hurried after her.

Entering the bathing room was like entering a little piece of heaven. It was as beautiful as I remembered—all golden and misty in the candlelight (I ignored the fact that the candleholders were skulls). Several barely clad nymphets jumped up and curtseyed, murmuring welcomes as I entered.

"Thank you. It's nice to be home." And I meant it. Their smiles were shy but warm. I singled out the taller of the nymphs, whose willowy beauty I suddenly realized reminded me of a kid named Staci, one of my all-time favorite students. My voice reflected the affection I had for her mirror image in my old world when I told her to, "Please tell the kitchen that ClanFintan will be eating the evening meal with me in my chamber. And tell them I am verrrry hungry."

"Of course, my Lady!" The Staci-nymph bounded out of the room.

"Would the rest of you please excuse us? I would like to be alone with Alanna." They curtseyed their way gracefully out the door.

"It will be so good to relax!" I watched as Alanna busied herself setting out the stuff for my bath. "Um, while you're busy I'm going to, well..." I nodded in the direction of the potties.

"Certainly, my Lady."

After an experience that I will describe only as satisfying, I returned and began stripping the filthy clothes off my body.

"Ugh. These things are just plain gross." I sat near the edge of the steaming pool and pulled off my crusty boots. "Hey, is there any bath oil over there that smells like the sand soap in the forest?" Alanna gave me a quizzical look. "You know, kind of like almonds and vanilla and, well, soap?"

"Yes, my Lady, I know." She turned and looked through the elaborate bottles that perched near the full-length mirror, stopping to smell several and discarding them, until she found one that fit my request. She brought the bottle over to the pool and poured it into the warm water. The soft scent of it hovered with the steam.

"That's it." I sniffed in appreciation, yanked off my pants and stepped gratefully out of the nasty thong. With a sigh of pure delight I lowered myself into the fragrant water. "Ahhh—this is beyond words."

"Yes, my Lady."

Somehow through the ecstasy of clean, warm water Alanna's behavior penetrated. I opened my eyes and watched her through the mist. She was busy rearranging brushes and makeup jars.

"Alanna."

She didn't pause, but answered in the cool voice of a stranger. "Yes, my Lady."

"Quit messing with that stuff and come over here and talk to me." I didn't mean for it to come out as an order, but she jerked stiffly around and moved to the side of the pool.

"What is it you wish me to say, my Lady?"

"I want to know why you're acting like I'm some stranger! Or worse yet, like I'm really Rhiannon!" My frustration made me sound grumpy.

"As you know, I am your servant, my Lady. I am only acting as befits my place in your household." Her eyes were downcast.

"Bullshit."

She glanced up at me, then quickly looked down again. I studied her face. She looked pale and tense. What the hell was wrong with her?

"I thought we got all that slave crap straight before I left."

"As you wish, my Lady."

"Stop this 'as you wish' and 'yes, my Lady' garbage! How many times do I have to explain to you that I can't see you as my slave? You're my friend."

Her eyes finally lifted to meet mine. I could see they were brimming with tears.

"Suzanna is your friend, not I."

"But you're a lot like Suzanna, and I can't help but want you to be my friend."

She drew a deep breath. "Would you have stolen out in the deep of night, going into danger and horror without telling your Suzanna you were leaving? Or asking for her aid and prayers?"

Yipes. Now I understood.

"No, I wouldn't have," I said quietly.

"So you see, my Lady, no matter what your words say, your actions show we are not really friends."

"Oh, Alanna, you are so right." I couldn't believe what a mess I'd made of this.

"It is better we remain slave and mistress only." Her voice was resigned.

"No! That's not what I meant." I cleared my throat, searching for the right words. "I meant you are absolutely right to be pissed off at me."

"Piss—" Now she really looked confused.

"Oops, I keep forgetting. Pissed off means mad. You have

every right to be mad at me. It was an idiotic thing for me to do."

"My Lady! I could not be mad—"

I interrupted, "Sure you could. You are. And you have reason to be." She started shaking her head, but I talked over her protestations. "You're right—I would have told Suz. I should have told you. I was wrong. Please forgive me and give me another chance at being your friend."

She looked at me as if I'd just grown another eye or something, but the tears were no longer threatening to spill from her eyes.

"I...I..." She seemed to be struggling within herself.

"I'm sorry I hurt your feelings and made you mistrust me."

"I forgive you." Her expression shifted as she spoke the words and a tentative smile raised the edges of her lips.

"Good! Next time I do something crazy I'll clue you in on it. Then we can both worry together."

"I would like that."

"Me, too." I sighed and relaxed back into the water, happy that we'd gotten that straightened out. "Could you hand me something to wash with?"

"Of course, my La—"

I had to interrupt her. "Alanna, I can't stand this 'my Lady' stuff. Can't you call me something else?"

She came back to the pool with another delicate bottle in her hand and a thick, cream-colored sponge. (I mean a *real* sponge. The kind they use at the ritzy spas.) She put the bottle on the ledge that ran the length of the pool and proceeded to crouch down, grab my arm and begin washing me.

"No offense, girlfriend, but I would really rather you just sat there and talked to me. And let me wash myself."

She looked vaguely disconcerted, but she handed me the sponge and my arm. "If that is what you wish, my Lady."

"I'd appreciate it." It's just too weird to be washed by your friend. "So—" I soaped myself up, loving the satinlike feel of the warm mineral water "—what else can you call me besides 'my Lady'?"

"I suppose I could call you Rhiannon." She didn't sound totally convinced.

"Rhiannon." I didn't like it. "I don't like it."

"It means queenly."

"That figures," I muttered as I scrubbed the crud off the bottom of my feet. "I wish you could call me Shannon, but I suppose that wouldn't be a good idea."

"No." She looked worried.

"I know! My friends don't call me Shannon very often, they shorten it to Sha. What if we shorten Rhiannon to something like Rhe or Rhea?" Jeesh, my feet were disgusting.

"Rhea?" She looked doubtful.

"Yep. I like it."

"Well, I will try."

14

"Alanna, can you find me something that will wash the yuck out of my hair?"

"Of course—" she paused, obviously struggling before she added "—Rhea." She looked through bottles until she found a tall golden one. "This is hair soap made from honey and almonds. Rhiannon's favorite—I thought you would probably like it, too."

"You're right, I do. It's strange how similar our tastes are, isn't it?"

Alanna gave a sudden, unladylike snort. "I think *strange* is not a strong enough word."

"Hang on, I'm going to dunk under and get this disgusting hair wet. Then I really would appreciate it if you could help me lather it up."

"I would be happy to help you, Rhea." This time the nickname came easier.

I held my nose and plunged under, shaking my head around so that the water soaked through my matted curls. Surfacing, I sputtered, wiping hair out of my eyes. Turning my back to Alanna, I sat near the ledge while she uncorked the bottle and poured the thick, soapy mixture all over my hair. Then we both attacked the dirty mess. We had to repeat the rinse-and-wash cycle three times before I felt really clean.

The bathing pool was remarkable. There was some sort of system that allowed dirty, soapy water to drain out one side, while fresh, hot water ran in from another side. And it was huge. The center was deep enough that if I stood, the soothing water covered me to just under my chin.

Finally clean, I lay back near the area where water bubbled in, soaking away the soreness in my muscles. Alanna sat near me, her legs playing in the water like she was a kid sitting on a riverbank.

"I am sorry you had to see the horror of what happened at MacCallan Castle," Alanna said sadly.

"I had to go. I didn't want to, but I needed to."

"Yes. But I am glad ClanFintan followed you."

"I don't know what I would've done without him." A sudden thought startled me. "Epi! I didn't even ask if she got home okay."

Alanna's brow wrinkled quizzically, then her expression cleared. "The Chosen—Rhiannon's mare. Yes, ClanFintan's centaurs escorted her home. She is resting contentedly in the stables."

"Her hoof's going to be all right?"

"She did not appear to favor it when last I saw her." She smiled at me. "The two of you have become friends?"

"She's wonderful." I know I sounded like a giddy school-girl. "I've always loved horses."

"Considering your new circumstances that is a lucky coincidence."

"No kidding."

We were both silent—contemplating deep thoughts of mirror dimensions and horse goddesses and sex with centaurs...

"I really like him."

Alanna blinked at me. Innocently.

"Who, my Lady?"

"Don't 'my Lady' me." I splashed water at her and she giggled. "You know who. Mr. Tall, Dark and Equine."

"So you are not upset at being mated with him?" Her eyes were sparkling.

"I can't seem to keep my hands off him." I think I had the good grace to blush, but it might just have been the heat of the water.

"Now you do sound like Rhiannon." Alanna's hands flew to her mouth and she tried to stifle another giggle.

"Now you sound like Suzanna." And we laughed together. "Oh, jeesh, that reminds me—he's going to meet me in my room and give me his—" pause, wink "—report. Please help me pick out something great to wear."

Alanna jumped up and grabbed a thick towel, in which I quickly wrapped myself. I sat at the vanity and we both started toweling my hair dry.

"And there is the problem of those horrid man-creatures." Both our hands stilled and our eyes met in the mirror. "Oh, Alanna, I had another of those dream things. The creatures have taken the women to Guardian Castle. They're mating with them." I turned and took her hands in mine. "I watched as a newborn creature burst from a woman's body." I shuddered at the memory. Alanna's eyes grew huge and her hands gripped mine tightly. "Tell me the centaurs are strong enough to kill those things. I know so little about this world. Do I have an army or something, too? Or are Rhiannon's guards just boy toys?"

"The centaurs are mighty warriors." Her voice was firm. "And Rhiannon chose her guards for their fighting ability as well as their…prowess and other, shall we say, endowments."

I squeezed her hands and turned back around. "At least she was a smart slut."

Alanna's grin answered me.

"Speaking of being smart…" I watched Alanna in the mirror as she started working a comb through my damp hair. "I feel like an idiot because I don't know my way around this world. Does Rhiannon have a map or something you could show me? I didn't even know Guardian Castle was Guardian Castle. ClanFintan must think I'm some kind of airheaded moron."

"Yes, there is a map of Partholon in your chambers." She cleared her throat and smiled sheepishly at my reflection. "You realize you will have to perform a blessing ceremony for the people on the morrow?"

"I forgot." Great, like I didn't have enough on my mind? "Can't you take my place or something?"

Alanna looked shocked. "No! You are not Rhiannon but you are still Epona's Beloved and our High Priestess."

I opened my mouth to interrupt.

"My Lady, you have been gifted with the Magic Sleep. That alone is proof of Epona's favor."

My mouth started to open again.

"And the mare loves and accepts you."

My mouth shut.

"You are Beloved of Epona and the people's spiritual leader." Her expression softened as she continued. "The people count on you, probably much like your students did in your old world. My Lady, I cannot believe you would let them down."

My mind wandered. I guessed I could come up with a brief morning blessing, heavy on Celtic sentiments. Yeats was one of my favorites—between him and Shakespeare (and whoever else I could cannibalize) I should be able to "borrow" enough material to get by (and perhaps not embarrass myself or my profession: teachers—the few, the proud, the broke). My mind scurried around rehearsing fragmented combinations of half-remembered poetry and partially recognized soliloquies…

"Tilt your head up, Rhea. Let me finish your eyes."

I blinked and did as Alanna ordered, vaguely surprised to find that while I'd been mentally rehearsing she'd been transforming me from the Wicked Witch of the West into Cinderella (at the ball—*before* midnight). She finished expertly highlighting my eyes, handed me a pot of bronze lip shine and held out two gauzy bits of silky nothing for my inspection.

"Do you have a preference?"

"Yes," I gulped. "I'd like to leave something to his imagination."

Her giggle bubbled. "You say the most unusual things!"

"I guess I like the green one with the gold threading." The other one was white with some kind of sparkly silver beading and I was certain that no matter how many times she wrapped it around me it would still be transparent. How's a girl to sit comfortably in that kind of outfit?

"The green matches your eyes." She held out a tiny scrap of silk. Experience had taught me it was a hankie masquerading as my panties. Experience had also taught me it didn't give much protection from the elements. But tonight the only element I'd need protection from would be ClanFintan, so…I quickly slipped on the thong and held my arms away from my sides while Alanna began wrapping and twisting the silk around me.

"That gold design is so pretty. What is it?" I craned my head around trying to recognize the glittering upside-down shapes.

Alanna had stuck the end of a brooch in her mouth and she answered me through pursed lips, "Skulls, of course."

"Of course." I should've known.

She pinned the silky garment at my right shoulder, then handed me a pair of sandals made of soft cream-colored leather. The shoes laced halfway up my calves and I was pleased to note that they had heels. Flats just can't be all that sexy.

Alanna was working her way around my body, tucking and pulling folds of silk into place. She studied me, nodding her head like she was pleased with herself, and turned back to the vanity to open the lids of intricately carved boxes. As she poked and prodded through the contents, I noticed sparkles and followed to peek over her shoulder.

The boxes were filled with jewelry. I felt my mouth go dry.

"Ohmygod, are all of those mine?"

"They are now." She sounded smug.

"I take it Rhiannon would have a litter of kittens if anyone touched her loot?"

Alanna's sudden laugh ended in a snort. "That is one way of putting it."

"Good. Let's dig through and load me up."

"Yes, let's," she mimicked.

As I have already mentioned, Rhiannon's taste was very similar to mine. That held true in the jewelry department (if not the panty department). The boxes before me were filled with gold. Shining, flat herringbone necklaces, twinkling diamond-cut ropes, intricate knots and twists of brooches and earrings. Precious and semiprecious jewels were sprinkled liberally amidst the golden mess—I noticed everything from earrings set with iridescent blue topaz to necklaces crusted with ancient teardrops of crystallized amber. And diamonds. Lots of diamonds. It was as if someone had emptied into the boxes several trays from Tiffany's estate collection.

I tried not to babble incoherently and to remember that I was dressing for my husband, not for a spot on a TV evangelism program.

Finally I decided to mix demure with Marilyn Monroe. I chose a long, thick diamond-cut rope necklace which nestled heavily between my breasts (which were mostly bare), an exquisite pair of dainty pearl and gold drop earrings and (this is the Marilyn part) around my left wrist I clasped a bracelet of enormous round diamonds held together by tiny gold links. I held my hand out, twisting it this way and that, while I admired the fire of the diamonds. I mean, they were really cool. Even Pammy, my flashy girlfriend who lived in Las Vegas, would be drooling.

"Do not forget this." Alanna held out the beautiful coronet I had worn before.

It was gorgeous, but I hesitated. "Are you sure it isn't a little much?"

"Rhiannon wore it always. It is sign of your nobility and station—a coronet can only be worn by a Priestess who is the Beloved of a Goddess."

I decided to follow my gut feeling. "Then I think I'll choose to leave it here. Tonight I want to be ClanFintan's Beloved." I looked at Alanna with belated concern. "I don't want to piss off my Goddess, though. Do you think Epona will mind?"

Alanna gave me a quick half hug that was so like Suzanna it made my breath catch. "Epona would want you to honor your husband and be happy."

"Good. Let's go back to my room." I led the way to the door. "And I'll go first—I have to start learning my way around. If I mess up I'll just act like a bitch. No one will notice anything out of the ordinary about that."

As we swept grandly out of the bathing room, the adorable door ornaments snapped to attention. I couldn't stop myself from tweaking the taller of the two's cheek (the one on his face).

"Nice job."

His eyes sparkled and his sensuous lips curved in a smile. I remembered that Rhiannon had probably known him well. In the Biblical sense. I blushed and started hastily down the hall.

"Psssst!" I slowed down and motioned for Alanna to catch up. "Walk next to me, I can't talk to you while you're back there." I whispered for her ears alone, "Did Rhiannon, um, well, boink that guard?"

"Boink?" she whispered back.

Sigh.

"You know." I wiggled my eyebrows suggestively and winked. *"Boink."*

"Oh!" She turned pink. "You can assume so. She *boink*ed all of her guards."

"Didn't you say there are one hundred of them?" I forgot to whisper.

"Yes."

"Damn, she must have been busy." It boggled my mind.

"She was very dedicated to her men."

I should say so.

"And she still had time to do goddess stuff?"

"She had many talents."

We came to the door to my chambers and I couldn't quit staring at the two guards as they snapped to and opened the door for me. It was like watching the aftermath of a car wreck. I wanted to look away, but I rubbernecked all the way into my room…

And right into the beautiful Staci-nymph.

"Oh, my Lady! Forgive my clumsiness!" She was bowing and quaking. I'm telling you, she looked like she was getting ready to prostrate herself at my feet.

I reached out to squeeze her shoulder and tell her not to worry about it, and she cowered down, protecting her face with her hands as if she expected to be beaten.

"I'm not going to hit you!" I blurted.

Her body was shaking and she peered up at me through her fingers. I looked at Alanna for help, and she mouthed what looked like the name Tarah to me.

"Tarah, please, it was my fault. I wasn't looking and I ran right into you." She blinked tears from her eyes and slowly her hands moved away from her face.

It amazed me how much she looked and sounded like Staci—shimmery, long dark hair, huge limpid brown eyes and bone structure a supermodel would die for (or, at the very least, commit bulimia for).

I smiled at her and held my hands very still, like she was a jittery colt. She smiled tentatively back at me.

"M–my Lady. I h–had your chambers set for your meal." She wiped away her tears. "I stayed to see if it met your approval."

I looked behind her and saw a lovely table setting for two. The chaise lounges were positioned so that the heads of the diners reclining on them would be very near one another.

"Everything looks wonderful. Just have them bring supper shortly after ClanFintan arrives."

She bobbed a graceful curtsy and began backing to the door.

"And, Tarah." She paused in her exit. "In the past I believe I have behaved badly." Her eyes opened wide as I continued, "And for that I apologize. Things will be different from now on."

"Yes, my Lady!" The responsive glow of her face made me even angrier with Rhiannon.

"Thank you, Tarah."

Her grin lit up the doorway as she left.

15

Alone again, I turned to Alanna.

"Did Rhiannon never control herself?"

"She is Epona's Chosen. She did not have to control herself."

"That's crap. It's that kind of thinking that allowed people like Caligula, Henry VIII and, well, certain presidents to make such asses of themselves."

"Who are they?"

"More sluts."

"Oh."

"How the hell could Rhiannon keep people loyal to her if she was such a bitch?"

Alanna gave me a knowing look.

"I mean *female* people. It's obvious how she kept her men happy." My hands were planted on my hips and I was tapping my foot in time with my anger. (I looked very teacherish—as a matter of fact, I felt the sudden desire to reprimand a teenager. But there's never one around when you need one.)

"Rhiannon was a very powerful woman." She didn't quite meet my eyes.

A thought came to me. "Alanna, you never did tell me how Rhiannon was able to exchange places with me through an explosive fire without either of us getting burned up." That was assuming Rhiannon had survived, too.

"I am not completely certain. She did not reveal everything to me." Her voice was hesitant.

"But you have a pretty good guess?"

Her sigh was deep and she raised her eyes to mine. "She went through several test rituals." She shuddered in remembrance. "They weren't successful. The people she attempted to exchange were… damaged…when they appeared. They did not live."

I nodded at her to go on.

"Then she came upon the idea of sending something inanimate from this world, something that could carry some of her power, with one of the people."

"The pot!"

"Yes, she sent a ceremonial funeral vase—one that had been used to pour libations over the graves of past generations of Epona's Chosen." She paused and swallowed hard. "Her next test was more successful."

"More successful?" I didn't like how that sounded.

"The servant lived. For a while."

"Ugh."

"Yes. Rhiannon went back to fasting and meditating. Then she seemed to have discovered an answer." Alanna sat on one of the chaises. This time I poured her a glass of wine, then poured myself a glass and sat next to her. "She had a favorite servant—a Shaman named Bres." She blanched visibly and her eyes darted nervously as she spoke his name. "He wasn't like ClanFintan, he worshipped dark gods whose names are better left unsaid."

"Well, don't say them then!" This whole conversation was giving me a walking-over-my-grave feeling.

Alanna nodded in agreement and continued, "They performed a dark ceremony the day you came to this world. A terrible storm blew in."

"There was a storm that appeared suddenly the afternoon of my accident."

"She and Bres walked to a deserted area near the Loch at the edge of Ufasach Marsh. She always insisted that I be nearby, so I went with them, but it was hard for me to understand what was happening because of the wind and the rain."

My Mustang and I understood exactly what she was describing.

"They chose an abandoned cottage to set afire. Even in the storm it burned with an unholy flame. Bres walked into the building, chanting an incantation that stung my ears with its intensity. He disappeared. Then another man, one with Bres's form, but who was obviously not the Shaman, burst from the building almost hysterical with confusion." Alanna stopped and took a long drink.

To save her the embarrassment of drinking alone I chugged with her.

"As he emerged, Rhiannon moved behind him and slit his throat. Then she caught his blood in a goblet and drank it. She spent the rest of the day speaking spells over his body. As dusk was falling she stripped off her clothes, flung her head back and arms wide, and moved into the still-burning building like she was embracing it."

I shivered, remembering the weird mirror vision of myself I had glimpsed in the pot as it burst into a fiery ball.

"Then the building exploded into nothing. And I found you lying unconscious in its ruins." She smiled bravely at me.

"I wonder if she was successful in getting to my world." It felt strange to wish ill on someone who could be my twin, or more accurately my clone. But I did wish it, vehemently.

"She was successful." Alanna's voice had gone flat.

"How do you know?"

"She was always successful. She settled for nothing less than exactly what she desired."

"Well, public school will be a rude awakening for her. I'd love to be a fly on the wall at her first parent–teacher conference." Not even tenure would be enough to protect her. "At least we're rid of her and that Bres character."

"Yes." We grinned at each other.

"Hey, was Bres tall and skeletal with real stinky breath and a fish belly–white complexion?"

"Yes!" She blinked in surprise at me. "Did you see him?"

"We met shortly before the storm hit. He was seriously creepy."

We shivered in unison.

"I'm glad you found me." I squeezed her hand.

"I am, too." She squeezed back and the warmth of our friendship brought the color back to a world that had turned temporarily pale.

"How about showing me the map before ClanFintan gets here and starts messing with my mind?" And (I sincerely hoped) my body.

She stood, refilled both of our empty glasses and then moved to a door at the far end of the chamber. It opened to a tastefully decorated sitting room, complete with love seats, a reading table, a chaise lounge (obviously a hot item in this world), a fireplace with an elaborately carved marble mantel and walls lined with rows and rows of—

"Books!" I yelped as I rushed into the room, practically knocking Alanna to her butt. "I thought this door led to a closet." I ran my fingers reverently down the leather spines. "God, I love books."

"So did Rhiannon. She kept the scribes busy." Alanna went to one wall and climbed to the top rung of a little wooden stepladder. She reached up inside the topmost shelf and pulled down a rolled-up map.

"This is Partholon."

"Wow!" Which was an understatement.

The map unrolled until it almost touched the floor. It was a little like the screen for an overhead projector, but it was made of some kind of intricately woven material that reminded me of silk, only thicker. It was amazing—its beauty drew me near and I longed to touch its softness. I stepped close to it and ran my hands in a light caress over its surface.

"Uh!" It was as though an electric shock had passed through the map to my fingers, and my hands shot back from the fabric. "It zapped me!"

Alanna looked pleased. "There is the last of your proof. The spark that passes between the sacred map of Partholon and the Beloved of Epona happens only when the Goddess's High Priestess touches it."

I rubbed my fingers and took a wary half step away from it.

"You could have warned me."

"Would you still have touched it?"

"Probably not."

"That is why I did not warn you."

"Smart aleck." I grumbled a smile at her as I began studying the map from a safe distance.

Epona's Temple was ornately marked by gold thread and situated in the southeastern part of Partholon, to the north of the wide vaguely east-west running river, which was labeled *Geal River.* The river originated in the northeastern end of the *Trier Mountains* as a split river, the west branch of which was labeled *Calman River,* and it emptied into the sea as a split river, too. At the B'an Sea the northernmost branch was labeled *Clare River.* I was interested to notice a structure labeled *Temple of the Muse* was nestled near the joining of the rivers on the Calman's western bank. My eyes were drawn to the far west of the map where the B'an Sea ran the length of the border, with cliffs of green drawn in dramatically. *MacCallan Castle* sat boldly near the edge. I sighed sadly and looked north from MacCallan Castle to see *Guardian Castle* situated in a cleft between huge white-tipped mountains. Looking down from Guardian Castle I was shocked to see a large blue lake labeled *Loch Selkie* (and I noted Ufasach Marsh hugged the eastern edge of the loch) between it and Epona's Temple. Another castle labeled *Laragon Castle* sat north of the loch and southeast of Guardian Castle. I didn't remember passing over a lake or another castle, and I felt a shiver of dread as I studied the area between Laragon and Guardian Castles.

A sudden noise broke my concentration.

"That will probably be one of your handmaids with word of ClanFintan." Alanna smiled knowingly as a flush bloomed over my face. "I will tell her she may announce him momentarily."

My eyes were drawn back to the map and I tried to take the rest of it in quickly. I could see at least three other castles labeled, but none as close to Guardian Castle as Laragon and MacCallan. I only had time to notice that the grassy lands which covered a great deal of the land outside Partholon were emblazoned *Centaur Plains,* when Alanna reappeared with a smile, followed by Staci-nymph.

"My Lady, ClanFintan asks if he may join you in your quarters." She gave me a sweet curtsy.

"Thank you, Sta…um…Tarah. Please show him in and bring our dinner, too."

"Yes, my Lady!" She certainly was cheerful.

Alanna and I went back into the main chamber (the one with my big bed in it).

"I'm a little nervous." I tried not to fidget.

"Just be who you really are." Alanna's eyes were kind and she patted one of my loose curls into place. "He is already predisposed to love you, you know."

I blinked in surprise. "No, I didn't know."

"You are Epona's Beloved. The Goddess always fashions a centaur High Shaman to be your mate."

A firm knock sounded and Alanna responded when I hesitated, "Enter!"

ClanFintan moved into the chamber and my stomach did several butterfly-filled flips. He'd obviously bathed. His coat shimmered like hot maple syrup and his long thick hair was brushed back and hung free in a dark curtain around his bronze shoulders. He wore a black leather vest embroidered with runes of gold that rippled almost as magically as his muscles when he moved.

Which made me realize he hadn't moved since the door had closed behind him. He just stood there, touching me with his eyes.

"Welcome, my Lord." I could hear the smile in Alanna's voice.

"Thank you, Alanna." The spell was broken and he moved gracefully into the space before me. "Forgive my silence, I was entranced by my Lady's beauty." He reached out and took my right hand in his, slowly raising my palm to his lips. Our eyes locked again and I felt my breath quicken.

God, he was big.

And muscular.

And hot (in all senses of the word).

"Good evening, ClanFintan. It's good to see you again." I realized as I said it that I'd missed him this afternoon.

"I find that it is good to see you again, too, my Lady." His breath was warm on my palm and his lips lingered near the pulse of my wrist.

For a second I wondered if he'd bite me again (not that I'd mind). He didn't and I sighed as he released my hand.

"If there is nothing else, my Lady, I will wish you a good evening and—"

"No!" Alanna paused in her flight to the door. ClanFintan looked at me, surprised by my outburst. "I mean, um, please stay until our dinner arrives. There are things we need to discuss." They both stared at me. Under their confused scrutiny I walked nervously to one of the chaise lounges and refreshed my glass of wine. "I would like Alanna to hear your report and, well, she has some really good insights about, uh, things." They were still staring and I looked to ClanFintan for understanding. "She is my friend, and I value her judgment."

"Of course, Rhiannon." That seemed to get through to him. "Then she should stay." He took his place at the other lounge. Alanna moved around the pillar-like table to pour him a fresh glass of wine and I tried to telegraph a "relax and help!" look to her.

"Wine, my Lord?" She slipped easily into her servant role.

"Yes." He sipped and I felt his eyes watching me over the rim.

I looked at Alanna and sighed. "Alanna, pour yourself some wine and sit here with me."

She nodded, looking at me oddly, but did as I asked. I think that sometimes it takes her a few minutes to remind herself I'm not going to shriek at her and pounce. But then again, I've seen teenagers give me the same kind of startled look, so who knows…

My attention returned to the centaur. "So, are the troops getting ready for battle?" I hoped I didn't sound too I-don't-know-what-the-hell-I'm-talking-about-ish.

"Yes. I've sent a call to the Plains, and the centaurs are gathering. They should begin arriving within the next few days. Your guard is, as always, ready to protect you and Epona's Temple. I have called a war council in your name—by the end of the next seventh day the heads of all the Clans will arrive, then you may inform them of what Epona has revealed to you—" he smiled grimly at us "—and we will forge a combined strategy to combat the Fomorian evil."

"ClanFintan, I would like you to lead that war council." He started to interrupt and I hurried on, "I would feel secure knowing you are in charge of seeing to our safety."

"But, my Lady, by right you should lead the council."

Great.

"Yes, but as my mate I am asking you to assume that particular place of leadership for me." I crossed my fingers (figuratively) and hoped what I was asking wasn't creating an enormous war council faux pas. I glanced at Alanna and was glad to see she didn't appear to be freaking out. Yet.

"If that is what you wish, I will, of course, do my best in your stead." He sounded hesitant, but I trusted his abilities much more than mine. After all—we were going to war, not studying rhetorical theories of writing succinct essays about war (yawn).

"Thank you. And there is something else I'm worried about." I looked at Alanna. "When we were studying the map I realized how close Laragon Castle is to Guardian Castle. Has Laragon been notified of what has happened?"

"Yes, carrier pigeons were sent the first day, and centaurs have been deployed to aid them in readying their defenses."

"So, you think the creatures will not stay at Guardian Castle? You think they will attack again?" My skin crawled at the thought.

"I know little about them, but I do not think they will be

appeased with what they have taken." His words were haunted by the memory of my description of the horror I had witnessed.

"Does nobody know anything substantial about these… things?" Frustration shortened my tone.

"Fomorians." Alanna helped me with the word.

"Yeah, Fomorians." I looked from her to ClanFintan. "Didn't you say you knew something of them from the legends?"

"It is not much. Only that they were defeated in ancient times and banished over the mountains. And that they dabbled in dark powers and drank the blood of living beings."

More good news.

"They're friggin vampires!"

"Vampires?" Alanna and ClanFintan spoke together.

Sigh. Guess they've never read Bram Stoker.

"Vampires are creatures that live off the blood of others—usually pretty nasty things." They both looked blank. "They don't like to travel during daylight. They can be killed only in certain ways, etc., etc., etc.…"

ClanFintan's blank look suddenly changed. "Perhaps the Fomorians have weaknesses like these vampires."

"Sounds good—how do we find out if they do?" The three of us looked at each other. Then the lightbulb over my head lit up. Clearly, we needed a teacher!

"Don't we have a historian?" I turned to Alanna. "You know, a teacher of ancient ideas and stories."

"Yes, of course, my Lady." Curiously, she went all pink. Even her ears blushed.

Wonder what's up with her?

"Good! Could you please contact the teacher, let her know what she needs to research, and bring her to me tomorrow morning, *before* I have to bless the people?"

"I will, my Lady." Her eyes shied away from mine and she plucked nervously at her wineglass. (Note to self: look into whatever the hell was the problem between Alanna and the teacher.)

"Good. I'm glad that's settled."

There was a knock at the door. This time I had the presence of mind to answer for myself.

"Come on in!"

Staci/Tarah-nymph skipped into the room with a big smile on her gorgeous face.

"My Lady, may I have dinner brought in to you?"

I grinned back at her young exuberance. "Yes, I would like that."

She moved aside and clapped her hands imperiously. Servants began swarming into the room. They were all carrying trays filled to overflowing with delicious-smelling food.

I grinned at Staci/Tarah-nymph. "Good job!"

"You said you were hungry, my Lady!" She was so excited by my approval I thought she would wiggle out of her porcelain skin.

"Yes, I am hungry." My eyes found ClanFintan's and we shared a secret smile.

Yep—we certainly were hungry…

As the servants loaded down our plates Alanna took the opportunity to stand and curtsy to me.

"I will tend to that problem of which we spoke, my Lady." Then she turned her curtsy to ClanFintan. "I wish you a blessed evening, my Lord."

"Thank you, Alanna." His voice was warm.

"Yes, thank you…" I paused so that all the eyes in the room were focused on me, then I continued, clearly so that no one in the room could mistake my words, "My friend. As always, you have my love as well as my appreciation for your loyalty."

To Alanna's credit she didn't blush or look shocked at what everyone else must have considered an uncharacteristic outburst from me. She just shot me a grateful look and exited gracefully with her head held high. There was a short space of dead air, and then the confused and silent servants followed her. (Although I did notice that the adorable Staci/Tarah-nymph was grinning like Saks Fifth Avenue Barbie as she led the exit.)

Rhiannon had been such an incredibly hateful bitch.

The door clicked closed.

I was starving (in all senses of the word).

And now that we were alone I felt incredibly nervous. I found myself lavishing intense interest upon the food on my plate.

"Gosh, this looks wonderful." I enthusiastically stabbed a piece of something that looked like chicken and popped it into my mouth.

"Yes…wonderful." That husky tone was back in his voice. It sent shivers from my back teeth to my toes. And everywhere in between.

His eyes locked with mine. His elbow was resting on the crest of the chaise lounge. His other hand held his wineglass. He wasn't even pretending interest in the food.

I swallowed hastily. "Aren't you hungry?"

His slow smile drew my eyes to his wonderfully full lips. "No. I ate before I came to your chamber."

"You did!" I sputtered, but at least food didn't dribble out of my mouth. "Why didn't you tell me? I would have eaten earlier, too."

"I enjoy watching you eat." His voice was deep and intriguing. "You do so love your food."

Well, he had me there.

I still felt uncomfortable. "But I don't want to eat alone."

He looked surprised. "But you are not dining alone. I am here."

"You sure are," I mumbled through the stuff that tasted like chicken.

He laughed. "You have such an odd way of speaking. I did not know that about you."

"Well, you learn something new every day."

"That is true." He looked enlightened.

Guess clichés worked well in this world.

I chewed my food and studied him. "You don't look like you've been traveling hard, carrying a passenger and going without sleep for the past several days." Actually he looked strong and refreshed—he looked yummy, to be more precise.

"You were a burden I enjoyed bearing." His husky voice deepened suggestively. "And my stamina is greater than a human man's."

I grabbed a hunk of lobster from an opened tail. It dripped with butter and I sucked it gently into my mouth.

I could hear his breath catch.

Slowly, I licked the liquid from my lips. "So you have mentioned before."

"Yes, so I have." I was pleased to notice his reply sounded strained.

"I don't think I thanked you for following me. It would have been unimaginable without you. Thank you."

The fine lines at the corners of his eyes crinkled as he smiled. "You are very welcome. The next time you feel the need to embark upon a quest, please allow me to accompany you from its inception."

Before I sucked another piece of buttery lobster into my mouth, I purred, "I wouldn't think of leaving home without you." My tongue slid out to catch a drop of butter from my upper lip, and then I sucked the wet white meat into my mouth, chewing slowly and deliberately. I swallowed and licked my lips (again). "I'll just call you Mr. American Express."

He looked hypnotized and vaguely confused.

"American Express? Who is that?"

The lobster was gone so I picked up a sugared strawberry and took it delicately between my teeth. Nipping the end of it gently, I watched him watch me.

"It is someone who allows me to have exactly what I desire." I sucked the strawberry juice off my middle finger. "Mmm, that is good."

"Yes, it was." My, my, my—I didn't think he was talking about the berry.

We sipped our wine. I attempted to look demure. (I said *attempted*.) And we studied each other. I could feel the wine bubbling in my head—it had (obviously) already begun to loosen my inhibitions. Okay, let's face it, I've never really had an inhibition problem. But the horse/man issue had seemed a little daunting at first.

And that was it! He had ceased to be a horse/man thing to me. I felt my lips turn up into what I sincerely hoped was a seductive smile. I suddenly understood what Beauty must have felt as she had fallen in love with her Beast. He was my husband, and I wanted him. All I had to do was reach out and touch him.

I put my wineglass down and leaned forward. His right arm was still resting on the curve of the chaise. Slowly, I reached across the short space that separated us and ran my fingers in a caress that moved from the swell of his bicep, down his forearm, and ended at his palm. His hot fingers closed over my hand. He didn't pull me over to him, like a human man would have. Instead, he stroked my wrist and waited, allowing me to decide when, or if, I wanted to come to him.

And that was a damn easy decision.

I stood and moved around to the other side of his chaise. He shifted his body so that he was facing me. As I might have mentioned before, he's a big guy. With me standing and him reclining, our heads were still not even, but at least this way he didn't tower over me. I stepped close to him and was immediately submerged in the inexplicable heat he radiated. Without conscious thought, I lifted my arms and rested my hands on his shoulders. Then, carefully, I slid my hands toward each other, at first loving the soft texture of his vest, then reveling in the springy feel of his chest hair as I found the opening in his vest. I raised my eyes to meet his. He was watching me with liquid intensity.

"I love touching you," I whispered.

"I am glad of it."

That voice—I don't think I had ever experienced any sound as seductive. It was a verbal caress. It ignited flames all over my already sensitized body.

My hands slipped inside the vest and traveled over his broad chest, finally moving downward until I traced the lines of his muscular stomach, lingering on the firm ridges and enjoying the way he quivered under my touch.

Down to where his human body met horse. And my hands stilled.

My hands refused to explore farther; unexpectedly I felt shackled by fear of the unknown. My eyes shot back up to his.

"There is something you must believe." He spoke with controlled intensity into the silence that had frozen between us. "I would never harm you. You must never fear me."

"This is all so new to me." My chin dipped down and I had to look away from him. If only he knew how alien this whole world was to me.

He took my chin in his hand and tilted it up so that our eyes met again. "You have my oath that I will do nothing that makes you uncomfortable."

"Do you want me?" My voice trembled and I wondered fleetingly if it was from anticipation of a yes, or of a no, as his answer.

"More than I could possibly make you understand." The erotic velvet had disappeared from his voice, and had been replaced by sad resignation. His hand slid slowly from my chin, and without actually touching my skin, he followed the outline of my shoulder and arm, down to where my hand had stilled against his waist, then he sighed and his hand came to rest against his own side. The heat of that touchless caress made goosebumps rise up and down my body.

The quiet resignation of his reply chased away the last vestiges of my fear. I felt like a diver getting ready to leap from the side of a cliff.

I held my breath and asked, "Would you take off your vest?"

His serious expression shifted into a smile, and he cocked one eyebrow, watching me closely as he pulled off the vest and dropped it to the floor beside us (just like a guy).

He was gorgeous, all bronzed muscles and chiseled lines. My hands found his chest again and I used my fingertips to circle his nipples. He snorted a quick laugh and grabbed my hands.

"Are you ticklish?"

"Just there." It struck us as funny and we laughed together.

I felt both of us relaxing, and after only a momentary pause I continued my exploration down his chest, back to his rippled stomach, and still farther downward. When my fingertips met his thick coat I glanced up at him. His expression was open and warm; an encouraging smile played on his sexy lips. I looked back down to my hands. His waist was tapered and strong, gracefully merging into sensuous equine lines. Without any further hesitation my hand traveled over his coat.

"You're beautiful." I stepped closer to him and my arms slid up around his neck. I finished speaking the thought into his lips. "All of you."

With a moan, his arms went around me and he drew me against his bare chest. Our lips met and I felt immersed in the familiar taste and heat of him.

I am a serious advocate of long, intimate kissing. There's something unbelievably erotic about taking a man's tongue into my mouth, and then exploring his mouth in turn, that makes me begin to feel all tingly just thinking about it. So I took my time. ClanFintan didn't seem to mind.

The heat of his body was incredibly seductive. As I nibbled on his lips and sucked at his tongue, I could feel him reining in his passion as his breathing grew deeper and his muscles continued to bunch and quiver under my roaming hands. He kept his hands still, resting low on my back, as he allowed me to become comfortable with touching him. The misinformed might think that his reticence would work against his original intention (which, I assumed—as would any American female—was to get into my panties). In truth, this style of seduction, perhaps we should call it the Non-Octopus Technique, was *seriously* working for him. By way of proof, let me offer the fact that in no time I was rubbing my body against his chest and, well, eventually I found myself reaching down, taking his hand off my waist, and putting it smack onto my boob.

I'm telling you, this guy could go on a lecture/training circuit and make a fortune teaching the Non-Octopus Technique to semi-bald, divorced, middle-aged men.

The heat from his hand and the roughness of his palm made my nipple harden, which was very obvious through the filmy material of my dress. His hand teased my nipple for a while, then his mouth made a hot trail down the side of my neck, lingered for a moment on the crevice of my neck bone, and then he began kissing his way slowly over the swell of my breast until his lips found my nipple. The fact that I was still clothed didn't cause him to hesitate and he ran his tongue over my nipple. Through the thin silk of my bodice, the warmth and wetness of his mouth brought my breath rushing out of my mouth in a moan. Then he opened his lips and drew the nipple, and the material that covered it, into his mouth, sucking and nibbling gently.

"Oh, that feels good." I arched against his mouth. I felt like my body was melting into him.

"Mmm." He raised his head and pressed his lips to mine. His arms wrapped all the way around me and he pulled me firmly against him. I reciprocated. Big-time.

Just when the top of my head was beginning to spin he broke the kiss, but he didn't loose his hold on me. Our eyes met. I know I was flushed and my lips felt delightfully bruised and wet.

"Is your fear gone?"

There was no hesitation in my answer. "Yes."

I moved half a step back from him. He looked at me curiously, but let me escape from his arms. Still holding his eyes with mine, I reached up and unpinned the brooch that kept my dress in place. I shrugged one shoulder and the material fell away to expose my breasts. A simple tug on an end of the fabric around my waist, and I was standing in a pool of silky material, wearing only a thong, sexy sandals and a smile.

I sucked in my stomach (not that I needed to, but, well, you know) and let him look, truly enjoying the ravenous expression on his face.

Then he reached out and crushed me against him—

Abruptly he stood up, lifting me off my feet. He slipped an arm under my butt and strode purposefully in the direction of my big bed. (It was very *Gone with the Wind*–esque.)

When we reached the bed he changed my positioning, causing my body to slide against his until I was sitting on the bed. Slowly, he untied my sandals, kissing the arch of each foot. After he removed my shoes, he lifted me by the waist till I was standing near the edge of the bed, my hands resting on his shoulders for balance. His hands glided down my body until they found the top of my thong, then they kept gliding down, but they took the filmy piece of material with them. I stepped out of it and he picked me up again, cradling me in his arms and kissing me softly. Then he leaned down and lay me on the bed, reluctantly releasing me before he took several steps backward.

"This will not take long, but I must ask you not to speak to me until the Change is complete."

Intrigued, I nodded.

He closed his eyes and bowed his head. His lips began to move as if he was speaking quickly and intently to himself. At first I couldn't hear his words, but within a few moments his voice became louder and the already quick tempo of his litany increased. Keeping his eyes tightly closed, his head slowly began to rise—with it he brought his arms away from his sides in an upward movement so that his head and arms were moving in tandem.

The volume and tempo of his voice kept increasing. I couldn't understand the words, but they sounded mysterious and ancient, and several of them were repeated over and over. His head kept moving up, as did his arms, until they were directly over him, and his face was pointed up to the ceiling. He was not shouting, but the intensity of the words was incredible and I felt the hair at the back of my neck and my forearms rise.

Then a shimmering began all over his body. At first it was like he was glowing, but the glow was moving. And then I realized it wasn't the glow that was moving—it was his skin. His skin was rippling and his muscles appeared to liquefy. My eyes shot to his face. His expression was one of intense pain. I wanted to scream at him to stop, but his warning about silence froze the words in my throat.

Then everything happened very quickly. His body exploded in a shower of light particles like the transporter on *Star Trek* as it beamed a person aboard the *Enterprise*. The light became so intense I had to hold my hand in front of my eyes and squint. A wordless shriek of pain echoed against the walls of the chamber.

Then the light disappeared. The room seemed dark in comparison and it took a moment for my eyes to refocus. As my vision returned, a figure took form. It was a human man. He was kneeling in the exact place ClanFintan had stood. His head was bowed and a thick blanket of familiar dark hair shielded his face. One hand rested on the ground and the other was still raised above him. He was breathing hard—his body was slick with a film of moisture, as if he'd been running a marathon.

He raised his head and shook the hair back out of his face. Our eyes met. The effects of pain lingered and deepened the lines of his face, causing him to look older and uncharacteristically vulnerable. Then he smiled at me.

His voice sounded raspy. "I probably should have—" he cleared his throat "—warned you about the light."

"The light!" That was *all* he'd thought he needed to warn me about! I scooted to the edge of the bed, but stopped there, afraid to get too close to him, not wanting to cause him any harm. "Are you okay?"

He took a deep breath and stood. His first step toward me was shaky, but as he got closer I could see the tremors in his legs still, and by the time he stood in front of me he looked strong and in control once more.

"I am unharmed." He smiled again and tapped the tip of my nose lightly with his finger. "Shape-shifting is difficult."

"I should say so!" I touched his chest tentatively. He felt reassuringly warm and solid. "It looked like you were in a lot of pain."

He took my hand in his. "Nothing of any value comes without a cost."

I thought about his words as I studied his new shape. He had shifted into an incredibly tall man—probably almost a foot taller than my five-seven. His skin was the same burnished copper color, only this time it covered all of his body. His legs were long and muscular. And he was naked. My eyes followed the line of his chest down to his waist, and down farther yet. Very naked.

He was built in every way like a human man—and he was quite obviously *very* happy to be here (he certainly had a short recovery time). Rumor has it you can tell the size of a man's penis by the size of his fingers. May I just say that he must have damn big hands.

He cleared his throat. I tore my eyes away from The View and brought them back to his face.

"Do I pass inspection as a human male?" I was glad to hear his voice had returned to its deep, sexy lilt.

"Absolutely." Actually, I wanted to yell, *Sheeet, yes, boy!* But since he wasn't from Oklahoma I didn't think it'd be appropriate. Instead, to show my appreciation for his maleness, I stood, wrapped my arms around him, pressed my body against his and gave him a big ol' Oklahoma hello.

He lifted me in his arms and sat down on the bed, with me in his lap. Cupping my breast in his hand, he lowered his head to my now bared nipple. Much too soon he lifted his head and looked into my eyes. His voice was husky.

"Tell me if there is something you would have me do. I have never made love as a man before."

I answered him by putting my arms around his neck and pulling him down next to me. I whispered against his mouth, "I have never made love as a man before, either, but something tells me we'll do just fine."

His chuckled reply was muffled by my mouth and replaced by a moan as I guided his hand to the wetness between my legs.

Oh—I was mistaken about one thing—we did better than just fine.

16

"I thought you said shape-shifting left you in a weakened state?" I said a little breathlessly, after the third incident of better than just fine. I was nestled against him, with my head resting on his chest. He blew some of my untamable curls out of his mouth before answering.

"I feel the effects after I have shifted back to my original form. And I cannot stay in any other form for more than the span of a single night." He tilted my chin up and studied my face, suddenly serious. "You understand I cannot remain a human?"

"Of course." I touched the side of his face, surprised to find no stubble there, and I realized that none of the centaurs had shaved or had facial hair over the days we had traveled together. "You're not a human, you're a centaur. I know that."

We looked at each other. I was afraid that the intimacy we had shared was going to evaporate. I didn't really understand what kind of a being he was—the whole shape-shifting thing was too science fiction-ish and totally alien to the world with which I was accustomed. But *he* wasn't alien to me.

"You're my husband—whether you're human or centaur." I gave him a crooked smile. "Or, um, whatever else you might happen to change into." I just hoped he'd warn me first.

A look of relief passed over his handsome face and he kissed my forehead gently. "Yes, I am your husband."

"I'm glad you are." I sighed with contentment and snuggled more firmly against him.

"As am I."

I curled my leg over his, and his hand found the back of my thigh. In a long, warm caress he began rubbing from the sensitive spot behind my knee, all the way up to the swell of my buttock and back down again. My eyelids fluttered shut; it felt like that massage was a drug. I struggled to stay awake, though, not wanting to waste any of our nighttime hours.

"Shh," he whispered into my hair. "Rest—I will be right here."

I nodded my head against him and allowed myself to relax into a deep, contented sleep.

A warm kiss against my cheek brought me slowly awake. The soft, clean light of predawn soaked through my closed eyelids, making me shut them all the more tightly. Another kiss on the cheek made me remember where I was, and, as I stretched and felt the intimate soreness of my body, who I was with. I smiled and yawned, letting my eyes come slowly open.

First, I noticed the source of the light, and I was surprised to realize it was coming through a nonexistent wall on one side of my room. Squinting, I saw that huge beveled windows looked out on a beautiful, rose-filled garden that lined the far side of the room, which obviously faced the east, because mauve-colored dawn was beginning to creep up over the flowers and into my room.

Then the shadowed mountain standing at the edge of the bed moved, bending to kiss me once more. I reached my hand sleepily out and it met the silk that covered his foreleg. I ran my fingers lightly over his coat, pulling playfully at some of the fur.

"Good morning." My voice was foggy with sleep. "The light surprised me. I thought those big curtain things just covered more wall, not windows and a garden."

"What? Rhiannon, how could you not know your own bedchamber?" His question brought me fully awake.

I realized my voice wasn't all that had been foggy with sleep. Great, I'd screwed up. I sat abruptly, rubbing my eyes and stalling for time. Through my fingers I could see ClanFintan studying me intently.

"Oh, gosh, um, I was having the strangest dream. My room had been changed around, and, um, it was so realistic I thought it had really happened…" My voice trailed off.

He opened his mouth to question me further. Deciding diversion was my best tactic, I stood on the bed and threw myself into his arms. Automatically he caught me, and I busied myself nuzzling and nipping at the side of his neck.

"I'm awake now." I felt his chest rumble with a chuckle and I relaxed.

I really do have to talk to Alanna about why I can't let him know who I am.

Two loud knocks sounded against the door. ClanFintan deposited me on the bed and I wrapped a sheet around my naked body before I called, "Come in!"

Alanna stepped into the room. She smiled knowingly at us, saying, "My Lord, my Lady, I hope you had an eventful night."

ClanFintan snorted (which I suppose meant that we had) and I felt myself blushing like a virgin (which I most thoroughly was not).

She continued through a big, face-splitting grin. "Rhea, I thought you might like to go to the bathing room and freshen yourself before you bless the people."

My cheeks still felt hot as I nodded at her.

Alanna's eyes shined with mischief and she addressed Clan-

Fintan. "Perhaps my Lord would like to join us. I am certain between myself and some of the maidens, we could wash and groom him properly, too." She paused, barely containing her mirth. "Several of the maidens have already said they would be happy to volunteer for the task."

ClanFintan's face lit up in a wolfish grin and I got quickly to my feet, being careful not to trip over my sheet outfit, and whacked him good and hard on his flat stomach.

I was satisfied to hear a grunt interrupt his laughter. He wrapped his arm around me and held me tightly against his side (probably so I couldn't hit him again, and, God knows, it certainly wouldn't do any good for me to stomp on his hoof).

Without looking down at me, he answered, "I think I will bathe in the warriors' chambers. I need to check with the night watch before the blessing ceremony. But thank you for your hospitable offer." He squeezed my shoulder.

"Huh," was my answer.

I pulled away from him and headed toward Alanna and the door. "Let's go, I need a bath." I had the distinct impression they were both laughing at me. Walking past the windows I caught a reflection of myself, wrapped in a rumpled sheet, hair standing out in all directions and head held high as I attempted a haughty exit.

The giggle began in my chest and bubbled out of my mouth before I reached Alanna. She put her arm around me and we both laughed. ClanFintan had followed me and I turned to smile up at him.

"Did they really volunteer to wash him?"

"Actually, they were arguing over the privilege."

We tilted our heads together and pretended to study the centaur as he stood in front of us, hands resting on his waist. His expression said that he was pretty certain we were nuts.

"Hmm, he is a rather nice-looking centaur. Do you not think so, my Lady?" Alanna said.

"I guess now that you mention it, he has good, wide withers and I can testify to his…uh…shall we say, *stamina*," I said.

I squealed as the object of our speculations lunged forward and lifted me off the floor and into his arms. Alanna jumped out of his way and opened the door for him. As he carried me through the door he was grumbling something about *"Wide at the withers, indeed,"* but I couldn't be sure because of Alanna's laughter. I peered over his shoulder and saw her holding her side as she hurried after us, trying futilely to control her giggles. I wrapped my arms around his neck and held on. I was pretty certain he would take care of keeping the sheet around me.

Too soon, we came to the door of the bathing chamber. The two guards snapped to attention. I noticed ClanFintan made a point of looking each of them directly in the eye, before he bent his head to mine and gave me a slow, thorough kissing. About that time, Alanna caught up with us and opened the door.

He set me back on my feet and we released each other reluctantly.

"You will join me for the blessing ceremony?" I realized I sounded wistful at the thought of being separated from him.

Damn, I had it bad.

"I will be by your side—" he glanced up at my guards "—where I belong." He kissed me once more, quickly. Before he turned to go, he addressed my two warriors. "Guard my Lady with your lives. If anyone touches her, I will kill him."

My, my, my, guess he'd heard those ugly rumors about Rhiannon's attachment to her men.

They saluted him. He looked satisfied and caressed the side of my face. Then he spun gracefully and headed down the hall, clomping purposefully and looking pleased with himself.

I floated after Alanna into the wonderful bathing room.

I used the facilities while Alanna rounded up the correct bottles and brushes, then I dropped my sheet and gingerly lowered my well-used body into the soothing mineral water.

Alanna plopped down on the ledge next to me and handed me the sponge and a bottle of the soap I liked so much.

I set to work repairing the damage of last night's intimacies, smiling secretly to myself as I discovered little bite marks on my inner thigh.

"It seems last night went well."

"Honey, last night was *spectacular.*"

We shared a girlfriend grin.

"So, you watched him perform the Change?" Her voice was filled with curiosity.

"It was the most amazing thing I've ever seen." I blinked at her in amazement. "You mean you've never seen anyone shape-shift?"

"Oh, no!" She looked shocked for a moment—then she smiled and tugged at one of my damp curls. "I forget you could not know these things. There are very few shape-shifters and the Change is sacred to them. It is something that only other High Shamans, or in your case, mates of High Shamans, ever get to witness. After Changing, a Shaman might perform a ceremony or service for the people in whatever shape he has assumed, but he or she would never Change in view of the public."

I thought about that. "Did you know it was painful for them to shape-shift?"

"No!"

"That must be why they don't like people to see them Change." I remembered the look on ClanFintan's face as his body shifted form. "They don't want people to know how painful it is."

Alanna took my soapy hand in hers. "Was it that hard on him?"

I nodded. "But he said nothing worth anything comes without a price."

"Do you think the night was worth the price of temporary pain?" Her voice was wise and I squeezed her hand in gratitude.

"He sure acted like it was."

"Then I would believe him and not let it shadow your pleasure."

Until we had spoken about it I hadn't realized just how much it had been bothering me.

"I guess he knows what he's doing."

"It would appear so."

I sighed wistfully as I lathered myself with the sweet-scented soap. "Alanna, he really was wonderful."

"And he is devoted to you."

I paddled out to the deep part of the bath to rinse and considered what Alanna had just said. Devoted...but was he devoted enough to love the real me?

"Alanna," I blurted out, "what if he's not devoted to me? What if he's only devoted to Rhiannon, and if he finds out who I really am, he'll change his mind about me."

Alanna's smile was kind. "It is you he loves."

I chewed my bottom lip.

"Perhaps you should tell him."

"What?" I squeaked. "But you said that I had to keep my identity a secret."

"That was before he loved you."

"I don't know, Alanna. What's happened between us is too new."

"You are afraid to tell him the truth," Alanna said.

"I'm afraid to lose what I've just gained with him."

"I think you underestimate the High Shaman, but I believe time will change that. When a man is truly devoted to a woman, he keeps her secrets."

I thought I detected a sad note to her voice and I started to question her further, when she chimed in with a perky "Rhea, you must get out. You need to bless the people shortly after the sun is high enough over the eastern horizon for it to shimmer off the river."

I climbed reluctantly out of the warm water and wrapped myself in the thick towel Alanna offered.

"How long do I have?"

"About as long as it will take for you to don your ceremonial robes—if we hurry." And she led me purposefully to the vanity.

"Why don't you summon a couple of the nymph-maidens to help us if we're so rushed for time?" My rumpled reflection was making me think a quick repair job would take more than two people.

Alanna was working some kind of hair-oil stuff through my wild curls. It smelled good, but I was doubtful it would have much effect on my incorrigible redheadedness.

"Last night, after I left your chambers, Tarah came to me and reported that several of your handmaidens are complaining of feeling ill." She smiled wryly at my reflection. "I think they are probably just worn out from attending to the needs of so many families. I put your maids in charge of keeping watch over the young children. I suppose you should make a point of rebuking them for their laziness."

"No way—I always hated babysitting. Let them sleep."

"They will be with you this morning during the ceremony. Perhaps a morning away from their young charges will refresh them and they will find they feel suddenly recovered."

I smiled but felt the definite stirrings of nervousness.

"What the heck am I supposed to do?" I began powdering my face as Alanna tugged at my hair.

"Near the bank of the river—"

"Named Geal, right?"

"Yes, it means bright. The western branch of the river that joins at the Temple of the Muse is called…" She paused.

"Cal-something?"

"Calman, meaning dove. Together they make the Bright Dove River, which you would understand if you could see how they look as they join. The rapids look like glistening, swooping birds."

"Cool—go ahead. Sorry I interrupted."

"You will ride Epona—" my face broke into a pleased grin "—to the sacred Tor, or hill, next to the river. There, while still astride the mare, you will bless the people as the sun blesses the river."

"Is there something in particular I am expected to say? Some ritual blessing I have to perform?" I was hoping Alanna would give me the lines.

"No, Rhiannon always authored her own prayers of blessing." She looked worried. "You did well on your wedding day, I assumed you would not have a problem evoking another prayer."

"No!" She gave me a shocked look. "I mean, yes, I can come up with a blessing."

She smiled her relief.

Good thing one of us knew what she was doing. And I didn't mean me.

"Honey, how long does this have to last?"

"Oh, not long—the morning blessing is a brief service Epana's Chosen performs once each fortnight designed to remind the people of Epona's love for them as they begin their day. It is on the first night of a full moon that you must perform the ritual dance and sacrifice."

Oh, goodie. I'll look forward to it.

"So, should I not mention anything about the Fomorian problem this morning? I assumed that was part of the reason I was going to speak to the people."

"Rhea, I think it should be mentioned that we are arming ourselves, and you should ask for Epona's protection specifically against their evil, but, well..." She drifted off, looking very uncomfortable.

"What? Really, Alanna, I don't just want your advice, I *need* it. Please tell me, as my friend, the truth. Always." I was sitting there, butt naked with my makeup only partially applied. I mean, how much more honest could I get?

Her expression showed she had come to a decision, and she met my eyes in the mirror. "I do not think you should discuss any aspects of the war with the people. Take this opportunity to announce ClanFintan as your appointed Chieftain of Warriors. He is wise in the ways of battle and men." She looked a little sheepishly at me. "I may be mistaken, but I do not believe you have been trained to lead men into battle."

What was her first clue?

"Nor do I believe you to be as, well, *experienced* in the ways of men as was Rhiannon."

I like to think I've attracted my share of men, but one hundred guards is just plain gluttonous.

"Uh, no. And, thanks for the advice. I agree." She looked relieved. "Jeesh, stop worrying about stepping on my feet."

She looked confused.

"I mean, you don't have to worry about hurting my ego. I depend on you—just be honest with me."

"That I can do."

"Good."

"And I was wondering—what does 'jeesh' mean?"

"It's something I say to keep me from cussing."

"Oh. It does not seem to work very well," she said very matter-of-factly.

"No shit," I said through my opened lips as I applied the finishing strokes of lipstick. "I think I'm ready for these ceremonial robes."

"Put this on while I get your garment." She handed me the coronet, and its beauty, again, took me by surprise.

"I hope there are matching earrings for this thing."

"Yes," she spoke over her shoulder as she opened one of the many wardrobes that lined the far side of the room. "Look in that box nearest you. There should be earrings and an armlet that match."

I was happily pawing through the jewels when she returned.

"Here." She handed me another silky thong. This time it looked like it was made of liquid gold. I was beginning to believe Rhiannon had a panty-line phobia.

"Now, stand and hold your arms away from your sides, this usually takes some complicated wrapping."

I faced her and did as I was told. The waterfall of what looked like liquid gold that she was maneuvering so carefully around my body intrigued me. I stood very still while she wrapped and wrapped and wrap—

"Hey! Where's the top to this thing?"

She was finished. She hadn't used any pins—I had no clue how the material was staying on my body. The skirt portion was long, but it had several slits in it (even more than Rhiannon's clothes usually had), so that I could imagine it would fall beautifully around Epi when I was seated astride her. That was okay. It was the top that was causing me stress. It crossed and wrapped intricately around my torso, leaving both of my breasts *totally bared*.

"Rhea—" she looked dangerously close to laughter as she noticed my horrified expression "—there is no 'top' to it. This is the ceremonial attire the Beloved of Epona wears during the morning blessing ritual."

"I thought you said it was a *robe!*" I looked down at my two very naked thirty-five-year-old breasts.

"Oh, of course. I wouldn't forget your robe." She hurried back to the wardrobe. And returned with another piece of liquid gold, which glistened with swirl after swirl of crystal beads, forming an intricate, delicate design.

"Let me guess—more skulls."

"Yes!" She looked pleased at my demonstrated ability to learn as she pinned the cloak neatly around my neck. It flowed down my back, glittering like stars on a clear Oklahoma night. But it didn't cover one damn bit of my breasts.

"You look beautiful—as always."

"Oh, hold on here! Are you telling me that I am supposed to go out in public, in front of *all* those people, with my boobs flopping around in front of God, or, uh, Goddess and everyone?" (Not to mention ClanFintan—although he's already seen them. Still...) I crossed my arms, already imagining the cool morning breeze and the staring eyes.

Alanna looked puzzled by my reaction. "In your old world were there no priestesses who wore ceremonial dress?"

An image of my Presbyterian pastor, Ted Foote, flashed through my mind. He's a friendly guy, and I like him (he's even let me teach adult Sunday school—which was pretty darn brave of him), but I couldn't imagine him baring his breast to the congregation on Sunday morning. Not even on Easter Sunday.

"Yes, but they don't bare parts of their bodies."

She looked aghast at our barbarism.

"Rhea, the baring of a priestess's body symbolizes the honesty and intimacy of her relationship with her goddess. If you cover yourself, the people will believe Epona has deserted you, or worse, that you are blaspheming your goddess."

"It doesn't seem to me that Rhiannon was very damn honest," I grumbled, trying to force my arms down to my sides.

"She was honest. She never pretended to be anything except spoiled and self-indulgent."

"But—" My arms found their way reluctantly to my sides.

"But the people loved her because she was Epona's Chosen. As are you."

"Okay. I'll try to ignore the fact that my boobs are flapping in the breeze for everyone to gawk at." A thought hit me. "But I don't want to talk to the teacher while I'm dressed like this. Can you send word to her to meet us in my chambers after the ceremony—*after* I've had a chance to change my clothes?"

"Yes." Alanna nodded and blushed a bright pink.

"Hey, is there some problem with—"

Alanna interrupted. "No! There is no problem!" She cleared her throat and began hustling me toward the door. "Rhea, we cannot be late."

17

"Oh, bloody, buggering hell." Using Brit cusswords might help me to maintain a certain level of dignity. At least in theory. I squared my shoulders, which caused my breasts to jut out even more prominently than usual.

Again, I'm not what you could describe as a small-breasted gal. And I've always been pleased that I'm not. To be totally honest, I admit that I've felt smug as my flat-chested girlfriends lamented over not filling out their bikini tops and scrambled to the local plastic surgeon for their augmentations. As I reluctantly followed Alanna out of the privacy of the bathing room, I found myself, for the first time in my adult life, wishing I hadn't been quite so blessed by the Tit Fairy (she's the more popular cousin of the Tooth Fairy).

Exiting the room, Alanna stepped aside so I could take my place as leader. She shot me an encouraging smile. I couldn't even glance at the two guards, but I felt their eyes on me. Or, more precisely, *I felt them staring at my bare boobs!*

I turned and began beating a hasty retreat down the empty hall. "My Lady?"

And was stopped by Alanna's voice. She was still back at the door to the bathing room. I turned—giving her a look that I'm sure was reminiscent of bitchy Rhiannon.

"Yes," I hissed through clenched teeth.

"Mistress, you are pressed for time. If there is something you require from your chambers, I will send a maiden to fetch it for you." She nodded subtly in the opposite direction from which I had been headed.

Okay, so I'd been going the wrong direction.

"Thank you for reminding me." I marched purposefully back to her and grabbed her hand as I passed her so she was forced to walk next to me.

"You'll have to show me where the hell we're going," I whispered.

"Rhiannon always had all who would be part of the ceremony await her directly in front of Epona's stables," she whispered in reply. "She loved the spectacle she presented riding up to the Tor, with her maidens strewing f lowers before The Chosen."

We turned a corner in the hall and it immediately widened. Two ornately carved double doors opened out to the beautiful courtyard I had noticed yesterday. Alanna continued whispering as we walked through the doors.

"Follow this walkway straight across the courtyard. See those doors over there?" I nodded. "We go through there, turn to the right and exit through the other set of opened doors. You will see the stables and your entourage."

I nodded again.

Alanna tugged on my hand. "Rhea, slow down. Remember that you are Mistress here. You are Epona's Beloved, High Priestess of Partholon, and you have performed this ceremony many, many times."

I followed her directions, and sooner than I was ready, we burst out of the main temple building and into the early-morning sunlight. My feet stopped, and I was grateful that Alanna didn't drag me forward, allowing me a moment to compose myself.

We had exited on the back side of the temple, which brought us to the rear of the stables. The corral was several yards in front of us. In front of the corral were probably half a dozen of my nymphet- maidens, scantly clad in gorgeous see-through white dresses (mine was the only outfit missing a top). They all carried baskets filled to overflowing with what I assumed must be rose petals. Epi and ClanFintan stood in the middle of them.

As if she could sense my presence, Epi's ears flickered in my direction and she let loose a vibrating whinny of welcome.

"Epona's Beloved…" Alanna gave my hand a last squeeze before releasing it. "You can do this. They are depending on you."

I took a deep breath, brought my chin up and stepped haughtily out of the doorway. If I was going to do it, I was damn sure going to do it right. As I approached the waiting group, I tried to keep my eyes on Epi, but I could feel Clan-Fintan's hot gaze almost as surely as I could feel my boobs jiggling merrily. I guess they must be happy to be free at last.

The nymphs executed their usual graceful curtsies, and Epi's whinny changed to a welcoming nicker as she thrust her velvety muzzle against my cheek. I smiled and kissed her softly.

"How have you been, sweet girl? I've worried about you, and missed you terribly."

Her nuzzle was a comforting reply.

"Have you missed and worried about me, too?" ClanFintan's deep voice passed through me like a hot finger that left a trail of shivers up and down my spine.

I turned to face him, leaning my back against Epi's warm side.

"I've missed you." I met his gaze with a teasing smile. "But

I'm very damn sure there's absolutely nothing physically wrong with you—so I needn't spend any time worrying. Or did you somehow hurt your hoof last night?"

My handmaidens tittered adorably, making me wonder if the "maiden" part of their title was just ornamental.

He leered rakishly at me, suddenly reminding me of a pirate, and took my hand in his, raising it to his lips. He kissed my palm and then my wrist, lingering at the spot where my pulse beat wildly.

"No..." He stepped close to me, still holding my hand in his. "We—I mean—*I* injured nothing last night."

His voice was an intimate caress, and for an instant I forgot all about my bared boobs. But Alanna's words brought me back to the real world. Well, relatively speaking.

"My Lady, are you ready to proceed with the ceremony?"

"Yes." I glanced at Epi, noticing how beautifully her tack sparkled in the clear morning sunlight. Her hackamore and saddle blanket were studded with carved gold (more damn skulls). Even the stirrups glistened and winked—and I wasn't surprised to notice jewels gleaming at me.

"Rhiannon, allow me."

ClanFintan put his arms around my waist and lifted me easily to Epi's back. I slid one leg over, and two of the maids stepped forward to guide my feet into the stirrups. I'd been right about the skirt. It was slit just right, so that it fell in lovely folds around Epi but left most of my legs bare. Oh, well, maybe my breasts wouldn't look so naked in comparison.

The nymphs scurried forward until they formed a double column in front of Epi. Alanna stood on the right side of Epi, ClanFintan on the left. I looked at Alanna and she nodded.

"Let's go," I said, and I clucked to Epi, who stepped forward like she knew what she was doing. The nymphets skipped ahead of us, moving gracefully like ballerinas. Every few feet one of them would grab a handful of rose petals out of her basket and strew them before Epi. I also noticed that every once in a while one of them would pirouette joyfully around. (My guess was they were happy because their boobs weren't naked, too, but I might have been wrong.)

We moved slowly out from behind the temple, heading in a northeasterly direction. The wall loomed before us in creamy glory. The rear exit was smaller than the grand front gates, and like the exit from the stables it seemed to disappear neatly back into the wall when it closed behind us. There was a softly rounded hill in front of us, and as Epi climbed over its crest a shout of welcome greeted us. We made our way down the hill, and I clutched her reins tightly so that no one could see how much my hands were shaking.

Before us waited a sea of people and centaurs. Behind the crowd I could see the wide Geal River, and as my eyes followed the river downstream, I could see the part of it that I had noticed from the air—it got even wider and formed a kind of harbor where several barges were docked.

We reached the edge of the crowd and they parted before the flower-strewing, cavorting maidens like I was a bare-breasted Moses. As we moved through them, the people spoke greetings with such warmth that I felt my stomach stop clench-ing. I spotted Dougal and Connor standing in a group of centaurs. Their shouts of welcome made my lips turn up in a happy grin. My hands stopped trembling. They were a great audience. I smiled back at them and waved (I wanted to look queenly, but more friendly than the Queen—she always looked so stiff, and, well, so British). We were making our way to a clover-covered hill. All around the base of it stood tall, ancient-looking stones that were the color of fog. My girls split up, and each moved to stand near one of the stones. Epi didn't hesitate. She picked her way between two of the stones,

climbing to the top of the hill. I was relieved to see ClanFintan and Alanna following us.

When Epi reached the top of the hill, she turned so that
the river was to our backs. The people faced us, and soon they
quieted respectfully. I looked down at Alanna. She glanced
pointedly over her shoulder to the river. I followed suit. The
water looked amazing. As we watched, the sun crested the trees
on the far bank, and its rays touched the water, causing it to
sparkle as if it were made of liquid jewels. When I could tear
my eyes from the incredible sight, I met Alanna's waiting gaze.

She nodded and I could barely make out her whispered,
"It is time."

Clearing my throat, I faced the adoring crowd—and sent
up a silent prayer to Epona, *If I really am your Chosen, please give
me the right words to say to these people.*

Using my best teacher voice, I opened with the obvious.
"Good morning!"

A ripple of laughter ran through the crowd, followed by an
enthusiastic "Good morning, Epona's Beloved!"

So far, so good.

"I come to you this morning with a twofold purpose."
Their silence awed me—I wished briefly that my students
could see what *really* paying attention looked like. "First, to
speak of an evil that threatens all of us, and, second, to ask
Epona's blessing for our cause." I looked intently at my crowd,
making eye contact with several of the listening people and
centaurs. "As you know, MacCallan Castle, and my father, have
been destroyed by Fomorians."

I paused here and allowed them to express their grief. After
they quieted, I continued.

"Epona has shown me that they have also overtaken
Guardian Castle." This time all that met my words was shocked
silence. I looked at their faces and couldn't add what I knew

about the women. I was pretty sure the centaurs knew the worst of it, but I didn't know just how far the knowledge had spread. I felt in my gut that I shouldn't go there right now. There would be time for that later, after the first shock of invasion had become easier to bear.

I turned and gestured to ClanFintan. He stepped closer to Epi.

"I have appointed my husband, ClanFintan, as Chieftain of Warriors." A cheer went up from the centaurs, which was echoed by the human men. I glanced quickly at Alanna and gave her a smug *see, there are more ways than one to inspire men* look (not many more, but…).

The cheers quieted and I continued. "ClanFintan has sent for the heads of all of the Clans and Herds." I made a quick decision that I hoped fervently would make sense. "After he meets with them, he will call for a meeting of all the heads of households." I mentally crossed my fingers that I was saying the right thing and using the correct terminology. "And he will inform them of our battle plans, so that all of you can prepare for war." I noticed nodding heads and I breathed a sigh of relief. "But the first step is for us to learn all we can from history about our enemy. If any of you have information, even if you think it is only from fairy tales meant to frighten children, come to the temple and ask for Alanna. She will take you to our historian so that this knowledge can be used. We will educate and arm ourselves because present fears are less than horrible imaginings." I sent up a silent thanks to Shakespeare for that great line.

"Remember, good has one enemy—evil. But evil always has two enemies—the good and itself." That sounded profound and I wished I could remember where I'd heard it, especially when several people cheered in agreement.

"Now, let us ask Epona's blessing." The crowd quieted. I

wondered what the heck I should do with my hands, and into my mind flashed a vision of the pot that had started this whole thing. Without conscious thought, I felt my body imitate Rhiannon's posture that had been captured so eloquently by the strokes of an unknown artist's brush. My body turned at the waist, so that I faced the sparkling river. My right arm lifted, palm up. I closed my eyes and focused on fragments of a Yeats poem that had been drifting through my mind like an answer to a prayer. My words rang bell clear as I recited the poet's beautiful verse.

> When day begins to break
> I count my blessings, good and bad,
> Being wakeful for your sake,
> Remembering the covenant we've always had,
> What eagle look your face still shows,
> While up from my heart's root
> So great a sweetness flows
> I shake from head to foot.

I paused, hoping Yeats wouldn't mind my tampering with his poem, and hoping this modified classroom would "get it."

"May Epona's blessing follow us daily, like a gentle mother guiding her children to safety. And may she help us to ensure that evil is never truly triumphant."

I opened my eyes and lowered my arm. Turning to face the crowd and smiling broadly, I finished with, "Live long and prosper!"

18

I breathed a sigh of relief as the people began to disperse. Before Epi retraced her steps, I looked at Alanna for approval. She was beaming, and I'll be darned if she didn't wink at me. The last bit of tension dissolved out of my shoulders. As Epi started back down the hill, I felt surrounded by love and acceptance.

"Rhiannon!" ClanFintan's sharp tone caught me by surprise. I pulled Epi to a halt and looked over my shoulder. He was behind me, still on the crest of the Tor. He wasn't looking at me, though; he was staring out toward the northern part of the temple grounds. His eyes squinted as he struggled to see, and he was taking in gulps of air through his nose, as if he was testing the breeze for a scent. Suddenly he pointed, and I followed his finger to the edge of the tree line.

"What is it?" Epi, too, began stirring nervously beneath me. It took very little urging from me to have her climb back to ClanFintan's side.

"In the northern wind I caught the scent of darkness." His tone made my skin crawl. "I have tasted this scent before." His attention was focused on the trees.

"At MacCallan Castle?" My voice trembled.

He nodded.

I heard a ripple in the crowd. Suddenly, centaurs surrounded us and members of my guard were rushing from the temple to join them.

ClanFintan began shouting orders. He spoke to the first of the temple guards to reach us. "There is something approaching from the woods. Get your mistress to safety, then gather the women and children within the temple walls."

Something inside me screamed, *Don't leave ClanFintan's side.* Without questioning this inner voice, I spoke.

"I stay with ClanFintan. Get the women and children to safety." My warriors saluted in acknowledgment and hurried away. Before he could say anything I looked into ClanFintan's eyes and repeated, "I stay with you."

"And I stay with Rhiannon." Alanna's resolute voice came from the other side of ClanFintan.

ClanFintan sighed, but didn't argue with either of us. His attention refocused on the distant tree line.

The gentle, seemingly harmless breeze caressed our faces. Dougal joined us on the Tor, and now Epi and I were sandwiched securely between the two centaurs, trying in vain to catch a glimpse of whatever they were scenting.

"It is mixed with centaur." Dougal's voice was grim.

ClanFintan's tight nod was his only answer.

"There!" Connor's shout shifted our line of vision from the middle of the tree line to an area closer to the river. Staggering, a lone centaur burst from the trees, moving swiftly, but erratically, in our direction.

"Ian!" Dougal's cry wrenched from his chest at the same moment I saw ClanFintan's start of recognition.

"Dougal, Connor, come with us. The rest of you position yourselves between the trees and Ian. If he has been followed, you must hold them off long enough for us to get him and ourselves to safety." He scooped Alanna off her feet and de-

posited her on his back. "Hold tightly, we will be moving fast."
She nodded. He looked at me. "Stay near me."

"I will." I grabbed a handful of reins and Epi's mane. I was
almost too scared to wish for a sports bra.

We exploded off the hill. I felt a thrill of pride at the way
Epi moved, which was immediately tempered with dread at
what we might be charging into.

Dougal was the first to reach the centaur. He came sliding
to a halt in time to catch the centaur's torso in his arms as he
stumbled, then collapsed to the ground.

I heard Alanna's intake of breath as ClanFintan, Connor, Epi
and I reached them. Dougal was on his knees trying to support
the centaur's bloody torso.

"Ian! By the Goddess!" ClanFintan's voice was anguished
and he, too, fell to his knees on the other side of the centaur.

Alanna slipped off his back and stood frozen, staring at the
gruesome scene.

"Have you been followed?" ClanFintan asked, and Ian
jerked his head from side to side.

"No—not—followed!"

"Breathe, Ian, then tell us what has happened."

Ian struggled to draw breath into his lungs as Dougal
murmured wordless sounds, trying to soothe him. The centaur
was covered with a horrible mixture of blood and sweat. He was
shaking violently. At first I didn't see any open wounds on him,
and wondered where all the blood had come from. Then his
body shifted as he tried to regain his feet, and I noticed an
enormous gash running from one side of his horse chest to the
other. I watched as his struggles brought a fresh torrent of blood
soaking his already darkened coat.

"No," ClanFintan and Dougal held him down. "Do not try
to get up."

I slid off Epi and tore the cloak off my shoulders. I knew

enough about horses and humans to know bleeding can be stopped by pressure. I looked at ClanFintan and he nodded in approval, then I crouched before the centaur and pressed the folded material against the terrible laceration.

"Connor, get a doctor!" I shouted at him. He spun around and ran back toward the temple.

Movement behind the fallen centaur's body caught my eye, and I glanced up to see a line of warriors positioning themselves between the trees and us. Knowing they were there, standing ready to confront whatever had done this to the young centaur, gave me a moment of calm in the midst of what felt like chaos.

I turned my attention to the bleeding centaur. Up close his wounds were worse than they had first appeared. He was so crusted with blood and foamy sweat that his human body and his coat looked as if they were a dark, dirty color. His body was riddled with slashes and cuts. I peered over his shoulder at the rest of him. Like a grotesque quilt, patches of silver-blond palomino coat were interspersed between pieces of crimsoned flesh laid open and oozing a mixture of blood and bodily fluids. At each new spasm of his muscles, blood seeped from the horrible gouges.

As he began to speak, my eyes flew back to his face, which was a terrible gray color beneath the blood and grime.

"Laragon…is…gone." He took deep breaths between each word, and his voice trembled. "The people…dead." He whispered the last word.

"The women, too?" ClanFintan asked.

Ian shook his head painfully. "No, they…did not…kill the women."

"The other centaurs?" ClanFintan's question hung in the air between them.

"Dead." The word fell from his torn lips into the terrible

silence of realized fears. Ian's body began to twitch violently and his eyes started closing.

"Ian! Stay with us!" Dougal's voice pleaded with him.

Ian forced his eyes to reopen.

"How many of them?"

"Many—too many." Suddenly, his breathing, which had quieted enough for him to speak, increased again. "Could… not…stop…" The centaur's quivering became uncontrollable and his words were lost as he strained to breathe.

I could feel the heat of his blood as it seeped through the material of my cloak.

"Dougal! Where are you?" Ian's eyes were open, but he flailed about like he couldn't see.

"Here! I am here, my brother." Dougal pulled the bloody torso closer, wrapping his arms protectively around Ian, trying to still his tremors. "All is well. You are safe now."

ClanFintan pulled me away from the dying centaur so that I was pressed securely to his side. I watched helplessly as red foam appeared at the corner of Ian's lips. I heard ClanFintan begin a chant, low and soft. As the sound of the chant reached Dougal's ears, I saw him look angrily at ClanFintan, who didn't pause in his litany, but shook his head sadly, affirming to Dougal what he must already know.

"ClanFintan." Ian's voice was amazingly clear as he spoke my husband's name.

"Yes—" ClanFintan worked the words into his prayer "—I am here. I will lead you home."

Ian's body relaxed as ClanFintan raised his face and voice to the sky, reciting words that seemed to place a calming spell over the centaur, blocking his pain and suffering.

I watched as Dougal closed his eyes and leaned his head against his brother's. I could see tears sliding down his face, mixing with Ian's blood.

"I love you, my brother. We will meet again in Epona's fragrant meadow." Dougal's quiet words carried through the air like a shout.

Ian's body convulsed once more, and then he sighed gently and was still.

ClanFintan continued his chant. Bowing his head and closing his eyes, he focused within himself. Gradually, his voice became softer and softer, until he, too, was still. Then he stood, pulling me gently to my feet and approached Dougal, who was clutching his brother and weeping openly.

"Dougal…" ClanFintan's voice was deepened with sorrow. "It is finished. He is gone."

Dougal opened his eyes and slowly looked up at his Shaman. "He was too young. It should not have happened." He sounded like a broken old man.

"True." ClanFintan's voice mirrored Dougal's loss.

I felt tears spill over at the corners of my eyes. I remembered how, just yesterday, Dougal had seemed so young and sweet, blushing shyly whenever I smiled at him. I moved from ClanFintan's side and shook out my bloodied cloak, spreading it softly over the worst of Ian's chest wound. Movement in the corner of my vision made me look up from the centaur's ravaged body. Alanna had followed suit. She, too, took her cloak from her shoulders and laid it respectfully over the centaur. Her face was wet with tears.

I touched Dougal's cheek lightly.

"He was very brave. Like his brother. I wish I could have known him."

Dougal pried one hand from his brother's shoulder and clasped my hand. "Would you ask Epona's blessing upon him, my Lady?"

"Of course."

Still clasping Dougal's hand in mine, I reached my other hand to find my husband's. I felt Ian's warm blood sticky between our joined palms. Alanna stepped to Dougal's other side and he reluctantly parted with his brother's body, taking her hand in his. Bowing my head, I let my eyes rest on the dead centaur.

"Epona, I ask your blessing upon this young centaur, who has died before his time. Touch him with your soft hands and help him never again to feel pain." I looked at Dougal's pale, strained face, and a small voice within me whispered the words I added. "And help us to remember that this world is the land of the dying, but the next world we go to will be the land of the living—where our souls will be joined again, never to be parted."

Dougal squeezed my hand gratefully before releasing it. He stood slowly, never taking his eyes from the body of his brother.

A flurry of hooves announced the arrival of Connor. He had a man astride him who leaped from his back before he had come fully to a halt. The man rushed to the fallen centaur's side. He carried a huge bag slung over his shoulder, like a leather duffel bag, which he had open and was searching through as he went to his knees in front of Ian.

He touched the centaur's neck and moved the robe away from his chest wound. I heard the man sigh heavily before he turned to face us.

The doctor spoke to Dougal. "My sympathies on your loss. If you allow, I will have his body cleaned, anointed and prepared for the bier."

"Yes," Dougal managed to say. "Yes." Then he looked at ClanFintan. "Our father and mother should be…" His voice trailed away.

"There will be time for that, son," ClanFintan said. "Connor, take Dougal back to the temple. I will see Ian is cared for."

Connor approached Dougal, and gently led him back toward the temple. Until he disappeared from sight, Dougal's head strained back to look at his brother's corpse.

I took all of this in, but I found it hard to stop staring at the doctor. I knew this man, or perhaps I should say I knew this man's mirror image—very well.

ClanFintan made a motion and an earsplitting whistle. The warriors who had been guarding us from what might have emerged from the forest immediately gave up their positions and headed to us.

"The centaurs will take Ian's body to your work site. I will be in your debt if you can clean the young one up, and make him presentable to his family." ClanFintan's voice sounded as if it had aged years in moments.

"There will be no talk of debt." Their eyes met and I saw a look of mutual respect pass between the two of them.

"Thank you," I said to him. "I know we can depend on you." My voice, though gruff from my recently shed tears, was filled with the warmth I felt for his mirror image. "Dougal deserves at least that much comfort."

"It will be done." I was taken back by the sudden look of coldness that sharpened his face as he answered me.

ClanFintan directed the centaurs to transport the Healer and follow him with Ian's body. The centaurs lifted the bloody corpse and began their sad journey back in the direction of the temple.

But instead of watching them, my eyes had been drawn to Alanna. She was staring at the Healer, and as he rode away I saw him send a furtive glance over his shoulder in her direction.

"Rhiannon, let us go back to the temple," ClanFintan said.

"Yes..." My voice sounded shaky.

I cleared my throat and called softly to Epi, who came obediently to me.

I smiled sweetly at the well-mannered mare, who had stood silently through the horrible death. As she came close to me, she nuzzled my face with her muzzle as if she needed comforting.

"It's over now, sweet girl," I crooned to her. I could see the damp trail tears had left down the sides of her face, more evidence that she was different from other horses.

ClanFintan's strong hands circled my waist and he lifted me to Epi's back. Then he turned and placed Alanna on his back. Together, we made our way slowly back to the temple.

19

ClanFintan led the way to the stables where we were met, not by my usual flock of maidens, but by several well-armed guards. First he helped me from Epi's back, and then he set Alanna gently on the ground.

"Have the lead warriors, centaur and human, gather in the temple audience chamber." He spoke a quick command to one of my guards.

The guard looked at me before moving to obey his order.

"I have appointed ClanFintan as Chieftain of Warriors. Why are you hesitating? Obey him as you would me." I made sure my voice carried.

The guard saluted me, and then turned to ClanFintan. "Yes, my Lord," he acknowledged before hurrying away.

I gave Epi one last pat and kissed her muzzle softly. "Take good care of her," I said needlessly to the guard who was waiting to lead her away.

"Of course, my Lady."

Alanna moved to my side. "Rhea, you must wash." She made a weak gesture at my bloodstained clothing and skin.

I looked down at myself, surprised to see blood smeared on my hands, breasts and the silky clothing that hid so little of my body. There was so much blood… My stomach suddenly felt queasy and my mind foggy, like I had taken too much Benadryl. I staggered as an overwhelming wave of dizziness washed over me.

"Rhiannon?" ClanFintan's voice was filled with concern.

I tried to blink the haze from my brain as I answered him. "It was horrible. That poor centaur…"

"Evil is only a shadow of good." He put his arms around me and cradled my shaking body against his. I felt his strength rush into me as the heat of his body enfolded me. "We walk in the light with good, while evil crouches, hiding in the darkness." His arms tightened around me as he continued. "But we will not allow it to continue to hide. We will burn it from its dark lair."

The wonderful mixture of the warmth and strength of his body, and the surety of his faith, combined to penetrate the fog of my shocked mind. I turned in his arms and spoke to Alanna.

"Before we meet with the Clan and Herd leaders, we need to talk to the teacher and find out exactly what is known about these creatures." I could feel ClanFintan's silent support. "Send for her to meet us in the library room that's attached to my chamber. What's her name, anyway?"

"*His* name is Carolan," she said.

Her cheeks had flushed pink again, and I gave her a questioning look, so she took a deep breath and continued.

"And he is not really a teacher, he is a historian." She paused, looking very uncomfortable. "And a Healer."

Suddenly it all made sense.

"He's the man Connor brought to Ian."

"Yes, Rhea." She looked decidedly sheepish.

"He seems a caring Healer." ClanFintan was oblivious to what was passing unspoken between Alanna and me. But he was a guy, so I didn't find that surprising.

I turned back to face ClanFintan and tugged on his arm until he bent for my quick kiss.

"Alanna and I are going to get cleaned up. Why don't you go get the Healer and meet us in my chambers."

"I will not be long." He touched my cheek lightly in parting.

As soon as we were alone, I said to Alanna, "My friend, we need to talk."

She nodded and followed me. Relieved that I was starting to figure out my way around, I headed back through the door that I knew would open to the courtyard. This time it was filled with chattering women and children, and ringed with warriors. At my entrance an emotion-laden silence fell. I understood what I must look like as I saw fear reflected in their faces.

I suddenly realized I had seen this kind of fear before in my classroom on a spring day when a student had been caught coming onto our campus with two loaded semiautomatic guns. I knew from that experience that hiding and prevaricating only made things worse; it works better to tell truth and deal with the ramifications of reality. So I held my hands to my sides, not attempting to hide the blood that stained them and the rest of my body. Squaring my shoulders, I met their frightened gazes with my don't-worry-I'm-in-charge look.

Bullshit is a prime weapon in any successful teacher's arsenal.

"A young centaur has been killed." A collective gasp filled the air. "We are not in immediate danger, but we must prepare for the enemy." I decided to use the same tactic I did in my classroom. When in doubt, give the general public something to do, it'll make them docile and useful. "I need your help. I want you to divide into groups. Some of you will begin preparing a place to care for the wounded—making linens into bandages, and that kind of thing." I saw several heads nod, and I felt encouraged. "My maidens will need help. Those of you who are the best cooks, please form a group and report to the kitchens. Warriors will need to eat well."

"My Lady! My sisters and I have carved and quilled arrows which we have bartered to the centaur traders." A voice came from the crowd.

"Who just spoke?" I yelled.

The women parted to let a tall, slender blonde step through the crowd. I felt my face break into a relieved smile as I recognized her resemblance to our school's best computer teacher. Now, *there* was a woman who knew how to organize.

"Your name?"

"Maraid, my Lady." She performed a cute curtsy.

I turned to one of my ever-present guards. "Send for the centaurs Dougal and Connor. Bring them to this courtyard. Have them instruct the women in what they can do to help support the warriors." I pointed to Maraid. "This woman, Maraid, will be in charge of organizing the women's groups."

The guard saluted and rushed away.

"The centaurs will tell you what they need." My teacher voice carried through the expectant silence. "By helping them you will help all of us—and I thank you for it." As an afterthought I added, "Epona's blessings on all of you." Then I beat a hasty retreat, with Alanna scurrying after me.

Rushing through the door that led to my private corridor, I breathed a relieved sigh and whispered to Alanna, "Do you think that was okay?"

She nodded, her head tilted toward mine as we hurried to the bathing-room door. "It gave them something to do. If they are kept busy, they have less time to be afraid."

"That's what I thought."

The guard opened the door for us. We stepped into the

bathing chamber, and I began stripping off my bloody clothes before Alanna could help.

"Are you certain you should have asked for Dougal, too?" Alanna was handing me a sponge and a bottle of bath soap. I sat on the pool's ledge and began scrubbing the blood from my body.

"I thought it would be best if he stayed busy." I submerged myself to rinse away the last of the blood. Alanna had laid a towel near the edge of the pool, and I stepped out of the water, wrapping myself in its softness.

Alanna was rummaging her way through one of the large wardrobes.

"Do you think you can find something that's not semitransparent *and* has a top to it?"

"I think you will find this acceptable."

She was holding a pretty piece of cream-colored material in her hands. I obediently held out my arms and she began her magical wrapping. I was pleased to notice the soft fabric wasn't see-through. She finished with a f lourish and another elaborate pin.

This outfit only showed off a nice expanse of my long legs, which I was used to, and, quite frankly, I enjoyed.

"I like it." We smiled. I turned back to the vanity and rummaged quickly through the plethora of jewelry. "The ability to accessorize is what elevates us from lower-life forms," I said in my lecture voice, choosing a pair of diamond-studded drops for my ears. "Like men." We shared a smug girlfriend look.

"Now, tell me about Carolan."

The smug girlfriend look fell off her face and was replaced by a bright f lush.

"Jeesh, quit blushing," I said. Which, of course, only caused her blush to intensify. I took her by the hand and led her to the bench in front of my makeup vanity. Pointing to the spot next to me, I said, "Sit and talk to me."

She sighed and looked into my steady gaze. And sighed again.

"Want me to help you?" She nodded. "You're in love with him."

Her eyes widened. She looked like Bambi.

"How did you—" I put up my hand to shush her.

"I'd like to say it's because of my wonderfully intuitive mind— or even because it's some kind of Beloved of the Goddess thing— but the truth is there's nothing at all mysterious about it." I smiled and playfully pushed my shoulder into hers. "He's the mirror image of Suzanna's husband, Gene." She blinked in surprise and I kept chattering. "They've been married forever and he still adores her like they were newlyweds. It's really pretty disgusting."

She was making little mewing noises, so I poured a goblet of wine from my unending supply and handed it to her. She drank deeply as I continued.

"Actually, it's weird how people mirror themselves—or however the hell I should say it." I poured myself some wine, too, and briefly contemplated grammatical problems caused by alternative dimensions before continuing. "In my old world Gene is a lawyer and a history professor. Suz and I call him Doctor-Doctor." I giggled. "She calls herself Mrs. Doctor-Doctor and says that his brains can kick sand in the face of any overmuscled Neanderthal pretty boy." I chased away the hilarious mental picture of Gene in a Speedo, which Suz's words never failed to conjure.

"What is a Neanderthal?" Alanna sounded on the edge of confused hysteria.

I frowned at her. "Don't worry about it. It just means she's crazy about him, too." She looked like that explanation helped. "You two aren't married in this world?"

"No!" She jumped as if the words held an electrical charge.

"Why not?"

Her eyes started to fill with tears.

Oh, great.

"Don't tell me he doesn't love you. I saw the way he looked at you out there."

"He loves me." Her voice was soft.

Then I remembered that Gene had been married once, briefly, when he was very young, long before he'd met Suzanna.

"Is he married to someone else?" I took her hand, ready to provide best-friend comfort and support.

"No! He loves no one except me."

"Then what the hell is the problem?"

"You." Her voice was a whisper.

"Me!" I glowered at her. "You mean that damn Rhiannon—not *me*."

"I am sorry. You are right. Rhiannon, and not you."

"I still don't understand."

"Once she discovered our feelings for each other, Rhiannon forbid the marriage. And she forbid the love. She would not let me be alone with him. Ever. She said I belonged to her and no other." She shrugged her shoulders sadly. "She said when she was finished with my services, Carolan could have me. That he could wait until then."

I was momentarily speechless.

"And so he has waited," she finished sadly.

"That selfish bitch." I shook my head at the absurdity of keeping them apart. "With all the damn men she had, you'd think she'd let you have one!"

"Oh, she would have let me have any other man. Just not Carolan."

"But you wanted no one except him."

She shook her head. We both drank our wine. Another thought popped into my head.

"Alanna, you don't have any children?"

"No, of course not. I have never been married."

I just stared at her and kept my mouth shut. How could I tell her that in another world she and the man she loves are happily married with three beautiful girls? I couldn't. Once again I felt the weight of Rhiannon's decisions hanging heavily on my conscience.

"He must hate me." I hadn't realized I'd spoken the words aloud until Alanna nodded slowly in agreement.

I stood abruptly. "Well, this I can fix. Marry him. Today."

Alanna shot to her feet. "Bu-but there is no time for a ceremony."

"What has to happen for you guys to get married?"

"A priest or priestess must speak an oath to bind us together."

"I'm a priestess. Right?"

She blinked like she was starting to understand. "Yes."

"So I can perform the ceremony," I said matter-of-factly.

"Yes," she repeated, looking faint. "But now cannot be the right time—we are readying ourselves for war."

"Sounds like a perfect time to get married." I looked hard at her. "You don't want to wait till after the fighting, do you?"

"No." I saw fear shadow her eyes.

"Then come on." I prodded her toward the door. "After this mess with the vampire-things gets cleared up, you can renew your vows." She wasn't saying anything, just nodding in a kind of dreamy way. "I'll throw a big party—it'll be great." I hastily decided that being the preacher was probably going to be almost as much fun as being the maid of honor.

We emerged from the bathing room and I paused only long enough to get my bearings. Striding purposefully to my chamber I was humming "Here Comes the Bride" to myself, and enjoying Alanna's dazed but happy expression. Being the Good Guy is a hell of a lot more fun than being the Bad Guy (something John Wayne certainly knew).

The maid who looked like Staci was just finishing supervising the laying out of my breakfast table. Smelling the enticing aroma of some kind of honeyed hot cereal made my stomach growl. I gave her an appreciative grin and remembered to call her Tarah. She surprised me by responding sluggishly, and she walked a little unsteadily as she left the room.

"You think the girls have been drinking too much?" I asked Alanna after the servants departed.

"What?"

"Never mind." She had that dazed expression still plastered on her glowing face, and I didn't think she'd heard anything I'd just said. And, anyway, sometimes wine creeps up on a girl (purely by accident). I was a real bitch to even mention it.

"Come on, eat something before you fall over."

We had just dug into breakfast (well, I'd dug in—Alanna was picking at her porridge) when two sharp raps sounded against my door.

"Come on in!" I yelled though a mouthful of sweet mush (it tasted kind of like oatmeal, only wilder—if that makes any sense).

My guards held open the doors and ClanFintan, followed by Carolan, entered the room. I had meant to watch Alanna's blushing reaction to her soon-to-be husband's entrance, but I found myself having what I liked to think of as a *Star Trek* Moment. ClanFintan's presence caught me like he was a big ol' black wormhole in space, and I was a little shuttle-craft. For you unknowing civilians, that meant he sucked me to him like a Hoover.

"Hi!" I sounded like friggin' Gidget.

He took my hand in his and raised my palm to his lips in a gesture that was becoming as familiar as it was intimate.

"Hello." His voice wrapped around me and made me shiver.

After his kiss, my fingers laced with his and he stroked my wrist slowly with his thumb.

"How is Dougal?"

A grimace of pain moved across his face. "It is not yet real to him." He shook his head sadly. "He and Ian were seldom separated. It will be difficult for him to bear." Then he squeezed my hand and said, "I hear you are keeping him busy. That was wise—it will give him less time for thought."

"I'm glad you're not upset with me for ordering around Dougal and Connor." I smiled into his eyes, and the rest of the world melted away. Really, and don't knock it till you've tried it.

Alanna cleared her throat and I remembered I wasn't a character in a book (sigh). I looked around ClanFintan's large body and saw that Carolan was standing quietly by the door, his eyes watching me warily. It was disconcerting to have a man who I would normally be friendly with treat me with such suspicion, so I decided that I would use the same tactic with him I had used with Alanna. I'd just act like myself and let him catch up—so to speak.

"Carolan, come on in." I smiled warmly as his eyes narrowed. "We need your expertise."

Alanna was sitting on one chaise facing me, and I was sitting on the other. ClanFintan had stopped within reach of the food (and of me). Carolan moved slowly to join us and I gestured in the direction of Alanna's chaise.

"Have a seat. Are you hungry?"

He halted next to the table, not looking at Alanna. "I would rather stand, Lady Rhiannon," he said stiffly. "And, no, I have broken my fast."

I shrugged. "Whatever, but we might be here for a while, so feel free to sit and pour yourself some wine. After all, grapes are my favorite breakfast fruit."

He was studying me like he thought I was a bomb getting ready to explode.

ClanFintan tugged on one of my curls. "You just like wine," he said as he looked pointedly at my half-empty goblet.

"It's medicinal," I teased up at him and playfully batted at his hand. Then I shot Carolan another smile, and asked in a conspirator's voice, "Am I right, Mr. Healer?"

"It has been called the nectar of life," he answered slowly.

"See!" I said to ClanFintan and he *hurmphed* at me. Turning to Alanna, I announced, "Then we'll have to make sure we have lots of wine at your formal wedding ceremony."

If possible, my words caused her to flush an even brighter shade of pink. But my words had the opposite effect on Carolan—his face blanched a horrible shade between white and gray; for a moment I worried that he would need a mortician instead of a priestess. Then he spoke through tightly clenched teeth. I felt ClanFintan stir at the obvious loathing in his words.

"Lady Rhiannon, I have known you capable of many hurtful acts, but this—" As his voice raised and his body began to tremble with repressed violence, ClanFintan dropped my hand and stepped protectively forward.

"Have a care what you say to my Lady, Healer." His voice was like death.

"If you knew what she really was, you would not defend her!" Carolan spat at the floor in my direction.

Alanna and I were on our feet as ClanFintan lunged forward so quickly that his large body was only a blur. Before I could say anything to stop him, he had forced Carolan to his knees.

"Ask her forgiveness," he growled.

"No!" I yelled as I pulled on ClanFintan's steel-like arm,

trying to get him to loosen his grip. "It's me who is sorry. I should have explained better—I just didn't think." ClanFintan looked confused, but he loosed his hold on Carolan, allowing him to stand.

Alanna was beside me, and I quickly grabbed one of her hands. Then, before he could spit at me again or anything, I grabbed one of Carolan's hands and placed hers in his.

"*You're* the one she's going to marry—today. You should never have been kept apart." I looked apologetically over his shoulder at my still ruffled husband and said, "I guess I wasn't very clear about that before, but I really didn't expect him to freak out."

Then I shifted my attention back to the almost newlyweds. Carolan's eyes were wide (and his mouth was kind of flapping open, but I thought it'd be rude to mention it). I nodded my head up and down and gave him an "it's true" look. He glanced at Alanna as if he was afraid she would turn into something horrible (in this world, you never knew), and as her misty smile of happiness registered in his mind, I heard him suck in a great gulp of air.

Before he could go all crazy again (and have my husband accidentally break something he might need later—like his neck), I put both of my hands over their joined ones, and jumped right in there with a makeshift wedding oath borrowed from Longfellow. "There is nothing holier in this life of ours than the first consciousness of love—the first fluttering of its silken wings—the first rising sound and breath of that wind which is so soon to sweep through the soul."

I squeezed their hands before letting go.

"I would say that now I've joined you, but I know that really you were joined long before today. So instead, let's just say I've finally made it official." I looked at Carolan's shocked face and continued, "Cherish her always." Then I stepped back and gave them a big smile. "Now you may kiss the bride!" What a great line.

But instead of kissing Alanna, Carolan dropped her hand and caught my eyes with his penetrating gaze.

"Who are you?"

20

I opened my mouth to answer, but Carolan cut me off.

"No! Do not try to disguise the truth with twisted words. I know Rhiannon. I have spent endless years hating her. I know her true nature is that of a spoiled, selfish child."

Alanna's sudden intake of breath made him turn to her. His face gentled.

"You know it is true, love." He touched her cheek in a lingering caress. "She rewarded your loyalty and sacrifice with jealousy and spite."

He turned back to me. His face had lost the wariness of before—now he just looked curious and pleased.

"I ask again, who are you? How could this happen?" He was studying me with a doctor's eye. "Physically you appear amazingly like her."

Well, I'd always known Gene was too smart for my own good.

He stepped closer to me, and I noticed that this time Clan-Fintan didn't move to stop him. Actually, the centaur had become very still. He was watching me with the same analytical eyes Carolan was using. Only *he* didn't appear very happy.

"Your hair may be a little shorter." He barked a quick laugh.

"And your speech patterns are certainly odd. But you are remarkably similar."

"Carolan, you are mistaken!" Alanna suddenly interrupted, not giving him time to say anything else.

This time I did the silencing.

"Let him finish, Alanna," I said firmly.

Carolan looked into my eyes again. "You are not Rhiannon. You may be Epona's Chosen, but you are not Rhiannon. When I look into your eyes I do not see my old enemy. You do not have the evil within you that she had."

I looked at Alanna's worried face and sighed. "I can't do this anymore," I said to her. My eyes sought ClanFintan's. "I don't want to lie to you anymore."

He didn't make any motion or sound. His face had become the guarded mask I had struggled against when we had first met.

But I couldn't take back what I had said. And, truthfully, I didn't want to. I'm me, and I was tired of being mistaken for some other bitch.

"I am not Rhiannon." I heard Carolan's satisfied grunt, but I didn't look at him. My eyes remained locked with my husband's. "My name is Shannon Parker. This is hard to explain. It's hard for *me* to understand, and *I'm* the person it's happened to. I come from a different world—a world where many of the people are the same, or as similar as a mirror image or a shadow would be, but the world itself is very different." I paused, wishing ClanFintan would say something. He stayed silent but nodded like he wanted me to continue. "Somehow Rhiannon found out about my world and she figured out how to trade places with me. It all centered around a pot that had an image of her on the front of it. From the second I saw the pot, everything changed." I searched for words. "I had no idea what was happening. It seemed like a terrible accident.

Actually, I thought I was dead at first." My eyes pleaded with him to understand. "Remember the day of our marriage? I could hardly speak because I had lost my voice?"

He nodded again.

"It was from the…I don't know what to call it…the *trading* of worlds."

Alanna stepped forward and stood by my side. "She is not Rhiannon, and we are the better for it."

"How can something that is based upon a lie be better?" ClanFintan's voice sounded flat and expressionless.

"But it was not her lie! It was mine." Alanna hurried on when I tried to shush her. "She never wanted to pretend, but she did it because I told her the people needed her." She looked at me, causing my eyes to break ClanFintan's cold gaze.

"I wanted you to tell ClanFintan, but I was afraid. At first I was afraid for myself, for what might happen if I was blamed for Rhiannon's disappearance. Then, after I grew to know you, I was afraid the people would turn upon you if they thought you an impostor." She looked pointedly at ClanFintan and continued, "Then I worried that those who were close to you would hurt you if your identity was discovered. But I have since realized that our Goddess must be working in this exchange, and that we all have been the better for it." She took my hand in hers as she spoke directly to the centaur. "If you are angry at being deceived, turn that anger upon me. And, Shaman, before you do, look closely at the gift you have been given. What would your future hold if you truly were hand-fasted with Rhiannon?"

Carolan's distinctive laugh surprised me. He put his arms around his new wife and hugged her. Then he, too, faced the centaur.

"*His* life? Rhiannon's vindictive nature has touched all of our lives. I will always be grateful that she has banished herself."

He smiled at me, and briefly lifted my hand to his lips. "Welcome, my Lady, Beloved of Epona. May our world bestow upon you the blessings you have so richly brought to us."

I returned his smile before looking nervously back at ClanFintan.

When he began speaking, his voice was contemplative but still emotionless.

"I knew you were different. Your manner of speech was odd, but at first I told myself that I had never really known you, and perhaps you were simply unique because you were Epona's Chosen." He looked at Carolan. "But you are right. I realized she lacked Rhiannon's malicious nature some time ago."

Carolan nodded in agreement. ClanFintan's gaze captured mine once more.

"I said nothing because I hoped that you would trust me enough to confide in me." His voice had finally regained its emotion, and I was upset to hear the sadness that filled his words.

"I do trust you! It's just that there didn't seem to be a right time. And then, well, I didn't tell you because I didn't want to chance losing your love." My voice had become a whisper.

Yes, damnit. I loved him. It was all so romantic I wanted to puke.

But, spend a night with a shape-shifter who is, well, hung like a horse, and see what happens to you.

Besides all that—he's one of the good guys, like John Wayne and James Bond. And I've always been a sucker for the good guys.

So, I stood there trying to blink away the tears that were threatening to spill from my eyes. ClanFintan sighed heavily and closed the space between us before I could start bawling.

He touched my face and cupped my chin in the warmth of his hand.

"My love is something you will never lose." He bent and kissed me softly, then smiled at my undoubtedly goofy expression. "My patience, perhaps, but never my love."

I wanted to throw my arms around him and bury my face in his heat, but I could feel Alanna's and Carolan's eyes boring joyfully into our romantic interlude.

So I tugged him down to me and reciprocated with a quick kiss and a whispered *"I adore you"* against his mouth.

About that time my stomach growled loud enough for the whole friggin world to hear, which caused ClanFintan to laugh as he propelled me back to the table. First he reclined, and then he pulled me down so that I could perch in front of him on the side closest to the food. It's a good thing the chaises were obviously made for at least two (I didn't want to spend much time contemplating the uses Rhiannon had probably found for them). ClanFintan wrapped an arm around my waist and pulled me snugly back against him.

"Have a seat, guys," I said contentedly.

This time Carolan didn't hesitate. Instead, he guided Alanna to the chaise and sat next to her. I noticed that he kept one hand always touching her, as if he was afraid she would disappear.

"I'll bet you really haven't eaten, have you?" I asked Carolan through a bite of some kind of yummy sweet roll.

He grimaced. "Actually, I missed the blessing this morning because I was helping to birth twins into the world. You are correct—I have not broken my fast."

"Eat! There's always plenty." I glanced over my shoulder at ClanFintan and teased, "It's like they make enough to feed a horse!"

Carolan almost choked on his porridge, and Alanna, who

was, by now, more used to my humor, had to pound him heartily on the back.

ClanFintan didn't say anything, but while our guests were busy he bit me on the shoulder.

"Yikes!" I gave a little scream. But when the two of them looked questioningly at me, ClanFintan had his deadpan face on again.

I shouldn't have been surprised. I already knew he was a biter.

"Just exactly what should we call you?" Carolan chewed thoughtfully while he studied me.

"Yes." ClanFintan tilted his head so he could study my face. "You said in your world you were called…" He hesitated, thinking "Shannon Parker." He made the name sound beautiful and exotic. I wished momentarily that we could throw caution to the clichéd wind, and he could call me by my real name, always.

Then I woke up. Figuratively speaking.

"Shannon is my name, but I don't think it would be very smart for you guys to start calling me something different. Unless…" I thought I might as well ask. "Do you think we should tell the people who I really am?"

"No!" Alanna, Carolan and ClanFintan all spoke at once.

There was a momentary silence (I guess while they contemplated the horror of letting the general populace know I was me), and then Carolan cleared his throat. We looked expectantly at him.

"Um, I cannot see any good that could come of informing the people. Especially at this volatile time." He paused and looked searchingly at Alanna. "And it is clear she *is* Epona's Chosen?"

"Yes, she is the Beloved of Epona," Alanna agreed, nodding her head vigorously.

Carolan looked relieved. "Then there is no point in upsetting the structure of the temple, and accordingly the people, by informing them of this—" he searched for words "—fortuitous change."

ClanFintan and Alanna mumbled a series of agreements.

"Well, okay," I said, "but Rhiannon did a lot of things I don't agree with."

"Good!" ClanFintan's exclamation made us laugh.

I kissed him lightly on the cheek.

"Rhea, the people love you." She smiled in the direction of my centaur. "And your warriors fear you, which is why they do not speak freely about Rhiannon's *habits*." Her gaze shifted back to me. "Be yourself. That will correct Rhiannon's errors."

That sounded good to me.

"But what do we call you?" ClanFintan asked.

"I like what Alanna calls me. Rhea. It's not Rhiannon—it's something that's distinctly me—but it's not so different that it would cause a big problem."

They nodded assent, and we all chewed happily for a while.

"Too bad everything's not as easily solved as that," I succinctly said.

They mumbled yes to that, too.

Unfortunately, I couldn't let it rest at that. I mean, if I was going to live in this world we were going to have to get rid of those vampire-things.

"Okay, Carolan…" My voice forced his attention reluctantly from his new wife. "Tell us what you know about the Fomorians."

"They are evil incarnate."

"No kidding?" I mean, hello, we knew that already.

He barely blinked at my interruption, and proceeded in his history-teacher lecture mode.

"They were a species that came from the far east."

I felt ClanFintan's startled reaction, which made me remember that the map that zapped me had shown all the land to the east of the river as centaur lands.

"Yes, before centaurs dwelt in the grassy plains." Carolan acknowledged my husband's chagrin, then continued, "The legends are obscure. At first there was very little contact between the people of Partholon and the Fomorians. But there seems to have been a long drought, followed by a great fire on the grasslands where the Fomorians dwelt. The fire could not be contained. The Fomorians were in peril of being incinerated, and they came to our ancestors for help. They needed to cross over the Geal River, which they said would be impossible without aid from Partholon."

"Huh?" I gave him a confused look.

"According to legend, Fomorians must stay connected to the soil of the earth. It is to them their life's blood, so they cannot cross running water."

"Wait a second—they have wings. If they have to stay connected to the earth, how can they fly?"

"Excellent point." He smiled. "There is never any reference to them actually *flying*. They were described as—" he cleared his throat and squinted his eyes, searching for the exact words "—gliding demons. Not *flying* demons. I assume their wings function like a flying squirrel's wings. Not real, birdlike pinions, just an apparatus that helps to manipulate the wind."

I remembered their horrible, ground-eating strides and had to agree with him.

Carolan continued, "The people of Partholon met and decided it would be an abomination to allow them to die in the flames, or to die of famine after the fire burned itself out. So an enormous bridge was constructed over the Geal River, one that was fashioned of timbers layered with soil, then more timbers and more soil. Actually, the remains of that bridge can be found not far from here." We just stared at him until he took a gulp of wine and spoke again. "The Fomorians crossed over and our two races attempted to live in peace together."

"I have only heard that the Fomorians were stories made up to frighten small children." ClanFintan interrupted Carolan's lecture. "Why is it not known that the people of Partholon aided them to come here?"

"There were very few written records of the Fomorians. Only scribes would know that the stories even exist, and most of the records are so ancient they are difficult to decipher, so few scribes bother to study the crumbling tomes."

ClanFintan's look told me scribes must be celibate—or girls (or nerds) or something.

As if reading my mind, Carolan chuckled. "Unless someone with scribe training happens to be a historian with too much free time and curiosity."

Alanna squeezed his hand and they smiled sweetly at each other.

He continued, "So, you see, the only legends that survived as oral tales for the bards to tell were those that originated after the war."

All three of us looked surprised. It was a relief not to be the only clueless one this time.

"Yes, the oral legends only tell about what happened after the Fomorians crossed the Geal River."

I thought about how things worked in my old world and decided that it all made sense. I mean, please, there were numerous politicians who would have thought life would be much easier if most of the people couldn't read or write (or hire lawyers and get on *60 Minutes*).

"So what do the oral legends tell us?" I piped in.

"The Fomorians were weakened, and their numbers were

few, but their true nature was soon known. It is written that they were a race of demons, generally monstrous and hideous, who dabbled in dark powers." He held up his hand and counted off items on his fingers. "They liked to drink the blood of humans. They were physically discomforted if they walked about in the sunlight. They could not cross running water. They thought themselves beyond all laws of nature and Epona." He grimaced.

I thought they sounded a lot like Fidel Castro, but that comparison would take a seriously long time to explain, so I kept quiet.

"Legends say a war ensued. The Fomorians were small in number. They were defeated, forced through the pass in the Trier Mountains, and banished to the far north. Then Guardian Castle was erected to stand as sentinel of the pass. It has blocked the pass for generations."

"Not anymore," I said.

"The northland should have destroyed them," Carolan replied. "It is too cold and desolate there. The sun shines brightly, but it gives off no heat. They should have disappeared into the bad dreams of children."

"Well, *they're back*." I said it with the *Poltergeist* inference. It was pretty safe to assume they hadn't seen the movie—but they understood the implication.

"How can they be killed?" ClanFintan's voice cut the air between us.

"Unfortunately, they are remarkably resilient. Cut off their heads. Burn them. That will kill them." He looked apologetically at the centaur. "Legend says they are difficult to kill."

"Did the legends say anything about them mating with humans?" I thought I should inquire.

"No!" Carolan looked shocked. "There were not many of them, but they had females of their own kind."

"Well, they still have females," I said, remembering the winged things that had grabbed the fetus out of that poor woman's womb. "But it doesn't look like they're making babies with them. They're making babies with human girls and letting the, uh, fetal *things* rip out of the mothers' wombs."

Carolan paled.

"That is what is happening to the women." ClanFintan's statement was like a death knell.

"Then they are multiplying," Carolan said quietly.

That sounded bad.

"Yes," ClanFintan answered. "Before Ian died he reported that there were many of them."

"You have to stop them." Alanna's voice was verging on shrill.

Carolan put his arm around her in a gesture that was so familiar to me that, for an instant, I could almost believe I was back in my condo, and Gene and Suz had stopped in for brunch. It was an eerie feeling, this blending of two worlds, and it made me disconcertingly dizzy. I had to avert my eyes…and my gaze was caught by the rear end of my husband—who was most definitely half horse. Which gave me a very decisive reality check. This world didn't play by the same rules I was used to. No cars. No planes. No TV (thank God) where violence was relegated to the realm of what happened only to other people.

For a moment I was overwhelmed by the reality of the situation. I didn't know what the hell I was doing, and I had been thrust into a position of authority at a time when these people really needed someone who knew what the hell she was doing. I closed my eyes and rubbed my forehead, a sure sign I was getting a tension headache.

And my husband's strong arms wrapped around me, pulling me securely back against his warmth. I felt the tension begin to drain from me as I remembered that I was not alone. I opened my eyes and smiled up at him.

"They were defeated once before," he said with finality. "They will be defeated again."

"And this time Partholon is allied with the mighty centaur warriors," Carolan reminded us.

ClanFintan bowed his head in acknowledgment of Carolan's compliment and gave me a rakish leer. "Aye, there are few things a centaur and a human together cannot accomplish."

Alanna giggled and I think I blushed. But I got his point. We needed to work together to get rid of the Fomorians. I could either sit here and worry, letting other people (and half animals) think for me, or I could act. I have always been a firm believer in facing problems. Experience teaches that there are very few bad things that will simply go away if they're ignored (a concept teenagers have a difficult time grasping). Quite frankly, I'd rather do something and be wrong than sit around and grow moss (which really couldn't be very attractive anyway).

"So they just attacked Laragon Castle," I said. "If I remember from my one look at the map of Partholon, the only things close to Laragon Castle are a big lake, and—" I cut myself off as I remembered what was on the other side of the lake.

"The Temple of the Muse!" Alanna's voice held the horror I was feeling.

"Ohmygod, aren't they just a bunch of women?" I asked Alanna.

Carolan answered me. "Yes. There are nine Incarnate Goddesses. Each is a mistress of her particular craft." His tone was sober and he sounded worried as he explained, "Each of them also has many attendants and neophytes. The Temple of the Muse is where the most beautiful and talented young women of Partholon are schooled in the arts of dance, poetry, music, the sciences, etcetera. Women who successfully complete their training are respected for their intelligence and education, as well as their grace and beauty." Then he added, "Rhiannon was trained by the Muses."

"But don't they have guards like I have here?" This was looking really bad.

"No. Epona is a goddess of warriors. It is only logical that guards should surround Her Chosen. The Muses are not warriors; they are teachers of art and beauty and science. They have no need of guards."

"They do now." My stomach felt sick. An image of my wedding celebration flashed through my mind, and with it came a mental picture of the woman who was a mirror image of my friend, Michelle. As Muse of the Dance she had been exquisite—beautiful and alluring. I didn't want to think about what the creatures would do to a temple filled with gorgeous women like her.

"Come on." I stood up. "Let's go in there and look at that map." I gestured to the door that led to the library room. "We have to figure out some way to stop them from getting any more women."

PART THREE

1

Alanna rolled the map down and I stood close enough to see it without actually touching it. Our eyes traced a path from Guardian to Laragon Castle. Laragon was a huge structure situated south of the Trier Mountains. The northerly tip of Loch Selkie jutted up to almost divide the land that stretched the distance between Laragon and the Temple of the Muse. The Temple of the Muse had been built on the western bank of the thick Calman River. Following the river south after it joined with the Geal River brought my eyes back to the elaborate structure marked *Epona's Temple.* Ufasach Marsh filled most of the area between the Muse and Epona, as did the large Loch Selkie.

"Can we assume the Fomorians are still at Laragon Castle?" Carolan asked.

"If they follow the same plan they used after the destruction of MacCallan Castle, they will have left Laragon and returned to Guardian Castle." ClanFintan stepped closer to the map and studied it silently before he continued, "But that is, perhaps, because MacCallan Castle was built in such a distant location. It might not have been convenient to their invasion plans for them to use it as a base from which to operate. I have visited Laragon. It is well located, and though it is not as easily defended as this temple, it could be used as a secondary site from which to launch an invasion."

That didn't sound good for our side.

ClanFintan motioned to the western side of the map, where MacCallan Castle stood its lonely watch over the B'an Sea.

"By neutralizing MacCallan Castle, they have wiped out the only concentrated threat from the northwest. Very convenient for them, whether they return to Guardian or remain at Laragon." He shrugged his shoulders. "So, even if they did not remain at Laragon, it was still an excellent strategy to first destroy MacCallan."

I could tell by the briefing-like tone of his voice that he was trying to take the emotion out of the situation and look at it with objective eyes.

I stepped a little closer, without touching the map.

"Is this map accurate?"

"Yes, the placement of structures and natural landmarks is accurate. But, of course, things appear much closer on the map than in actuality, and the castles and temples are not to scale." Carolan smiled. "It is a lovely map, but the weaver took artistic license when it came to the structures."

Personally, I thought it was beautifully done and couldn't see what difference dressing up the buildings made. Then I remembered that Gene had always been a stickler for detail. Guess borderline obsessive-compulsive tendencies stay consistent in mirror images.

It made me wonder about *my* mirror image and my own tendencies. (Note to self: think about being less sarcastic. Later.)

I refocused on the map. After the Geal River looped around beneath Epona's Temple, and continued to the west, it widened into something that looked as if it could rival the Mississippi. South of the river was forestland, and I noticed a structure labeled *Woulff Castle* nestled amidst the forest, which eventually gave way to more of the sweeping Centaur Plains.

Following the river west, there was a small area labeled the *Blue Tors,* and then I encountered a huge structure named *McNamara Castle* situated in the far southwest corner of the map. Like MacCallan, it was near the coast, but it had the added benefit of being smack in the middle of where the Geal River resplit, with one branch renamed Clare, before it dumped into the sea. So, for all technical purposes, McNamara Castle was isolated by water.

"I guess the Fomorians wouldn't be interested in that castle." I gestured toward the water-locked structure. "Or probably that one, either." I pointed at Woulff Castle.

"The forest men of Woulff Castle are mighty archers," Carolan said thoughtfully.

ClanFintan nodded his agreement.

"And how about that other castle?" I asked.

ClanFintan snorted. "Old McNamara is almost as cantankerous as the wilderness over which he is Chieftain."

Carolan looked as if he agreed. "He certainly is a land unto his own."

"Makes an excellent brew of whiskey, though." ClanFintan sounded appreciative.

"Well, that's certainly in his favor," I added.

Alanna looked surprised. "Rhiannon could not tolerate the taste of whiskey. She said it was a common drink."

"I adore a good single malt." Ha! All of us looked pleased that my tastes didn't always run parallel to Rhiannon's. And I felt my psyche relax a little.

"I take it we don't have to worry about Fomorians targeting either of those castles."

They shook their heads.

"Would they send us some warriors?"

Carolan and ClanFintan exchanged glances.

"Woulff can probably be counted on for aid," ClanFintan said, and Carolan seemed to agree.

"McNamara?" I asked.

ClanFintan shrugged his shoulders. "Perhaps, if we made it worth the old Chieftain's while."

"How about letting him know he would be helping to save lives?" I realized I sounded disgruntled.

"We can send him word." ClanFintan didn't sound very sure of the outcome of the request.

I had a sudden inspiration. "Hey, with that word, be sure to make it clear that the Fomorians are stealing human women, and that they've already had a taste of West Coast girls. And they like them. A lot."

"That would anger him." ClanFintan smiled.

"Good," I said. "Just don't mention the little detail about their aversion to water. And it wouldn't hurt to emphasize the woman-stealing-raping-and-impregnating point to Woulff, too."

The four of us smiled at each other in full agreement.

Before we could turn our attention back to the map, two sharp raps sounded on the door to my outer chamber.

"I will see to it," Alanna said. She kissed Carolan softly on the lips before leaving the room. His eyes followed her hungrily.

Watching them I suddenly felt like I was being a little too voyeuristic, so I turned my attention back to the map.

"I realize I know next to nothing about any of this war stuff, but it seems to me that we need to try and box them in someplace."

"Guardian Castle could hold off a siege indefinitely. It was built to be self-sufficient and to withstand attack." ClanFintan studied the map as he spoke.

"I'd like to know how the hell they broke through the castle to begin with," I mumbled to myself. "Okay, from this map Laragon Castle is very close to the northern end of Loch Selkie. Right?"

"Yes," Carolan answered.

"How far are the mountains from the castle? They look like they are close." I felt an idea forming.

"Very near. The southern part of the range ends at the edge of the castle's grounds." Carolan's voice sounded wistful. "It is a beautiful castle, built in a valley filled with green clover and wildflowers. Laragon is where we get our dyes and perfumes. All along the base of the mountains stretch field after field filled with flowers and berries."

I tried not to get distracted by the lovely image he was painting, and the thought of what it might look like now.

"But Laragon can only be approached from either the east or west. That is, if you're unable to approach it from over the Loch."

"Yes." ClanFintan's voice sounded as if he had captured the essence of my incompletely formed idea. He stepped up to the map, touching it with sweeping gestures as he spoke.

"If we could be certain that the main force of the Fomorians was at Laragon Castle, we could surround them from here." He brought his hand in a trail from Epona's Temple up past the Muse to the east side of Laragon. "And here." This time his hand traced a path around the Loch's left edge to approach Laragon from the west. "And, finally, here." Clan-Fintan drew his fingers from the south bank of the Loch, almost directly north of Epona's Temple, up the middle of the huge lake, to enter Laragon grounds from the south. "Our combined forces could easily surround and entrap them at Laragon. There would be no escape. The castle is well built and conveniently situated, but they could not last through a protracted siege or combined invasion—not like Guardian Castle could."

"It would work—" Carolan rubbed his chin thoughtfully "—but only if the majority of the Fomorian force was at Laragon. If enough of them remained at Guardian Castle, they could flank us, divide our warriors and destroy us in pieces."

"So, the trick seems to be to make sure a lot of them need to be at Laragon." I thought aloud. Suddenly, the idea that had been half-formed in my mind crystallized, like it had been whispered into my subconscious by…well…a goddess. Reluctantly, I spoke the idea aloud.

"I…um…" I cleared my throat, which felt rather thick. "I think I may have a way of getting them interested in being at Laragon."

ClanFintan and Carolan looked at me respectfully, as if I really might know what the hell I was doing.

"It seems that the main focus of their invasion is to collect women." I paused, waiting for them to "yep" me. They nodded in agreement. "Do you think they know that the Temple of the Muse is filled with beautiful women?"

"Probably not," Carolan answered. "It was not until this century that the Muse built a combined temple and school. In ancient times the nine Goddess Incarnates traveled throughout Partholon, instructing young women at each of the major castles."

It was weird to hear Carolan talk like these were modern times. But, then again, civilization doesn't necessarily depend on things like dishwashers and computers. After all, they did have wine, toilet paper and jewelry. That's modern enough for me.

"What do you think the Fomorians would do if they got the idea that there was a temple just to the east of Laragon filled with gorgeous, fertile, nubile women?"

"They would attack that temple." Carolan's voice sounded certain.

"And what would they do if they thought the temple was guarded by a troop of centaurs?" I smiled at my virile husband.

"They would come in force to attack the temple." ClanFintan's eyes widened as he answered.

"And it would be logical to assume that their force of warriors would use Laragon as headquarters instead of the more distant Guardian Castle." Carolan's voice was warm with appreciation. "It is an excellent plan—except how are we going to plant the idea within the Fomorian camp?"

That was the part that made me uneasy, but, once again, I felt a slight subconscious prod. This Beloved of the Goddess stuff might drive me to drink. How unfortunate.

"I think I can do that," I said slowly. The centaur and the man looked at me like I was Santa Claus.

"How?" they said almost together.

"It's something that happens during the…dream things." I sighed again. "The first time it happened was when I saw my dad, I mean, Rhiannon's dad, that awful night. I knew the creatures were attacking the castle, and I had to warn him. Her dad heard me, kind of. Anyway, he knew what I was saying, and he looked like he could almost see me, or sense me, or something. It happened again the night I traveled to Guardian Castle, twice." My voice must have reflected the fear I felt in the remembrance, because ClanFintan moved to my side so that I could lean against him. With his arm around me I felt better—not great, but better, and able to continue. "A young girl sensed me. And then there was that…thing. The leader." I searched my memory for the name, and it came easily to me—like it had been whispered into my mind. "Nuada. He more than sensed me, he knew I was there. And he said he had known I was at MacCallan Castle, too. If I had tried, I know I could have spoken to him. And I know he would have heard me—or at least understood what I was trying to say to him." A shudder went through my body and I leaned more heavily into ClanFintan's warmth. "That's how they'll know. I'll tell them."

"I do not want you to be in danger." ClanFintan's deep voice rumbled over my head.

"Didn't you guys say Epona is a warrior goddess?" I asked, looking at Carolan.

"She is—" Carolan's gaze met mine "—and Epona makes certain those who belong to her are protected." He looked as if he wanted to say more, but I interrupted him.

"I'm counting on that." I sounded much calmer than I felt. The sensation of subconscious prodding was back, and I spoke the thoughts that came to my mind. "But we need to hurry. How soon can the combined forces be ready, and how long will it take for them to reach Laragon?"

ClanFintan studied the map before he answered.

"Within five days the majority of the forces can be gathered. With hard marching, we can be in position to attack Laragon in two more."

"Seven days." A week had never seemed so short—or so long. "Then I need to start tonight," I mumbled, more to myself than to my husband.

"Start tonight? What do you mean?" ClanFintan sounded worried.

Carolan saved me the trouble of explaining. "She cannot persuade the leader…"

"Nuada," I supplied.

"Nuada—" he nodded his thanks and continued his explanation to ClanFintan "—with only one manifestation. She must appear to him more than once, as a taunting vision with which he will become obsessed, until he is compelled to follow her."

"Is Epona talking to you, too?" I smiled at him.

"It seems she must be," he replied.

"I still do not like it." My husband didn't sound happy.

"Epona will look after her spirit. You will protect her body." Carolan reached up and put his hand reassuringly on the centaur's shoulder.

"And I don't particularly like it, either," I said. "But this world doesn't have telephones, or a media that can plaster the facts on the nightly news—so it seems I'm stuck doing things the old-fashioned way. Myself."

To their credit, they didn't comment on my otherworldly vocabulary.

"I will be with you every moment." ClanFintan hugged me tightly.

"As will I," Carolan seconded him.

"I will, too." Alanna stepped back into the room. "But what are telephones and the nightly news?"

2

I laughed and pulled a face at Alanna. "Telephones and the nightly news are very effective demonic forces. Be happy we don't have them here."

"I will," she replied with such seriousness she made me laugh all over again.

Carolan took her hand and pressed a lingering kiss to her palm. "What was the interruption, love?"

Worry creased her forehead, and as she answered she looked back and forth between Carolan and me.

"An illness has broken out in the temple." She spoke slowly. "Several of your maidens complained last week about not feeling well after returning from a retreat." Alanna looked apologetically at me. "I did not think much of it. The maidens usually made excuses to stay away from Rhiannon." I nodded my head in understanding, and she continued, "Then I was so busy, first with the new Rhiannon—" we grinned at each other "—then with the people who poured into the temple, that I gave the maidens' complaints no credence and admonished them to serve the Goddess with more diligent spirits."

"I remember you mentioning to me that the girls were

playacting, and I said I thought they just needed a break from their babysitting load," I chimed in.

"Yes, well, it seems we both were mistaken." The lines over her forehead had become even more pronounced. She turned to her husband. "Many of the maidens are very ill, as are several of the children and old women. They need your attention." She turned back to me, "And your prayers."

"Of course, love." Carolan kissed her on the cheek, and let his thumb brush her worried forehead in a light caress. I could see her relax at his touch.

"I'd better come, too, and see what the heck's wrong with them." Alanna looked surprised, but pleased, at my pronouncement.

"You do not wish to attend the meeting with the warriors and explain our plan?" ClanFintan inquired. I loved the way he looked at me—all serious, like he really expected me to want to speak to a room filled with smelly old warriors about stuff I really didn't understand. Actually, I'd almost rather solve math problems. Almost.

"No, honey." I tried to look sorry. "You go ahead and explain it to them. I'd better be sure my maidens are okay."

"If you feel you must, I am certain the warriors will understand."

Sometimes he reminded me of Worf (as in the Klingon from *Star Trek The Next Generation,* for you civilians).

"When you finish with your maidens, please be sure to join us. You will be good for the warriors' morale."

Now, *that* I did like. Just like Marilyn Monroe.

"Not a problem." I tugged on his arm and he bent down for my kiss. "Knock 'em dead, big boy," I purred. He looked confused, but he returned my kiss, nodded at Carolan and Alanna, and trotted his cute butt from the room.

Attempting my best bad imitation of Madeline Kahn as Lilly

VonSchtupp in *Blazing Saddles,* I sighed dreamily and said, "What a nice guy."

Carolan ignored me completely. Alanna rolled her eyes and said, "Are you coming?" over her shoulder as they turned and left the room.

I guess I needed to get some new material.

I hurried after them, but they were waiting at the door so that I could exit before them and maintain the façade of bitchy goddess-in-charge. Not that I minded. Just outside the door a guard waited for us. He was holding an enormous bag made of worn leather, which he handed to Carolan. Carolan thanked him and the guard bowed, turned on his heel and stepped back into his position of door ornament.

"I sent for your bag of medicines," Alanna said.

"As usual, you anticipate my needs." He smiled dreamily into her eyes.

Ugh. Newlyweds.

Starting down the hall, in what I hoped was the right direction, I "*psst*-ed" and motioned for them to catch up with me.

"Hey," I whispered. "Where the hell are we going?"

"To the quarters of your maids." Alanna supplied that nonhelpful answer.

I gave her an *I'm clueless* look and she seemed to remember I was me.

"Oh, just keep going straight, like you are returning to the courtyard. Before you come to the door, turn left, and keep walking and the corridor will lead you to their quarters." She paused. "When you smell it, you are near."

Carolan's eyes narrowed at her description, and we increased our pace.

I followed her directions. I turned left when I came to the exit that I recognized as the door that would open out on the center courtyard. We walked down a long, marble corridor that was decorated with colorful murals on one side and large windows that overlooked the courtyard on the other. The murals were predominately of lovely maidens frolicking gaily in flowered meadows, with me (or, rather, Rhiannon) astride Epi (bare bosomed, of course—me, not Epi) benevolently overseeing it all. As we hurried down the hall, I glanced out the beveled windows and was pleased by the scene of industriously working women. Maraid was in the thick of it all, walking from group to group (no doubt she was in organizers' heaven). We rounded a bend in the hall—

And the smell struck me. At first it was almost sweet, like sugar that had been scalded. Then it changed to a thick, purulent aroma that caused me to gag. I put my hand to my mouth and paused, looking at Alanna. She motioned to the unguarded door that was closest to us, and nodded.

"I will enter first." Carolan moved past us toward the door. "It may be best if you wait here."

"No." I took my hand from my mouth and made my voice sound firm. "I'm coming with you. They're my girls."

"I have already been in there—it holds no surprise for me." Alanna's voice sounded sad.

Carolan nodded at us, and opened the door.

The scene that greeted us was like a vignette taken from a weird horror flick. If it hadn't been for the smell making it real, I would have thought I was having my first authentic nightmare. The room was enormous, and had obviously once been lovely. The ceiling was tall and intricately lined with creamy-colored crown molding. The walls and the matching sheer curtains, which draped over floor-to-ceiling windows and pooled in shimmery waves on the marble floor, were tinted a soft peach color that should have evoked feelings of harmony and comfort, but now it seemed to cast everything in a diseased off-color light. Soiled bedding and linens were piled all over the floor—on each pile lay a person. Other women shuffled between the piles of bedding with beakers of water and wet clothing, stopping briefly to help one of the sick drink or to wipe a fevered face.

As I stepped into the room I forced myself not to retch, but I couldn't keep my hand from covering my mouth. Vomit and other bodily wastes mixed with something that I didn't, at first, recognize. Then I realized where I had smelled the odd scent before—MacCallan Castle. It was the scent of death.

Alanna and I stayed by the door as Carolan hurried into the room. He went quickly to the pallet closest to us, and bent to touch the fevered brow of a young girl. Thick, down-filled blankets covered her, but I could see she shivered and thrashed about. I watched Carolan examine her—he drew back the blankets and began feeling her neck with one hand and taking her pulse with the other. His face was set in an impassive mask as he murmured soft words to her and opened the bag, which lay at his feet.

He pulled out something that looked like a crude stethoscope and began listening to her chest. I felt helpless and inept standing there, watching him move from pallet to pallet, examining the patients and calling for water, fresh linens or cool compresses.

I wanted to misquote Bones and yell, "Damnit, Jim, I'm a teacher not a miracle worker!" But I knew no one would get it. I glanced sideways at Alanna and decided I was going to have to start telling *Star Trek* stories, if for no other reason than just so someone would be able to appreciate my wit.

"My Lady?" A raspy voice caught my attention. I looked around, trying to identify who was calling me, and about halfway into the room I saw a hand make a vague motion in my direction and a head raised feebly so that I glimpsed long, dark hair.

"Tarah?"

Alanna nodded her head sadly.

Well, that did it. I sure as hell couldn't just stand there when a nymph who looked like a favorite ex-student needed me. I took a deep breath through my mouth and made my way to where she lay.

As I came to her side, I took her hand in mine. It was cracked and dry, and the fragile lightness of her bones surprised me.

"I am sorry, my Lady." She tried to smile, but her expression turned into a grimace. "We are too busy for me to be ill."

"Shush," I quieted her. "Don't worry about it. Just rest and get better." She closed her eyes and nodded.

She didn't want to let loose my hand, so I sat next to her and studied her face. It was pale and her lips looked dry, but what was most disconcerting was that the skin of her face and neck were covered with an angry-looking red rash.

"Chicken pox?" I mumbled aloud to myself.

"Yes, I believe it is the pox." Carolan's voice startled me. "Are you familiar with it?"

"I think so. I had it when I was a child," I answered him, still looking at Tarah's drawn face. "But I wasn't this sick." I remembered hearing stories of people who had died of chicken pox, but these had always seemed to me like old wives' tales. I had caught chicken pox when I was a kid, and I remember missing several days of school and being itchy, but nothing like this. These people were severely ill.

"I, too—" Tarah's weak voice trailed off, and I had to bend down to catch the rest of her words "—had the pox as a child."

"She says she had pox when she was a child." I blinked up at Carolan in surprise. "That's weird. In my—" I almost said *world,* but caught myself and changed words with a cough "—um, *experience,* people can only get pox once. They are unable to be infected again."

Carolan nodded in agreement then motioned for me to follow him back to the door. Before letting go, I squeezed Tarah's dry hand and whispered that I'd be back soon.

The three of us huddled together near the entrance, and Carolan spoke quietly and urgently.

"I have only performed a rudimentary examination of several of the patients, but what I have already found concerns me deeply. I believe this is all the same disease, but it develops in three distinctly different stages." He pointed at the first girl he had examined. "The beginning stage seems to be high fever with headache, backache and vomiting." He gestured toward Tarah and continued, "Then a few days later the fever breaks and the rash begins. It appears to move from the face throughout the body and extremities." He nodded his head in the direction of a cluster of pallets, all occupied by children. "The rash changes into blisters, which become filled with pus and putrefaction. The fever returns, bringing delirium. This stage is dangerous and deadly. These children are dehydrating. Some are developing fluid in their lungs. Some have throats that are closing. This is not the childhood pox that brings uncomfortable itching and is only fatal to the very young or very old and weak. Many of these women and children were young and strong—but they are dangerously ill."

"Smallpox." The name washed into my mind from the recesses of my memory. Growing up in Oklahoma I was very familiar with tragic stories of tribes of Native Americans being wiped out after being infected with the disease. Almost without conscious thought, my hand lifted to trace the old inoculation scar on my left arm. A shudder of fear fluttered in my stomach.

"What is this smallpox?" Carolan asked.

"I don't know a lot about it. In my world, or at least in the civilized part of my world, it has been entirely eradicated. But from what I can remember, this sounds like it might be a similar disease." I gave him an apologetic look.

"Anything you can tell me I can put to use."

I searched my memory, wishing the biology electives I had taken in college hadn't been ten-plus years ago.

"Under what you might call normal circumstances, which means if a race of people had been periodically exposed to the pox, it killed those who were very young, and those who were old and already ill. But let's say a certain country and the people who lived in the country had never been exposed to the pox. It could devastate them, killing probably ninety-five out of every one hundred exposed. It is like a plague." My remembrances only made me more worried. "Has this disease ever been seen in Partholon before now?"

Carolan rubbed his chin while he thought. "It seems to me that I do have some records of a pox that has sprung up periodically in the people who live near Ufasach Marsh, and spread sporadically to the general public. But they are a strange, secretive people who do not look to outsiders for aid, so the references are few."

That gave me a thought. "Alanna, you said the maidens were complaining of being sick when they came back from a retreat. Right?"

"Yes," she agreed.

"Where was the retreat?"

"The Temple of the Muse."

"Isn't that near the marsh?" I tried to visualize the map.

"Yes," Carolan answered. "The marsh makes a picturesque southern border for the temple grounds."

"I'll bet if we check this out, we'll find the retreat was where this stuff originated. Which means the Muses are probably dealing with the same illness there that we are dealing with here." I dug through my memory (which tended to be cluttered with old pieces of half-memorized literature and poetry), trying to remember everything I could about smallpox.

"Oh, God." I hit my forehead, upset that the most obvious thing about smallpox had just now popped into my mind. "It's *really* contagious. Through bodily fluids and contact. Like if you sleep in the same bedding someone who is infected has slept and sweated, or whatever, in—you get the disease. Or if you drink after them out of the same cup. Anyone who takes care of someone who has it risks contracting the disease." I wondered briefly if they understood about germs. An image of Carolan calling for fresh water and soap and washing his hands between patients set my mind somewhat to rest.

"Then you and Alanna must stay far away from those who are sick."

"You're right." I looked at Alanna. "You have to stay out of the sickroom…you've already been exposed too much."

"As must you," Alanna said.

"No, I can't get it." I brushed aside the soft fabric of my half sleeve to expose my faded scar. "When I was a kid I got a shot."

Carolan's face was a total question mark. I sighed and made a motion with my hand of a needle sticking into my skin and something being injected into my arm, deciding quickly to give him the short version of the story and leave out my (now very fortunate) decision to say yes when the school nurse asked if we wanted smallpox boosters along with our annual flu shots at school. "It made my body build up something called anti-bodies against smallpox. If I'm exposed to it, my body will fight off the disease."

"It sounds like a miracle." Carolan's voice was awestruck.

"Yeah, I wish I were a doctor so I could explain how it works." I shrugged my shoulders helplessly. "Sorry, you got the English teacher not the doctor."

"The teacher is fine with me," Alanna said sweetly.

I smiled my thanks at her before turning back to Carolan. "Well, what do we need to do?"

"The first step is to quarantine the sick."

"And everything they use," I added. "And their families."

Yes." He nodded in agreement. "I think it would be wise to limit contact with the sick to my assistants, and, perhaps, a few healthy volunteers, probably family members of those who have already been exposed to the disease. Then I must look through my records to see if I can find references to this disease." He glanced sadly back at the room that was already filled with sick people. "The only thing we can do is make them comfortable and attempt to keep them filled with liquids."

"Boil the water first, before they drink it." Sounded like a good thought. They sure didn't need wine, and I had no way of knowing how clean the water supply was—I hadn't gotten sick yet, but I hadn't been drinking much of my water straight (I prefer my water in wine form). "You should also make sure that the dirty linens are kept quarantined from the rest of the temple, and they need to be washed in boiling water, with lots of harsh soap."

"Boiling water cleanses the evil from contagion." He sounded pleased.

However he wanted to put it was okay with me; I was just happy he agreed.

"Yeah, as well as most germs."

Carolan raised his eyebrows at me, but he didn't argue or ask for an explanation.

"I am concerned about the origin of this outbreak. It would serve an ill purpose to have our warriors become sick as they are moving into position to entrap the Fomorians. If this pox originated at the Temple of the Muse, the warriors must stay away from that area."

"Wait, you're right about that, but—now, correct me if I'm wrong—I don't think I've ever heard of horses coming down with a pox. Have you?" My mind was whirring like a hamster in a wheel.

"No…" Carolan was rubbing his chin again. "I can think of no instance of a horse pox."

"How about a centaur pox?" I asked.

"Your husband would be more knowledgeable than I, but I do not believe I know of any such pox that has ever infected the centaurs."

"Good." I felt a load lift from me. "Then we'll just be sure we have only centaur warriors go through the Temple of the Muse to attack Laragon from the east."

"That would be wise, but we still must be certain we contain this outbreak."

"Okay. Let's get busy." If I thought too long about what I was going to volunteer to do, I'd run screaming out of the room. This was one of the times it was better to act than to think.

"Love," Carolan spoke softly to Alanna, "you cannot aid us here. I will not have you put in danger of contagion."

"But you are exposing yourself." She moved close to him and his arms went around her.

"I must." He kissed her forehead. "You know I must. But I cannot do what needs to be done here if I am worried about your safety. You can help me by sending for my assistants, and then going to the kitchen to oversee the boiling of water and making of herbal tea."

"And I need you to make sure the women are doing what they should be doing," I added. "I'm sure Maraid is dependable, but she's not you. And you have to round up the families of those infected, and keep your eye out for people who might be just coming down with the sickness."

I heard Alanna's sigh as she gave in. And I knew she would—her sense of responsibility and integrity would never allow her to be selfish or childish. It wasn't in her nature to insist she stay here with Carolan. Alanna and Suzanna were women who put the needs of others before their own desires.

Not for the first time, I wished I could be more like them.

She kissed her new husband on the lips and I heard their whispered adoration for each other. Then she turned to me and gave me a hard hug.

"Keep watch over him for me." She yanked one of my loose curls, reminding me of my own husband. "And keep watch on yourself, too."

"Not a problem. Oh, and would you find ClanFintan and explain to him what's happened? And ask him if he would come here when he has finished with the warriors."

Alanna nodded and said, "I will see you this evening. I love you both." She left quickly, as if she had to force her legs to start moving before her heart could order them to stop.

Neither of us said anything; we just watched her leave. Her quiet dignity touched our hearts.

"Okay…" I clapped my hands together, purposely breaking the moment before either of us did something ridiculous like start bawling. "Give me something to tie back this friggin hair with, and I'm yours to command. Just tell me what we need to do."

"First, let us begin by arranging the patients in areas of most to least ill. Then we can get these linens and pallets changed and cleaned. And we must try and keep the patients hydrated and comfortable." He pointed to a pile of what looked like clean strips of cloth. "And there is something you can use on your untamable hair."

"Aye! Aye!" I saluted his back as I grabbed the makeshift scrunchie and followed him out into the room. "Hey, is it okay for me to crack open these windows? It's nice outside and nasty in here."

Carolan gave me a "yes" nod and I hurried to pull open the huge windows. Outside, the warm breeze held the heady scent of honeysuckle in bloom. I tried not to retch as the sweet smell mixed with vomit and disease.

I could already tell this was going to be a really long day.

3

While I was going to college I worked part-time as a unit secretary for a large Catholic hospital near the campus of the University of Illinois. As a rule, unit secretaries don't do much dirty work. They're just what the name implies—a secretary for a nursing unit. I usually worked on a general-medicine floor. For a while I worked on the birthing unit (which was pretty cool). There were two major things I learned from my part-time-helping-to-put-myself-through-college job. Number one was I didn't particularly like being a secretary. People were just too damn stuck up and they didn't think secretaries knew anything, when usually a good secretary knew just about everything—or at least everything that was important. Lesson number two was that I absolutely never, ever wanted to be a nurse. Don't get me wrong, I liked them. I respected them. I appreciated them. I just didn't want to be them. Blood, feces, vomit, sputum, looking at people's private parts (which were usually anything but attractive) and sticking things into bodily orifices while being surrounded by sickness and yuck—nope, it wasn't for me.

My thoughts drifted back to what my college experience had taught me as I held the head of woman number six who, in the last few moments, had felt the compelling need to retch violently into what looked like a chamber pot straight out of *Oliver Twist*. Ugh.

In the ten years since I graduated from college I have changed my opinions and tastes about many things, but this is one thing that I hadn't changed my opinion on one bit.

I am not, nor will I ever be, cut out to be a nurse. Period.

After she had finished puking, I wiped the woman's face, surprised to notice under the layer of perspiration and sickness that she was young, probably only a teenager.

"Better?" I asked gently.

"Yes, my Lady." Her voice was weak, but her lips fluttered up in a smile. "Your touch is so nice and cool."

I helped her lie back, and brushed the hair from her damp forehead.

"Would you bless me, my Lady?" Her feeble-sounding question caught at my heart, as it had every time one of these people asked for my blessing.

As I had done so many times already that day that I had lost count, I bowed my head, closed my eyes and prayed, "Epona, please watch over and comfort this girl."

Then I opened my eyes and smiled at her. "I'll come back and check on you later," I promised for what seemed like the zillionth time.

My feet dragged as I walked over to one of the pitchers that Carolan's assistants kept filled with clean, hot water. I held out my hands and one of them poured water for me to wash with, and another dripped soap from a bottle into my chapped palms. As I rubbed my hands together I caught sight of Carolan making his way purposefully from one bed to another. His movements were steady and sure. He seemed inexhaustible.

After drying my hands I took a moment to stretch my back and roll my head around to try and loosen my tense neck muscles. Damn, my shoulders were killing me. I heard a weak voice call my name, and automatically I replied with an "I'll be right there." But I couldn't seem to make my body move. My stomach growled and I wondered how long it had been since two of Carolan's assistants had delivered to us a lunch of cheese, bread and cold meat. The cheese had been cut into hearts and Carolan and I had laughed aloud at Alanna's gift to him.

Now I marveled at the fact that I had been able to laugh. Exhaustion tugged at me—and not just simple bodily exhaustion. I was overwhelmed. Here I was, trying to comfort people who were seriously ill. Me—an English teacher from Oklahoma. And they believed in me. They even wanted me to bless them.

Tell them stories, yes. Recite poetry to them, yes. Even explicate the symbolic meaning of Coleridge's most obscure and bizarre writings, yes.

But be a goddess or a priestess, no.

I felt helpless, inept and uncharacteristically close to tears.

"Goddess," a weak voice beckoned from the far side of the room.

"My Lady," I heard Tarah calling from the part of the room where we had grouped the cases of medium severity.

"Lady Rhiannon," another voice, a child's, from the area of the most seriously ill.

I drew myself up, pushed strands of hair back into my makeshift ponytail and tried to collect myself, both mentally and physically. It was horrible. It was like being in a classroom filled with sick teenagers who were all begging for me to help them complete a page of complex algebraic equations. And I can't do friggin algebra.

As I moved slowly toward the most ill of the voices calling me, I realized that was exactly it. They were like my students. And I needed to quit feeling sorry for myself and do what needed to be done.

So I didn't like being a nurse.

The bottom line was I couldn't get this horrible disease.

They were mine. I was responsible for them. *In loco parentis* was more than just an abstract term. It transcended worlds. And I needed to suck it up, quit whining and do my job. (Actually, one bright spot was the pay. I was pretty sure I made more in this world as a Goddess Incarnate than I did in Oklahoma as a schoolteacher. I mean, who doesn't? I could look at it like it was kind of a promotion. And it certainly wasn't as bad as being "promoted" to a position in administration.)

"What it is, sweetie?" I took a beaker of water that was sitting on a nearby stand and helped the child to take a sip. Her lips were cracked. Horrible pus-filled blisters covered her face, neck and arms. As she opened her mouth to try and drink, I saw red sores all over her tongue.

The water dribbled uselessly down her chin, and I wiped it up with the end of her sheet.

"Is Epona wonderful to ride?" Her young voice was raspy, as if she had been smoking for twenty years.

"Yes, honey." I carefully dabbed her face with a damp cloth one of the assistants handed me. "Her gait is so smooth it's like riding the wind."

"Is it true she talks to you?" Her eyes, already bright with fever, captured mine. I recognized the fervor of a true horse lover.

"I think she does. She's very smart, you know."

The sick girl nodded weakly.

"What is your name, sweetheart?"

"Kristianna," she whispered.

"I'll make a deal with you, Kristianna." Her eyes never left my own. "You get well, and I'll take you to have a talk with her. Perhaps she will even tell you she'd like to take you for a ride."

I was almost sorry I'd made the offer, because immediately she began trying to sit up.

"Hey! That means you have to rest and concentrate on getting well."

The child settled back into the soiled linens with a sigh.

"Goddess," she asked wistfully, "do you think she might really want to talk to me?"

Something within me whispered the words I spoke aloud. "Epona is always looking for young ones who are willing to hear her voice."

"I want to hear her…" The child's voice trailed off as sleep, or unconsciousness, overtook her.

I put the cloth down and looked sadly at her swollen face. "I hope you do, honey," I whispered.

I felt the presence of heat encompass me from behind before I heard him say my name.

"Rhea?"

I turned and almost ran into ClanFintan's muscular chest.

"Oh, hi." I was acutely aware of how I looked. Something like the friggin redheaded stepsister of Medusa. And he looked strong and handsome and wonderful. As usual.

"We missed you at the warriors' meeting." His voice was like warm molasses pouring over my sore body.

"I'm sorry," I said, trying frantically to retie my hair into some semblance of propriety. But as I glanced down I noticed the vomit stains covering most of the front of my dress, so I gave up.

"I hope you explained to them why I was, uh, detained."

"Yes, they understood and commended your sense of responsibility to the people." ClanFintan had taken me by the arm and was propelling me toward the door as he spoke. I saw Carolan nod at him as he wrenched open the door and we emerged into what I realized with surprise was the waning light of the late afternoon sun as it peered sluggishly through the beveled glass of the hallway.

I found myself suddenly encompassed within the centaur's strong arms.

"Ugh…" I tried futilely to pull away. "I'm disgustingly filthy."

"Be still." His deep, hypnotic voice washed over me. "I have missed you."

That did make me be still. He missed me. I was sure I was smiling foolishly against him.

"And I worried about you, too." He held me a little away from him so he could look into my face. "What is this magic Alanna tried to explain to me? Do you really have a talisman against the pox?"

"Yes." I loved his worried expression. "It's not really magic—it's medicine. But, believe me, it works. I can't get smallpox."

"Good." He crushed me against him and I felt his lips touch the top of my head. "I would not have any harm come to you."

"I wouldn't have any harm come to me, either," I tried to joke.

He squeezed me even harder against him. "This is not a matter for joking."

"Sorry," I squeaked, and he loosened his grip. "It's just that I don't particularly like this turn of events. I don't want to shock you, but I'm not cut out to be a nurse."

"That does not shock me. You do not like things that smell bad, and sick things smell bad."

"Boy, that's the truth." I smiled sardonically. "Anyway, did Alanna tell you we think this pox is probably at the Temple of the Muse, too?"

"Yes," he sighed. "That complicates our plan."

"I'll say—if we send human warriors up in that area they will be susceptible to this stuff. That can't be good for an army." I leaned back a little, still supported by the warm cradle of his arms. "Have you ever known of any centaurs getting anything like this pox?"

"No." He sounded sure of himself. "The centaur race is not susceptible to pox."

"That's what I hoped."

"Which means only centaur warriors will be allowed near the Muses. I have already sent a group of centaurs to their temple. They will tell them of our plan and report back to us of the health of the women at the temple."

"It's probably a mess. As awful as it might sound, we need to quarantine the temple and the area around it. We can send them supplies, but we cannot let humans from the temple further contaminate the rest of Partholon."

"I agree. I have already spread word of the quarantine." He eyed me critically. "And now it seems I must take care of you, too."

"Huh?"

"Are you remembering that you have a rather full night ahead?" He looked at me quizzically.

In my best sexy Marilyn Monroe voice I cooed, "What did you have in mind?"

"Communicating with the Lord of the Fomorians."

That certainly threw cold water on my X-rated thoughts. And, yes, somehow I'd forgotten all about that.

"Oh, yeah."

"I wish there was another way. I still do not feel comfortable with you taunting this dark Lord."

His thumbs traced lazy circles on the pulse points inside my elbows. I didn't want to be involved in any scary dream-magic crap. I wanted to take a long bath, eat a big dinner and screw his brains out. But an insistent voice whispered that I had a job to do.

It was just too dang hard to ignore a goddess when she was inside your brain and tapped into your guilt button.

"I'm not particularly looking forward to it myself, but it has to be done." I sighed and nuzzled against him. "You did say you were going to stay with me. Didn't you?"

"Of course. I will always protect your body."

I could think of many things I'd like for him to do to my body, protecting was the least of which.

"Good. Well, let me go in there and finish up. Then I'll have some dinner, and you can help me figure out how to make this dream thing work."

"The Goddess will lead you." He took my chin in his hand and tilted my face up. "I will give you only a short time more. Then if you have not left, I will come carry you out of that room of contagion. You may not be able to get the pox, but you must be mindful of your health."

"And of my husband, too?" I attempted to sound coquettish, but I didn't think the puke on my clothes helped to set a sexy mood.

"Yes, your husband, too." He ruffled my already mussed hair and turned me around. With a gentle push he propelled me back toward the sickroom door. "Remember, if you do not finish soon, I will come get you."

"I love it when you're rough," I said over my shoulder as I reentered the room.

Coming back into pox hell was a serious wake-up call. The first thing I saw was Carolan slowly taking the end of a linen sheet and covering the face of one of the children who had been among the most severely ill. I hurried to his side.

"This is the first one—" his voice was low, so only I could hear it "—but she will not be the last."

"ClanFintan says centaurs do not get the pox."

"That, at least, is good news. Do you realize that twelve more cases were reported since this morning?"

No, I hadn't realized. I'd been too busy dealing with what was in front of my face. I had thought the sickroom had seemed more crowded, but I'd chalked that up to my aversion to nursing.

"And five of the seven most serious cases will probably not live through the night."

"How about that little girl?" I pointed discreetly to the small horse lover.

He shook his head sadly. "She is in Epona's hands."

"Damnit."

Carolan motioned for a couple of his assistants to take the body away.

"The body is still contagious," I said.

He looked at me in surprise, but he didn't hesitate to say, "Take her to the room adjoining my clinic. We must build a pyre outside of the temple grounds in which to send her remains to Epona."

I nodded my head, careful to make a distinctly public display of agreeing with him. "Epona wants all of the victims of the pox to be cremated in one place, away from the temple. She will receive their souls, but she does not wish the dead to contaminate the living."

We watched them carry the small girl away.

Carolan spoke to one of his several competent assistants. "Have the parents of the girl notified of her death."

"No." This time I didn't need a voice within to prod me into action. "It's my job." I spoke directly to the woman. "Bring them here. I'll tell them."

"As you say, my Lady." She curtsied and hurried away.

"You do not have to. Rhiannon would not have done so."

"I am not Rhiannon." My frustration with his comment was obvious.

"No, you are not. Forgive me for evoking a comparison." Carolan's tired voice was rich with warmth.

"You're forgiven." We smiled at each other. "Hey, while we're on the subject of your forgetfulness, are you remembering that this is your wedding night?"

I swear, underneath the layer of sweat and yuck he blushed. "Perhaps it has slipped my mind."

"That could get you in trouble."

He looked around helplessly. "How can I leave them?"

"You have wonderful assistants. Trust them. You have to take a break to sleep, or whatever." I managed a tired grin of encouragement. "Clean up and go to her. Life is too unpredictable to waste a moment."

"But—" he stammered.

"Take eight hours. You won't be any good to your patients if you're too tired to see straight. I'll stay for a while and make sure things are in order."

"Rhea, you have a good heart, but you are really not experienced in caring for the ill."

"Tell me about it. Don't worry, I'll just delegate and look goddess-like."

"Now, *that* you have experience in."

Seems everyone had my number. I made a face at him as he began calling his assistants to him and giving them their orders. I could overhear him dividing them up into shifts, so that some could rest, then come relieve the night shift.

"Lady Rhiannon?" A tentative voice called me from the doorway.

It was the assistant who had been sent to get the dead child's parents. I could see the shadowed forms of two people standing behind her in the hallway. I squared my shoulders and walked toward them.

During my first year of teaching I had the privilege of teaching one of *those* students. You know—the kind of student that completes the teacher. Sarah had been bright and funny and full of promise. She had also been more deeply troubled than any of us knew. She committed suicide shortly before her seventeenth birthday. Walking up to the podium to speak at her funeral, I had felt then much as I felt now, sure of only two things: a horrendous tragedy had happened, and whatever I could think to say wouldn't change that.

"My Lady—" the assistant's voice was hesitant "—these are the child's parents."

I turned to face the couple. They could have been the parents of any of my students. They held hands and had that look about them that said they knew what I was going to say but they wanted desperately not to hear it.

"I am so sorry, but your daughter died this evening." I would have gone on, but the mother began sobbing. She clung to the husband as if she was unable to stand by herself. Suddenly, she straightened and, between sobs, asked, "May we see her?"

Oh, God. This was awful—they couldn't even see their little girl.

"Her body still holds the disease. She has to be cremated quickly, at the behest of Epona." Their looks of desperation made me change my mind and finish with, "You may not touch her, but you may say your goodbyes to her."

I made a motion to the assistant for her to take them to see their daughter. Before they turned to go, the father reached out and grasped my hand.

"Goddess—" his voice shook "—were you with her when she died?"

I didn't even hesitate. "Yes," I lied. "I was by her side, as was Epona."

"Thank you. May you be blessed for your kindness." They followed the assistant slowly, like their bodies were being turned to living stone.

Then I realized it wasn't their bodies—it was only their hearts.

"Rhea, come away now." ClanFintan stepped out of the shadows. He quickly occupied the space in front of me the parents had just vacated. His hands lifted to my face, and his warm thumbs wiped the tears from my cheeks.

"Come," he repeated.

I nodded silently and let him lead me away from the scent of death.

4

"I smell bad." I sniffled back my tears and mumbled at him as we walked down the torchlit hallway.

"*That* I know—which is why I am taking you to the bathing room."

I nodded numbly, thinking how nice it would feel to be clean. If nothing else, the thought alone was good for morale. Mine.

We walked without speaking. I noticed campfires burning in the courtyard, and I could make out the dark shapes of women cooking over the open fires. The aroma drifted in through the floor-to-ceiling windows, and my stomach growled in response.

ClanFintan chuckled. "Dinner is waiting in your chambers."

"Thanks."

"It is not a problem."

"You're starting to sound like me."

"There are worse things to sound like." His deep chuckle rumbled through his chest, and I felt my depression lifting in response. The guy would make one heck of a vibrator. Hell on the grocery bills, but one heck of a vibrator.

Before you could say *Billy Jo Bob loves his cousin,* we were walking through the door to what was quickly becoming my favorite room. I noticed that the guards didn't flinch from my husband's possessive stare.

"Where's Alanna?" I looked longingly at the steaming water.

"She has a husband of her own who requires her attention." He smiled at my confusion. "I will be your servant tonight."

Before I could make my tired brain conjure a witty response, he had taken the back of my filthy dress in his hands, and with a quick motion, ripped it neatly in two.

"Eeek!" He could have warned me.

"You did not want to save it, did you?" His voice almost sounded innocent. Almost.

"Absolutely not. Oh and make sure you burn that nasty thing later. I don't want any of the girls touching it." I reached for his arm to steady myself as I stepped out of yet another tiny thong. Kicking off my sandals I practically ran, again hoping desperately my ass didn't jiggle too much, into the pool of hot water and submerged myself up to my shoulders with a groan.

"Rhea?" he caught my attention.

Before answering him, I felt along the side of the pool until I found my sitting ledge. Situating my butt, I succinctly said, "Hmm?"

"Give me a moment." He was shedding his vest as he spoke. "And, I must remind you again, please do not speak."

"What?"

"Shush."

Then his concentration turned within and he began the chant I recognized from the previous night. At the same time I felt a shiver of desire, I felt a rush of fear when I remembered the pain The Change had caused him. Again, I wanted to cry out as the shimmering became his flesh shifting and re-forming. Almost too late I remembered to close my eyes—the light against my lids was sharp and penetrating.

Then there was darkness.

Blinking, I refocused on his kneeling, temporarily human, form.

He wiped the sweat from his eyes and tried to control his accelerated breathing.

"You—" he paused to take a deep breath "—may speak again now."

"I hate that it hurts you."

He stood, still a little shaky. "If I could not shape-shift, we could not be together as husband and wife."

"I know, and I'd hate that, too."

He walked to the pool, his steps growing steadier with each stride. Using the stone stairs that led down into the water, he joined me.

"I didn't notice that *you* smelled bad." I was, apparently, a little nervous.

"I told you I would be your servant tonight." He took a sponge and a bottle of soap from the edge of the pool. "Turn around."

I complied happily, resting my forearms against the ledge on which I had been sitting. He swept my hair out of the way and began rubbing soap all over the back of my body.

"Mmm," I breathed. Soon he set the sponge back on the edge, and used his strong, warm hands to rub the soap around my back, stopping at my shoulders and neck to work the knots out of my overstressed muscles. I felt myself turning to liquid.

After ministering to my backside (and I do mean *all* of it) he lifted me onto one of the higher ledges so that most of my torso was out of the water and he had access to my legs. Then he soaped up the sponge and began washing the front of me. I realized that, although his touch was intimate, it was not sexual. Instead, it was gentle and soothing. I watched him through my half-lidded eyes, struggling to stay awake.

"Just lean back and relax." His voice was warm. "You have been through much today. I did not Change to be intimate with you in a sexual way—that is not what you need tonight."

I felt a definite sense of relief at his words. I loved him, but he was right, tonight I needed to be cared for, not seduced. I closed my eyes as he started at my toes, holding first one foot, then the other, out of the water. With one hand he used the suds-filled sponge, with the other he rubbed and kneaded my sore muscles. After he finished with my legs, he moved slowly up my torso, using the sponge to gently circle the soap around and over my arms and shoulders. It seemed that with every swipe of the sponge my muscles relaxed more and more and the horrors of the day were becoming almost bearable.

"I am moving you again," he warned.

"Okay," I sighed, keeping my eyes closed.

He grasped my waist and let my buoyancy in the water help him move me down to a lower ledge.

"Lean back and get your hair wet, I will hold your shoulders."

I did as I was told, rinsing the rancid smells of puke and sickness from my hair. After soaking my head, he situated himself behind me on the ledge, and began working shampoo through my wild tresses. All I could do was lean back into him, enjoying his firm touch.

"Now, rinse." He supported my shoulders again as I lay back into the warm water, swishing my hair from side to side until it felt clean.

"Float for a time, allow your body to absorb the healing of the bath's heat. I will not let you go."

I lay back in the warm water, keeping my eyes closed and my mind blank. I felt bruised inside and out. Under his breath, ClanFintan began a melodic chant. I couldn't understand the words, but his deep voice was beautiful and hypnotic.

"What are you saying?" I whispered.

"I am saying relax, love. Your cares are mine and I will never let you go."

Lulled by the water and his love, I barely stirred when he lifted me out of the pool. By some wonderful feat of manual dexterity and raw, brute strength, he was able to wrap me in a thick towel and set me on the chair at my vanity.

"You will not fall over, will you?" he asked.

I opened my eyes just a little to see him squatting in front of me, his hands resting on my knees. I shook my head.

"This will take very little time." He squeezed my knees and stood.

"Where are you going?" I was starting to wake up.

"Shush."

I watched silently as he began the chant that would shift him back to his original form. It seemed to take less time than it took for him to become a human, and the light began earlier and was more intense, causing me to close my eyes and bury my face in the towel.

I heard the familiar clomp of his hooves and knew it was safe to look (and to talk).

"Are you awake?"

"That light is a little hard to sleep through. Does it hurt as much to change back into a centaur?" I asked as he scooped me into his arms.

"Stop worrying." He tucked my head into the crook between his shoulder and his neck, and fussed around until he made sure the towel covered all of me. "I am fine."

I nuzzled against him and kissed his neck. "Bet you couldn't run a marathon."

"I could run one," he chuckled as he carried me out into the hall and headed toward my chambers. "I just would not run very fast."

My stomach growled and we both laughed.

5

My room was softly lit with about a zillion candles (yes, most of them were in the shape of skulls, but I was learning to ignore that), and my table had been heaped full of delicious food. As usual, I was starving.

ClanFintan reclined on one of the chaises, tucking me in front of him. He leaned over me and grabbed a huge golden leg of what must have been a mutated turkey.

"Eat," he talked through the bite of leg. "I know you think you are starving."

I tucked the towel around me and fell to. There was a great selection of meat, vegetables and pasta. And, once again, I felt a foodlover's appreciation for the chef's expertise. (Note to self: give the cook a raise—or whatever.)

The wine was, as usual, a deep, rich red. Rhiannon had her bad points, but she certainly knew her food and wine.

"You remind me of a centaur female the way you love food." ClanFintan's chuckle rolled against my back.

"Are you telling me I eat like a horse?" I teased.

"A centaur is *not* a horse." He sounded stuck-up, but I still thought he was cute. "Although we do appreciate the equine's limited uses."

"We only have horses in my old world," I said between bites.

"What?" He sounded shocked, as if I'd just said babies came from cabbage patches or something equally as ludicrous.

"Yep." I talked as I chewed a wonderful piece of fish that tasted like halibut. "In my old world, centaurs are make-believe—the stuff of fairy tales and myths."

"How can that be?" He sounded truly offended.

"I don't know. It's certainly their loss."

"Hurmph," he snorted in agreement while he chewed. Then a thought struck him and he said, "It must have been quite a shock for you to find yourself married to a being you thought existed only as myth."

"Tell me about it." I smiled and took another drink of wine.

He nodded in sudden understanding. "Little wonder you were so afraid at first." He brushed the hair back from my face in a familiar caress. "There are no shape-shifters in your world, either." It wasn't a question.

"You took a little getting used to." I leaned intimately against him.

"You were very brave. I wish I had known."

"We did just fine. You made me feel it was safe to trust you."

"I am glad." The worry was leaving his face. "But if I had known, I would have…" He hesitated.

"What? Waited longer?" I gave him a mock frown. "I don't think I would have let you."

"Well, I certainly would not have wanted to." He bent down and kissed my neck.

"There is something I want you to know—now that you do know who I really am." I turned at the waist so I could look directly into his eyes. "Unlike Rhiannon, I am a faithful woman. I have never been—" I struggled to find the right words that would span worlds "—inclined to sleep with a lot of different men." His look said he understood. "You don't ever have to worry about trusting me."

"I already believed that of you." His voice was hypnotic; I felt like I could get lost in its warmth. "But I cannot help but be pleased to hear you say it. I will not share you."

I remembered his little tête-à-tête with my guards and grinned. "You won't have to."

He looked smug and happy.

"Hey!" I felt the need to add, "This goes both ways, you know. It's not okay for you to mess around, either."

He looked shocked. "Of course not. I will always be faithful to you."

"Good." I raised my eyebrows at him menacingly. "I'd hate to have to chase down and beat up some lady centaur. I guess Epi could help me, but I think it'd be very stressful." And probably not particularly attractive.

His laughter rolled over me. We ate in companionable silence. I was thinking how easy he was to be around, and what a witty sense of humor he had. And he definitely wasn't a short guy. Actually, the fact that he wasn't technically a *guy* didn't seem very important.

I was finally feeling full, so I poured myself a new goblet of wine. Before I could curl comfortably against him, the mood was broken by me having the Mother of all Yawns.

"Come." He rose gracefully from the chaise. "You are exhausted."

"No, really, I'm not tired." I tried to hang back and drag my feet as he pulled me toward the bed. But try stopping a horse from pulling you somewhere. It wasn't exactly an equal tug-of-war contest.

We got to the bed and stood looking at it. It was, as I may have mentioned before, a really big bed. But, as I glanced from ClanFintan to the bed and back, I realized that no matter how big it was, it would be incredibly awkward for my centaur husband to sleep next to me on it.

I walked over to the edge of the bed and pulled back the gorgeous golden embroidered comforter and sheets so that I could inspect the mattress. It was a huge, thick, down-filled bag, which hung suspended on lots of leather straps. I retied my towel into a more secure position, and started stripping the bedding from the top of the mattress. When the linens were out of the way, I grabbed one side of the mattress and started to tug.

"Well, aren't you going to help me?" I asked over my shoulder as I struggled to pull the mattress off the bed frame.

"Yes." He sounded doubtful as to my intentions, but he added his considerable strength to the maneuver and pretty soon we had the mattress lying on the ground. I put the sheets and comforter back on it and stood back to survey my work.

"It looks like a giant marshmallow." Which wasn't necessarily a bad thing.

"I have two questions," he said.

I gave him an attentive look as I crawled onto the marshmallow bed.

"First, why did you do that?"

"Well, it didn't appear too likely that you were going to climb your half-horse body onto that bed and be comfortable." I looked him over carefully and added, "And you might have broken the dang thing if you'd tried. I want you to sleep with me, so I thought we'd be more comfortable down here together."

"Oh." He looked enlightened, and stepped gingerly onto the marshmallow with me.

"What's the second question?" I asked as he folded his equine legs and lay down next to me.

"What is a marshmallow?"

I snuggled into his body while I answered him. "It's kind of a dessert. It's puffy and white and very sugary. They're good toasted over an open fire."

He pulled me against him, spoon style. The sides of our feather bed fluffed up around us. He smiled and kissed the side of my head. "It is certainly puffy."

"That's what I thought." I ended the word on another big yawn.

"Relax, you need to sleep."

I felt myself starting to relax, when a shudder ran through me and I jolted awake, remembering the mission that waited for me in my sleep.

"I don't think I want to. I'm scared."

"I will be here with your body, and Epona will be there with your spirit." ClanFintan's hand found the outside of my leg and he began a hypnotic caress that ran the length of my thigh, to the sensitive spot behind my knee and all the way up to the small of my back—and then repeated over and over again.

I felt my body relaxing and my eyelids fluttering.

"Don't let go of me…" I whispered, and felt his arm tighten in response as sleep claimed me.

I was a guest at an exclusive spa getting a massage from…I looked over my shoulder…Batman (must be one of my "bad boy" dreams). The massage table was on a terrace, which overlooked a countryside that reminded me of the Lake District of England, except instead of shaggy English sheep, fat black-and-white cats grazed in meadows of mice grass.

Batman had just bent down to whisper in my ear that I had the most perfect ass in the world, when—

My body was sucked up through the ceiling and I found myself looking down on what had become a familiar view of Epona's Temple. The night was clear but the moon wasn't fully risen yet, so the stars were really showing off by lighting up the sky with a brilliant display of priceless jewels. From overhead it was easy to see how crowded the temple and the surrounding grounds had become. Tents and campfires spotted the land. It was late, but I could make out the forms of centaurs and humans who were still awake, busy with uncompleted tasks.

My body floated in the soft breeze, which was blowing toward the river. The river, too, was alive with motion. Barges jockeyed for position, lanterns were lit and voices carried over the water. I watched the action below me as my body turned slowly north, then began to pick up speed. The sensation of traveling so quickly was the same as it had been the other two nights my spirit had been sucked from the comfort of Dream-Land. It was like I had become a gust of wind that had been blown from the mouth of an irritable giant. The sensation was as unpleasant as the analogy made it sound, especially now that I had a pretty good idea of where I was heading.

I left the river's side and veered to the west. Looking down, I saw a huge expanse of dark water passing swiftly by, obviously Loch Selkie. Much faster than should have been possible, I came to the northern bank of the Loch. I noticed a large stone structure a little way from the water's edge. It sat silent and dark. I averted my eyes and sent a silent plea to Epona that she not take me there. I didn't want to see what the creatures had left at Laragon Castle. It was probably cowardly of me, but I breathed a spiritual sigh of relief when my body didn't slow or change direction toward the dead castle.

Far too soon I began to see lights ahead of me. I recognized the dark stone of Guardian Castle's walls as I floated over them, and my body began to slow and descend.

"Please don't make me stay here too long," I whispered to the air around me.

Be brave, Beloved. The words flitted through my mind so quickly I couldn't be sure that I hadn't made them up myself. I drew a deep breath and tried to prepare myself for something awful.

My descent brought me over the middle of the same courtyard I had visited on my previous dream trip. Apparently, it was still being used as a campground for women, because I could see shabby tents reflecting the dim glow of flickering fires. Blanketed shapes huddled around the fires. I drifted closer and I could tell that the number of women had increased considerably. An unusual silence hung over the courtyard. Normally, this many women, even late at night, would be chattering and gossiping in friendly groups. This gathering was so silent I could hear the popping and crackling of the campfires. This time none of them seemed to notice my presence, and I did not pause over them. Instead, I felt myself moving off to the western wing of the castle. My body stopped when I reached the flat balustraded roof of a section of the castle that was lit brightly by many flaming torches.

The whispered words *Prepare yourself, Beloved* echoed through my mind. Then suddenly I was dropping down through the roof below me.

I snapped through the ceiling into a large bedroom chamber. The room was filled with lit torches and candles. Two hearths large enough for several men to stand upright within were ablaze. Well-illuminated in the firelight overkill, the predominant feature of the room was the huge bed situated directly below me.

At first I thought the room was empty. Then a rustling sound drew my eyes to the center of the bed. The thing on the bed stirred and pulled his wings back, and I realized with a shudder of revulsion that what I had thought was an empty bed draped with blankets was really a bed on which lay a creature whose wings had been outspread, like a bat-winged bedspread. Ugh. Without willing it, my body drifted down.

The creature's wings shifted again, and I saw that they covered more than its own body—they had been covering the naked body of a human girl. She was so pale and she lay so very still that I thought she might be dead, then I saw her jerk convulsively as the creature reached his hand down and cupped her naked pubis.

"So sweet," he hissed.

His hand kept traveling down to her inner thigh, and his fingers slid in a circular motion, playing in the wetness he found there. Her legs spasmed, allowing the flickering candlelight to illuminate the liquid, so that I could see it was thick and red with blood.

"Oh!" My breath left me in a horrified rush.

Instantly, the creature's head swiveled up in my direction and his eyes narrowed as he searched the area above his bed.

I recognized him as soon as I saw his face—it was Nuada.

"Get out," he ordered. With a taloned foot he pushed the girl to the edge of the bed. She fell to the floor, then picked herself up and staggered quickly to the door. As soon as she had left the room, Nuada crouched near the headboard of the bed, still looking intently above him.

"I know you are here." His breathy voice was fearless. "I have felt your presence before."

My body, which was floating directly above the foot of his bed, sank a few feet lower. I studied the smug creature. His face looked as if it had been carved from pale granite—it was all hard, sharp lines. His body was lean and free of hair, except the silver mass that fell from his head past his shoulders. Huge batlike wings kept shifting, as if to cover his nakedness, but they did little to hide the bloodstains that were smeared all along his thighs and now-flaccid genitals.

I had thought I would be terrified, so it was with surprise that, instead of fear, my foremost emotions were anger and revulsion.

"You make me sick," I spat at him, and saw his eyes narrow in response.

"I can tell you are *female*." He enunciated the last word slow and long, like it was a curse. "Show yourself, unless you are too weak and afraid."

I had heard about guys like him. They were the kind of "men" who found pleasure in abusing women and children. As anger filled me I felt a change in my floating body. I glanced down to see myself become suddenly semivisible. I was naked, and I floated enticingly over the bed, like I was a dream made almost substantial.

His eyes widened and he licked his lips as he stared.

"Do you like what you see, Nuada?" My spirit voice resonated with an unearthly quality.

"Come closer, and I will show you what I like," he leered cruelly.

"Maybe I will…" I let the sound of my words hang in the air between us. *"Or maybe you should come to me."* I extended one hand and beckoned to him, like a snake charmer teasing a cobra. My other hand reached up and touched the pulse point in my neck, then moved in a long, slow caress down my body to finally come to rest on my inner thigh. There I made my fingers mimic what his had done to the newly raped girl.

His eyes watched me with an obscene hunger that made my stomach roll. As he began to collect himself to lunge at me, I noticed that his wings, as well as his all-too-human-looking penis, had begun to stir and swell.

Through my mind drifted the words *Laugh at him, Beloved,* and I obeyed, letting my ghostly, taunting laughter echo off the walls of the fiery chamber. The moment he lunged at me my body shifted, disappearing up through the ceiling. I burst into the night with the sound of his enraged shriek shattering the deceptively peaceful silence.

And my eyes flew open.

"You are safe."

I had a horrible moment of panic as I tried to remember where I was. Then feeling rushed back into my body, and I knew ClanFintan's arms were wrapped around me. I rubbed the mist out of my eyes so that I could look clearly at his face. He smiled at me, but his brow was creased with lines of worry.

"You have returned to your body." He sounded almost as glad as I felt.

"Yes," my throat felt scratchy. "I need something to drink."

He let me slide out of his arms so I could retrieve my wineglass from the table. Filling my goblet, my hands were shaking so badly that I made a mess, splattering red drops on the white marble table. I found my eyes were drawn to those scarlet spots. The liquid transformed into spattered drops of blood—red against the inhuman white of Nuada's skin. I couldn't pull my eyes away and shake the image of how the girl's blood had been splattered across the creature's body.

"Rhea?" ClanFintan's voice broke the spell, and I breathed a shuddering breath then hurried back to bed. Rearranging myself comfortably against him, I took a long drink, trying to steady my frayed nerves.

"Tell me," he coaxed.

"Epona took me straight to him. He had just finished raping a young girl."

"Did he sense your presence?"

"More than that. He could hear me, and Epona did something to my spirit-body so that he could see me. Kind of."

ClanFintan nodded in understanding. "Epona is using her powers to get our message to the Fomorians."

"I just hope she remembers to watch out for me during all of this, too." I know I sounded kind of whiny, but this whole dream-magic-goddess-creature stuff was more than a little nerve-racking.

"You are Her Beloved, she will always protect you."

I was about to open my mouth and make a snide comment about wishing I could be so sure, but then I remembered the voice in my mind that had whispered the warning *Prepare yourself, Beloved,* and kept my mouth shut.

I took another long drink of wine.

"Did you tell him of the Muse?"

"I didn't get to it this time. Epona jerked me out of there just as he was leaping at me." I remembered Nuada's frustrated shriek at not capturing my body, and I took another long drink.

"He leaped at you? It will please me to skewer him on my sword. Soon." His voice was hard and angry.

"I'm not usually a big proponent of violence, but this time I'll make an exception. That thing seriously needs skewering." I took another drink, and was mildly surprised to find it was the last in the goblet. I yawned. "I hope Epona's done with me for tonight. I'm tired."

ClanFintan took the empty goblet from my hand, and used his long arms to put it on the floor next to our marshmallow.

"I think the Goddess will allow you what remains of the night to sleep." He pulled me close to his body.

"Good." I patted a down-filled pillow into place and snuggled up into a comfortable ball. My husband's hand found the small of my back, and I sighed gratefully as he rubbed up and down my spine.

"Sleep, my love," he whispered. "I will let no harm come to you."

I'm pretty sure I fell asleep with a big smile on my face, Nuada and his evil temporarily rubbed away by ClanFintan's gentle touch.

6

"**R**hea?" The distant voice broke into my dream of being granted an unlimited shopping spree at Tiffany's.

"I'm over here, in the diamond-tiara section," I mumbled sleepily without opening my eyes.

"Why are you on the floor?" The voice was closer, and I was (unfortunately) awake enough to realize it was Alanna.

I opened my eyes slowly and stretched, noticing that my husband had disappeared.

"Have you ever tried getting a horse into bed?"

She covered her giggle with her hand, shaking her head from side to side.

"Hard to imagine, isn't it?" I noticed I was naked and asked, "Could you toss me something to cover up with? I really need to visit the little girls' room."

She gave me a quizzical look as she handed me a night robe—probably because by now it was obvious I wasn't a "little girl," but she got the idea and followed me as I scrambled to the door, pulling on the robe.

The hall that joined my room to the bathing room was unusually crowded with guards and women, who solicitously moved aside and bowed or curtsied a good-morning at me. I nodded sleepily in return, wishing I'd taken a few minutes to fix my hair or pick the sleep from my eyes.

Soon, I darted gratefully into the privacy of my bathroom, glad that my ever-present guards were there to close the door securely behind us.

"Jeesh," I shouted from the "facilities" section of the bathing chamber. "What's up with all the people?"

"More people are arriving constantly—even a temple the size of Epona's has to get crowded eventually."

I rejoined Alanna, pulled the robe over my head and walked down the stone stairs into the warm pool to give myself a quick morning bath.

"So, you're telling me lots of people are here?"

"People and centaurs," she said with a stressed-out undertone to her voice. "I gave the order for the men to set up the Great Tents that Rhiannon kept for our yearly Gathering, and for the cooks to get extra provisions from our stockpiles. I hope that does not make you angry."

"Angry?" I asked as she handed me a towel. "Of course not—do what you think is best. You know better than I do what needs to be opened and closed and whatever."

She looked relieved as she began wrapping another short tunic around me. This one was made of a shimmery aqua-green fabric that reminded me of sea foam. Happily, it covered all of my breasts. Sitting at the vanity, I picked through the makeup as she began combing out my hair and twisting it into a sturdy French twist. Our eyes met and I smiled mischievously up at her in the mirror.

"Did you get plenty of *rest* last night, my friend?"

As I expected, pink blossomed over her cheeks—which made me laugh and quote Juliet's bawdy nurse in my decidedly bad Cockney accent, " 'Now comes the wanton blood up in your cheeks, they'll be in scarlet straight at any news.' "

Which only made her blush even more furiously. I laughed again, happy at the way her eyes danced—even in her embarrassment.

"It was a wonderful night." Such simple words, but her voice made them sound like the pronouncement of a miracle.

"I am so glad for you, Alanna." We stayed silent for a while, each of us, no doubt, thinking of her own husband. I'll admit that my own cheeks felt a little hot as my mind wandered.

"Rhea, last night, did Epona guide you to Guardian Castle?"

"Yes. She took me to Nuada." Our eyes met again in the mirror, and we exchanged a sober look that said we acknowledged the evil we were up against. "I challenged him, and Epona got me out of there. I don't look forward to my return trip tonight."

"Epona will protect you." Her voice sounded as sure as ClanFintan's.

"That's what everyone keeps telling me. And, I admit that I think I can hear her voice sometimes, but I don't think I'll ever get used to flitting around the country, naked in body and soul."

"Even Rhiannon could be disconcerted after nights when Epona's Dream Magic visited her." Alanna's hands stilled and I saw a pensive frown cross her face.

"What is it?" I asked.

"I was just remembering how very upset Rhiannon had been right before she crossed The Divide into your world. She slept little. It was as if she wanted to avoid Epona's visions."

"I'll bet that bitch knew those Fomorian things were coming." It made perfect sense. "Epona would have wanted her people warned." As I spoke, that feeling was back—the one that whispered encouragement into my mind and soul. "She probably showed Rhiannon what was going on and, selfish bitch that she is, she chose to run away rather than stay and fight with her people." I hated that someone who looked like me pissed me off so badly.

Speaking to the back of my head, Alanna combed and pinned my hair. "Perhaps Epona allowed her to run because the Goddess wanted you to lead our people against the Fomorians."

I started to reply with a big *no way,* but she wasn't finished.

"Epona had to have known Rhiannon's true nature—and the Goddess must have known yours, too. It was you Epona chose. You are her Beloved, not Rhiannon."

Alanna finished off my hair with a beautiful golden band, and I kept my mouth shut. It was a daunting thought—that a goddess might have really chosen me. I hoped fervently Epona knew what she was doing.

I stayed silent and Alanna reached over to retrieve the coronet from its spot on my vanity. She placed it on my head. It nestled against my forehead comfortably, like it had been made for me.

"I think you should wear this more often."

I reached up and touched the golden circlet with hesitant fingers. It felt warm under my fingers.

"Maybe I should," I heard myself saying. My stomach felt fluttery. I tore my eyes away from the reflection of the crown and searched through the nearest jewelry box for some matching earrings.

And changed the subject.

"How are Carolan's patients?"

Before she could answer, we were interrupted by a double knock at the door.

"Come in!" At my command the door swung open to admit several servants who were laden with trays of breakfast food.

"Yum!" I smiled in pleasure at the servants. "I'm starving."

"Good morning, my Lady." One of the men bowed nervously (I swear he looked like a kind of zitty kid who had flunked my freshman English class. Twice). "Lord ClanFintan ordered us to serve you breakfast here as soon as you awoke."

"He did!" I smiled like a lovesick fool. "Isn't he adorable?" I said to no one in particular.

"If you say so, my Lady." The servant looked slightly flustered as he bowed his way out of the room.

Alanna's laugh rang through the room. "You are freaking them up."

She almost caused me to shoot oatmeal out of my nose. "Alanna, honey, it's freaking them *out,* not up."

"Oh." She shrugged her cute little shoulders and sat next to me. We daintily dug into breakfast.

"Carolan's patients?" I repeated through a mouth filled with some kind of wonderful cinnamon roll, which I washed down with a strong, green tea fragrantly sweetened with honey. I guessed the servants had decided to restrict my breakfast drinking. (Note to self: tell the friggin servants to bring back…never mind. Tea was probably better for me. At least for breakfast. Sigh.)

"I do not know." Her brow wrinkled with worry. "He would not allow me to accompany him to the sickroom. But last night we were sent word that several more families had fallen ill with the pox."

"That's not good." I dreaded what I knew I had to do. "I'll go see what I can do for them as soon as we finish eating." And I felt my appetite dwindle at the thought.

"ClanFintan asked that you come to him first."

"Where is he?"

"Before I came to wake you, he was in the inner courtyard overseeing the ladies with Connor and Dougal."

"How did Dougal seem?"

"Busy." We exchanged a satisfied look.

"Well—" I swallowed the rest of the tea "—I better get going. I guess I should look on the bright side of this. At least I don't have to bare my breasts this morning." I gave her a slanted look. "Do I?"

"Not for another fortnight," she laughed.

"Great—I have that to look forward to."

Her laughter bubbled around us.

"What are your plans today?" I asked as I finished the tea.

"I will oversee the household servants, check on the cooks, make sure there is room for the arriving families and warriors and be certain you and Carolan have the needed supplies for the sickroom."

"Just another boring day of nothing to do, huh?"

"Yes, my Lady," she sighed as if she had not a care in the world—except perhaps whether to have her finger or toenails manicured.

"Yes, yes." I walked regally to the door. "Being ladies of leisure is certainly tiresome." We giggled like girls as we stepped out into the crowded hall—where our giggles turned into coughs.

"Rhea, I need to go make sure the cooks are not having attacks of apoplexy." Then she lowered her voice for my ears only. "Do you know your way from here to the courtyard?"

"Yes," I whispered back.

"Good— Oh, please give Carolan my love when you see him."

"I'll do that." I smiled. Then I straightened up and said in a very Goddess Incarnate–like tone, "Thank you for all of your hard work, Alanna. You are a diamond amidst a group of CZs."

Her blank look was reflected in the faces that had paused to bow in reverence to me.

Oops.

"As I said, you are a diamond amidst any group, which is easy to see." I knew how lame I sounded.

She tried fairly successfully to hide her smile behind a submissive "Thank you, my Lady."

I started purposefully down the hall with my mouth shut, before I could say anything else that would make no sense at all to the local populace.

I remembered the way to the courtyard, and a double set of well-muscled guards bowed and opened the doors for me. I paused for a moment, observing the activity in front of me.

The courtyard had been transformed from a lovely garden area to an efficient working area. Women clustered at different stations—it seemed they were doing everything from carving shafts of arrows to tearing strips of linen and boiling huge vats of water. Everyone was busy doing something. Working side by side with the human women were *ohmygosh* female centaurs.

I stepped back into the shadows of the doorway, intrigued by my first look at female centaurs. The first thing I noticed was that they were smaller. No. I take that back—the first thing I noticed was that they were stunningly gorgeous creatures. They carried themselves with a grace and fluidity that was a cross between the way a beautiful Arabian mare would move, and a prima ballerina. There were at least a dozen female centaurs scattered throughout the courtyard, their coats and coloring ranging from blond palomino to a dusky dappled gray. They each wore intricately decorated leather vests, a little like the ones ClanFintan and his warriors wore, but the females' vests were brightly colored and sparkled with jeweled beading.

Several of them were clustered around the area where the human women were carving arrows, and my eyes were naturally drawn to that group of alluring horse-women.

In the middle of which stood my husband.

I suddenly decided it was time to leave the shadows and make my Goddess-Incarnate-Beloved-and-Chosen-of-Epona presence known. Drawing myself up to my full height (which would probably come about to the shoulders of the female centaurs), I stepped out into the courtyard.

"Good morning, Goddess!"

"Epona!"

"Blessings upon you, Epona's Beloved!"

I smiled gratefully at their adoration, which made the incredible beauty of the centaur females somehow easier to digest, and returned their greetings as I made my way slowly (so their loving welcome could sink in) to my husband.

As I joined his little group, he moved into the space in front of me. His eyes held mine—they sparkled with his own, decidedly more personal, form of adoration. He lifted my hand to his lips and kissed first my palm, then the pulse point at my wrist.

"Good morning, Rhea." His deep voice gave me shivers. Or maybe it was his lips that gave me shivers. Or maybe it was...

Anyway, you get the idea. He gave me shivers. Not that I minded.

"Good morning, love."

He registered my greeting by stepping even closer to me and leaning down to lightly kiss my lips.

"I missed you this morning," I whispered to him.

"And I did not want to leave our *marshmallow.*"

I smiled at his accented pronunciation.

"Thank you for having breakfast sent to me."

He bowed his head briefly in acknowledgment before saying, "I know you are always hungry."

"Well, yes, I am." I did my best to give the words a double meaning. His grin widened.

At the sound of a delicate throat clearing we remembered where we were, and looked away from each other to find the entire courtyard watching us with happy, knowing smiles on their faces. I felt my own face begin to get warm. One of the female centaurs cleared her throat (again) and my gaze shifted to her. And my face flushed from warm to hot.

She was probably the loveliest creature (human or otherwise) that I had ever seen. Her hair and the coat of her body were the same color—a shimmery platinum blonde. Her hair hung in a thick waterfall of silk down her back, well past her shoulders. (Not one wild, crazy curl.) She had incredibly high cheekbones, which framed startling aquamarine eyes. Her lips were full and lightly dusted with some kind of sheer lip shine (where the hell had she gotten that?). She wore a scarlet-colored leather vest (just the shade that made a redhead like me look like an orange-head) encrusted with crystal beads that glistened in the morning light. Her full, perky breasts weren't exactly bared, but they weren't exactly covered, either.

ClanFintan still held my hand in his, and he pulled me forward to her.

"Rhiannon, I want you to meet a close friend of mine, Victoria Dhianna, Lead Huntress of Centaurs."

She gracefully executed something between a curtsy and a bow.

"Lady Rhiannon—" her voice was as silky and perfect as her hair "—at last I meet the woman who managed to marry ClanFintan."

I bowed my head slightly and said with the perfect inflection of surprise, "*Managed* to marry him? Gosh, the tenacity with which he pursued me left me little choice." I smiled and added, "But I am glad he made sure he caught me."

I heard ClanFintan's snort of humor, but my gaze stayed locked with Ms. Blue Eyes. I was pleased to see her eyes crinkle (laugh lines!) as a smile broke out over her face.

"Touché, Lady Rhiannon," she laughed.

"Call me, Rhea." I grinned back at her. It looked as if she had girlfriend potential.

"Rhea…" ClanFintan regained my attention. "I must go see to the warriors. Many more have joined us last night and this morning. I need to make certain that they are organized, and that their leaders are apprised of our plan." He raised my hand to his warm mouth again. This time his kiss was followed by a quick nip on the fleshy part of my palm. "I will look forward to dinner tonight."

His parting look said dinner and beyond. I sighed happily and watched him leave.

"Obviously, what I heard about your mating is not true." Victoria had moved to my side, and was speaking softly.

I looked up at her. "What is it that you heard?"

"That duty alone made you mate with ClanFintan, which is why it is only a handfast and not a permanent marriage covenant."

I didn't know what to say, so I told the truth. "What started out as duty has changed. Much like a handfast can be changed into a permanent covenant."

"I am pleased for both of you." And she sounded as though she really was—my jealousy radar didn't detect any latent hateful vibes to lock on to.

"Me, too."

"Let me introduce you to the rest of us." She turned and caught the attention of the group of lady centaurs.

All except five of them had wandered off during our exchange. The five that remained were easily recognizable as the most exquisite of an already attractive group of females (horse or not).

"Kaitlynn, Cynthia, Elaine, Alexandra and Cathleen." As Victoria called each name, the corresponding centauress (female for centaur?) executed an agile mixture of curtsy and bow in acknowledgment of her introduction.

"These are my Huntresses." Her proud gesture took in the five beauties.

"Welcome to Epona's Temple," I said, trying not to feel dwarfed by the statuesque horse-women. "I am pleased to have you here, although I wish it was under different circumstances."

Victoria's serious expression mirrored my own. "As Huntresses we oversee the crafting of bows and arrows, as well as the provisioning of game for our Herds. When we received word of the Fomorian invasion, we thought our expertise could be of use."

"You're right. We need all the help we can get."

Victoria looked pleased at my acknowledgment of their worth, then she said to the Huntresses, "Continue to instruct the women in techniques that will lessen the time it takes to carve and form arrows. I will notify the cooks that we are at their disposal if they need fresh game."

The Huntresses went back to working with the other women, and Victoria and I found that we were left standing together in a small pocket of silence amidst a throng of busy people. It was hard for me to stop looking at her—not only was she stunning, but she intrigued me. I had gotten used to ClanFintan and "the boys." Amazingly enough, I didn't think of them as bizarre or unusual anymore. They were just, well, guys. But these female centaurs were something else. Not only did their beauty draw my attention, like standing next to Michelle Pfeiffer or Sophia Loren, but I was dying to ask a zillion questions about what the heck a Huntress was, how did she get to be one and how they figured into centaur society.

And, well, I knew I couldn't mention it—but I was bubbling with curiosity about stuff like, um, well, centaur sex. If I were a cat I would be as dead as a big ol' pile of poopie.

Instead, I settled for a safe question that I hoped would be appropriate for Rhiannon to ask.

"I'm not very familiar with the role Huntresses play in centaur society, but I would love to know more about you and your…" I hesitated for a second, stressing about what noun to use as only an English teacher could stress. "Colleagues."

"As the name implies, each of us is Huntress for our Herd, or Clan, as you would call them. We supplement the domestic meats with a supply of fresh game, we are master trackers, and master crafters of arrows, cross- and longbows. We even occasionally attach ourselves to a human Clan, but you already know that."

I nodded like I'd already known that, and quickly asked, "So centaur men don't hunt?"

"Only for centaur women."

"Men are men," I said. She nodded and we exchanged a knowing look.

"We are not warriors—we leave that to the males—even though our patron goddess is Diana. But we are not virgins, either." She smiled. "And we do respect Epona and pay tribute to her at the beginning of each phase of the full moon."

I heard a whisper in my mind and repeated it aloud, "Epona thinks highly of Huntresses."

"Thank the Goddess for her favor." Her expression was pleased and open. "I do not know if you plan to travel with ClanFintan to Glen Iorsa, but if you do, I would like to ask your Goddess's blessing upon a new birthing grove, Glen Shurrig, which will be opened with the next spring season."

I could only guess that Glen Iorsa was where ClanFintan was from, and I felt an instant of awful insecurity. I mean, he was my husband, and I didn't even know the name of his hometown.

Before I could become a neurotic mess, the voice in my mind whispered, *He was born to love you.* With a rush of surprise and appreciation, I sent a silent thanks to Epona for the reality check. He loved me, and it really didn't matter where he was from.

Answer the Huntress flitted through my head, and I shook myself and said, "I'd be happy to, after we take care of the Fomorians."

"Yes…" Victoria lowered her voice and continued, "Is it truth that they have captured, and are mating with, human women?"

"You can't really call it mating." My voice echoed my loathing. "They rape them to impregnate them. I have only witnessed one woman giving birth—but that was enough. She was killed by the hybrid creature as it was born."

"Diana help them," she breathed the prayer.

"Diana, Epona and all of us have to help them."

"Lady Rhiannon!" A woman calling for me across the courtyard interrupted us.

"Yes. I'm over here." I waved and the woman hurried over to me. As she got closer, I recognized her as one of Carolan's assistants.

"My Lady," she curtsied. "Carolan sent me to find you. He asks that you come to him in the sickroom. He must speak with you." She looked frazzled and tired.

"I'll be right there." I turned to say goodbye to Victoria. "I hope we have more time to talk again soon. It was a pleasure meeting you and your Huntresses. Thank you for your help."

"You are gracious, Lady Rhea." Her lithe body executed the female centaur's distinctive bow. "As our Goddess teaches, females must support one another."

"I'm with you there, girlfriend," I called back over my

shoulder as I headed toward the sickroom. I saw her eyes widen, and then her laugh lines were back as her face split into a smile.

Yep—definite girlfriend material.

7

I thought about the beautiful centaur as I followed Carolan's assistant across the courtyard. This world didn't have technology. No computers, cars, TV, etc., but it was rich in diversity and replete with ancient culture. For some reason, I felt at home here, which was strange because I was nothing but a plain old (well, not too old—and not too plain, either) white girl. Ms. Middle America Schoolteacher, and a registered voter. Now I found myself the Chosen of a Goddess, married to a centaur (decidedly *not* a white boy), battling vampire-things (they wouldn't even be considered Americans—not even in New York) and becoming friends with a Huntress who just happened to be half horse.

Somehow I didn't think this was what my mother had in mind when she said things happen in life you don't plan for (if I remember correctly, she was talking about saving money versus buying a new Ann Taylor outfit). I hoped I had bought the damn outfit.

We left the courtyard and walked through an archway, then turned left and entered a hall. I recognized that it was the same hall I'd followed yesterday to get to the sickroom. Another quick turn and the smell told me we were near before I saw the door. This time it was guarded by a young male centaur I didn't recognize. He acknowledged me with a bow and opened the door.

It was worse than yesterday. The number of patients must have at least doubled. Their groupings of least to most ill were no longer discernible. Pallets were crowding each other, and any free space had been filled with bedding laid directly on the floor. Muffled noises and weak cries came from different areas of the room, but mostly an unnatural silence hung over the chamber, like someone had pushed a bizarre mute button.

I counted three assistants, plus the one I had followed, and had to search around for a while before I found Carolan. He was over in the far corner of the room, bent over a pallet. As I watched, he stood slowly, then reached down for the end of a soiled bedsheet so that he could cover the small patient's head. He turned, moving like an old man, and caught sight of me. First, he motioned for an assistant to carry out the body. Then he nodded in the direction of the makeshift hand-washing area, asking me to join him there.

I made my way to him, returning the pitiful greetings of the sick with quickly uttered blessings.

"It looks bad," I whispered to him as he washed his hands. "There are so many of them!"

"And more are becoming sick as we speak. Two more died in the night. This morning I lost three children and one aged woman." He glanced over his shoulder, then looked back at me and lowered his voice even further. "I estimate five more will not last the day. And for every one that dies, three more are brought here in various stages of the illness." He wiped his hand across his brow. "I need more quarantined space."

"Whatever you need is yours."

"Not far down the hall from here there is a grand ballroom.

Rhiannon loved to host huge masquerade balls where she disguised herself so she could come to her own party incognito."

"She was just friggin weird."

He nodded in agreement and continued, "We could use that space for the milder cases, and the cases that have just begun to show symptoms. Then I would be able to save this room for the most seriously ill."

"Sounds like a good idea to me. How can I help?"

"I need a little over half of these people moved, but I do not want any unexposed humans transporting the sick ones. I thought, perhaps, you might convince some centaurs to help us."

An image of Victoria and her more than capable Huntresses flashed through my mind. "I think I know just the centaurs to head up this job. You start getting them ready for transport, I'll bring in the marines."

"Marines?"

"It means I'll come back with the good guys to save the day."

He looked relieved. "Thank you, Rhea."

"Not a problem." Before I left I gave him a teasing smile and said, "Uh, I saw your wife this morning. She asked that I give you her love. I hope that doesn't mean I have to kiss you or anything."

His eyes sparkled and he looked more like himself as he answered, "I think the sentiment is enough—no kiss will be required."

"Except from her." I grinned.

"Yes." He grinned back at me. "Most definitely from her."

"I'll go get the marines." As I left I could see he was still smiling while he began giving orders for the forthcoming move.

Retracing my steps back to the courtyard gave me time to wonder if I'd spoken too soon. Overseeing women making bows and arrows was one thing, hauling around sick, stinky folks was another. But my feet were still moving, and I didn't see that I had much choice—unless I wanted to go running to ClanFintan to ask for his help.

I loved him and everything, but Carolan had asked for *my* help. And I wanted to be able to give it. I also wanted to be able to act independently in my new world. I'd never been a follower—and, obviously, neither was Rhiannon. I thought it was about time that I exerted some of her/my authority without my nervous compatriots acting as trapeze nets in case of my failure or major screwup. It was kind of like being happily married but wanting your own money. Some people would say it was a destructive thing, this need for independence in modern women. I think it's simply not being a clinging vine. I'm not a militant man-hater or anything like that. I just have a brain and can breathe on my own. Jeesh.

The courtyard was still humming with activity, but the Huntresses were easy to spot—they were the tallest, most gorgeous things in the area. I could see that Victoria was talking earnestly with Mariad, so I waited for them to conclude their conversation before I *pssst*-ed at her to catch her attention. She saw me and smiled as she came toward me.

"Lady Rhea." She brushed her shimmering mass of blond hair back as the wind blew it in front of her face. "I am pleased to see you again so soon."

"You may not be so pleased after I tell you why I'm back." She gave me a questioning look.

"Did you hear that we are dealing with an outbreak of smallpox?"

"Yes, ClanFintan briefed the warriors, and, as lead Huntress, I was included in the meeting." Her expression was sincere. "It must be a terrible disease. I was sorry to hear your people have become infected, but he said Epona has given you a talisman against the disease."

"Yes, well, I can't catch it." If only she knew. "But the rest of my people can." She nodded, and I continued, "Even though we have quarantined the sick, many more are becoming ill. Our Healer, Carolan, has asked that I open the ballroom and use it as a kind of intermediary sickroom, so that the quarters of my maidens can be used for those who are most severely ill."

"That seems logical."

"The problem is we need to move the patients who aren't severely ill to the ballroom, and Carolan has only a few assistants. Centaurs can't catch smallpox. I know it's an awful job, but they're my people and I'm responsible, and—"

"What is it you require?" Victoria's voice was very businesslike. She would have been a great corporate executive for one of those ritzy companies that build gazillion-floor highrises (if she could've fit in the elevator).

"I need you and your Huntresses to help us move the people. And I think Carolan would appreciate it if he had some extra help. He's looking pretty frazzled, and last time I checked, he was down to about four assistants. The rest are either exhausted, or more likely, they have become sick." I looked her in the eye and asked, "Will you help us? I know this isn't the job you came to do, but we need you."

She studied me silently for a moment, then said, "Excuse me, Lady Rhea, if I seem taken aback. You are so different from what I expected."

I quelled the urge to scream, *I'm not that stupid, selfish, hateful Rhiannon,* and let her finish.

"Yes, the Huntresses will aid you." Her vibrant blue eyes pierced my worried greens. "And after meeting you, I believe you would return the favor should we need to call upon Epona for her aid."

I nodded gratefully. "Of course I would. Women need to stick together."

"As we shall." She called to the female centaur nearest to us. "Elaine, gather the Huntresses. The humans need our help in tending to their sick."

The beautiful bay centaur nodded at Victoria.

"And call Sila—we have need of a Healer. Have them meet us at—"

"My maidens' chambers," I supplied.

"Yes, Mistress." Elaine left us to begin calling together the Huntresses.

"Show me the way to the sickroom, and tell me what needs to be done. My Huntresses are at your disposal."

"This way," I gestured and led, walking quickly so that her brisk stride didn't clip my heels. As we made our way down the hall, she reached back and began efficiently braiding her long hair. She noticed I was watching her.

"If I am to care for the sick, it is better that my hair is out of the way."

"Yeah, you're telling me." I pointed to one of my escaping curls. We had, by now, come within smelling range of the sickroom, and I wasn't surprised when Victoria paused, sniffing suspiciously.

I studied her face, thinking I saw a familiar expression.

"I don't like nursing the sick, either," I offered.

Her expression perked up, and her laugh lines crinkled again as she made a face like she'd just bitten into a lemon. "It is truly not a job I enjoy."

"Smells bad," I said.

"Yes," she agreed. "I would rather hunt wild boar."

"Well, I think I've been hunted by several bores before, and while it wasn't any fun, it was certainly more enjoyable than friggin nursing."

"*Friggin* nursing?" she asked.

"I'm trying to quit cursing."

She rolled her eyes before she nodded. "I, too, have a propensity for using inappropriate words."

"You? I'm shocked!" Surely not Centaur Barbie!

We had come to the door, and I watched the young centaur guard's blank expression change to adoration as he caught sight of Victoria. He drew himself up to his full height, and made a sweeping bow of greeting to Victoria (he glanced briefly my way to semi-include me, too).

"Well met, again, Mistress Victoria!" he said with enthusiasm.

The Huntress's face didn't register any recognition, so the centaur babbled on.

"Last evening's meal—we supped at the same campfire."

I worried for a second that he'd blow up if he didn't relax and quit puffing his chest out. Then Victoria's expression shifted into a benevolent half smile. "Oh, yes." She paused and thought before she added, "Willie. How could I forget the name of the chivalrous centaur who gave up his place at the campfire for me?" She touched his arm in a friendly caress and I thought he'd wiggle out of his skin. "Willie," she breathed, "would you do me another service by directing my Huntresses within when they come?"

"Anything for you, Mistress!" His voice broke adorably on the word *Mistress,* like the poor thing hadn't finished going through puberty yet.

"Thank you." Her voice was husky as we passed him and entered the sickroom. "I will remember your devotion."

The door shut (reluctantly) behind us, and Victoria and I exchanged amused glances. She rolled her eyes.

"Was he a centaur or a puppy?" I asked.

"Both," she laughed. "Colts are so endearing."

"Rhea!" The strain that was evident in Carolan's voice sobered us. He quickly crossed the room. "I see you brought the marines."

"I'll explain later," I said in answer to Victoria's look of inquiry. Turning back to Carolan, I made the hasty introductions.

"Victoria, Lead Huntress of the Centaurs, I would like you to meet our Healer, Carolan." They nodded a greeting to each other.

"We are at your disposal, Carolan. My Huntresses and our own Healer will be joining us shortly. How can we be of assistance?" Victoria's brisk voice said she could handle anything, and Carolan gratefully began explaining what he needed. I felt the urge to belt out a verse of "I Am Woman," but I settled for silently mixing the lyrics around in my head to fit the occasion ("I Am Centaur Hear Me Neigh?" Nope, it didn't rhyme).

"Lady Rhiannon?" A weak voice interrupted my bad songwriting. I looked around and caught sight of a small hand raised weakly in my direction. I swallowed a sigh and headed toward the pallet.

"Hi, Kristianna." It was the little horse lover. She looked awful, but she was still alive. The blisters on her face, neck and arms that yesterday had been pea-size and watery, were now pus-filled and angry-looking. Her face was flushed and her lips were cracked.

"C-c-centaurs…" She managed a ragged whisper, and her unnaturally bright eyes shifted in the direction of the door, where Carolan and Victoria had been joined by half a dozen female centaurs.

"Yes, centaurs. They're beautiful, aren't they?" I made eye contact with a passing assistant, and she handed me a cool, wet cloth, with which I tried to blot some of the sweat from the girl's forehead. I cringed internally every time the fabric touched a pustule—I was afraid I was causing her more pain than I was helping. But her gaze had fastened upon the Huntresses and she seemed almost oblivious to me.

"S-s-s-so p-pretty." I had to bend to hear her.

"Honey, you rest. I'm going to go see if I can get you some tea to soothe your throat."

Her eyes shifted back to mine; she refocused on me and nodded painfully.

"Hurts."

"I know. Close your eyes and rest."

Rejoining the group by the door I wished fervently for something that would make that little girl feel better.

"Don't you have anything you can give them for the pain?" I blurted at Carolan.

"I have been giving them mixtures of willow bark and chamomile, but those who need it the most cannot swallow well enough to get enough of it into their systems," he said sadly.

A petite roan-colored centaur I had not seen before stepped forward. Her curly auburn hair had been cropped short in a chin-length bob, parted at the side and tossed back behind one small ear. She wore a leather top that was more formfitting and utilitarian than the Huntress's ornate vests.

"A patient has to swallow only a small amount of juice from the poppy for it to relax them. Perhaps if they were given the poppy extract first, they could then be coaxed into drinking more of your tea mixture." Her voice was a pleasant surprise—gentle and easy to listen to. I was instantly drawn to her.

"Let me introduce our Healer, Sila," Victoria said.

"The poppy extract is an excellent idea. Unfortunately we have very little of the elixir. Our supply comes from the fields around Laragon Castle." Carolan shrugged helplessly. "Laragon is no more."

"Poppies grow in profusion on the centaur plains, I have an ample supply with me, and I will send immediately for more."

"We would be in your debt," I said gratefully. "You are an answer to our prayers."

"If I am an answer to your prayers, Beloved of Epona, it is the Goddess you are indebted to, not me." The Healer's expression was gracious and open.

The thought passed through my mind that she must be an exceptional Healer if just the sound of her voice was so soothing.

Then she turned her attention to Victoria. "Huntress, please have a runner bring my trunk of medicines so that we can start relieving these people of their pain."

Victoria caught my eye and raised her eyebrows at me. "I know a young centaur who would be happy to be our runner."

"Yours, anyway," I mumbled and she turned, flicking her tail at me as she opened the door. I could hear her sexy voice calling for Willie. The sound of his eager hooves scrambling to do her bidding echoed off the walls.

"You're going to cause that boy to have cardiac problems," I said as she rejoined us, looking smug.

"His heart is young, he will be fine," she said, but her satisfied grin said she enjoyed the thought of the possibility. Then she shifted from Flirtatious Naughty Centaur Barbie to Corporate Executive Centaur Barbie. "Carolan, show us which patients need to be moved. We can use the pallets as litters to transport them."

"All the patients who have yellow ribbons tied to their wrists need to be moved. The others must remain here."

"The ones who are staying are the most seriously ill?" Sila asked in a hushed voice.

"Yes."

"Then it is here that I will concentrate my efforts." She went to the washup area and began scrubbing her hands.

The rest of the centaurs got to work.

8

It was amazing how quickly things fell into place. The Huntresses were fast, efficient and well organized. Victoria seemed to be in several places at once, and it amused me to see that the adoring Willie looked exhausted long before the lady centaurs began showing any signs of slowing down.

I tried to be helpful, but mostly I just stayed out of their way. Interestingly enough, I found myself assisting Sila as she worked among the seriously ill. It was a testimony to her talent when, after watching her tend to the first few patients, Carolan announced that he was going to the ballroom to get the patients there situated and medicated, and he would be leaving Sila in charge with only one of his assistants and me to act as her "team" of nurses.

Great.

Like the previous day, time blurred as my world narrowed to caring for the sick. Sila worked tirelessly to ease her patients' pain. First, I helped dribble thick poppy liquid down the closing throats of the most ill, relieved each time the drug took effect and I saw their grimaces of pain relax. Then we began following the poppy dosages with tea. Sila explained to me which was willow bark, used to fight pain and inflammation (sounded kind of like liquid aspirin), and which was chamomile. I already knew chamomile was soothing for upset stomachs and helped relieve stress (my students give me copious amounts of herbal tea for Christmas and end-of-year presents, probably thinking it might make me "chill out"—silly children).

Carolan's prediction of the day's casualties had been close to correct. Five new patients were admitted to our ICU, and I counted four deaths—two young girls, one of my maidens and one infant boy. It seemed as if I had only taken one long, sustained breath, and hadn't really had time to let it out, when I realized that the torches and candles had been lit for several hours. I felt like my feet were going to pulse out of my sandals, and my shoulders were vibrating with tension.

"Lady Rhea, Sila." Victoria's voice caught my attention. I looked up from the bed of a wheezing boy to see that she had entered the sickroom with six new female centaurs who looked fresh and awake. "These postulants of Diana are here to relieve you."

"Good," I tried not to cheer. Actually, I was too tired to cheer. "Come on, Sila, let's wash up and go eat."

I watched Sila as she bent over an elderly woman, coaxing her to swallow just a little bit more tea. She looked a lot like she had when I'd met her this morning. Her auburn hair curled around her face, softening her prominent cheekbones. Kindness and compassion radiated from her. She looked content and rested, which confused me because I was sure I looked like an exhausted bag lady.

"You go ahead, Lady Rhea, I will stay and oversee the young ones." She gestured to the eager young centaur females.

I started to open my mouth to protest, but (thank God!) Victoria stopped me by saying, "ClanFintan told me to carry you out of here if I had to." She looked askance at me and continued, "But I would truly rather not lift another human today."

"Okay, okay! Sila, I'll have supper sent to you."

"I have already ordered it." Victoria gave me an insulted look. "I knew our Healer would not leave the sick so soon."

So soon! We'd been nursing all friggin day!

"Go to your husband," Sila ordered when I just stood there like an idiot.

I gave in gracefully. "Have someone come wake me in the morning." As I passed by Kristianna's bed I paused to look at her flushed face. She appeared to be sleeping, but her breathing was labored.

"There is nothing more you can do for her." Sila had joined me beside the child's bed. "She is in the hands of your Goddess."

"Come get me if…" I didn't want to say it.

"I will. Now, go." She pushed me toward Victoria. Before we were out the door I could hear that she was already issuing orders to the newcomers.

Victoria and I walked slowly down the hall in silence. I glanced at her and was pleased to see that she, too, looked dirty and tired.

"How's a soak in my mineral bath sound?"

"How large is it?"

I let my eyes travel the length of her body before answering. "Large enough."

"Good—humans sometimes do things in a small way." She didn't sound like she was trying to be offensive; she just sounded like she was stating an unfortunate fact.

"Not Lady Rhiannon, Beloved and Chosen of Epona." I stuck my dirty nose up in the air.

Her eyes crinkled in a tired smile. "Of course, how foolish of me to forget."

"That's because goddesses aren't usually covered in puke and poop." I picked at a dried ball of yuck that was half stuck to my coronet, and half stuck to my hair. "And I think I have snot in my hair."

"That could have something to do with it." She rubbed at a spot on her cheek that was crusty with something as equally disgusting. "Being High Priestess should be more glamorous."

"Well, I always thought I wanted to be a goddess." I sighed theatrically. We looked at each other, smiling at our fatigue-induced silliness.

Thankfully, we were soon at the door that led to my bathing chamber. My guard opened the door. I noticed he was staring at my general state of disheveledness with a stunned expression. I gave him a haughty frown, and before he closed the door I said, "Get a life. I'm too damn busy to be immaculate."

His eyeballs bugged out in shock. Rhiannon's boys were certainly in for some confusing days ahead.

My bathing room was familiar and comfortable, and I inhaled a deep breath of pure sensory delight as the mineral fumes from the steaming pool wafted over me.

"This is a lovely chamber." Victoria was already shedding her skimpy vest.

"Thanks, I really like it." I followed suit and awkwardly disentangled myself from Alanna's morning wrapping job. Over my shoulder I said to the beautiful, now bare-chested Huntress (yes, her breasts were large and perfectly rounded—the bitch), "Go ahead and get in. Be careful, though, the steps are a little steep."

I finally rid myself of my dirty dress and stepped out of my teeny thong, just in time to see Victoria making her way gingerly to the deepest part of the pool, which covered her about midway up on her well-formed breasts. I stepped down into the warm water and was soon settled comfortably on my ledge, leaning back so that the water sloshed up to my chin. Victoria must have done some unhorselike maneuvering of her legs, because she relaxed in water that was suddenly up to her neck.

"Mmm," she sighed contentedly. "We have no mineral springs in the Centaur Plains, just cold, clear water from springs."

I remembered my little dalliance with ClanFintan at the country pool. Little wonder he knew his way around the sand soap.

"It's great to soak in. Here…" I threw her one of the several bottles of my favorite soap, which just happened to be lying beside the pool within my arm's reach (Note to self: thank Alanna). "This stuff is great."

She uncorked the bottle and sniffed delicately, then said with surprise, "It smells like sand soap, only with more—" she sniffed again "—vanilla."

"Yeah, it's cool." I grabbed a bottle for myself and started to lather up.

"Cool? I feel nothing cold." She was holding a puddle of soap in her hand, staring at it like it was a glob of bugs.

"It's just an expression," I explained. "It means something's nice, or you really like something."

She shook her head at me as she began scrubbing herself free of smallpox scum. "You have an odd way of speaking."

"Well, uh, it's an Epona thing." And I made myself very busy with unbraiding and washing my hair, hoping she wouldn't press the point.

Two quick knocks sounded against the door.

"Come in—" I glanced at my very naked bathing partner and added "—if you're not a male." Girlfriend or no girlfriend, I wasn't about to let my husband come in here and fill his eyes full of buxom naked centaur.

I mean, please, I *am* an English teacher. Some things just aren't acceptable.

Alanna breezed through the door, arms loaded down with clothes and a large jug of what I desperately hoped was wine.

"Hi, Alanna!" Seeing her familiar face made me realize how much I'd missed her today.

"Rhea!" She smiled her sweet Alanna smile at me and rushed forward to empty her arms of stuff, nodding pleasantly at Victoria.

"Alanna, meet Victoria, Lead Huntress of Centaurs."

"It is an honor to meet you, Mistress."

"Alanna is my best friend—proof of that lies in the fact that I'd bet my coronet that jug is filled with my favorite red wine."

As I spoke, Alanna was pouring me a goblet of red magic and placing it on the ledge next to me.

"Any red wine is your favorite red wine."

"Any *dark,* dry red wine—I have my standards," I quipped as I took a quick swallow.

Alanna, always Ms. Manners, was already pouring a second cup for Victoria. "Please join us, Mistress," she said politely as she handed the wine to the centaur.

Victoria gratefully accepted the cup, and I watched as Alanna began to pick up my dirty clothing—

"Stop!" I screamed and jumped up, spraying water and wine everywhere. "Don't touch my clothes!"

Alanna dropped the dirty mess as if she'd been burnt, and stood there looking miserable.

I grabbed her hand and led her over to the waterfall area where clean water bubbled into the pool. Pouring a lavish amount of soup on her hands, I ordered, "Wash—really, really well."

"I forgot," she said apologetically.

Mumbling to myself about blondes and best friends, I

marched my naked body over to the pile of nasty clothes, picked them up and threw them into the blazing hearth that was built into the far wall. Then I jumped back into the pool and repositioned myself on my ledge. I looked up to find Victoria watching me as if I had suddenly sprouted wings or, worse, a penis.

I took another drink from my goblet, which I was pleased to see still had some wine left in it, before I explained.

"Smallpox is very contagious."

"I knew that. It is why humans should not tend those who are already ill."

"It's more than just tending the ill that spreads the disease— the blankets, clothes, cups, anything someone has gotten—" I searched for the right words "—body fluids on, can spread the disease just as surely as if the person were standing there."

"That I did not know." Her keen eyes searched mine. "This is something your Goddess has revealed to you?"

"Yes," I said, glancing sideways at Alanna, who was still scrubbing her hands as she watched me.

She acknowledged my worried look by reiterating, "The Goddess reveals many things to Rhea."

Victoria looked satisfied with the divine-intervention explanation, and went back to washing her hair while she talked. "It has been said that you are taunting the leader of the Fomorians and drawing them into our trap."

"Yeah—" I attacked my hair, too "—and it isn't much fun."

"I have found that there is only one compensation for dealing with great evil." She paused and I waited expectantly for her to continue. "It teaches great lessons."

She spoke with such profound sadness that I suddenly wanted very much to ask what had happened to her—I wondered what horrible lesson evil had taught her.

Instead, I said, "I wonder what lesson it will teach me."

Into the silence the two knocks on the door seemed to echo.

"What?!" I yelled in my most annoyed-teacher voice.

"Rhea?" My husband sounded uncharacteristically tentative as the door opened a crack. I could see the reflection of the candles glimmer in his eyes as he tried to peer into the room. "May I enter?"

"No!" I screeched. "Victoria doesn't have a damn thing on!"

He paused, holding the door open a little farther than a crack, and I could hear his amused snort. "I grew up with Victoria. I have seen her bathing many times."

"I don't care how many times you've seen how many zillions of gorgeous naked centaurs *before* we were married." I was still yelling as I jumped out of the pool and sped to towel dry my body while I made shooing motions at him. "From now on you don't get to see any naked females except me—centaur or not."

I could hear his laughter, and I could see the door was still cracked open.

"Unless you want me leering at my guards while they bathe!"

The door slammed quickly closed. I continued drying myself, mumbling something about this not being the Playboy Mansion, so we were certainly not bunnies on display.

A noise from the pool made me look, just in time to see Victoria explode in laughter as she surged from the pool and shook water all over the room.

I noticed that Alanna (my supposed best friend) had plopped down on her butt and was joining the centaur in a big belly laugh.

"What's so damn funny?" I asked as I wrapped my wet hair in a towel, turban style.

"You and ClanFintan!" Victoria said between her ringing laughter.

"What about us?"

"You are jealous!"

"So?"

Alanna was laughing so hard she snorted. I shot her a look and said, "I don't know what you're laughing at, Ms. Newlywed." She tried to sober her expression, but only succeeded in causing her eyes to tear with suppressed laughter.

"Lady Rhea," Victoria hiccuped as her laughter subsided, "do not be offended. It was just so unusual to see the woman I have heard so many—" she stopped, clearly choosing to discard several offensive words "—tales about showing such obvious affection for her mate."

I frowned and continued to dry myself.

"And then to see ClanFintan's equally jealous reaction—it was just so unexpected."

"Why?" All ears, I waited for inside ClanFintan info.

Alanna had herself back under control, and she was able to hunt up an extra towel for the centaur. Victoria talked as she dried herself (Alanna poured more wine for all of us—God bless her, I forgave her momentary hysteria).

"ClanFintan has long been pursued by females, centaur and human. He has always reacted with the same polite indifference."

She saw that she had my full attention.

"I am not saying he has been disinterested in females, he has just never let his heart become involved." Her lovely smile lit up her face. "It is quite obvious his heart is now involved."

"Much to his chagrin," Alanna piped in, and they started giggling all over again. This time I joined them.

"I did not mean to offend you with my laughter. It was motivated by joy not ridicule. I saw earlier that he cared for you, and you him. I just now understand the extent of your relationship. You are in love."

I heard Alanna sigh romantically. I would have puked if it hadn't been so true.

"Yes." I was sure that goofy grin was back on my face.

"I wish you joy. He is an exceptional centaur."

I searched her eyes for dissembling or any hint of anything that wasn't true and honest, and found no evidence that she was anything but forthright and sincere.

"Thank you, Vic." We grinned at each other, well satisfied with our new friendship.

"I brought this for you, Mistress Victoria." Alanna handed the centaur a brilliant blue, silky piece of material.

Victoria fingered it carefully, and looked at Alanna with a questioning gaze.

Alanna smiled at her. "I can show you how to secure it."

"Let her," I said. "She's really good at wrapping that stuff around a body."

"It is quite lovely." She sounded wistful. I recognized the voice of a fellow clothes lover.

"Mistress, I must ask you to kneel so that I can reach around you."

Before she complied, the Huntress gave Alanna a stern look. "Only if you stop calling me Mistress. I am Victoria to my friends."

Alanna smiled and Victoria dropped gracefully to her knees. I watched, fascinated by the wrapping and weaving of what looked like nothing but a long, pretty scarf. After just a few twists and turns, Alanna had morphed it into a sexy top that left just enough of Victoria bared to draw second and third looks without getting her arrested. Victoria stood and trotted (literally) to the full-length mirror.

"It is beautiful!" She moved her body around so she could admire her entirely too sexy reflection. Then she grinned mischievously at me and said, "Be careful, Rhea, that I don't tempt Alanna away from you. Once my Huntresses see this, they will implore me to find a way to coax her from you."

I gulped and tried not to look worried.

"Victoria, it is an easy skill to learn. I will simply teach your Huntresses how to wrap the fabric." Alanna's sweet voice put my fears to rest.

And a great idea came to me—why not gift the Huntresses with lots of beautiful cloth when they leave? (Note to self: remember to set the present up with Alanna.)

"Here is yours, Rhea." Alanna handed me a silky butter-cup-colored nightshirt. It was cut with a deep V in the front, and cascaded in delicate folds to the floor. Almost see-through but not quite. I didn't have to look in the mirror to know how erotically it outlined my breasts and hips. Alanna certainly knew what she was doing.

"It's gorgeous. Thank you, my friend." I gave her a quick hug before I started hunting through the large selection of combs and brushes for a thick-toothed comb that I thought would suit Victoria's platinum masses. Finding one I thought would work well, I handed it to the Huntress. Then I grabbed my own and smiled at my two friends.

"If you'll excuse me, I think I'll take my comb to my room and work it through my hair there."

"Rhea, I can dress your hair for you." Alanna sounded confused as she looked skeptically at the towel turban I still had wrapped around my hair.

"Don't worry about it. I'm sure Carolan will be coming to find you soon. You should make sure he has a good dinner, and *dessert*." As I said the last word, I gave her a suggestive look that made her cheeks flush.

"And you have *dessert* of your own waiting in your chambers." Victoria gave me a knowing look.

And I felt my own cheeks turn pink.

"Good night, you two," I said as I escaped out the door. Their giggles made me want to break into a chorus of "Young Love." But, well, I seriously can't sing, so I just hummed internally while I walked down the hall.

The adorable guards snapped to as I approached.

"My Lady, Lord ClanFintan awaits within," one of them informed me.

"Good." I wanted to tweak his sword, but I realized it wouldn't be appropriate. "Thanks for telling me." He saluted and opened the door for me.

ClanFintan was reclining on a chaise that sat before a laden and delicious-smelling table. At my entrance his face broke into a welcoming smile.

I couldn't help myself—like a goofy teenager I rushed into his arms, loving his eager kiss.

"So, you want to leer at your guards as they bathe?" His deep voice was playful, but I heard the serious undertone he tried to hide.

"Only if you want to look at naked Huntresses." I nibbled at his bottom lip.

"There is only one naked female I wish to look at." He kissed me slowly.

When I came up for air, I asked. "How many legs does she have?"

His laughter shook his chest as he hugged me against him. "Only two."

"I'm glad." We smiled at each other until my stomach growled. Well, actually it roared.

He chuckled. "Eat."

I swiveled and took up my perch on the chaise next to him. Everything looked so delicious that I decided I would have to try a little bit of every single thing. As I grazed my way across the table, ClanFintan asked me questions about the smallpox patients. He was sorry to hear of the number of dead and newly ill, but we agreed that neither of us was really surprised. After a while my appetite started to slow down, and I could ask my own questions.

"Are the warriors still arriving?"

"Yes." He sounded pleased. "I believe we may be able to begin moving on Laragon earlier than I had originally anticipated. Do you think Nuada can be convinced to attack the Muses in less time?"

I thought of the expression on the creature's face as I had taunted him.

"Yes," I said quietly.

He squeezed my shoulders and said nothing.

Suddenly, the weight of my exhaustion was back. My head felt heavy and all I wanted to do was comb out my hair and sleep. I kissed his cheek and got up, unwinding the towel from my almost dried hair. Situating myself cross-legged on our mattress (I noticed our bed had been made, but it was still on the floor), I started to comb my way through my stubborn hair.

"Let me." ClanFintan knelt behind me and took the comb from my tired fingers. "Lean back and close your eyes."

"Mmm." I felt my body become leaden under his touch. "You have the most wonderful hands."

I leaned back until I was curled up on my side against a bunch of propped-up pillows. The sensuous feeling of his hands working the comb through my hair made me want to stay awake and enjoy it, and maybe even try and coax him into shape-shifting again tonight, but the stress of the day won, and I felt myself falling into a deep, exhausted sleep.

Tom Selleck and I were at a wonderful Mexican seafood restaurant somewhere in northern Italy. The margaritas were made with real lime juice and gold tequila, and the white cheese dip was totally calorie free. Tom was just in the middle of explaining to me why he was only attracted to voluptuous women over thirty, when the scene dissolved and I was lifted up through the ceiling and shot out into the clear Partholonian night.

Tonight I didn't feel like spending any time sightseeing or trying to avoid what I knew I had to face.

"Okay, I'm ready. Let's get this over with," I said aloud to the air. I felt my spirit body heave forward, as if I had been thrown out of a slingshot. Familiar landscape blurred beneath me as I rocketed toward the increasingly less distant mountains...

And came to an abrupt halt over the inside courtyard. The scene wasn't much changed from the previous night. Women were huddled in unnatural silence around smoky campfires, blankets shrouding most of their features. I felt anger begin to build inside me.

"Take me to him," I whispered through clenched teeth.

My body moved forward toward the part of the castle that I had visited the night before. Through the windows of the uppermost rooms I could see lights blazing and I knew who I would find on the other side of the roof beneath me.

Prepare yourself, Beloved. The words whispered through my mind.

"I'm ready," I said resolutely, and the bottom dropped from beneath me. I sank through the roof and into Nuada's chamber.

It took a moment for me to refocus in the bright, overly lit room. The bed was empty, but before I could feel relieved, a movement from across the room caught my attention. My body turned and I felt a shudder of revulsion as I realized what I was witnessing. Nuada was holding a naked young girl in his arms in a sick parody of a lover's embrace. She was tilted backward, as if they had just danced and he was finishing a

romantic dip, but her head was thrown back to the side unnaturally. Nuada's mouth was pressed firmly against her neck,
and as I drifted closer I could see his jaws working in a grinding
motion as he bit through her skin. Blood welled out of his
mouth and began running in a dark stream down her body and
to the floor. As he lapped and sucked at the wound, his wings
began to rustle, growing taut and erect, spreading up and over
him like a giant predatory bird. The girl began to twitch and
moan in pain, and the movements of her body allowed me to
get a better look at Nuada. He, too, was naked, and it was
obvious that his wings weren't the only things growing and
becoming erect.

"*Eeww, that is seriously disgusting.*" I spat the words.

At the sound of my voice, Nuada's head shot up and he
hissed, "Are you here, female?"

My body drifted forward and, once again, I experienced the
shivery feeling that told me I was becoming semivisible.

"*I'm right here.*" The ghostly sound of my spirit voice echoed
off the walls.

Nuada flung the girl to the ground.

"Get out!"

The pale girl scrambled weakly on her hands and knees, and
fled out the door. Nuada wiped his bloody mouth with the
back of his hand and crouched on his haunches, studying me.

"So, you come to me again." He sounded self-satisfied.

He made my stomach feel tight and sick.

Draw him to you, Beloved. The words drifted through my
mind.

"*I came to you because you are not strong enough to come to me.*"
I cupped one of my breasts suggestively.

His wings twitched and his eyes narrowed.

"*It is such a shame that all you can handle are weak, pitiful little
girls.*" I cupped my other breast and pouted at him.

He licked his lips; his eyes never left my breasts. I let my hands move from caressing my breasts down my body, my fingertips drawing shapes and patterns over my naked ribs, waist and stomach. His eyes stayed locked with the seductive play of my hands, and I could hear his breathing deepen.

"But maybe anything except a helpless little girl would be..." I paused. My hands traveled down to caress my inner thigh, while the other cupped my pubis, much as I had seen him do to the violated girl the night before *"...too much for you."*

His breath turned into a hiss as he shot to his feet and lunged forward, reaching clawed and bloody fingers into the air below me.

Tonight I didn't need the Goddess to prompt me, and my mocking laughter echoed around him as he paced back and forth beneath me.

"If I knew where to find you, I would show you my strength," he hissed.

"You want to know where to find me?" He stopped pacing and stared up at me. *"I am a Goddess Incarnate. My home is the Temple of the Muse. Ask any of your weak captives, they can tell you how to find my temple."*

His face split into a leering grin. "I will come for you myself, and instead of your laughter this room will be filled with your screams."

My taunting laugh caused his pacing to resume.

"Finding me is not the difficult part, Nuada. Possessing me is. My sister Goddesses and I are well protected by an army of centaur warriors." My hands began caressing my breasts again. *"I am almost sorry that you cannot possibly defeat them. It would have been amusing to dally with you."*

His chalky-colored face was suddenly mottled with a flush of rage and he screamed, *"Amusing!"* He took several long, running strides. His muscles gathered and he leaped up, taloned hands reaching into the air. I felt a sharp pain as the tips of his claws brushed through the bottoms of my transparent feet...

Suddenly I was out of there like a fat boy playing dodge-ball.

"Damnit! Ow!" I sat straight up, grabbing for my feet.

"What is it, love? What has happened?"

The fire had burned low, and he must have extinguished the candles and lamps before he fell asleep, so the light in the room was dim, but I could see three strips of welts across the bottom of my left foot. They stung, like someone had just beat me with something hard and sharp. As I watched, the welts swelled, looking even more angry and red.

"He hurt me," I said as I tried to rub the sting off my foot.

"Show me."

I changed positions so that I was propped up on my elbows. I watched him inspect my sore foot. He looked grim as he stood and headed toward the door.

"Where are you going?"

"Nowhere." He gave me a reassuring look before opening the door. I could see one of my guards salute him. "Go to the Healer. Tell him I need some soothing balm, like what he would apply for a burn or an insect bite." He closed the door and poured us two cups of wine.

"Thanks." I smiled at him.

"How did this happen?"

"Nuada leaped at me. His claws raked through my feet just as Epona was getting me out of there."

I saw ClanFintan's jaw clench. "Was tonight's visit enough? Do you think he will mobilize the Fomorians to attack the Muse?"

"I think so. Of course, I won't know for sure until I actually see them leave Guardian Castle. But he was sure pissed off."

ClanFintan gave me a puzzled look.

"It means mad," I clarified. "Really, really mad."

He walked over to the edge of our bed and bent so he could touch my face, smoothing the hair back out of my eyes. "He will pay for hurting you." His voice was flat and dangerous. I was glad he was on my side.

Two knocks sounded and ClanFintan strode quickly to the door.

"The balm, my Lord." I could hear the voice of the guard. "Carolan asks if you require his assistance."

"Tell him no, not at this time."

Before ClanFintan returned to his position at the end of our mattress, he lit an oil lamp and carried it to a niche in the wall behind us. Then, once more, he took my foot in his hand, studying the lines of welts.

"It's really not that bad. It just stings." Actually, it stung like I'd stepped on a nest of yellow jackets, but I didn't want to be a whiner.

He looked up from my foot, his expression was serious. "Rhea, do you not know that wounds to the spirit can be far more dangerous than wounds to the body?"

I shrugged my shoulders. "I really don't know much about this kind of stuff."

"Listen to your inner voice. I think you know more than you realize. Now lie back and concentrate on ridding your spirit of any dark influence."

I did as he ordered. My damn foot did hurt more than a few welts would normally cause. As his gentle fingers began rubbing the balm onto my foot, I couldn't help but suck my breath in at the sharp pain.

"Repeat after me—concentrate on your spirit—concentrate on being well and whole." His deep, hypnotic voice began a chant that I repeated, *"Cuimhnich, tha mi gle mhath…Cuimhnich, tha mi gle mhath… Cuimhnich, tha mi gle mhath…"*

On and on the chant went as he rubbed the cool paste into my foot. I closed my eyes and let the sound of his voice wash over me as I concentrated on being well. And I realized he had been right. Part of me had felt dirty and damaged by my encounters with Nuada. By touching myself for his benefit, teasing and taunting, it was like I had allowed some of his darkness to seep into my spirit. As soon as I realized it, I began to let the darkness go. That creature wasn't going to control my feelings or ruin my spirit.

And the stinging stopped. I opened my eyes to ClanFintan's relieved smile.

"Look," he said, and he helped me to sit up so I could fold back my leg and look at the bottom of my foot…which was now smooth and free of any welts or pain.

"What was it we were saying?" I asked, still amazed that my foot was welt free.

"Remember, I am well," he answered.

"That's all? I thought it was some kind of magic spell."

He laughed and pulled me against him, kissing me soundly.

"The words are from the Old Language, but the only magic they hold is already within you."

I snuggled comfortably against him. "Are you sure it was just me? I think you cast some kind of spell or something."

He tapped the tip of my nose with his finger. "Not tonight." His look was intimate and I thought the room might have grown warmer as his voice deepened. "You need your sleep."

"Are you sure?" I nibbled at his neck, and he bent to capture my lips with his own. Our tongues began a seductive game of tag. Now I was sure the room was hot, and I moaned against his mouth and whispered, "Why don't you do that voodoo that you do so well."

"If you are talking about shape-shifting," he whispered

back, and his hands stroked my waist and buttocks, up and down, up and down, "I cannot tonight."

I wriggled around, pressing myself against his hard chest so that I could breathe in his ear, "Why not?"

Gently, he pulled me back from him, then tucked me under his arm (where I could do less damage, I guess). I was gratified to see his breathing had increased and he looked flushed, too.

"We begin our march to the Muses' temple tomorrow. I cannot afford the energy drain of shape-shifting tonight," he said, brushing a curl out of my face. "No matter how much I would like to."

"We're leaving tomorrow?" I felt my stomach clench. "So soon?"

"After what happened tonight, I believe Nuada will be on the move, and we have a full legion of centaur warriors ready to depart."

"And my guard is leaving when?"

"Early in the morning they begin their march to the Loch."

"What about the men who are supposed to attack from the west?"

"McNamara and Woulff have both sent word that their armies are joining. I sent Connor there with a group of centaurs to lead the march."

"I guess they didn't like that little stealing-and-raping-our-women info."

"Well, what our runner said was that it angered the men—" ClanFintan grinned at me "—but it really, how would you put it, *pissed off* their women."

I laughed. "Yeah, I'll bet they were pissed."

"Seems old McNamara's first wife died last winter, and now he has a young and beautiful new wife. When she heard the news, she told him if he wanted his bed warmed by her this winter he would make sure the Fomorians were stopped."

"Smart girl." I yawned. "Remind me to thank her someday."

"Sleep first. We leave at midday."

I nestled against him, lulled into sleep by the warmth of his body and the gentleness of his hand as he stroked my hair.

9

"**I** still think I should be coming with you." Alanna almost sounded whiny.

I sighed as I pulled on a new pair of soft leather breeches, marveling at their supple beauty. "Alanna, I wish you could come with us, too, but you have to stay away from the smallpox."

"But the pox is here, too."

"We already talked about this. The pox is quarantined here. At the Temple of the Muse it has probably infested everything."

"I do not like the idea of you going without me."

"I don't like it, either, but I like even less the thought of you dying from smallpox." She handed me one of my boots. I turned it over, smiling at the carved star I found on the sole, and tracing it with my finger. It's so cool that my footprints leave stars everywhere I stepped. I looked up to see Alanna watching me with an I'm-going-to-cry expression on her face.

"Rhiannon never even noticed those stars."

"I think they're great." My grin started to make her lips twitch. "Rhiannon was such a bitch." At those familiar words, her lips turned up in an answering smile.

"My friend—" I reached out and took her hand, pulling her

down beside me "—I couldn't stand it if something happened to you just because you felt you had to take care of me."

"I will worry about you every day." Her voice was soft and shaky.

"Don't—you know ClanFintan won't let anything happen to me. You just focus on taking care that Carolan doesn't exhaust himself. Now that Sila's going with us, he's back to too little help and too many sick people."

"He does need me," she said with the wistful voice of a newlywed.

"And don't forget, I've put you in charge of temple management. You have to make sure everything runs smoothly. Who would do it if you went with me?"

"There is no one else."

"Well, when this Fomorian mess is over we'll train an assistant for you so you and Carolan can go on a long vacation. Maybe then you could get started on a baby." I butted into her with my shoulder as her face lit up. "If you haven't already."

"Rhea!" She hit me playfully.

"Come on." I jumped up, stomping my boots more snugly on my feet. "You know ClanFintan is already annoyed at how long it took for me to say goodbye to the patients this morning."

I probably had spent too much time in the sickroom, but saying goodbye was more difficult than I had imagined, even if it was only temporary. Six more of the most seriously ill patients had died, and more ill people were being admitted to both rooms. Carolan said he thought the disease had peaked, but I wasn't so sure. The good news was that it looked like the little horse lover, Kristianna, was going to live, and, although Tarah had been moved to the room with the most seriously ill, Sila had said she thought that she, too, would survive the awful disease.

Alanna sighed miserably and followed me out the door. The hall was deserted, which I thought was odd because just an hour ago when I'd left the sickroom to bathe and get dressed for the trip I'd had to dodge people and centaurs. I was just thinking what a nice change it was to have the hall back to being a more private walkway when we came to the door to the courtyard. The guard bowed and opened the door, and a rush of noise exploded over me.

"Goddess!"

"Blessed of Epona!"

"Luck be with you, Lady Rhiannon!"

"Our love goes with you, Chosen of Epona!"

The courtyard was crammed full of people and centaurs. They cheered and waved as I straightened my shoulders, swallowed hard, grabbed Alanna's hand so she wouldn't be separated from me and stepped out into the narrow path. I was instantly surrounded by my adoring masses (who had just scared me so badly that I'd almost peed my pants).

"Thank you. I appreciate it. I'll miss you, too. Thank you." I waved and babbled what I thought was the correct Goddess Incarnate response.

I made my way through the courtyard and out what I considered the front door of the temple, which opened out on the horse fountain and led to the Big Front Gate and the outside wall. The sight that met me was incredible. Stretching before me was a sea of centaurs. Their beauty and ferocity made the breath in my throat catch. They were equine lines of strength and muscle, melded with man and woman. They rippled with power, and confidence hung over them like a physical entity.

They caught sight of me, and as one they let loose a cry of "Hail Epona!" that sent gooseflesh up and down my arms. I suddenly remembered something that Ovid had written about beauty, that it was "favor bestowed by the gods." If that were true, surely all the gods smiled on this group of warriors.

The most handsome (at least in my opinion) of the warriors detached from the front of the group and regally bowed to me before raising my palm to his lips. At his greeting another cheer went up, this time from the centaurs and the humans together.

"Are you ready, my Lady?" he asked.

I gave Alanna one last hug, then I turned to face the human crowd that spilled out of the castle and stood around the base of the temple and the huge fountain.

With my loudest voice I projected as far into the crowd as was teacherly possible.

"Lady Alanna carries my authority while I am gone." I saw a ripple of smiles pass through the crowd at my announcement. I didn't have to look at her to know Alanna was blushing again. "While I am gone, keep me close to you in your prayers." I smiled and felt my eyes fill unexpectedly with tears. "Know you will always be with me in my thoughts, and in my heart. May Epona's blessing surround and fill you like the air you breathe."

I turned to ClanFintan and held out my arm so he could lift me to his back. Then he spun around, and at his command our army moved out at a smart trot while the people cheered and children ran back and forth strewing flowers in our path.

Suddenly, I heard a loud, familiar neigh, and I shouted in happiness as Epi galloped up to us. She slid to a graceful halt, as did the entire army of centaurs. Her neigh turned into a low whicker as she nuzzled my side. I bent to kiss her soft muzzle, murmuring to her how glad I was to see her, and how clever she was to manage to come out here to say goodbye. I glanced up to see several nymphets who were running from the direction of the stable, trying to catch up with her.

"You have to stay here, love," I whispered to her and

stroked her velvet muzzle. "I couldn't bear it if anything happened to you."

She blew through her nose, and lipped my chin. Then she backed a couple of steps, threw her head in the air, spun around on her rear legs and raced back toward her stable, snorting with her tail held high—once more leaving the frustrated girls in the dust behind her.

"Clever mare," ClanFintan said as he gave the order for us to proceed. I could hear chuckles of appreciation for Epi's antics from the centaur warriors behind us.

I recognized that we were headed in the direction of the river, just as I had gone a couple of days earlier on the morning of the blessing ceremony. I leaned forward, resting my chin on my husband's shoulder so I could speak in his ear.

"Are we going to follow the river north?"

He tilted his head back so I could hear him. "Yes, but we must cross over the river and travel up its eastern side. We don't want to pass through Ufasach Marsh…it would be impossible for a centaur legion to navigate through the wetlands. And we must travel quickly. The eastern edge of the Geal River begins the Doire nan Each, which is forested land. Traveling through it is considerably quicker than picking our way through the swamp."

"Makes sense," I said and gave him a quick kiss on the earlobe. "Doire nan Each, sounds pretty—what does it mean?"

"Translated from the Old Language it means Grove of the Horses, probably named thus because it is the forest that separates eastern Partholon from the Centaur Plains. But the name is misleading, it is an ancient forest filled with giant oaks, not a mere grove." He snorted. "And I have never noticed any horses there at all."

I nodded in an understanding kind of way. Then a sudden thought made me frown. I remembered how wide and beautiful the river had looked the morning of the blessing ceremony. It had been lovely to look at, but I sure as hell wouldn't want to swim across it.

"Wait—are you telling me we have to swim across the river?"

I felt his deep chuckle. "No, there is a bridge just north of the temple. Actually, it is quite near the ruins of the ancient bridge Carolan told us about. We'll cross there."

"Good, these leather pants would take forever to dry out."

"I certainly would not want to be the cause of your wet pants," he said, glancing over his shoulder at me with a gleam in his eye.

I nipped at his neck. "Don't get fresh—you're supposed to be conserving your strength."

"I was only trying to be helpful." He tried to sound innocent.

"The kind of *help* I need from you can't happen in your present form, Mr. Too Big For My Bed."

"You might be surprised." His voice had deepened.

Before I could ask him to explain his last intriguing comment, we followed a bend in the river and before us stretched the bridge. It was a high, flat structure made of logs tied together with what looked like giant binder twine. And it really didn't look all that safe.

"Why does it have to be so friggin tall?"

"So the barges can sail beneath it. The Geal is normally a very busy waterway."

I did remember seeing barges and other ship-type things floating down the river on my first couple of nightly spirit excursions. Oh, well, crossing bridges was, no doubt, probably safer than driving a car.

The bridge was only wide enough for the centaurs to cross two abreast, so ClanFintan started barking a series of orders that were echoed by several old and grizzled centaurs (like John Wayne in *The Green Berets*) that were situated at intervals down the lines. It sounded like, "COLUMN ATWOSTOTHE-RIGHT! HUUUH! FORHUUUH! STANDHAST! MARCHHUUUH!"

A military man just makes my heart go pitter-patter.

The army swung in a neat motion, and a column, two centaurs abreast but about a zillion deep, marched out in a perky trot. ClanFintan cantered ahead of the line. The bridge loomed closer and closer.

"Hold tightly—the climb is steep."

I shut my eyes and held on as he plunged up the bank.

I could feel his footing falter as it slipped on the bridge's crude logs, and my stomach sank somewhere around my ankles, then his hooves echoed dully like we were a million miles up. I had a flashback of the time I tried to walk across the Royal Gorge Bridge in Colorado. Not even my girlfriend dangling a bottle of my favorite red could coax me past the halfway point.

Keeping my eyes squeezed closed. As a neurotic tribute to one of my all time favorite movies, French Kiss, I started to sing under my breath, to the tune of I Love Paris in the Springtime, "I hate bridges in the springtime."

"Rhea, is there a problem?"

The sound of hundreds of hooves following us almost drowned out ClanFintan's inquiry.

"Nope," I said with my eyes still closed. "But let me know when we're across the damn bridge."

I felt the solid ground underneath his hooves. He stepped to the side and said, "Dougal, you and ClanCullen lead the column up the second path to the north." Dougal and an extremely muscular roan centaur saluted and galloped to take up positions at the head of the column.

I had relaxed my eyes open enough to notice Dougal was looking less pale.

"Dougal looks well," I said as we watched the centaurs pass.

ClanFintan glanced over his shoulder at me and said under his breath, "Better than you do. Your face is drained of color." Then he added, "Oh, we have crossed the bridge."

I glanced at bridge/accident waiting to happen, and shuddered. "I don't like bridges," I whispered in his ear.

His laughter caused the passing centaurs to grin in response.

"You can taunt the leader of a demon horde and put yourself in mortal danger night after night, but crossing a bridge makes you faint?"

"Yeah…so?" I said succinctly.

He took my hand and kissed my palm. "You are a constant surprise."

"Yeah, well, uh, don't you forget it." I felt sure his continued laughter reflected the fact that he was overwhelmed by the depth of mystery and allure that made up a modern American woman. That or he thought I was just goofy as hell. I didn't ask which one it was. In every marriage there are things better left unsaid.

"Lady Rhea!"

I smiled and waved enthusiastically as Victoria and a whole group (pack? herd? gaggle?) of Huntresses thundered over the bridge.

"I will find you when we camp tonight!" she yelled.

I yelled back an enthusiastic "Okay!"

We stood there watching the majesty of the centaurs trot by us. They seemed to stretch endlessly.

"How many centaurs are in a legion, anyway?"

"One thousand," he said with obvious pride.

I hoped it would be enough.

"Hagan!" My husband's voice carried above the hooves, and a huge black centaur stepped out of the column to join us.

He exchanged greetings with ClanFintan and bowed his head respectfully to me. I tried not to stare. He was the biggest friggin horse I'd ever seen. And the blackest. His skin was black, as was his thick, wavy hair. His coat was so dark it gleamed highlights of purple and dark blue, like a raven's wing. Even his hooves were black. The only things white on his entire gigantic body were his teeth, and two patches of silver-white hair that streaked his temples. It was amazing. And, quite frankly, very attractive in a rakish, Zorro sort of way. I found myself having a sudden urge to lick him. (Oh, please—I wouldn't really lick him, I'm just saying he was seductive-looking. I'm happily married, not entombed.)

After a brief discussion with ClanFintan, Hagan assumed our position, I reined in my risqué mind, and we set off at a quick gallop to rejoin the front of the army.

We overtook the column easily, and Dougal and Cullen saluted us and fell back to their previous positions. ClanFintan slowed the column, allowing the centaurs to re-form so that they were now trotting four across. Then, with a shouted order the centaurs lengthened their strides into the ground-eating canter "the boys" had traveled with on the way to and from MacCallan Castle.

As I already knew, it was a fairly comfortable way to travel, but it was pretty hard to carry on a conversation with your husband if he happened to be your source of conveyance. That was okay; I enjoyed gawking at the scenery.

ClanFintan had been right, Doire nan Each was no grove. The path we traveled was on the edge of the forest, between the tree line and the high eastern bank of the Geal River. The river was beautiful, wide and wild, with a clean, rocky smell that reminded me of the night Epi and I had spent next to it. But it was the forest that drew my eyes. It was easy to believe it was ancient. Oaks grew to such enormous heights that I could have barely reached the bottom branches standing on ClanFintan's back. Just a short way into the forest I could see that there was very little ground cover, just a thick rust-colored blanket of old leaves and dry branches and logs. The passing army caused birds to scold and squirrels to chatter; I even glimpsed a doe and her fawn springing away in fright. The leaves rustled in the gentle breeze melodically, and soon I felt my head grow heavy.

ClanFintan reached back and pulled my arm around his waist. "Lean on me and rest. You have been getting too little sleep."

I yawned and burrowed against him, breathing deeply of his unique scent. I mumbled sleepily, "It seems like you're always telling me to rest."

The breeze brought his deep voice to me. "I like caring for you."

"Good." I yawned again. "Please don't let me fall."

"Never." He put his arm over mine. The sounds of the forest lulled me into a surprisingly deep sleep.

I was on a cruise ship, which was rocking gently in the blue Caribbean Sea. Lying next to me on a bright fuchsia sunbathing chair was Sean Connery, circa 007. In the ship's pool in front of us frolicked a whole school of dolphins. They kept telling me to forget 007 and to come play with them. The dolphins had a ball-shaped thing that they were tossing around on their noses, and swatting soundly with their tails. I looked closer and realized it was my ex-husband's head…

I laughed as my spirit body rose from ClanFintan's back to hover briefly over the huge oaks. Mentally shaking off a feeling of numbness that I could only explain as me being way over-tired, I turned so that I could look down the line of the centaur army, and felt a rush of pride at its numbers. They were so powerful and brave. How could anything stand against them?

"Okay." Even my spirit voice sounded weary. "I'm ready."
And as I said, "By the way, how often do we have to do this
twice in one daaaaayy…" my body shot forward with the
familiar catapult-like explosion. I followed the line of the river,
which blurred under me like a big silver ribbon, and then I
changed direction and headed to the west. I was surprised to
see that the sun was setting—guess I'd been napping longer
than I'd realized. The Loch came into view. I tried to catch
sight of my warriors who had left the temple this morning to
march to the Loch and then sail to the rendezvous point with
the other two armies, but I was moving too quickly to see
anything except a blur of dark blue.

Laragon Castle passed beneath me, and I made myself look,
but nothing was moving except some dark birds. I turned my
head away, knowing where my spirit would be traveling to
next. I turned once more to the west, and the mountains
loomed huge ahead of me and to my right. They gave me a
creepy feeling, which I thought was odd because I usually liked
mountains. (No, I can't ski well, but I have totally mastered
sitting in the lodge drinking mulled wine.) The closer I got to
the mountains, the stronger The Feeling. It was like…when
you're walking alone at night and you just know someone's following you, or…

Oh, no. I knew what it was like. It was like the night of my
spirit visit to MacCallan Castle when I'd first felt the inklings
of the presence of Fomorian evil. I tried to calm the sudden
pounding of my heart while I looked around me. Guardian
Castle was nowhere in sight. I was hovering over the beginning of the mountain range, and wasn't nearly far enough into
the mountains to be close to Guardian Castle. My body drifted
lower, and I studied the jagged terrain below me. The twilight
made it hard to see. I drifted down the far side of the crest of
one of the first large peaks.

And my heart froze.

Below me, spilling over the side of a mountain and into a small valley was an avalanche of creatures. Even though the terrain was too rugged for them to use their wings to help their advance, they moved swiftly and silently. In the waning light something about them struck me as reptilian.

Find him, the Goddess whispered into my mind. My body drifted lower still, until I floated near the heads of the leaders of the creatures. From above it was impossible to distinguish individuals—they all looked alike. Their wings were semi-erect; their heads were tilted down, as if they needed to watch where their talons were stepping. They were all tall and skeletal-looking, and I couldn't friggin find Nuada.

Frustrated and not knowing what else to do, I drew a deep breath and yelled, *"Hey, Nuada! Where are you, sweet thang?"*

A horribly familiar hiss erupted from one of the lead Fomorians. He halted abruptly, causing the synchronized line behind him to falter and stop. They milled around in confusion as Nuada searched the air above him. I drifted down until my spirit body was floating almost directly behind him. I sent a silent plea to Epona that she would lift me back up and out of reach before he turned around.

Do not fear, Beloved.

Without breathing, I leaned forward and whispered my breathy spirit voice almost directly into his ear, *"Looking for me?"* As I begun speaking, my body was already lifting—which was a good thing because Nuada spun around, grabbing only empty air with his distended claws.

"Up here, big boy!" I felt the shiver that told me I had become visible, and Nuada's eyes were slits as he caught sight of me. His companions, too, could see me, as was obvious from their reaction. I glanced down at myself, realizing that I was naked again. I gritted my teeth. My body was still kind of see-

through, so somehow that should make it okay that I was naked. At least that's what I told myself.

"We come, female," he spat.

"Good." I blew kisses at his leering companions, which made him snarl. *"The centaurs are looking forward to your defeat almost as much as I am."* My mocking laughter echoed from the side of the mountain as Epona made me transparent once again, and lifted my body away and back to…

"Uh!" I sat abruptly upright, blinking in the golden-tinted twilight.

"Rhea?"

I cleared my throat and said, "They're on their way."

10

We made camp as it became fully dark. ClanFintan said there would be light as soon as the moon rose, but not enough to risk snapping off a centaur's leg. Besides, the Temple of the Muse was only a day's march ahead. It was possible that they would be going into battle within forty-eight hours, so this night might be their last chance to rest before engaging the Fomorians.

The thought of the battle to come made my stomach hurt, but surrounded by one thousand strong, well-armed centaurs it was hard to imagine that anything could stand a chance of defeating us. Not even demonic, vampiric creatures like the Fomorians.

Soon after halting for the night, campfires flickered and the Huntresses returned with fresh meat that was quickly spitted and strung over the open flames. I excused myself, heading in the direction of the river to find a convenient bush and a trail down to the river so that I could wash some of the travel grime off me. ClanFintan, Dougal and a host of other smart-alecky centaurs made loud offers to accompany me, but I declined gracefully (telling them to mind their own friggin business).

The bank was much steeper than I had anticipated, but it

was lined with a lovely assortment of low, leafy bushes. I smiled as I chose my facilities.

Then I scrambled down the bank in a spot that looked like it might have been a deer path. The Geal River glistened in the pale moonlight as if someone had broken a giant thermometer and spilled silver mercury over the top of it. It was more turbulent here than it had been downstream and it growled as it tumbled over rocks and crevices, beautiful in a wild, untamed way I would have never experienced in my old world. I'd seen many spectacular rivers: the Colorado River, Red River, the Rio Grande and the Mississippi. And I'd thought they were lovely and scenic, but this river felt different. It hadn't been tamed and commercialized and touristized. It was still the pulse of its country. As I dipped my hands in its icy wetness and washed my face, then drank from it, I could almost taste its power. Surprisingly, instead of being overwhelmed by its primitive strength it invigorated me.

You belong here, Beloved. The words were spoken clearly in my mind.

"Could that be true?" I said aloud to the Goddess. "I think I want to believe it. I know I want to believe. But I'm…I'm just *me.* Nothing special." Or at least not special enough to be chosen by an ancient goddess.

What does your heart tell you, Beloved? The gentle words soothed through my mind.

My heart said that this was my home, and the wonder of it caused the flesh on my arms to prickle and raise.

Remember to follow your heart, my Beloved… The sweet voice faded away like wind-blown leaves.

I stood beside the tumbling river for a long while trying to wrap my mind around the concept of belonging to a new world and age—and being called *my Beloved* by a goddess.

Feeling more than a little overwhelmed, I struggled back up

the bank, which must have grown steeper as I'd communed next to the river. I was breathing hard and losing ground, when a strong arm reached down and pulled me the rest of the way up.

"I was beginning to worry about you." My husband gave the path I'd just been trying to navigate a frown. "This bank is really too steep for you to be climbing—it could give way and you would find yourself in the river."

I brushed my breeches off and muttered, "*Now* you tell me."

"I would have come after you sooner, but I know how you value your privacy, and I thought I would wait until you were finished."

"Darn nice of you." I started walking back to our campfire. He fell in beside me, looping his arm around my shoulders and adjusting his long stride so that he didn't walk over the top of me. His warm, solid presence grounded me, and I realized that whether or not I believed I should be the Chosen of a goddess, there was one thing I did not question, and that was that I belonged with ClanFintan.

The smells of our campfire were welcoming and made my mouth water. Something that had probably been Bambi was sizzling on a spit over the fire—I could hardly wait to dig in. I was happy to see Sila had joined our campfire, and we exchanged warm greetings.

"My Lady!" Dougal's cute self hurried up. "I pulled this log over for you." He pointed to a log that made a perfect seat by the fire.

I smiled at him and patted his arm like he was a cross between a teenager and a puppy. "Thank you, Dougal. It's perfect."

He blushed and gave me a shy smile.

"Do you think you could find me a wineskin, preferably filled with a nice red?"

"Of course, my Lady!" And off he trotted. Literally.

"He is young." My husband's voice sounded amused.

"He's adorable—don't you make fun of him."

ClanFintan snorted in reply.

"I'll bet you were an adorable young thing once, too."

ClanFintan snorted again, and several of the centaurs within hearing range experienced coughing fits, which sounded suspiciously like laughter.

Dougal returned with a full wineskin, followed by several young centaurs, all of whom bowed nervously to me. ClanFintan spoke to each by name. I recognized two of them from our excursion to MacCallan Castle, the others looked vaguely familiar, and I figured they must all be from ClanFintan's private guard. Victoria joined us just as Dougal handed me a piece of sizzling meat on a stick, to the very obvious joy of the young centaurs.

"There is room here by me, Huntress," one cute sorrel said.

"But you would be directly in line of the smoke from the fire there," a muscular bay chimed in. "Here you would be free of smoke, Huntress."

Several other centaurs opened their mouths to make their own bids for her attention, but Victoria silenced them.

"I need to speak with Lady Rhiannon, but thank you for your generous offers." She accepted a succulent-looking piece of meat offered to her by Dougal, whom she rewarded with a grateful smile.

I thought poor Dougal might faint.

She took her place next to my log, and folded her knees gracefully. As she did so she caught my eyes and rolled her own, mumbling something about *silly fresh colts.*

"They adore you," I whispered to her.

She shrugged her shoulders and bit daintily into her Bambi-on-a-stick. After she'd chewed she whispered back, "Young males would all like to tame a Huntress."

She said it as if there was very little possibility of that happening.

"You don't have a mate?" I kept my voice low, thankful the centaurs were distracted by talking to my husband.

She gave a horselike snort through her nose. "No! Males take up too much time."

I laughed, but my eyes gravitated to my husband's handsome profile. As if he felt my gaze, he turned his head in my direction and smiled warmly from across the fire.

"But they can be awfully nice to have around." I knew I sounded love-struck, and I didn't care.

"That is because you love him. I have not found love—so I have taken no mate." She didn't sound particularly bothered by it. As if to verify that, she added, "Some Huntresses never mate."

"Guess you're kept pretty busy."

"As Lead Huntress it is my responsibility to travel from herd to herd, training and overseeing all of the young Huntresses." She shrugged her shoulders again. "It leaves little time for courting."

"Well, Vic, maybe someone should tell them that." I gestured to the young centaurs who were still sending her looks filled with longing.

She laughed and winked at one of the staring centaurs, who promptly dropped the meat he was pulling off the flank roasting on the fire. As he frantically tried to grab it out of the hot coals, Sila, who was reclining comfortably across the fire from us, laughed aloud.

"Take care with what you are doing, colt. I will not mend burns caused by foolishness." At that, the young centaurs all chuckled at themselves good-naturedly.

But they didn't stop sneaking looks at Vic.

"They are intrigued by the power of a Huntress. When one

is intrigued by who *I* am—Victoria, not the Lead Huntress—
then I may be willing to make time for him. Until then they are
sweet diversions, and no more."

I was dying to ask her about centaur sex, but ClanFintan
chose that moment to join us, and, well, when girlfriends talk
about sex it is a girl-exclusive subject, even when one of the
girls is part horse.

"Huntress, this is exceptionally choice venison. May I
commend you on your hunting today?"

See, I knew we'd been eating Bambi.

"Hunting is easy in this forest. It is brimming with game."
Vic sounded nonchalant, but I could tell she was pleased by
ClanFintan's praise.

I started to tell her that I thought it was good, too, when
Dougal cleared his throat and caught my attention.

"Lady Rhiannon—" his eyes were shining and his cheeks
were flushed "—I have been asked to inquire if we could
entice a story from you tonight."

Oh, jeesh. Here we go again.

"That would be lovely, Rhea." Victoria gave me a girlfriend
grin. "I have heard you are a master storyteller, trained by the
Muse."

Great. Actually I'm a master teacher who memorizes well
enough to plagiarize pretty easily.

I could see ClanFintan shifting nervously at my side, obviously worried that Shannon couldn't hold up to Rhiannon's
reputation.

He should have known better by now.

I wiped my hands on my pants, tossed my hair back and
stood.

Smiling at Dougal, I said, "I would be delighted to tell
you a story."

At my words, exclamations of happy surprise went up from

the group around our campfire, and I noticed several centaurs within hearing passed the word that Rhiannon was telling a tale, so my crowd began to grow.

For a teacher, that's a good thing.

I cleared my throat and put on my storytelling voice, which was part actress, part teacher and part siren. Tonight I made sure it was heavy on the siren part, while my mind was questing ahead, changing and rewriting the romantic legend of the *Phantom of the Opera*.

"Once, long ago, a child was born with a horribly disfigured face. His eyes were mismatched, his lips were deformed, his skin was thin and yellow, like old parchment, and where his nose should have been, there was only a grotesque hole." My audience made murmurs of disgust. "His mother abandoned him at birth, but a kindly goddess—" I searched my brain frantically "—the Muse of Music, took pity on him. She carried him to her temple and allowed him to live in the catacombs beneath it. To make up for his terrible disfigurement, she gifted him with that which was most important to her, a magical ability to make music, both with instruments and his voice. So, the child grew into a man, living in the bowels of the temple, worshipping music and perfecting his craft. His only love was music; his fondest joy was to listen to his Goddess training the voices of the neophytes who came to study at the temple."

The centaurs were rapt with attention—a seriously good class.

"He never allowed himself to be seen, he even fashioned a mask, white as moonlight gleaming on snow, which he wore always to shield his face from the shadows and spirits that were his only company. He even believed himself to be a shadow, or a spirit, and he called himself the Phantom of the Temple." (Well, it worked.)

"He convinced himself that he was content with his life, convinced himself he needed nothing more than music to fill his dark days and endless nights. Until the day he happened to hear a young neophyte auditioning, and he made the mistake of glancing at her through a hidden mirror. He fell instantly and irrevocably in love. Her name was Christine."

I moved around the fire, weaving a bastardized version of the timeless story. I loved teaching the story to freshmen— every year I had them read Gaston Leroux's original, then I would read aloud to them from Susan Kay's 1990s romantic retelling. Then we would listen to Andrew Lloyd Weber's amazing musical. By the time the final scene was played, there were very few dry eyes in my classroom.

For my centaurs I mixed the best of the three versions together, recreating a tale that mesmerized them.

"…and when he finally had Christine alone, down in his chamber beneath the temple, he knew there was only one chance she would love him—and that one chance was if his music could move her heart enough that she could forget the horror of his face. So he wrapped her in his words and sang to her of The Music of the Night."

"What did Christine choose?" My husband's voice was thick with emotion. The world had narrowed so that it seemed we were alone.

I smiled through tears and told a big ol' whopping lie. "She overcame her fear of his appearance and chose the beauty within him—and they lived happily ever after."

A cheer went up from my audience, followed by lots of loud clapping and stomping of hooves. In the midst of it all, Clan-Fintan pulled me into his arms and kissed me long and hard, which caused a lot more cheering and stomping. Then he picked me up and, to the accompaniment of lots of ribald shouts, carried me quickly away from the campfires. Over his shoulder

I was surprised and touched to see Sila smiling wistfully as she wept openly, and Vic wiping tears from her shining eyes with one hand, and waving at me with the other.

Clearly, I'd been a hit.

"And you didn't think I could do it." I kissed his muscular shoulder, then (on second thought) gave it a sharp bite.

"You know I can bite back." He looked down at me with mock seriousness.

"I'm counting on it." I kissed the place I'd just bitten.

"It is not that I did not think you capable of entertaining them…" He paused. I stayed silent, allowing him to continue as he carried me away from the firelight. "It is just that I know you do not like to be thought of as Rhiannon, and storytelling is a very…"

His voice trailed off and I offered, "A very Rhiannon thing to do?"

"Yes." He looked relieved that I understood.

"Our lives overlap—" I shrugged "—I can't help that. All I can do is make what was hers my own." I wondered briefly what kind of mess she was making of my life. Then I squelched that thought. This was my life; there was nothing I could do about what she was or was not doing in another world. If I dwelt on the possibilities, like how badly she must be hurting my friends and family, it would drive me insane with frustration. There was no going back, no fixing it. I looked up at my husband's strong profile, and admitted to myself that even if there was a way for me to go back, I wouldn't. I understood it was a selfish decision, but he was my love and with him was where I chose to make my life. I closed my eyes and rested my head against his chest, wishing sincerely that Rhiannon would get hit by a bus.

11

"You are not asleep, are you?"

"No." I opened my eyes and looked around.

ClanFintan had been traveling north, and we had passed out of the area in which the army was camping. I heard him answer a sentry's hail, pausing only long enough for him to acknowledge the centaur's salute before he continued moving. He veered to the right, and we were soon encased by the darkness of the forest. The moon had risen, and points of silver light drifted down through the ancient trees, washing everything in a surrealistic glow.

"Where are we going?"

"I have a surprise for you."

"Really?" I started patting his vest for pockets.

"What are you looking for?"

"A jewelry box."

He laughed. "Not that kind of surprise."

He began looking around at the floor of the forest, like he was searching for something. Then I heard his satisfied grunt as he came to an old fallen tree. It looked as if it had been split almost exactly in half, probably by lightning. ClanFintan walked over to the largest half.

"Stand on this," he said as he carefully deposited me on the log.

It was wide and sturdy, and I didn't have any trouble balancing on it. I looked at him and grinned happily.

"Hey! I'm almost even with you now." And I was. Almost. My eyes came about to his chin. I looped my arms around his shoulders and leaned into him, kissing the cleft in that chin.

He responded by wrapping his arms around my waist, finding my lips with his, and beginning a slow, sensuous kiss that seemed to have no end. I parted my lips and let him devour me, losing myself in the heat of him. I was glad he had his arms around me, because my knees began to feel decidedly weak. He pulled me against him. His lips began a hot trail down the side of my neck. I leaned into him, letting my hands travel over the hard muscles of his shoulders and back.

Without pausing in his exploration, I felt him untying the laces of my leather top, which he deftly pulled off me. His head lowered to my breasts as he began alternating erotically between nibbling, sucking and kissing. Then I felt his hand untying the laces of my pants. I held tightly to him and stepped out of them, so that now all I was wearing was one of my tiny thongs. I whispered, more than a little breathlessly, "I thought it wasn't smart for you to shape-shift right now."

His hands cupped my ass and he pulled me roughly against him again, whispering back into my mouth, "I am not going to shape-shift." He playfully took my bottom lip between his teeth.

"Oh," I said when he released my lip. "Then what—"

"That is the surprise."

Staying in the safety of his arms, I leaned back a little bit so I could see his eyes.

"I don't understand."

He kept one arm around me as he talked; the other was busy with my body. First he caressed my breasts gently.

"I had a talk with Carolan—" His voice was low and seductive, and what his hand was doing was making my head feel dizzy. "About human female anatomy."

I blinked, not sure if I'd heard him correctly.

"What? I still don't understand."

His hand traveled from my breasts to my waist and stomach. "Relax, you will." His hand dipped down, slipping inside my thong and sliding easily over the hot moistness he found there.

I sucked in my breath and leaned my head against his shoulder, letting my own hand roam under his open vest.

"I asked him how I could pleasure you when I was not able to shape-shift." His fingers moved back and forth. "He explained several things to me." He bent and captured my mouth again, while his fingers kept up their erotic dance.

Slowly, he broke the kiss, and whispered to me. "And our talk gave me an idea. Trust me, and I think you will enjoy yourself."

"I'm already enjoying myself," I said breathlessly.

He smiled. "There is more."

"Oh, God," I moaned.

He smiled again and explained, "I am going to put you on my back. I want you to scoot forward, press your body against me, and wrap your arms tightly around me. Then move with my rhythm." He kissed me again.

I made a mewing sound when his fingers stilled, then retreated. He held me with one hand, and with the other he quickly stripped off his vest, leaving his torso bare. Then I felt his strong hands encircle my waist, and he lifted me, placing me firmly on his back.

He turned his head and spoke over his shoulder. "Hold me tightly."

I moved myself as far forward as I could, loving the feel of my naked breasts against the heat of his back. I wrapped my arms tightly around him, stroking my hands from his chest down to his hard stomach, while I kissed and nibbled on the line of his shoulder blades.

"Now press yourself against me as I move." His voice was thick with desire, and I felt chills travel down my inner thighs in response.

He started out, moving in a rolling canter. I felt my pelvis rock with him, back and forth, back and forth, as if his hand was still caressing me. I moaned and buried my face between his shoulder blades. His arms covered my arms. Then, slowly, his gait increased, and the rhythmic rocking increased…and increased…and increased…until suddenly I found myself exploding and dissolving into him.

It was so good it made my back teeth ache—I swear.

His gallop decreased in speed as he circled back to our log. By the time we were back where we started, I felt as if I had no bones left in my body. Not that I minded.

"Rhea, I'm going to set you on the log."

I nodded sleepily against his back, and he gently lifted me to the log.

"Open your eyes so I know you will not fall when I let go of you."

I opened my eyes and stretched like a cat.

He watched me for a moment with a pleased expression on his face. Then he asked, "Did you like your surprise?"

"Absolutely." (Note to self: thank Carolan.) I looked at him dreamily. "But what about you?"

"Me?" He was putting his vest back on and searching around for my shirt and pants.

"Yeah. You know, is there something I can do to, um, *pleasure* you?" I held my breath waiting for his answer.

It came in the form of a horse-size belly laugh.

"I think not, love," he said when he was able to control himself.

He handed me my clothes, still chuckling to himself.

I was feeling a little disgruntled and slightly embarrassed as I jerked my clothes back on, trying to tie the intricate laces myself.

"Let me do that." His fingers took over for mine as I swept my hair out of the way.

When he was finished he noticed my (unusual) silence. I didn't meet his eyes, but I felt him study me, and when I did allow myself to glance up at him I saw his eyes widened in sudden understanding. He took my chin in his hand and tilted my face so that I had to meet his gaze.

"I did not mean to belittle or embarrass you. I am pleased that you offered, but—" his smile lit up the night, and I felt my lips turning up in response "—you are such a small human." He chuckled again and kissed me gently.

I let my arms slide around his shoulders, and he put one arm around my back and one arm under my legs, carrying me close to him as we headed back to the camp. I rested my head on his shoulder.

"But it doesn't seem fair. I want to please you, too." Although I did really enjoy the fact that he thought of me as "small."

"Your pleasure is my own," he said in a matter-of-fact tone of voice and kissed the top of my head. "Do you not understand that I was born to love you?"

You belong to one another, Beloved.

The Goddess's words filled my mind. "Yes, I understand." My voice was choked with emotion. I watched his strong profile in the moonlight, and saw his lips turn up in a contented smile.

It was at that moment that I vowed to myself, *I will never be parted from him.*

12

The sounds of horses' hooves rustling through dried leaves called me from my deep, dreamless sleep. Then I smelled something that reminded me of scrambled eggs…and frying meat. I rolled over, trying to find a comfortable spot on the hard ground so that I could drift back to sleep, but deep voices shouting orders made me crack open my eyes. It was still dark, but I could see that a pale hint of dawn was beginning to push night away.

"Good morning, Lady Rhea!" Sila's cheerful voice assaulted me.

"Morning," I muttered in reply, rubbing my eyes.

"Victoria found a nest of partridge eggs, do they not smell delicious?" She beamed at me as she reached down and stirred the contents of an iron pot that was perched between two rocks so that it hung above the campfire.

"Yeah, they smell great." They did, but the aches and soreness in my slowly awakening muscles sucked the life out of the pleasure I took in the yummy smell.

I'd forgotten how horrible traveling centaurback for a protracted period of time was. Every muscle in my body screamed for my mineral pool and a nice massage. I stood slowly, feeling each second of my thirty-five-plus years, multiplied by ten. My hair was a nest. My back hurt. And my breath probably smelled like someone's dirty toes.

I really hated camping.

I tried to return Sila's perky smile (great—another morning centaur). "I'm going to, uh, freshen up."

"Wonderful! The eggs should be ready when you return."

How could anyone be so happy before the sun had risen?

"Okay," I mumbled and began limping toward the riverbank. On the way centaurs kept calling me by name and wishing me a good morning. I did my best to be polite, especially when several of them commented graciously on the *Phantom of the Temple* story. I found a receptive bush, and managed to scale my way to the river, wash my hands, face and scrub my teeth with my finger, then scramble my way back up the bank.

Ah, the Wonderful World of Camping—may it rot in hell.

A huge amount of scrambled eggs mixed with reheated Bambi was hot off the grill as I grumbled my way back into camp. ClanFintan, Dougal and two more young centaurs I recognized from the night before were already eating. I wondered where Vic was, but common sense told me Ms. Huntress was probably already scouting around, looking for something tender to kill.

"Good morning, my Lady." ClanFintan gave me a quick smile and handed me a wide leaf filled with steaming egg and meat.

"Morning." I tried to smile back. I sat on the log and carefully scooped the hot mixture into my mouth with my fingers, and noticed my bedding was already packed away somewhere. Everyone looked eager to hit the road.

"Will we reach the temple today?" I asked ClanFintan as I chewed the surprisingly scrumptious egg mixture.

"Yes, we should arrive just before dusk."

"They do know we're coming, don't they?" I asked.

"Runners were sent, as well as carrier-pigeon messages. They know our plan."

"Any word on the condition of the ladies?"

"None. The centaur runners were directed to stay there and prepare for our arrival, and nothing was mentioned through pigeon messages."

"Rats with wings," I muttered around a piece of egg à la Bambi.

ClanFintan gave me a questioning look.

"Just ignore me—I'm grumpy in the morning." I looked around at the lack of light. "And especially grumpy in the premorning."

ClanFintan laughed good-naturedly. "You just need to get going. Once we have started you can go right back to sleep." He lowered his voice and brushed a curl away from my face. "If I remember correctly, you are quite comfortable astride me."

I playfully slapped his hand away and smiled through my eggs. "You're so fresh."

"Come!" He grinned and lifted me off the log and onto his broad back. "You can finish the rest as we travel."

"Yeah, great," I said as I brushed his thick hair out of my leaf plate so I could eat the last bites of my breakfast, and seriously wished for some coffee.

The centaurs broke camp quickly, and soon the army was on its way. I had to admit it was a gorgeous morning. It was still too damn early, but even I could appreciate an exuberant display of Mother Nature Morningness. The sun rose over the forest, shining precociously with a clear, brilliant tint. Today our path took us more toward the picturesque bank that had been growing ever steeper. It was beautiful, though, lined with weeping willows, cottonwoods, and I was even pretty sure I glimpsed an occasional wild-cherry tree. A thousand centaurs' hooves muted the noise of the river, but its majesty was visible when the foliage thinned out, and its tumultuous rush downriver impressed me.

About midday we paused long enough to pass around dried meat and hard biscuits. ClanFintan deposited me near the bank so I could stretch my legs. While I was attempting a runner's lunge, the direction of the wind changed. It had been blowing softly from east to west, now it originated in the west, and it was blowing harder. It lifted the branches of the willows, making them look like a woman's long hair blowing in the breeze.

I turned my face into the breeze, shaking out my own hair, liking the way it was lifted off my shoulders. I breathed deeply, stretching my sore muscles, and…

"Shew! What is that nasty smell?" The breeze brought with it a decidedly gaseous scent.

"Ufasach Marsh." ClanFintan wrinkled his nose as he, too, tested the air.

"Ugh, it's horrible. Smells like my grandma's compost heap."

"Those who live near the marsh say it has its own unique beauty."

"Yuck—they can have it. How close is it, anyway?" I walked over to stand on the precipice of the bank, squinting and shielding my eyes from the reflection of the midday sun off the turbulent water. I could barely make out the far bank. I could tell it wasn't high like the eastern bank, but all I could see were more willows—no clinging moss hanging from branches or snakes or alligators.

"What I have been told is that it begins about the length of twenty-five centaurs inland from the western bank, and stretches almost the entire breadth of the land from the Temple of the Muse to the northern border of Epona's grounds." He shrugged his broad shoulders. "I have never traveled through the marsh. Centaurs avoid swampy ground."

"Well, I'm with you on that one. Snakes, leeches, stinky water…yeesh! Makes my skin crawl just thinking about it."

Movement of the troops behind us caught our attention. I stretched one more time, then held up my arms so that Clan-Fintan could redeposit me on his back, and we could take up our position at the head of the army.

Smallpox, or no smallpox—I was going to be really glad to get to the Temple of the Muse. My butt felt like it was adhering to my husband's back, which is not a particularly good thing.

The day progressed pretty much as the previous day. The farther north we traveled, the thicker the forest became. Soon the line of centaurs was forced to re-form and travel in columns of twos. But they kept up their ground-eating canter. Even though I'd witnessed it before, their stamina amazed me. Clan-Fintan's breath came just as easily after he'd been traveling for several hours as it had this morning before the sun had risen. I'm telling you, centaurs could seriously kick butt in an aerobics class… My head snapped up and I realized I'd been nodding off.

ClanFintan's head began to tilt back in my direction and I spoke before he could.

"I know—" I cuddled up against him, and he looped his arm over mine "—you won't let me fall."

"Never," he repeated.

I smiled against his warm back and let myself drift off into a deep sleep.

I was in a parent–teacher conference with one of our school's counselors and our vice principal in charge of discipline. Across the table from me sat a student and his mommy. Even in my dreams I'm too professional to mention any names, but I will describe said student as a replica of The Missing Link, if The Link had been introduced to marijuana, so that his general appearance had become reminiscent of a Neanderthal-like sloth. His mommy was blond, perky and extremely well dressed—begging the question: just exactly how much alcohol and/or recreational drugs had she consumed while he was in utero?

I was just explaining to Mommy, accompanied by a standing ovation from the counselor and vice principal (who, by the way, was being played by Pierce), that her sixteen-year-old "baby boy" was neither underchallenged nor too bright to be interested in sophomore English, he was simply a lazy, whiny, pot-smoking brat who could be the poster child for why we should bring caning into America's public schools…

…When I was sucked off of my husband's back and found myself suspended over the middle of the violently churning river.

"I don't mean any offense by this, but this time you interrupted one of my top ten favorite dreams," I said to the air around me. "And I was just getting to the real fantasy part where the vice principal actually backs up a teacher." There was no response, but my body did begin hurling north, following the river.

"Someday, do you think I'll be able to sleep without these little…excursions?" I asked aloud.

Patience, Beloved.

"Not one of my virtues," I mumbled.

Then my attention was captivated by the huge building I was rapidly approaching. It was a domed edifice, and even from a distance the stately arches of carved marble were impressive. As I got closer I saw that what I took at first to be one enormous building was really several graceful structures, joined together by elaborate walkways and gardens. The center building was the focus, and the surrounding structures were situated like spokes in a wheel. I was close enough now to see that women dressed in flowing robes walked the pathways between buildings. Many of their heads were tilted together, as if they were in the midst of lively discussions.

Although all of the buildings were beautiful, the central building was the most impressive. I studied it, intrigued by the lifelike statues that ringed its entrance. In the garden before it, a woman was speaking to a group of young women sitting all around her feet. She gestured gracefully with one hand, and with the other she held an exquisite cane carved of ivory. Her beauty was so striking that if she hadn't moved I would have thought her one of the perfect marble statues.

As I hovered nearer, she suddenly stopped speaking, and cocked her head like she was listening to a voice in her mind. Then her face broke into a delighted smile, and she tilted her head up, speaking directly to me.

"Welcome, Beloved of Epona!"

The girls at her feet (I was close enough now to see that they, too, were unusually beautiful) murmured excitedly and began searching the air as though they were trying to see me.

Thalia, Incarnate Muse of Comedy, the voice in my mind volunteered.

"Thank you, Thalia," I answered politely, trying to project my spirit voice.

She cocked her head again, like she could hear but not see me, and asked, "Are you and the centaurs close?"

"We'll be here a little after dusk," I yelled.

Her smile broadened and she turned her head, speaking to the girl nearest her feet. "Fiona, run to the main temple and announce that the centaurs will be here shortly after dusk!"

Delighted cries and giggles went up from the healthy, obviously smallpox-free girls. I wondered if we had been premature in isolating humans from this temple.

"We will be pleased to welcome you this evening, Lady

Rhea." She tilted her face up, and I had the sudden realization that her eyes could not see my spirit body, or anything else. Her milky orbs had no pupils—she was blind.

All I had time to do was sputter a quick "Goodbye!" and I was on the move again, this time heading directly into the west, where the sun had already begun its descent.

The land surrounding the Muses' temple was reflective of the women's beauty. The mountains to the north made a picturesque backdrop to a valley painted with fields of wildflowers and irrigated with bubbling streams. I was preoccupied with gawking at the scenery beneath me, so when Laragon Castle loomed suddenly before me, I felt myself startle in surprise.

Torches burned brightly from the battlements and the interior rooms and courtyards. Tall, winged figures scurried around the surrounding grounds, shooing away flocks of dark birds so that they could drag pieces of bodies into a gruesome pile at the edge of the castle grounds.

I closed my eyes and whispered, "Please don't make me go down there."

Be strong, Beloved. Remember, I am with you was my only answer, but, thankfully, my body didn't pause at the carnage outside the castle. Instead, I floated quickly toward an inner towered room that was lit up with an overabundance of torches, candles and hearth fires.

Epona didn't have to prepare me. I knew what I would be facing as my body dropped through the ceiling of the room.

Nuada was alone, sitting in a thronelike chair before a blazing hearth. His abnormally long, ivory-colored fingers were wrapped around a goblet of red liquid. I hoped it was a nice Merlot, but I had my doubts.

"Worrying about the battle to come, Nuada?" my ghostly voice asked.

He didn't hiss and lunge toward me, as was his custom.

Instead, he sipped delicately at the liquid in his cup, and smiled over his shoulder at me.

"Not worrying, female, anticipating tomorrow night, when you will be mine to claim." As he spoke, his lips glistened with the red wetness from the thick liquid in the cup.

"Good idea. You have one last night of freedom. You might as well stay deluded and make it easier on yourself," I said in a matter-of-fact tone of voice.

He stood slowly, like a snake uncoiling, and turned toward my voice. He rested one hand on the high back of the chair, in the other he still held the goblet.

"I have decided that I will not kill you. Instead, I will keep you alive for a very long time, so that you will have the opportunity to pleasure me over and over again."

"Really?" I laughed and felt my body shimmer into view. *"I'm afraid my centaur husband will not approve of your little plan."*

"Husband!" His hiss was back. "Sever your ties, female. You belong to me."

I felt anger fill my soul and I spat the words at him, *"You disgusting creature! ClanFintan will squash you under his hooves like the roach you are, and send you back to rot in hell where you belong! Take a good look at me, because this is as close as he will ever allow you to come."*

His wings began to rustle in angry response and he shrieked, "Tomorrow night, female! You will belong to me!"

As he hurled the goblet at me, Epona pulled me away from that disgusting scene. I kept my eyes tightly closed until I felt myself resettle into my body.

I breathed deeply and tightened my grip around my husband. He squeezed my arm in response.

"They're at Laragon Castle," I said.

He took my hand and raised it to his lips.

"They're going to attack the Muses tomorrow night."

"That is according to our plan."

"He'll be looking for you."

"Good." His voice was flat and dangerous. "That will save me the trouble of searching him out." He barked an order at the centaur closest to us in the column. "Tell Dougal to loose the pigeons to send word to the human armies. We attack Laragon tomorrow night."

I started to tell him to be careful, but just then we rounded a bend in the river and a joyous cry went up from a crowd of enthusiastic girls on the opposite bank. The Temple of the Muse stood brightly lit by the setting sun. The centaurs began shouting and waving in reply. ClanFintan called a command and the entire army broke into a synchronized gallop.

Which would have been an exhilarating experience, except I could see that we were headed directly for a delicate-looking suspension bridge that was obviously the only means of crossing the raging river.

"Oh, crap," I said.

ClanFintan shouted above the cries of the welcoming women, "Close your eyes and hold on! You know I will never let you fall."

I shut my eyes and buried my head into his thick hair, muttering, "Great, that means we'll both hurtle to our deaths when the damn thing breaks."

I could feel his laughter shaking his shoulders as he stepped onto the bridge.

"I just hope I don't puke."

"If you do, turn your head. And remember, they are here to welcome you, too."

"Ohhhh!" I felt us swaying with the breeze and the weight of the centaurs who followed us.

"You couldn't choose now to make me go on one of my spirit-trip things?" I asked my Goddess.

Trust him, Beloved. He will never let you fall drifted through my mind, but I swear it was accompanied by goddess-like laughter.

13

The Temple of the Muse was even more impressive from the ground. We followed a flower-strewn path to the central building, then beautiful young women divided up the army, leading each group to their quarters amidst lots of young human voices giggling and centaurs laughing. Thalia was on the steps of the great building to greet us. She wore a long, silver gown that sparkled like it had been threaded with zillions of tiny diamonds. Her thick, honey-colored hair was braided with fragrant gardenias and hung past the middle of her back. The deepening twilight cast her blind eyes into shadow.

"Welcome again, Epona's Chosen." She smiled warmly. "And Shaman ClanFintan, we are always pleased to have you visit us."

"Thalia…" ClanFintan walked forward and took her hand as she offered it, raising it briefly to his lips. "You never age."

Her laughter was infectious. "Save your flattery for your new wife," she said, but with obvious affection. Then she tilted her head toward me. "Lady Rhea, I have waited long to welcome you."

I had the disconcerting feeling that she knew who I was. On impulse I slid off ClanFintan's back, and took her hand in mine, squeezing it warmly.

"Thank you, it's nice to meet you, too." From close up I could see her face was etched delicately with laugh lines and small creases that said she was not as young as she appeared.

She squeezed my hand in response. "Come, our maidens will show you to your quarters. After you have refreshed your-selves you can join the feast we have prepared for you." She turned, and her robe rippled and shimmered as she moved with graceful confidence up the steep stairs to the open doors of the temple, her ivory cane tapping occasionally in front of her the only evidence of her blindness.

She sees more than most, Beloved. The words in my mind didn't surprise me.

We were led through halls that made Epona's Temple look modest. The ceilings were impossibly high, decorated with crown molding that was carved with lifelike scenes of the Priestesses and their students. I was amazed to see colorful songbirds flitting above us, filling the air with welcoming trills. Our opulent chamber had its own private bath, complete with a sunken pool of steaming water. I noticed a filmy-looking gown, much like Thalia had been wearing, draped over the end of the huge bed.

ClanFintan smiled as I cooed in delight.

"Oh, man! I'm going to take a long bath! Want to wash my back?" I was already peeling off my dirty riding clothes and heading to the sunken tub.

"If I know Thalia and the rest of the Muses, we do not have time for much intimate bathing." His eyes followed my naked body with what I was pleased to recognize as lustful longing.

"I'll hurry." I looked at the bath, then at him. "Come here, I'll share my sponge with you, there's just no way you're going to fit in here."

He grinned, stripped off his vest and approached the tub with a leer.

"Be good." I slapped his hands away with the wet sponge. "Hold still, you smell like a horse."

After much splashing and laughing, I declared both of us clean, and my husband wrapped me in a towel. I held tightly to his arm so I didn't slip on the water that we'd caused to spill from the tub.

"We made a mess," I said as I dried myself and headed over to the bed, where my hands caressed the diaphanous material of the dress.

ClanFintan stood behind me and took the towel from around his shoulders and began helping me to dry my damp hair.

"You will look edible in that." He leaned down and kissed a sensitive spot on the side of my neck.

I shivered in pleasure, then turned and walked into his arms, resting my head against him.

"Please be careful tomorrow. Nuada is…" I didn't know how to describe such perfect evil. "Horrible beyond words." I faltered.

"I will not allow him to touch you."

"I know you won't."

He held me tighter.

Two knocks sounded at the door, and a voice said, "My Lord, my Lady, the banquet is about to begin."

"Thank you," I called. Before I pulled away, ClanFintan bent and kissed me.

"I love you," he said simply.

"I love you, too. That's why I'm scared."

He smiled and tapped the tip of my nose. "Do not be."

I smiled back at him before I turned and pulled on the beautiful dress. But I couldn't shake the empty feeling in my stomach—and, for once, I knew it had nothing to do with food.

ClanFintan held my hand as we joined the crowd that was

making its way to what must be a humongous banquet room. The centaurs were all smiles, looking relaxed and happy as they followed their hostesses to dinner. It was hard for me to imagine they would be going into battle in twenty-four hours.

We stepped into the banquet hall, and I gasped with appreciation for the exquisite room. It was filled with tables and chaises, and food and wine were being set out everywhere, but my eyes were drawn upward. At least a dozen huge crystal chandeliers hung suspended from the high domed ceiling, which was painted with a mural depicting the night sky, complete with constellations encrusted with sparkling jewels. The entire room glistened with a glow that made the stars appear to move in the painted sky.

"There has to be magic in here," I whispered to ClanFintan as we were shown to our places at the head table.

"Yes," he whispered back, "there is always magic present at the Temple of the Muse."

"Wow!" He bent so that I could keep my voice soft. "Now, *that* is amazing!"

His eyes glistened with laughter, and he kissed me on top of my head. "You will find magic is much like life, its gifts are best when they are unexpected."

"Then this room is a great gift." As was this surprising new life of mine, I added silently as we made our way to the center table.

"Ah, Lady Rhea, ClanFintan! Please, join us." Thalia motioned to a large chaise that sat between her regal chair and another beautiful woman's chair. I was happy to see Victoria was already reclining on the other side of Thalia.

Our chaise was set up so that ClanFintan and I could position ourselves in our preferred mealtime positions, with him reclining, and me perching next to him.

I wonder how the hell she knew so much about us?

As if she could read my mind, she said, "I know more than just that, Shannon." The Incarnate Muse of Comedy leaned close to me so that our voices wouldn't carry.

I blinked at her in surprise, a clear question on my face, before I realized she couldn't see me, and I attempted to babble something that sounded like, "But—I—don't…"

Her infectious laughter sparkled between us. "Do not worry, I am pleased that Epona's *true* Chosen has finally arrived—as are we all."

"Oh," I said, feeling completely out of my league.

Concern passed across her face and she quickly explained, "Do not fear what you do not immediately understand. Your Goddess is with you. That is all that is really important." She patted my hand kindly, suddenly reminding me of my mother. I felt unexpected tears catch in my throat.

"What is it, child?" she asked.

"I'm just glad to be here."

She reached out unerringly and touched my cheek, exactly as my mother would have done. "You must be hungry." She clapped her hands together, and servants carrying trays laden with steaming food began circulating around the room.

As I devoured a delicious stuffed quail, I winked at Vic. "Hey, did you kill any of this food?"

"Not tonight, Rhea." She winked back. "I offered, but they said they had already been preparing for our arrival. So I had to content myself with sipping a goblet of wine and waiting for you to finish—" she raised her eyebrows suggestively in ClanFintan's direction "—dressing."

"Stop, you bad thing," I giggled at her. "What can I say, he's big, so he takes a lot of—" I raised my eyebrows suggestively, too "—washing." We dissolved into girlfriend giggles. Clan-Fintan pointedly ignored us, but Thalia joined our laughter.

With the next course I noticed Sila entering the room and

being led to our table, and I was chagrined that I'd forgotten completely about the threat of smallpox. Before Sila took her appointed place next to Victoria, she paused to address Thalia.

"You seem to have the outbreak quite under control." Her voice was filled with respect. "Melpomene asks that I inform you that none of the young ones have worsened, and the marsh people will soon be well enough to be on their way." Her brow wrinkled as she continued, "But Terpsichore has become ill, and will be unable to attend the feast."

"Thank you, Sila. Please rest and refresh yourself."

I leaned over and whispered to ClanFintan, "Isn't Terpsichore the Muse that danced at our handfast?"

"Yes," he replied, keeping his voice low.

"And Melpomene is Muse of Tragedy," Thalia surprised me by leaning toward me and volunteering. "She feels she needs to be in charge whenever there is an illness."

"Then you're familiar with smallpox?"

Thalia's expression remained serene. "It is not unusual for illness to come out of Ufasach Marsh, and we have dealt with the pox before. But we were saddened to learn it had spread to Epona's Temple."

"We have the sick quarantined, and our Healer says it is under control."

"Excellent." She took a sip from her crystal wineglass before she continued in a voice pitched low for my ears alone. "Perhaps you would like to know that next to your husband sits Calliope, Muse of Poetry. Beside her reclines Cleio, Muse of History." She tilted her head, listening, before she continued. "At the head of the nearest table, Erato, Muse of Love Lyrics, is entertaining young Dougal, who has so recently lost his brother."

My eyes followed her introductions and I was pleased to see

Dougal's face glowing with rapt attention as the lovely Erato spoke animatedly.

"Seated at the table with the leaders of the warriors are Polyhymnia, Muse of Song, Rhetoric and Geometry, who is wearing a violet robe, and Urania, Muse of Astronomy and Astrology, who should be attired in her typical velvet robe the color of the night sky."

"Yes, it's exactly as you describe."

"You have already heard that Terpsichore, Muse of the Dance, has fallen ill…" Her voice lowered with sadness. "And Euterpe, Muse of Lyric Poetry, became ill two days ago."

"I'm sorry. Terpsichore danced at our wedding. She was beautiful."

"And if her Goddess wills it, she will be again."

"Thalia, thank you for explaining all of this to me. And thank you for accepting me."

"You are very welcome, child." She straightened, still smiling, and clapped her hands together twice. The room fell silent in expectation. "Allow us to entertain our brave centaur warriors." Her smile was as bright as the chandeliers. "And may all of our Goddesses bless you tomorrow."

The Muse Erato was the first to rise. She began a touching song about a young peasant girl who won the heart of a Chieftain's son, and the feats he had to accomplish before his father would consent to their marriage.

I tried more delicious food than I could keep count of, then, satisfied, I leaned back against my husband's warm chest to enjoy the talent of the Muses, and the delicious quality of their red wine.

Erato was followed by Calliope, who expertly recited a rousing epic poem about the first centaur High Shaman, which concluded to the thunderous applause of her audience. Then Polyhymnia sang a hauntingly beautiful ballad that reminded me

of something I could have heard on an Enya CD. As several
dancers entered the huge chamber and began a sensuous dance,
accompanied by pulsing drums, I felt my eyes begin to grow
heavy.

ClanFintan's arms encircled me, and I tried to swim back
to wakefulness.

"Shh, child, sleep." Thalia's motherly voice drifted into my
semiconscious mind. "Your Goddess calls."

And blackness overcame me.

This time I wasn't eased out of my sleeping body by a delicious dream. Instead, I felt my spirit wrenched upward, through
the diamond-encrusted dome in response to the order *Come!*

I hung above the enormous temple, momentarily disoriented. The temple looked misty and confusing—and I realized
that clouds had rolled in with the night, obscuring the familiar
landmarks of the mountains and river. But laughter and music
floated in the night around me. Despite the bad weather, the
Muses' temple was alive with esprit de corps—in other words,
morale was damn good.

Too soon my body began moving in a westerly direction. I
began passing over the fields that separated Laragon Castle from
the Muse, catching only occasional glimpses of the green
beneath me through the low-hanging clouds. I hadn't gone far
when I began to feel an uncomfortable sensation in the pit of
my stomach.

My body slowed—then stopped.

My heart was racing, and I heard the blood pounding in my
temples. Below me, just outside the western edge of the
temple's grounds, the misty fields were thick with the moving
bodies of the Fomorian army. They were approaching silently,
using their wings to increase their insect-like gliding strides.

No! I closed my eyes and willed my spirit back into my body...

★ ★ ★

I leaped up, interrupting the lovely dance as I screamed the word aloud, "No!"

"Rhea!" ClanFintan reached for me. "What is it?"

I gasped for air—my body was shaking violently. "They're coming! Now! The Fomorians are almost on the temple grounds."

The room erupted in pandemonium, and ClanFintan shot to his feet, raising his arm and shouting for silence. Centaur and human obeyed.

"Then the time has come," he addressed the centaurs with the confidence of an experienced leader. "Herdsmasters, assemble your warriors on the western lawn. Dougal, send our swiftest runner with orders to skirt the Fomorian line and get to the humans. Tell them we await their aid. Loose the pigeons with the same message. And remember, centaurs, they must not break through our lines."

Bless them, Beloved.

I was filled with a sudden calm, and my voice rang out across the huge chamber. "We are counting on your courage. And you are courageous. I know it because courage is not measured by the crude vulgarity of claws and fangs overpowering women and hacking apart unprepared men. Courage arises from a sense of duty, and the firm resolve of goodness and right. And that is what I see before me—your nobility and integrity. May Epona's blessing and grace go with each of you. My love surely does."

A shout of "Hail Epona!" rang to the domed ceiling. Then the room exploded into a sea of moving centaurs.

The Incarnates of the Muse were making their way toward Thalia. The blind priestess's face was serene. She spoke in a calm voice to the women who surrounded her.

"Priestesses, our students know they are to assemble here.

Keep them busy, it will help to keep them calm." The Priestesses murmured agreement, and they began calling to the young students who had begun arriving as the centaurs were leaving.

"Mistress Thalia," Sila addressed the Priestess, "have your students begin boiling large quantities of water, and tearing linen into strips for bandaging. I will check on the ill ones and inform them of what has happened. Then I will return here to help your students prepare for the injured."

"Thank you, Sila."

"Victoria!" ClanFintan called the Huntress to his side. He put his hand on her shoulder and looked into her eyes as he spoke. "While I am away, I entrust to you the safety of my wife."

Vic covered his hand with her own. "Fight the battle with a clear mind, my friend. I will protect Rhea with my life."

ClanFintan put his arm around me and led me a few paces away from the women. For a moment we just looked at each other, then he bent and his mouth covered mine. I clung to him, wanting to drown in the taste and heat of him. Reluctantly, he broke the kiss and took my face in his hands. I felt my lip tremble, and I blinked my eyes rapidly, willing the tears that were waiting there not to fall. I didn't want to send him into battle with me blubbering like a sissy.

"Remember always, I was born to love you. You are as much a part of me as my soul. If you stay safe, a part of me will always remain safe."

"No, it doesn't work like that." I knew I sounded frantic, but I couldn't stop myself. "Nothing can happen to you—don't tell me all that crap about if I'm safe, you're safe. It's bullshit unless you really *are* okay." I put my hands over his. "Promise me you will live and come back to me. I couldn't bear it if you did not."

"Rhea, you—"

"Promise me!" I said with a violence that surprised even me.

"You have my promise." He pulled me against him roughly, and I felt his lips press the top of my head. "Stay with Victoria. I will find you when it is over." He released me, and without looking back, turned and left the room.

I heard Vic's hooves clip sharply against the marble floor as she came to stand beside me.

"Thalia has told me of a way we can reach the roof of this temple. She says it will be tricky, but the Huntresses and I should be able to climb to it. Let us go watch from there."

"It's dark." My voice sounded numbed.

"It will not be for much longer. Dawn is only a few hours away."

I could see the other Huntresses had entered the room. I noticed they were all carrying an impressive array of crossbows and quivers filled with deadly-looking arrows. The sight of their quiet confidence broke my numbness.

"Vic, I need to change out of this dress and back into my riding clothes."

She nodded in understanding. "We will wait here for you."

As I hurried back to the banquet room, it was easy to tell that the scene was already more organized. The students were quietly clearing away the feast and pushing the tables to the sides of the room. Several large pots were suspended over the hearths in the walls. The Priestesses were moving among their young students, stopping here and there to speak words of calm encouragement. I saw Victoria and the five Huntresses I knew from Epona's Temple standing in the far corner of the room. Vic made a motion for me to join them. As I moved across the room, Thalia intercepted me, handing me a long bronze tube.

"It will help you to see," she explained.

I took the small telescope and tried to thank her, but she had already moved away and was speaking to a group of nervous young girls.

The Huntresses were standing in the arch of an exit that led to a circular stairway that wrapped its way upward.

"Come, Thalia says this leads to the roof." Victoria began climbing the precariously small stairs first, followed by me, then the other Huntresses.

The passage was narrow. The Huntresses could stretch their arms out and touch the smooth walls on either side, which they did to help them maneuver their way up the tight spiral.

"If you trip and fall backward, you'll squish me," I informed Vic.

Without turning her head, she said, "Huntresses do not trip."

"That's a good thing," I muttered.

I heard the Huntress directly behind me, I think her name was Elaine, snort a quick laugh at my response. Nope—they sure didn't act nervous.

Just when I thought the spiral would never end, Victoria heaved herself through another carved doorway. I heard her hooves clatter on the roof as she moved aside so that the rest of us could emerge.

We spilled out onto a narrow passageway that wrapped around the domed roof. It was not quite a horse's width across, which meant the Huntresses had to stand sideways and hug the wall to pass by one another. The outer wall was lined with balustrades. Between each column were large earthenware planters filled with geraniums and overflowing ivy, trailing a green waterfall of wide-leafed plants over the side of the temple.

In the murky light of predawn, Victoria surveyed the rooftop.

"This was meant to be a garden, not a place of defense." The Huntress sounded annoyed.

"It's a school for women, Vic, not soldiers." I felt the need to come to the Muses' defense. After all, this was the equivalent of Rhiannon's university, and I sure wouldn't want anyone making fun of the University of Illinois (go Illini!).

Vic made a disgusted noise, which was echoed by the other Huntresses.

"Spread out. Take up positions several lengths apart, all facing the west. Let me know when the armies become visible." The Huntresses moved to obey her. I took up my own position next to her.

I peered out into the gloom and worried.

"He is a great warrior," Vic said.

"Even great warriors bleed when they're cut." I sighed. "Maybe I should try and sleep so that my spirit body could go find him."

"He would sense your presence," she said gently. "You would distract him."

"I hate waiting."

Vic nodded in agreement.

14

We sat in silence. I strained to see or hear any sound of fighting, but the only noises came from the light breeze whispering through the ivy, and an occasional call of a lark that was greeting the new day with innocent exuberance.

The sky behind us began to lighten, and the gray lifted, but only a little. The clouds from the night before were obviously there to stay, and even a weird fog was drifting out of the marsh to hang suspended over the temple grounds. My body jerked with understanding.

"Carolan said Fomorians don't like to move around in the daylight. But they're attacking today because of the damn weather."

Grimly, Victoria nodded.

To the north the mountains swam into and out of view. I raised the lens to my eye, turning the wheel in the middle of it until the misty side of the closest mountain came into focus. No creatures visible there. Yet.

I turned and looked over the deep forest. Overshadowed by clouds it looked sleepy and harmless. I continued turning, and got occasional glimpses through the fog of the verdant green of what must be the beginnings of Ufasach Marsh.

Before I could complete my circle, Victoria yelled, "There!"

I yanked the telescope from my eye to see Victoria pointing into the west at a dark smudge that spread across the western horizon. I lifted the glass back to my eye, surprised by the sudden trembling in my hands.

"Take it." I handed it to Vic. "Look for me, my hands won't be still."

The Huntress took the glass and calmly put it to her eye, focusing the wheel as I had done before.

"It is the rear line of our archers," she said as she looked.

I remembered the group of centaurs I had noticed who carried dangerous-looking longbows slung across their backs, along with quivers filled with long, pointed arrows.

"Are they good archers?" I asked.

"Except for Woulff's men, they are the best in Partholon."

"I wish Woulff was here, too."

"As do I." She kept watching. "The warriors must not have engaged the Fomorians yet. I can see the archers firing rounds, their bows pointed high into the sky." She adjusted the focus again. "There, I can see the line of our warriors. They are waiting for the archers to finish."

It started to drizzle as I looked intently into the west. I was able to make out the distant line of archers and the rain of arrows that flew at intervals up and out, then down, as though the clouds were belching death. Between the rounds of arrows, I saw something that glistened intermittently in front of the archers' line.

"What is that shining?"

"Our centaurs have drawn their claymores," she explained.

I felt a chill travel down my spine.

"They are advancing." Her voice was emotionless and loud so that the Huntresses could hear what she was saying. Listening to her I felt an odd detachment, almost like we were watching a bizarre TV program. It was hard for me to believe my husband was part of that line of glinting swords.

"What's happening now?"

She took the telescope from her eye and handed it to me. "The battle has begun."

I wiped droplets of moisture from the lens before resting my elbows against the rail that ran around the top of the balustrades, which kept my hands from shaking. Then I raised the telescope to my eye and focused on the distant scene.

Through the dreary morning I could see the moving line of centaurs, several thick, as the archers parted and, brandishing their own claymores they dispersed to join the left and right flanks. I tried to focus on individual centaurs, but they were too far away. I couldn't even see any Fomorians, just the straining, heaving backs of the centaurs as the line moved forward in some places and surged back in others.

"I can't tell what the hell is going on." I took my eye from the glass and handed it back to Vic.

"It could go on like this for hours." She smiled gently at me. "The first battle you witness is always the most horrible."

"Basically, all we can do is stand here and watch?" I asked.

"That is all we can do."

And that is what we did. As the morning changed to midday, five young students brought us sandwiches of hard bread, meat and cheese, along with skins of sweet wine.

"Tell Thalia there is no change," I said to one of the girls.

"She already knows, Lady Rhiannon," she said as she left the roof.

"Thalia sees many things," Vic said.

"She sure does."

We chewed our food, taking turns looking through the telescope. As I finished my sandwich, the Huntress to the right of me, Cathleen, handed me the telescope so I could take my turn. I took several drinks of the sweet wine to clear my throat, and then I raised the glass to my eye, refocusing until the battlefield came into sharp view.

And I felt a sudden urge to puke up my lunch.

"Vic!" The Huntress moved quickly to my side. I handed her the telescope. "The line is moving."

She raised the glass to her eye, looking intently. Her breath sucked in, and her body grew very still. "The centaurs have broken." Her voice was a death knell. "These women are doomed."

15

"No!" I grabbed her arm. "Fomorians cannot cross water. Being separated from the earth by flowing water causes them unbearable pain. If we can get the women across the bridge to the other side of the river, they will be safe."

She handed me the telescope, and while I refocused it she called orders to the Huntresses.

"We must move the women across the bridge. The creatures have broken through our warriors. The only way the women will be safe is if they cross over the river. Help them get to safety. Now!"

I pressed my body against the balustrade as the Huntresses passed me to retrace their path down the treacherous stairwell, and gazed in horror through the telescope. Now I could see the winged shapes of the Fomorians as they inundated the centaur ranks. There was no longer a discernible line—instead, there was a jumble of bodies as the battle swelled toward us. I was still unable to recognize individual centaurs, but I could clearly see creatures being hacked apart by claymores, and centaurs being clawed to their knees as groups of the creatures broke off to single out and surround individual warriors. As I watched, masses of creatures were slain, only to be replaced by more and more of their fellow creatures, who used the bodies of their fallen comrades to stand upon so that they were more equal in height with the battling centaurs. Wave upon wave of claws and teeth washed over the centaurs. They had no choice but to give ground.

"Come, Rhea, we have work to do."

"I don't see him!"

"Rhea, he said he would find you. It does no good for you to stay here watching. But you can help us get the women to safety."

I made myself lower the telescope and turn away from the battle scene. "Let's get the women out of here." I hurried from the roof with Victoria close behind me.

As we entered the banquet chamber, the fearful chatter of the girls quieted. Thalia walked silently to stand before us.

"The centaur army cannot hold the Fomorians. They will overrun the temple," I said, surprised at how calm I sounded.

"Yes, my Goddess has already spoken thus to me. What must we do?"

"You must have all the women make their way quickly to the bridge. Fomorians cannot cross the Geal River. Once you are on the other side of the river, you will be safe."

I looked around the room until I spotted Sila.

"Sila, get those who are ill onto pallets, the Huntresses will transport them."

The centaur Healer nodded and cantered from the room.

"It must be now, Thalia, the army cannot have much time remaining."

"Ladies…" Thalia's regal voice filled the room. "Follow the Priestesses to the bridge—we must leave our temple. Take nothing with you except your lives." Then she tilted her head to the side, and the room remained silent while she listened to an internal voice that I understood all too well. "My Goddess assures me this is not the last time we will see our beloved temple—what is lost will be regained. Now, quickly, and as we leave let us each pray fervently that the brave centaurs will join us across the river."

The Priestesses were the first to hurry to the exit doors, each followed by an orderly group of her students. Erato took Thalia by the hand, and together they encouraged those at the rear to keep up with the others.

Thalia would have made a really good high school teacher. (But she would've had to take a big cut in pay.)

"You should go with them, Rhea," Vic said.

"Where are you going?"

"To help move those who are ill." Her fellow Huntresses were already cantering through the door Sila had used.

"I stay with you." Before she could argue, I reminded her, "ClanFintan told me to stay with you."

She sighed, but said, "Then come here, we can move more quickly if you are astride me." Much like ClanFintan, Vic grabbed my upper arm and I grabbed hers, then she tossed me easily onto her sleek back. I held tightly to her shoulders as she sprinted to the exit, following her Huntresses. We skidded around corners and turned down elaborately decorated halls, following the clear echo of hooves in the otherwise silent temple. We burst through an opened door to an outside garden in time to see the back of one of the Huntresses disappearing through a door across the courtyard. She leaped across the space in several long strides.

"You are damn fast," I yelled into her ear.

"I am Lead Huntress," she yelled back, like that explained everything.

We caught up to the Huntresses just as I smelled a familiar odor. Vic and I wrinkled our noses.

"This must be the place," I said as our group came to a large door.

I slid off her back, and Vic opened the door. Sila was in the middle of the room, helping patients from their beds and onto thick blanket-like pallets. She looked up as we entered.

"Those near the door are ready to be moved," she said, then turned back to the pustule-marked teenager who was leaning heavily on her arm.

"There are more of them than I anticipated." Victoria spoke in low tones to her centaurs. "Work quickly, Huntresses."

"Sila!" Vic caught her attention. "We have very little time."

Sila's eyes widened, but the centaur Healer's gentle voice did not betray the worry reflected in her eyes. "Listen, ladies!" The room became abruptly silent. "Those of you who are able must be transported astride the Huntresses. Stand if you think you are able to ride." About a dozen young women rose slowly to their feet.

The Huntresses moved quickly to the standing women. I followed them, helping to lift the sick girls to the centaurs' backs. As each Huntress turned to exit the room, a tall woman dressed in black blessed them and admonished them to hold tightly so they wouldn't fall.

"Priestess," I heard Sila addressing the woman when the last Huntress had left the room. "You must join the others at the river crossing."

"I will not leave until this room is emptied," was her dramatic reply.

She must be Melpomene, Muse of Tragedy. I wanted to roll my eyes and say, "That figures," but I thought it'd be rude.

As I helped another teenager out of her bed, a dark-haired woman who was propped up against pillows caught my eye.

I almost called her Michelle, but caught myself in time.

"Terpsichore." I stopped at her bedside, studying her. "You look well enough to ride, be sure to get on the next Huntress who returns."

"My students leave first." Her eyes were bright with fever and her face was flushed. She was obviously in the beginning stages of the disease.

"They need you with them." I tried to reason with her, but I recognized the familiar stubborn set of her jaw. (Usually she was being stubborn about buying a $250 silk blouse when she could only afford a $40 cotton pullover, but it was the same immovable stubbornness.)

"And those who leave last will need me, too."

"Fine." I knew better than to waste my time arguing with her. "Just watch your butt when time gets short. You do not want to be caught by those things." I started to walk away, and her voice stopped me.

"Rhiannon, I hear you have changed."

"Yes, I am not like I used to be."

"Then I truly do wish you happiness in your mating." This time her blessing was genuine.

"Thank you." I smiled at her, and went back to work, helping the sick girls get ready to be moved. I hoped she would show enough sense to get across the river—I didn't want to think about what would happen to her if the creatures caught her. Except for the unnaturally bright flush of her skin, she was still breathtakingly beautiful.

I was lifting a wraith-thin girl from her bed and making her smile by telling her that she wouldn't weigh ninety pounds soaking wet with a squirrel in her pocket, when the Huntresses slid back into the room in a clatter of hooves and began loading up for their second evacuation trip. The girl I was carrying shrieked suddenly with much more strength than I would have thought possible. I looked up to see Dougal burst through the open door.

"Get across the river now!" he shouted between ragged breaths. "The warriors are keeping them out of the temple for as long as possible, but they are close behind me." His sides quivered, and he was spattered with blood and gore. There was an angry-looking slash across his shoulder, and another gash across his cheek was steadily seeping blood. He looked so much like his dying brother that I had to choke back tears.

Sila rushed to his side and began examining his many wounds.

The room broke into a cacophony of sound and motion until the tall Priestess, Melpomene, raised her black-robed arms, clapping her hands together in a bursting ball of sparks.

Yep, there sure as hell was magic here.

"This is what we shall do." She spoke in an imperious tone. "Those of you who are able to ride will climb astride the Huntresses. Those of you who can walk, go down the rear pathway to the river. If you cannot make it to the bridge, conceal yourselves in the foliage near the water. The rest of us will remain here."

"If you remain here, you will die." I spoke with surety into the stillness of the room.

"Epona's Chosen, you should know that we are not without defenses." The Priestess smiled at me, and I was amazed at the transformation that occurred in her appearance. Her smile softened the harsh lines of her face, and let her underlying beauty become visible. "Wait no longer. Save yourselves. We have placed ourselves in the loving hands of our Goddesses."

I saw that Terpsichore was walking purposefully to stand by the dark woman's side. She looked serene and lovely and spoke in a calm, unhurried voice.

"Lady Rhiannon, did you not send word that your Goddess has revealed to you that the way to combat the pox is to isolate those who have been infected with it from other people?"

"Yes, smallpox is very contagious," I answered quickly, not sure why she was taking time to repeat old instructions.

"So contagious that it can spread easily if an infected person mingles with those who are healthy?"

"Yes, it can be spread easily, but there needs to be contact between the ill person and the well person."

"And are the Fomorians not humanlike?"

"Yes."

"Then I will remain and have contact with them," she said simply.

"No! They'll kill you. Or worse. Anyway, even if they can get the disease—and we don't know for sure that they can—it can be transmitted to them through the diseased waste left on these blankets." I gestured at the mess of linens that lay abandoned around the room.

"What would creatures like that want with these soiled linens?" Her laughter was like music. "No—" her lovely face sobered "—my Goddess and I have decided. This is how it must be."

"We have to leave now!" Dougal's strained voice interrupted the silence that the Muse's words evoked.

"Whatever happens to me is a small price to pay to give the creatures so *priceless* a gift." Terpsichore's thick-lashed eyes sparked with the irony of her words.

"What you do here will not be forgotten," I said, awed by her sacrifice. "I give you my word."

"I am pleased my final performance will be remembered," she said before melting into the graceful bow of a prima ballerina.

"It will be," I promised before shifting my attention to the rest of the room. "Let's go!" I yelled and the room exploded back into action as sick teenagers scrambled aboard Huntresses.

Sila approached me and paused long enough to hand me a leather purselike pouch suspended on a long leather thong. I looked at her questioningly.

She spoke quietly. "Within the pouch is ointment that numbs and helps to close wounds." She glanced across the room at Dougal. "Apply it sparingly, many may need it. And be certain you take a skinful of wine before you leave, too." She pointed to a table filled with full leather bladders.

I nodded my understanding and slung the thong over my head so that the pouch rested snugly against my left side near my waist, and grabbed one of the wineskins and slung it over my other shoulder. Then I went back to work loading the Huntresses with sick girls.

As the last patient scrambled aboard Elaine, I looked around the room and saw that Sila was supporting four stumbling girls as they slowly made their way out the back exit of the room.

"Sila!" I shouted after her.

She turned and I heard her angelic voice from across the room. "I will go with these sick ones. If the Goddess wills, we will meet you across the river." Without taking any more time, she and her entourage moved through the door.

"Lady Rhea, we have no more time." Dougal held a shaking, blood-covered hand out to help me mount. All of the Huntresses except Victoria were already out the door; the fading echo of their hooves rang as they galloped down the hall.

Victoria moved quickly to my side, brushing away Dougal's hand.

"You are in no shape to bear even her slight weight." She grabbed my arm and tossed me to her back. As we thundered toward the exit, I craned my neck around in time to see Melpomene and Terpsichore holding hands in the middle of a circle of about half a dozen women who were too sick to move. Their heads were bowed and they looked like they were suffused with light. Then we, too, burst out into the hall.

16

The Huntresses were out of sight somewhere ahead of us, but Victoria confidently dodged around corners and cut through gardens, until we finally cleared the internal maze of the temple and found ourselves on the front lawn. We veered to the left, but a movement on our right caught my eye.

"Victoria!" I yelled, pulling on her shoulder with one hand and pointing with the other. Dougal and the Huntress skidded to a halt, turning in the direction I was pointing. Spilling onto the northwestern edge of the lawn was a ragged line of centaurs. They attempted to stand their ground, and their claymores sang as they hacked at one winged creature after another. But, just as I had witnessed in the telescope, as soon as one creature fell, another stepped in to take its place— all teeth and claws, standing atop its fallen comrade. Step by step, they beat back the centaur line. As I watched, one exhausted centaur fell to his knees and six creatures leaped on his back, raking their claws over him, turning his coat red with his own blood.

"Get to the bridge!" Dougal yelled. "The warriors will hold them off as long as possible." And we resumed our flight.

We followed the lush green lawn around a corner, and came

face-to-face with a group of four students who were running fearfully back in our direction.

"Stop! You cannot go back this way, you must get over the bridge." Victoria and Dougal put their bodies in the path of the terrified group, forcing them to halt.

The girl who appeared to be in the lead shook her head violently from side to side.

"T-t-they are t-t-there already!" She was shaking so hard she was difficult to understand.

"What? Who do you mean?" Dougal asked frantically.

"Them!" Her voice was shrill. "The Fomorians. They are ch-chopping d-down the bridge!"

"Oh, Goddess help us," Victoria breathed.

"They must have flanked our army and circled around the temple to the north to cut off the river escape." Dougal's voice was flat.

"Go toward the swamp." I said the words aloud as they whispered into my mind.

"Yes!" Victoria spoke to the frightened girls. "Go into Ufasach Marsh…the Fomorians will be loath to follow you there."

The girls nodded and darted off in a new direction.

"That is where we must go, too," Dougal said, staring back the way we had come. "There is nothing the two of us can do to stop the Fomorians at the bridge."

Victoria nodded tightly.

"Not yet," I said firmly.

"We must." Dougal sounded exhausted.

"No, I'll go to the edge of the swamp, but I won't go into it unless ClanFintan is with us."

"Lady Rhea, he sent me ahead to be sure you were moved to safety. He said he will join you when he is able."

"Then he's still alive." My stomach wrenched as I asked the question.

"He lived when last I saw him."

"Then I wait for him to find me, *before* I go into the swamp."

Victoria and Dougal exchanged glances as they began a flat gallop in the direction the girls had taken. We quickly overtook them. I felt Vic sigh as she and Dougal slid to a halt beside them.

"Scoot forward, Rhea, you have company." Vic's voice attempted light humor. "Come on, girls, we do not have time for riding lessons."

Dougal grimaced in pain as he lifted two girls up behind me, then he put the other two on his own blood-flecked back. We took off again with the frightened kids clinging like crabs to the backs of the centaurs.

"I hope the swamp is not too damn far away," I said into Victoria's ear.

"As do I," she whispered between labored breaths. "You humans just seem to get heavier and heavier."

We smelled the marsh before we saw it. Again, I thought it reminded me of an old compost heap, but this time the smell was much more inviting. We came to a halt on the edge of a steep incline, at the bottom of which bunched a grove of trees, mostly moss-laden cypress, intermingled with a few willows and some trees with yellowish bark that I thought were probably hackberry. Along the edge of the incline, at intervals of about ten feet, stood an enormous ring of old stones, reminding me a little of the rocks at Stonehenge.

"They look like they're standing guard."

"That is the legend, Lady Rhiannon." The kid sitting behind me, who was clutching me around the middle so hard I felt short of breath, spoke.

While I helped the teenagers behind me drop off Vic's back, she continued educating me.

"Thalia taught us that the first Incarnate Priestesses of the

Muse erected the Stonewatchmen to help stop Ufasach Marsh from spreading to their new temple." She suddenly looked apologetic and embarrassed. "Oh, forgive me, my Lady, you must already know that."

"Don't worry about it, kid. It never hurts to hear one of Thalia's lessons again."

When all the teenagers were on the ground once more, Vic spoke urgently to them. "Now, hurry into the marsh, but keep as close to the eastern edge as you can. As soon as you are far enough south, try to find a way to get across the river. If you cannot, stay within the marsh until you reach the boundaries of Epona's Temple. Help will be waiting there."

They thanked us, then ran bravely down the incline and disappeared into the swamp.

"We have to join them," Dougal said.

"I'm waiting for him."

The two centaurs turned, and we stared down the lawn that led back to the temple. The land sloped gradually down from the lovely buildings, so from where we stood it was apparent that the network of Muse temples had been built on a raised plateau, which, even in the gloom of the cloudy day, allowed us a good view of the south side of the grounds. I realized that the stand of ornamental shrubs that Vic and Dougal had crashed through to get to the edge of the swamp looped in a decorative line before us, serving to shield us from the sight of anyone standing on the southern grounds.

The temple had become a battlefield. Hordes of Fomorians blackened the steps of the central temple and the surrounding lawns as they attacked groups of retreating centaurs. There was no more organized line of centaur warriors; instead, they had broken off into clusters, heroically attempting to keep the creatures from getting past them. But even as we watched, creatures slipped around the battling centaurs and sped past them, entering the temple and racing past it toward the river.

"I hope the women got across the bridge." Dougal's voice sounded strained.

"I wish I still had that telescope," I said, straining my eyes to try and make out individual centaurs.

"We must enter the swamp." Vic didn't sound happy at the prospect.

"I won't go without ClanFintan."

"Even if you see him, he has no way of knowing you are here." Vic's voice sounded exasperated with my insistence.

"I could try and find him," Dougal said.

"A lone centaur? You'd be killed for sure." I shook my head.

"I could go with him," Vic offered.

"Then you'd both be killed."

My mind was whirring, trying to come up with a plan, but my thoughts were all jumbled together. Everything had happened too fast. We hadn't been prepared. They had attacked too soon. Where were the other armies? And where was Clan-Fintan where was ClanFintan where was ClanFintan…?

Peace, Beloved—let yourself hear my voice.

At the Goddess's words I forced my mind to clear, closed my eyes, put my face in my hands and took a deep, cleansing breath, letting Epona's wise words drift through my addled brain.

"Yes!" My eyes shot open. "Vic, get me over there to one of those stones."

Victoria gave me an odd look, but she didn't argue as she trotted over to the nearest stone. It was huge. I'd have to stand on her back. Hopefully, I could grab the craggy ridges near the top of it and haul myself up.

"Um, I'm going to have to stand on your back, Vic. Sorry about that. And you'll need to hold this wineskin for me."

She grabbed the leather bladder from me and backed up against the rock. "You should probably stand on my rump."

"You're a good friend."

"I know."

I stood on her rump and grabbed the rough side of the rock. "Dougal, help boost me up on top of it."

I lifted my right foot and set it in Dougal's hands so he could boost me up, just like I was mounting a horse (which, I realized, was vaguely ironic). He counted to three, then shoved, and I scrambled, till I was sitting on the thing.

The top was flat and about as wide as the bottom of a folding chair. Slowly, I got my feet under me and stood, with my arms out to help me balance.

"Be careful," Vic called.

"It's damn high," I said, feeling my stomach flutter.

I was facing the temple grounds. The scene of carnage now visible was horrendous. There were only a few clusters remaining of living centaurs. Fomorians dominated the scene. I closed my eyes, not wanting to see the defilement of the temple.

Concentrate on your love for him.

I nodded my head in response, and focused my mind on ClanFintan. Images flashed against my closed eyes: of Clan-Fintan carrying me, tipsy and giggling, into my room—rubbing my tired feet as we made our way to MacCallan Castle—holding me gently in his arms so that I could overcome my fear of him—shape-shifting so that we could join together as man and wife—and telling me he was born to love me.

I tilted back my head, took a deep breath, and with all the strength of my body and soul, I loosed a shout that Epona magnified until it was almost a physical thing.

"CLANFINTAN! COME TO ME!"

I opened my eyes to see that all movement had ceased on

the temple grounds. Every being, centaur and Fomorian, had turned in my direction, and they stood frozen, like they were a part of a macabre painting. Then my heart began to beat again as a small cluster of centaurs from the far right of the scene broke the immobility and began an all-out run in our direction. Even from this distance I recognized the silhouette of the centaur leading the group.

"He's coming!" I yelled. Then my breath caught as the Fomorians, too, became unfrozen and they gave chase. "Oh, no—they're after him."

"Get down from there!" Dougal held out his arms to catch me.

"Wait." I kept watching as ClanFintan and the centaurs fought off the seemingly endless stream of creatures while they made their way toward us. I could hear the screams of the creatures as the centaur warriors hacked at them with renewed strength, but it seemed to no avail as one by one the mighty centaurs fell under swarms of dark winged shapes. As I watched, a single Fomorian broke ranks and sped after the group of retreating centaurs ClanFintan led. Then another followed him, and another...

The way the lead Fomorian moved drew my eye. He didn't have to get any closer for me to recognize him.

"Catch me," I said to Dougal as I faced the rock and let myself drop over the side. I took the wineskin back from Victoria and said grimly, "The centaurs are trying to fight the creatures off, but they are being overwhelmed by sheer numbers."

In response, Dougal unsheathed his claymore, and Victoria pulled her crossbow and quiver from the sling at her side.

Then ClanFintan exploded through the hedge. Up close he was barely recognizable. His claymore and the hand that held it were drenched in blood. His body was covered with gore.

His vest was gone, and in its place were deep claw marks that bled freely. His hair was matted with blood and grime, and a laceration ran from his right temple down to his jawline, barely avoiding his right eye. He skidded to a halt in front of us as Dougal yelled.

"They cannot follow us into the swamp!"

He grabbed me with arms that felt like slick iron, and threw me to his back. I caught a glimpse of a set of deep gouges on his rump. I couldn't tell if the blood that covered his back was his. I put my hands lightly on his shoulders, and tried not to tighten my legs around him, afraid I would break open an unknown wound. Normally, his skin felt warmer than mine, but beneath my hands his shoulders felt like they were burning.

He spun around and faced the hedge.

"The centaurs who were following me?" His voice was raw.

"There were too many creatures. They didn't make it," I said quietly. His only response was to reach up and lay a hot, blood-soaked hand over mine.

The first Fomorian leaped over the hedgerow.

In a motion so fast it blurred, Victoria fired an arrow that embedded itself to the quills in the creature's forehead. It fell, and another creature sprang onto its body, snarling. Vic dispatched that one with an arrow through its throat.

The centaurs began backing quickly down the slope of the incline, with Victoria firing arrows as if she was shooting a machine gun. As we entered the grove that bordered the swamp, a long, sharp hiss focused our eyes on one of the Stonewatchmen.

I knew that hiss.

He hid behind the giant rock, with only the outline of his erect wings visible, but his voice echoed eerily to us.

"I see you, *female.*" His wings quivered. "Remember, I have claimed you for my own. This will not be the last time we meet."

Victoria sighted and let fly an arrow, which tore neatly though an exposed flap of his wing.

We entered the swamp as Nuada's scream sounded behind us.

17

After we left the cover of the grove of trees, the land changed dramatically. It was like we had been transported from a lovely villa in Greece to the middle of the Louisiana bayou. Before us stretched a trackless wetland—a world of still water, and seen and unseen (yeesh) reptiles and bugs. The air was very quiet, and the saturated ground sucked at the centaurs' hooves as they surged ahead, determined to get as much of the wetlands between them and the Fomorians as possible.

The soft ground gave way to a stagnant lake, but the centaurs didn't hesitate. Soon they were flank high in soupy, green-tinted water, pushing their way through thick mats of algae.

As time passed, ClanFintan slowed and fell behind Victoria and Dougal. I saw them sending worried glances over their shoulders at him. Vic pointed in the direction of a stand of trees that appeared to be on semisolid ground. We changed direction and made for the trees.

As we got closer, it was obvious it was some kind of island shooting up in the middle of the shallow lake. Along the edges of the solid land, huge cypress roots were exposed. They looked like thick, brown-gray snakes. I was sure they housed all sorts of crawly things.

One at a time, the centaurs hauled themselves out of the water and onto solid ground. As soon as ClanFintan's four hooves were on the island, I slid off his back and handed the wineskin to Victoria. She uncorked it but handed it to Dougal before she drank. Then I began untying the pouch Sila had given me (and I said a silent prayer of thanks for her thoughtfulness—please let her have crossed the river). Inside the pouch was a jar of thick, yellow salve, a couple of rolls of gauzy linen strips and (I was surprised to discover) several hooked needles and a black thread that felt like fishing line. I gulped when I realized they were clearly meant to sew up wounds and not to replace a button on a dress.

"Show me where you are hurt." I looked up at him, overwhelmed by what I saw. He was breathing hard, and where he wasn't covered with blood and grime, his ordinarily bronzed skin was pale and gray. His muscles twitched and I could see blood trickling steadily out of the slash on his head.

"I heard you call me," he rasped.

"I wouldn't leave without you." I felt tears wash over the corners of my eyes. "Are—are you going to be okay?"

He reached his hand toward me. I rushed forward and clung to it.

"I'm afraid to touch you," I said shakily.

He raised my palm to his lips, closing his eyes as he kissed my hand.

"Do not be afraid." I felt his lips move against my palm.

Salve his wounds, the voice in my mind ordered.

Before I started working on his wounds, I took a strip of gauze and motioned at Dougal to bring me the wineskin. Then I soaked the linen, took a drink, then soaked the linen again.

"You'll need a drink of this, too." I handed the wineskin to ClanFintan, who drank deeply.

"Bend down so I can reach that cut on your head, and hold still, I'm pretty sure this is going to hurt. A lot."

"Tend to Dougal's wounds first."

I looked at the young centaur, who shook his head pointedly at me. "Dougal's not bleeding, you are. Now bend down and hold still."

"I will tend to Dougal," Victoria said in a businesslike voice. She, too, took a strip of gauze and soaked it in wine. I watched out of the corner of my eye while she approached him. He looked as if he didn't know whether to wriggle with enthusiasm or bolt. He chose neither and froze as the beautiful Huntress began cleaning the wound on his cheek. I wasn't even sure he was breathing.

"You can breathe," I overheard Victoria chiding him.

"Yes, Huntress." The young centaur expelled a long breath.

I guess I had a silly smile on my face, because my husband's rough voice whispered, "Don't laugh at the colt."

I gave a guilty jump. "I'm not laughing," I whispered back, pleased beyond words that he felt well enough to tease me. "You know I think Dougal's adorable."

"Perhaps so does Victoria." I was pleased to see his lips relax into a smile.

"That would be nice, but right now I want you to quit talking and hold still."

He grunted a response, but he kept silent as I worked on his head wound. As I got the blood and dirt cleaned out of it, I was relieved that it didn't appear as deep as all the blood caused me to think. I spread Sila's salve over it, and began working on his chest wounds, which were far deeper. There were four long, ugly slashes that began up over his left breast and traveled in a diagonal line to the bottom of the right side of his rib cage. They had quit bleeding, but I had no idea if that was a good or bad sign. I looked up at him and found him watching me.

"Do you have any idea how badly you're hurt?" I asked, trying not to sound as incompetent as I knew I was.

"I will recover." His voice was starting to sound more normal. "Centaurs are very resilient."

"I know, I know." I smiled, relieved at his answer. "You're probably way better at healing than a mere human."

"Among other things." He bent to kiss me, but the effect was lost when I saw him grimace in pain.

"There'll be time for that later. Let me get you cleaned up."

I went back to work on his cuts. He stood quietly, and soon I was able to lather in the salve. That done, I reluctantly moved to the rear of his body.

"You're too matted with dirt, and, uh, stuff, for me to tell. Are the cuts on your rump the only big wounds on the rest of your body?"

He turned at the waist, looking up and down his horse body as if it didn't belong to him.

"I believe so."

"Okay, well, you're too tall, so you're going to have to lie down for me to take care of these."

With a sigh, he folded his knees and dropped to the ground.

Warnings from my memory file titled Stuff You Don't Let Sick Horses Do flashed in my mind. "You will be able to get up, won't you?"

"I hope so."

Great. Where the hell is a veterinarian when you need one, anyway?

The cuts on his rump were terrible. It looked as if the claws of a giant bear had raked him. Three L-shaped gashes, huge flaps of skin and muscle, had been gouged out, then laid back down. I pulled one of the flaps up a little, and heard ClanFintan's sharp intake of breath.

"I think these are going to have to be sewn up." Just the thought of it made my head feel faint.

"Do what you need to do," he said quietly.

"I'm going to clean them first." I wet another strip of linen with more wine, trying to use it sparingly, but it was hard not to just douse his entire rump in wine. The wounds were deep and scary. After I worked as much of the grime as I could out of them (I would've given all of Rhiannon's jewels to have a big bottle of peroxide and a syringe filled with penicillin), I applied a thick layer of Sila's ointment, and was relieved to see his face relax as the numbing salve took effect.

"Just rest, I'm going to go talk to Vic." I patted his shoulder and handed him the wineskin.

Vic and Dougal were talking amiably. I noticed his wounds looked clean, glistening with yellow salve, and his skin had returned to a more normal color.

"Vic." I sounded like I was having an anxiety attack. Probably because I was having an anxiety attack. "I think the wounds on ClanFintan's rump need to be sewn up."

"That is very likely."

I spoke tightly under my breath. "I can't sew up his skin!" I felt like I was going to cry, which really made me mad. "I could sew up your skin. I could sew up Dougal's skin. But I just can't friggin sew up *his* skin." I paused in my tirade. "No offense meant."

"None taken," Dougal's sweet little self assured me.

"I can do it," Vic said, as if she was talking about driving down to the corner to pick up pizza.

"Good." I grabbed her hand and pulled. "Come on. I'm sure the longer we wait, the more swamp dirt and crap will fester away in it, and his butt will probably fall off in the morning...or something."

"I hope you realize I can hear you quite well." ClanFintan's amused voice carried across the few feet that separated us.

"You didn't hear anything," I said as Vic and I approached him. "You're probably delirious."

"Or you will soon wish you were," Vic said sadistically as she began threading one of the needles.

I was horrified, but ClanFintan and Dougal shared a big belly laugh.

"I'm glad you three are having a good time." I crossed my arms, and felt a serious teacher leg-tap coming on.

"Come here, love." ClanFintan held his arm out to me.

I stepped into the shelter of it, even though he was still covered with all sorts of scabby unmentionables.

"The worst is over now." He kissed my cheek.

"Is it?" I asked as I watched Victoria head toward his rump, needle in hand.

"I will need something to cut this!" she yelled, and Dougal unsheathed his sword and moved quickly to her side.

"We are together," he said simply.

His words made my heart beat more regularly, so I shut my mouth and peeked over his shoulder at Vic.

"Brace yourself," Vic said.

I watched her jab the needle through the flaps of his skin, and I heard the distinctive *pop* sound every time she poked through one side and the other—then I listened to the *shuuuuuu* sound the thread made as she pulled it taut, tied it off (with the help of Dougal's sword) and started anew.

I thought I was going to be sick.

"Do not forget to leave room for the drainage." ClanFintan's voice sounded remarkably calm.

Victoria threw him a look that said, "I know that, dummy."

"Rhea—" my husband's voice was soft in my ear "—the salve has numbed the wounds. She is not hurting me."

I looked into his face, wanting to believe him, but seeing the film of sweat over his upper lip made me have my doubts.

"I just don't like needles." I snuggled into his shoulder, watching Victoria as she sewed up my husband's flesh.

It seemed like hours had passed before Victoria tied off the final suture and asked me to hand her the salve, which she applied generously all over the freshly sewn-together skin.

"I believe you will have a scar." Victoria sounded jealous.

ClanFintan grunted, and acted as if he was starting to get back to his feet.

"Oh, no!" I pushed down on his shoulders. "You need to rest." I looked over at Dougal. "So do you. The creatures can't follow us in here. You two have just been through a major battle. You need to stay put."

"Rhea." ClanFintan's voice sounded strained. "I have to gather the centaur survivors, find the women and get back to Epona's Temple. Quickly. The Fomorians have not finished with us."

"You can't do anything if you don't get some rest." I glared at him.

Before our own little private war could begin, Vic cleared her throat and said, "Does anyone have any idea how far we are from the river?"

The centaur know-it-alls were silent.

"Nope, doesn't look like any of us does. Centaurs don't like the swamp, and I sure as hell have never been in here before," I said.

"Then I propose I scout and find out where we are. It might be a simple thing for us to cross the river—and it might not." Victoria had turned into Centaur Barbie In Charge.

"Sounds like a great idea, Vic," I said. "Just be careful."

"I am Lead—"

"Huntress," we said together, and smiled at each other.

"I will accompany you," Dougal said.

"No, I hunt alone." But as she passed by the young centaur she touched his cheek gently, which took the sting out of her words.

Nimbly, she leaped from the island with a splash, but soon the thickness of the swamp swallowed all sound of her passage.

Dougal sighed and took a position near the edge of the island, peering into the distance after her.

ClanFintan shifted his weight to his other side so he could lean his torso against the craggy edge of a cypress tree. He patted the ground next to him.

"Come, I need you beside me."

His words made me feel a rush of warmth for him, and I sat down, nestling against him on the soft ground. He tucked me under his arm and rested his chin on my head.

"Are you sure you're okay?" I asked, trying to get another look at his wounds.

"Be still. As you have already said, I need rest."

"Oh, sorry."

His chuckle vibrated through his chest and I felt his warm lips on the top of my head. I pressed myself against him harder, trying to be careful of his wounds but needing the comfort of his body to reassure me that he was truly here and alive. He seemed to understand my need, because he laced his fingers with mine, pulling me against him.

"I was so afraid you were dead." I couldn't stop the words from coming.

"You would have known."

"Let's not test that theory, okay?"

He squeezed me, and I was pleased it was with enough strength that I felt the air rush out of my lungs.

"I watched from the roof of the temple."

"We could not hold them—there were too many." His voice was suddenly hollow.

"I should have known there were too many of them. I saw them coming. I just didn't realize."

"It would not have mattered if you had known." His voice

lowered, and I wasn't sure he knew he was speaking aloud anymore. "It would not have mattered if the human forces had joined us. There are too many of them."

A chill crawled down my spine. Too many of them? For even our combined armies? Then what the hell were we going to do?

18

The gloom of the cloudy day gave way easily to night. Dougal and ClanFintan slept fitfully, and I stayed awake, listening to the hum of what must be a zillion cicadas, and a symphony of mewing, chirping and croaking frogs mixing in gross harmony with other unseen slimy, crawling things.

And I swatted mosquitoes. I'd thought Oklahoma had a mosquito problem. This place must be Insect Heaven.

And I was starving.

And it was really dark.

I kept feeling ClanFintan to see if he was feverish, but his body was always so hot that I couldn't tell if he had a raging temperature, or if he was just "normal." Plus, he had started getting annoyed at me for waking him up every few minutes. So I sat back and tried to rest, without actually falling asleep because I really, really, really didn't want to go on another one of those spirit-dream things. I just couldn't handle seeing what I was sure was happening back at the Temple of the Muse.

Rest, Beloved drifted through my tired mind.

I felt my eyelids droop in response, and I breathed a silent plea that I would, please, be allowed to stay in my body…and sleep enveloped me.

The thrashing sound of a large body sloughing its way through water made me come suddenly awake. I sat straight up, wondering for an instant just where the hell I was. Then the smells of the swamp registered in my foggy brain.

"It is Victoria," ClanFintan's deep voice rumbled against me.

There was little light. It seemed the marshy landscape soaked the moonlight up, but the silver-blond of the Huntress's coat glimmered ethereally.

"It took you long enough." My worry came out as bitchiness.

"It was—" she paused, and I realized how hard she was breathing "—more difficult than I had imagined."

"Tell us," my husband said as he moved me gently to the side, then rose stiffly.

"I traveled into the east, attempting to find the edge of the river. This lake goes on for quite some time before it gives way to a field of tall, sharp grass." Her voice drifted in the darkness. "There are dangerous bogs within the grass—I was almost trapped in one."

I remembered ClanFintan's comment, *centaurs avoid swampy ground*. No wonder.

"It is slow going through the bog, but when it finally gives way it is bordered by a thick growth of trees, much like we saw at its beginning. Only the grove that runs along the swamp's eastern edge is probably twenty centaur lengths in width. Then that ends at the edge of the Geal River."

I felt my heart flutter. All we had to do was get across the river. Then it would be a straight shot south back to Epona's Temple and home, where we could regroup and come up with plan B.

But Victoria wasn't done.

"The Fomorians have stationed guards along the perimeter of the marsh so that they can catch anyone who tries to flee from the swamp to the river."

"He's looking for me." They knew I meant Nuada.

"He is looking for all of us," ClanFintan assured me.

"Okay, how about going toward the Loch instead of the river?" I asked.

"Loch Selkie is even farther away than the river. And if Nuada has creatures posted between the swamp and the river, he will certainly have them posted between the Loch and the river," ClanFintan reasoned, "and we would only be safe as long as we were in or on the Loch. Crossing it is out of the question, its width is too great to swim, even if its waters were not icy."

"Bad news," I said.

"Exactly," Vic replied. I could hear her rummaging around in what I assumed was her quiver (since she wasn't carrying a purse). Then she began searching the island, gathering what sounded like loose leaves and twigs. I heard her crouch down, striking two sharp objects together—from which sparks flew. Soon she was breathing life into a spark, which she fed into a friendly blaze. The fire reflected off her white teeth as she smiled at me.

"Males never have flint. When you need a campfire, call a Huntress."

"I'll remember that." I stood up and moved closer to the warmth of the fire. My stomach let loose a mean-sounding growl. "Now, if only we had something to roast over it."

"How about this?" Victoria had moved from her spot by the fire, over to the leafy side of one of the cypress trees. She reached out and plucked a golf ball–size thing off one of the leaves, then returned to the fire.

"What is it?" I asked, studying the thing that lay in her hand.

"Apple snail." She grinned as she searched the ground around her. Finding what I supposed was the appropriate twig for the job, she grabbed a stick and jabbed it up into the brown shell, fishing out the soft-skinned creature. Impaling it like a snail shish kebab, she held the squirming thing over the fire.

"Does it taste like chicken?" I gulped.

"No, more like oysters."

Well, oysters were cool with me. So I swallowed my squeamishness and joined the centaurs in the Great Apple Snail Hunt and Fry. Thankfully, the little island seemed to be some kind of snail vacation spot—probably snail Florida—there were zillions of them. And Vic was right—if you discounted their little eyeballs and antenna-thingies, they tasted a lot like oysters. I wished I had some crackers, Tabasco and an icy Coors.

Later, we were contentedly picking snail guts from between our teeth and swatting mosquitoes, and I, for one, was feeling full and sleepy.

"They will be watching for three centaurs and one human," ClanFintan said suddenly.

"Yes," Victoria said.

"Then we split up. Separately we will have a better chance of getting past their line."

"I'm *not* being separated from you!" I said.

ClanFintan put his arm around my shoulders and squeezed. "No, you and I will not be separated."

Dougal remained silent, looking miserably at Victoria. The Huntress's gaze rested on the ground while she said, "Dougal and I should stay together, too. Two couples would still have a better chance at getting past their line than one group of four. Besides," she continued, "there are alligators in this swamp and we each need two sets of eyes to watch for them."

I saw Dougal flush in happy surprise. When Vic finally raised her eyes to meet his, I thought I detected an unaccustomed shyness in her gaze.

"Victoria and I will travel together." Dougal's voice sounded strong and confident.

ClanFintan looked pleased that the two centaurs were

staying together. "At first light the four of us will travel south until the sun is midway in the sky. Then you and Dougal will branch off to the east. Rhea and I will travel farther south, then we, too, will turn toward the river."

Dougal and Victoria nodded in agreement.

"The night is still young. Let us rest, my friends." Clan-Fintan's voice was hypnotic in the waning fire. I leaned against him, pleased he sounded like himself. Maybe everything would be okay...

Exhaustion caught up with me and a deep, thankfully dreamless sleep claimed me as its own.

The *rat-a-tat-a-tat-a-tat* of a woodpecker woke me.

"God, what an annoying bird." I grumbled as I rubbed the sleep from my eyes.

Then I smelled something that was cooking—something that smelled yummy. The three centaurs were standing around the fire. Cooking over it on a spit was a long, thick piece of white meat. I got up and stretched my way over to them.

"Good morning!" Dougal said cheerfully. ClanFintan pulled a leaf out of my hair. Vic nodded.

"Morning," I grumped. "What is it? It looks too thick to be snake," I said hopefully.

"No, caiman," Vic said.

"Oh, good. What's a caiman?"

"Small crocodile—easier to kill and skin than a large one." She smiled proudly. "They are a little tricky to catch, but—"

"I know, I know—tastes like chicken."

They laughed. Were they all morning people/centaurs/whatever?

"Here." ClanFintan pulled something that looked like a burnt sweet potato out of the coals. With one of Vic's sharp arrowheads he slit it to expose steaming pulp. I picked a small piece out and blew on it, then popped it into my mouth.

"Not bad, a little bitter and barky tasting, but not bad. What is it?"

"The tuber part of a cattail." Vic motioned at a grove of cattails just off the far side of our little island.

"You Huntresses are just dang handy to have around."

"Of course we are," Vic said with her normal lack of modesty.

The caiman was pretty good, too. What they write in books is the truth—sometimes you get too hungry to care what you're eating.

Before we left, I checked ClanFintan's wounds. His head and chest wounds looked good, especially under the definite lack of sterile circumstances. But the sutured slashes on his rump looked ugly. They were weeping bloody fluid. They worried me, especially given the stiff way ClanFintan was hobbling around. I told him to hold still while I rubbed more salve on all of them.

He met my eyes, smiling gently, and pulled me into his arms. "It is normal for the wound to drain."

"You can hardly walk!"

He laughed. "Perhaps I am simply not a morning centaur."

"Don't be a smart aleck, you're hobbling around worse than Epi did when she went lame."

"I am older than Epi."

I put my head against the side of his chest that wasn't wounded. "Tell me the truth, are you really okay?"

He ruffled my hair. "Yes, I will move more easily when my muscles are warm."

"Maybe I should ride Vic again." I peeked over at her where she and Dougal were stomping out the fire. "I don't think she'd mind."

"I would mind. I want you close to me." He kissed the top of my head. "But I would appreciate it if you would refrain from fondling my rump—" he paused and gave me a teasing look "—*today.*"

I pulled away from him and went back to salving his wounds, muttering, "You probably need a good smack on the rump."

We left the island and traveled south, into the ever-thickening marshlands. Thankfully, the water stayed at a depth between the centaurs' knees and their flanks, but it made for slow going. The mud sucked against their hooves like a living thing. Shortly after we had started out, a log drifted past us. I caught sight of movement on it and shouted an alligator warning.

Vic's crossbow was in her hand, and Dougal and ClanFintan unsheathed their long swords, taking up a defensive stance with their backs to each other. As it floated closer to us we got a better look at it. It wasn't an alligator; it was a log teeming with writhing snakes.

"Yeesh, that's disgusting. Are they poisonous?" They made my skin crawl.

"Yes, but they are mating. If we let them drift by without bothering them, they should not bother us." Vic's voice mirrored my disgust.

Needless to say, we gave them a wide berth.

Except for all the bugs, crawling things and green, slimy water, I was surprised by the hidden beauty of the marsh. Tall, pointed-nosed birds stood in the water, blinking at us like lazy blue-haired old southern women. High in the moss-dripping cypress trees, brilliant scarlet birds nested.

"That must be a scarlet ibis." I pointed at one as it floated gracefully to the water.

"Yes." Vic nodded. "They are a rare bird. Have you seen one before?"

"Only in a story," I sighed, remembering the poignant

coming-of-age story that I read to my freshmen every year entitled *The Scarlet Ibis.* "Remind me to tell you the story about Doodle some day."

"I will," Dougal said with endearing enthusiasm.

A little before midday we came to another patch of dry land, too small to even be called an island. There the centaurs took a break from the constant water. I searched the leaves for more apple snails.

"They only come out at night," Vic informed me.

"I don't suppose we have time for a fire anyway." And I didn't think I was hungry enough to eat one raw. Yet.

"No," ClanFintan said. "Victoria and Dougal must be on their way. And so must we." He turned to Victoria. He clasped her upper arm, and she his. "Take care of each other." Then he faced Dougal. "If you reach the temple before we do, tell them they must evacuate to the other side of the river. Head to Glen Iorsa. From there we will decide what is to be done." They clasped arms. "But you must get the humans across the river. It is no longer safe for them, no matter what has become of the other armies."

His words shocked me, and I could read my shock mirrored in Victoria's expression, although she didn't speak. But Dougal simply nodded, as if he had expected the news. I walked over to Vic, and gave her a girlfriend hug.

"Stay safe," she said.

"Allow yourself to be loved," I whispered.

Her eyes widened at my words and I was amazed to see a hint of color sneaking into her cheeks.

"I am too old to bother with such nonsense," she whispered back to me.

"No one is too old for such *nonsense.*"

Then I went to Dougal, who tried to kiss my hand, but I pulled him down and gave him a hug, kissing him soundly on the cheek.

"Watch out for her—and for yourself." I turned away so that I wouldn't have to see them leave. I heard them leap off the dry land and back into the water, but soon the swamp covered all sounds of their departure.

"We will see them again soon." ClanFintan stood behind me, resting his hands on my shoulders.

"I know," I said with false bravado.

"We must go."

I reached up and he swung me onto his back, and we, too, immersed ourselves back in the unending marsh.

It seemed like days instead of hours had passed when Clan-Fintan finally made an abrupt left turn.

"This should be enough space between us," he said as he changed direction.

"Good!" I agreed cheerily, to cover up the worry that had begun inside me. ClanFintan's amazing stamina was beginning to wane. His coat beneath my legs was damp with more than water; it was flecked with white sweat—something I'd never seen on him before. The gashes on his rump were constantly dripping yellowish drainage. I could hear his breathing deepen as he strained against the muddy ground.

"I think I should walk for a while."

"No," he said between breaths.

"Really, it's okay. I'd like to stretch my legs."

"I said no!" he snapped.

I just sat there, not sure if I should smack his butt and tell him not to yell at me, jump off his back and tell him I'll damn sure do what I want or just sit there and cry. Confusion won, so I shut my mouth and sat there in a tight ball of emotions.

Soon he came to a halt and wiped the sweat from his brow wearily with the back of his hand.

"Forgive me, love," he said with a voice that sounded like

it came from a grave. "I shame myself by taking my exhaustion out on you."

I leaned forward, carefully wrapping my arms around his chest. I rested my chin on his shoulder. "You're forgiven."

"When the water becomes a little more shallow you may walk, if you would like."

"I would like." I kissed his neck. He lay his arms over mine briefly, then took a deep breath and forced his hooves out of the soggy ground. The horrible sucking sound made me want to cringe. We continued to move slowly forward.

When the water had subsided to his knees he halted again.

"How about if I walk for a little while?"

He nodded, and helped me to dismount. My booted feet sank down in the mucky ground until I was standing in water up to my thighs.

"Yuck, this stuff is seriously gross." I took his hand and we started walking.

"Seriously gross?" he asked.

"Yeah, like that log that was filled with snakes."

"Oh." He nodded tired understanding.

We struggled on. After we had only gone a short way, I was breathing heavily. It amazed me that he had been traveling in this mud all day—with me on his back and a butt that was all torn up.

"It can't be much farther," I said between breaths.

He didn't reply. It seemed that he was focusing all of his energy on continuing to move forward.

Soon the water level had noticeably subsided, which would have been wonderful, except that the level of the mud increased. The water came only to my knees, but every time I put a foot down, I sank to midcalf in mud. In the dwindling light we didn't see the grass until it was right before us. It was an incredible sight; much of it even towered over ClanFintan.

We stopped, both of us breathing heavily.

"Didn't Vic say a field of tall grass came right before the edge of the swamp?" I asked hopefully.

"Yes, and she said it was sharp. You should remount me so that I can shield you from its cuts."

"No, let me try walking through it." I could see he wanted to argue, so I rested my hand on his arm and said, "If it's too sharp, I'll climb back aboard."

He agreed reluctantly, and we stepped into the forest grass.

As usual, Vic had been right; the grass cut. And now that I thought about it, I remembered seeing red slashes across her skin, but we were all so mud spattered and insect bitten that I had given it little thought.

Well, now that I was walking through the stuff, I gave it lots of thought. I put my arms up to try and shield my face from the worst of the grass. Soon I could feel warm blood trickling down my forearms from the scratches on scratches as the razor-edged grass sliced across my skin like a giant paper cut.

"Rhea, stop. You must ride now."

"Just a little farther, then I will." I had managed to draw a small distance ahead of him, and I didn't even pause to look back, afraid he'd see the blood on my arms. The mud still sucked at my feet, and I knew he didn't need the burden of my added weight.

I pulled one foot up, and put it out in front of me, set it down—

And my foot continued to sink down, down, without stopping. I cried out and struggled to pull it back, but I fell off balance and floundered, suddenly finding myself up to my waist in a soft, sandy mixture. The more violently I struggled, the more it sucked me into it.

"Rhea!" ClanFintan yelled, and with a ferocious strength he grabbed my arm and yanked me backward, almost causing my shoulder to be wrenched out of its socket.

ClanFintan went down, and I fell back into his arms, where we stayed for a moment—happy that what was beneath us was just mud. My husband's hands were traveling over my body, like he was checking to make sure everything was still there.

"Did something grab you? Are you hurt?" His voice was shaking.

"No, I'm okay." I laid my head against him, breathing deeply. "It didn't have a bottom. It felt like it was sucking me down. Ugh—it must be quicksand."

"Yes." He sounded calmer now that he knew I was in one piece. "I have heard of the sinking sand." He attempted a smile. "It is one reason centaurs stay out of swampy land."

"Well, it's a damn good reason."

He surged to his feet, lifting me with him.

"We must go around it." He started working his way to the south, stepping carefully. "And now you cannot ride me."

He didn't need to say what we both knew. He could pull me out of quicksand, but there would be no way I could do the same for him. We kept moving, and I sent a silent prayer to my Goddess, begging for help.

19

Eventually, we traveled far enough south so that we skirted the quicksand, and were able, once again, to turn to the east. The cutting grass felt as if it was ripping the flesh from my arms, and my footsteps became slower and slower.

"Rhea, let me walk ahead." He had stopped. "Rub some salve on your arms and walk behind me, give them a chance to rest," he coaxed. "After a time we can change positions again."

"But what if you step into some quicksand?"

"I will be careful."

"Okay." I gave in with something that sounded very much like a sob, and stumbled back to him. He took the pouch from my shoulder, and I wished we had some wine left, but the four of us had finished that off before midday. I held out my arms, flinching as his gentle fingers applied the sticky ointment. Almost immediately the burning stopped, and I breathed a long sigh of relief.

"That feels good." I noticed the scratches on his arms and chest. "Here, I'll put some on you, too."

"They are just small scrapes—my skin is not soft, like yours." He touched my cheek.

"I'll just put a little on you. I know how badly they sting."

He smiled indulgently at me while I doctored the scratches. Then I put the jar away and moved reluctantly behind him.

"Be careful!" I called.

"I will." He started out, and we began our timeless struggle forward again.

Just as I thought the field of grass would never end, Clan-Fintan called over his shoulder excitedly, "I can see the tree line ahead!" He surged forward with renewed vigor.

And right into a bed of quicksand.

His equine body floundered, struggling against the sucking sand. His arms flailed out, trying to grab something, anything, that he could use to pull himself to safety.

"Stay back!" he yelled as I tried to go to him. "I am too far in—you cannot reach me."

"What can I do?" I yelled, feeling panic rise in my throat.

He looked frantically around. "If you can make it to the trees, find a long branch and bring it back here."

I nodded, and started searching for a way around the quicksand, but I knew I would never make it in time. I couldn't even see the stand of trees, and I couldn't run in the marsh's sucking mud.

I knew he was going to die—and all I could do was watch him.

He must call The Change. The thought burst loud and clear through my panicked mind. I rushed to the edge of the quicksand. He had sunk to midway up his human torso.

"Stay back..." His breathing was ragged.

"Listen!" I dropped to my knees and crawled around the side of the pit. "You must shape-shift." I stretched out my arms to him. "See, if you reach out, I can grab you. Try!"

He did, and our fingers touched.

"Now, shape-shift. I can pull out a man—but not a centaur."

I saw understanding flash through his eyes. Then he closed

them and bowed his head. His body became very still as he began the chant, raising his arms and head synchronistically. The shimmer started. Before I had to close my eyes to the brilliance of the light, I watched his face twist in unimaginable agony.

Then the light extinguished. Immediately, I stretched forward.

"Help me! Reach!" I yelled at him.

With weary determination he reached for me, and our fingers touched. Then our hands grasped one another's. I dug my heels into the murky ground and pulled with everything within me. Inch by inch I won ground over the deadly sand, until ClanFintan's torso lay on the wet ground and he was able to help me pull the rest of him free.

He rolled over on his side, and for a long time we lay there against each other. Our only movement was to breathe.

"Thank you, Epona," I said aloud.

"Your Goddess is good to you." I was reassured by the normal sound of his deep voice.

I brushed some of the clinging sand from his face, then kissed the spot I had cleaned.

"Can you walk yet?"

He nodded and stood with painful, stiff movements. As he turned, I was afforded a glimpse of the rear of his body. The gashes were huge, horribly flapping wounds, tacked together obscenely with dark sutures. They ran from just above his buttocks, all the way down to the back of his thighs, and oozed fluid, which mixed with the sand and water of the pit.

"Oh, God!" I couldn't stop the exclamation. "Change back!"

"I think—" his slow answer was painful to hear "—I should stay in human form until we have crossed the river. Remember, they are not looking for a human man and woman. They search for Epona's Chosen and her centaur mate."

"But your wounds." Just looking at them made me ache.

"Put more salve on them and it will be tolerable."

I didn't want to touch those horrid gashes in his flesh. I was petrified I would hurt him more than he hurt already.

He reached for the bag and drew out the half-empty jar.

"I can do it," he said when he noticed my reticence.

I dipped my fingers into the jar.

"I'll do it." I gritted my teeth and forced myself to smear the ointment over and into the gashes. He didn't move, and he didn't speak. He also didn't breathe until I was finished.

"Better?" I asked, wiping my fingers across the slashes on his forearms to rid them of the lingering ointment.

"Yes." He made a great show of acting brave, but his skin had taken on a sickly pale hue. "I saw the tree line just over there." He pointed. "It is not much farther."

We started out, careful to pick our way around the pit of quicksand. I gave his naked body a sideways glance.

"You want to borrow my thong, or something?"

His bark of laughter made him flinch with the pain it caused his wounds, but his eyes sparkled as he looked down at me.

"I think not. If we were captured by the Fomorians, think of the stories they would tell."

"I can see the headlines now, Cross-dressing High Shaman of the Centaurs Finally Captured."

"Headlines?"

"Gossip that everyone reads about."

"Yes, that would be embarrassing."

"It certainly would."

"Perhaps we should talk about what we can do with your thong at a later time."

I was heartened to hear a sexy tease in his voice.

"Save your energy, big boy. Who do you think you are, John Wayne?"

I knew he was going to ask.

"John Wayne?"

Now here's a subject I could pontificate on for hours. I cleared my throat and assumed my teacher-lecture mode.

"John Wayne, real name Marion Michael Morrison, born in Winterset, Iowa. He was what we called a Great American Icon in my old world. Personally, I think of him as a patriot and a hero."

He gave me a curious glance, which was all the encouragement I needed. "Let me tell you about him…"

I was in the middle of retelling the plot of *The Cowboys,* and choking myself up, when ClanFintan put his hand out, stopping me.

"Shh," he said. "The end of the grass." He pointed, and I saw that, sure enough, the field of cutting grass ended just a few feet ahead of us as abruptly as it had begun.

I peered around in the fading light. A line of trees began on the other side of the grass field. Not a pretty grove with a carpet of dried leaves, like we had traveled through on the opposite side of the river. Here the trees were wild and thick, an impenetrable jungle of cypress, willow and hackberry, interspersed with huge, red-tipped elephant ear and something that looked like mutant hibiscus.

But, as we stood there silently, a delicious sound came to our ears. We realized what it was at the same time, and our eyes lit up as we smiled at each other.

"The river," ClanFintan said in a low voice.

"Thank you, Goddess! Finally!"

"Shh." He put his arm around me and spoke into my ear, "If we can hear the river, that means the creatures are somewhere between here—" he nodded his head back at the marsh behind us "—and the bank."

"How do we get past them?" I asked quietly.

"They are expecting a centaur to crash through the under-brush with his mate riding boldly astride his back, not two humans who can duck and dodge through the trees stealthily."

"And what two humans can do that?"

He squeezed my shoulders and kissed the top of my head. "We can."

"Oh, yeah. I almost forgot."

"That is why you married me—so that I could remind you of things you have almost forgotten."

I was glad to see a mischievous smile playing on his lips.

"And I thought I just married you for your great foot rubs."

"That, too." His expression sobered. "We must move like our Huntress friend, slowly and soundlessly. Try to disturb no brush. Place your feet softly on the dampest part of the ground. Avoid twigs and dry leaves."

I listened intently, psyching myself up for the task before me.

"What if we are seen?"

He took me by the shoulders and turned me so that he could look intently into my eyes. "You run for the river. Do not stop. Do not worry about me. Just get to the river and swim across it."

"But—"

"No! Listen to me. They will not recognize me. They will think I am only a human male. I can buy you the time it will take for you to cross the river. When you are safe I will call The Change to me and join you."

It sounded like a line of crap to me. I started to tell him so, but his fingers dug into my shoulders.

"If they catch you, think of what they will do to you. I could not bear it." The pain reflected in his eyes was palpable. "All they can do is kill me—they can do much more to you."

"Okay, I'll get to the river."

His expression relaxed, as did his grip on my shoulders. He bent and kissed me gently.

"Now let us get out of this marsh. Step only where I step."

"Okay, you're in charge."

He gave me a huge grin.

"For now," I added.

We started forward slowly, leaving the grass behind and entering a world of primeval trees and dense underbrush. In a way, it was worse than the mud and the grass. At least amidst the grass we could blunder ahead, concentrating on putting one foot in front of the other. Here it was different. ClanFintan moved in slow motion, and I mimicked him. We couldn't travel in a straight easterly line. We had to zig and zag our way through the brush, avoiding piles of dried leaves and mounds of twigs. It seemed for every step we were able to take forward we had to take two to each side. And, to make an already difficult situation worse, dusk was falling, making it difficult to see the next clump of noisy dry foliage.

From my position behind him, I was afforded an excellent view of his naked backside. Each step he took caused his wounds to seep bloody fluid. His back was covered with a film of sweat. I watched the muscles in his back twitch and shake as he slowly shifted his weight from side to side.

Every moment I expected something winged and snarling to leap at us, but we kept moving, with only the sound of our own breath and the noise of the river as companions.

Then ClanFintan's hand went up, and he froze. In front of us was the river, powerful and gray in the fading light. Between the tree line where we were standing and the bank was a rocky area, probably twenty or thirty yards wide.

And in that area between the river and us crouched three winged creatures.

They were a little way upriver from where we stood. Their backs were to us—actually, they were hunkered around a blazing campfire. As we watched, one of them fed it more dried branches. They didn't speak, but once in a while one of them would look at the river and hiss.

ClanFintan motioned for me to move up beside him, and I did so carefully.

"When I give you the word, I want you to run to the river. Do not look at me. Do not wait for me," he said with quiet intensity.

I opened my mouth and he put a warm finger against my lips.

"Trust me," he whispered.

I swallowed my complaints and nodded reluctantly.

He bent and searched the ground around us. Finally satisfied, he grasped a fallen branch that lay close to his feet. He looked at me.

"Ready?" He mouthed the words.

I nodded.

He reached his arm back, and hurled the green branch to our left, toward the line of trees directly behind the creatures.

"Go!" he whispered.

I shot from the trees, fear and adrenaline giving me a jolt of unaccustomed speed. I heard ClanFintan following close behind me.

And I heard the creatures. They were snarling and spitting. I glanced over my shoulder in time to see them bounding for the trees behind them.

"Don't look, run!" ClanFintan said between breaths.

Unfortunately, I wasn't the only one who heard him.

"There!" one of the creatures hissed, pointing at us.

The rocks crunched as he rushed after us, with the other two following close behind him.

"Faster!" ClanFintan yelled.

I reached the bank as one of the creatures caught ClanFintan. I heard an awful tearing sound as his claws raked my husband's shoulder.

ClanFintan pivoted, putting his body between the Fomorians and me. He ducked another slashing attack from the creature, and landed a blow of his own on its jaw. I heard it crunch—the thing backed off a few paces to recollect itself, ready to attack ClanFintan again.

"Jump! I'll join you as soon as I can!" he yelled over his shoulder at me.

I looked down at the surging water, and back at my husband and the three creatures that were getting ready to hurl themselves at him.

"Not without you!" Before he could answer I ducked under his arm and ran straight toward the surprised creatures. My arms were raised over my head and I waved my hands wildly, shrieking, "Get the fuck back, you slimy, perverted bastards!"

The Fomorians skittered backward, away from me, looking justifiably confused. I mean, really, how many human women actually run *to* them? And I was a human woman covered in swamp yuck, with wild red hair sticking out in matted hunks and arms flailing like a demented Bride of Frankenstein. *I'd* run from me. Before they could recover, I turned and faced my husband.

"If I jump, you jump!" I yelled. Remembering everything I'd ever heard Dad tell his football players about blocking, I ran forward and tackled ClanFintan with my shoulder, low and hard, knocking us both over the bank and into the swirling water.

I kicked my way to the surface, pleased to hear ClanFintan sputtering beside me as the roaring current grabbed us and carried us away from the edge of the river.

"Relax," he yelled above the water. "Swim with the current!"

I did as he said, stroking with the fast-moving water, always angling toward the opposite bank. The water was cold, and soon the numbness began to scare me.

"Stay with me!" ClanFintan yelled. "Almost there!"

A finger of bank jutted out in front of us, and ClanFintan grabbed my hair with one hand and a low-hanging branch with his other, hauling us both into the rocky shallows.

"Ouch!" I said as he tried to disentangle himself from my hair.

"Come." He took my hand and we walked unsteadily together out onto the shore, where we collapsed.

I heard his painful groan as he shifted his weight from his backside.

"I hate to say this, but you really should go back into the shallows and wash the mud out of those wounds."

He nodded tightly and forced himself to his feet, stumbling back into the river. I followed him, helping him splash the cold, clean water over his damaged body. Happily, the pouch that held the remaining ointment was still around my neck, and I spread the rest of it on his wounds. He was shaking violently. The fresh cuts on his shoulder bled freely.

"Can you change back now?" I asked.

He gave me a tired nod, and I stepped away from him so he'd have room to call The Change. I closed my eyes against the light and the sight of his pain. When the brightness faded and I opened my eyes, I was relieved to see that he looked more solid and powerful in his true form.

"Let's go home," I said, holding out my hand to him. He took it and helped pull me up the steep bank.

20

We easily found the tracks the legion had made on the way to the Temple of the Muse, and began retracing our steps. At first I walked next to him, refusing his insistent offer that I remount.

"No, you've been through too much." I tried to reason with him.

"As have you."

"Oh, sure. Look who has all the gaping wounds."

He snorted at me.

"And, correct me if I've forgotten, but I think you're the only one who's changed his body's form in the last twenty-four hours."

"You are my wife." He said it as if that explained everything.

"Yes, and I'm more than capable of walking for a while."

He opened his mouth to continue the argument.

"Wait, let's compromise," I said reasonably. "I'll walk until the moon rises to the middle of the sky, then I'll ride you without arguing about it."

He made a noise under his breath that sounded like he didn't totally believe me.

"You are a stubborn woman."

"Thank you."

That made him laugh, and he looped his arm around me.

"We smell bad." I smiled up at him.

"Again?" He chuckled.

"I guess that's what I get for marrying a horse."

I could see him cocking one of his eyebrows at me in the new moonlight. "That is not all you get."

I laughed and sent a silent thank-you to my Goddess. He sounded like himself again.

We walked in companionable silence. I breathed in the fresh night air, and enjoyed the solid feel of my husband's arm around me. We would make our way back to the temple, and from there figure out how the hell we were going to get rid of those damn creatures.

A noise in the forest to our left startled me, and I laughed in relief as the white tail of a deer blazed in the silver night. But the deer brought something else to mind.

"Do you think we'll run into any of the women from the Muse? Or Dougal and Vic?"

"Dougal and Victoria are probably well ahead of us. I do not know about the women." His voice was sad and low. "When it became apparent that we could not hold the creatures, I sent part of the legion to the river, and part to the temple. No centaur would have passed a woman without giving her aid. If they made it across the river, the centaurs would have hastened the women to Epona's Temple. They, too, should be ahead of us."

If any of them had made it…I knew we were both thinking it, but we left the thought unsaid.

"The moon is over our heads," he reminded me of my compromise.

I stopped and looked intently up at him.

"Are you really okay?"

"Yes, love." He brushed a curl back from my face. "My wounds will heal."

"Then I'll ride. I admit I am kind of tired."

He lifted me to his back.

"And hungry?"

"Don't even mention food. You know I'm starving."

"Alanna will have a feast ready for you." He glanced over his shoulder at me, and his eyes widened. "Look," he said, pointing down the path in the direction from which we had just come.

I looked, and saw that my footprints each had a star in the middle of them. As we watched, they shimmered and glittered, as if they had just fallen from the sky and landed where my feet had been. Then I blinked, and the play of light vanished.

"Magic?" I spoke reverently, like I was in church.

"Perhaps there is more magic within you than you realize."

ClanFintan took a few strides forward, and then broke into his familiar ground-eating canter. I leaned against his back, thinking about magic and goddesses and love…and fell immediately asleep.

I was curled up on a big rocking chair in the café of my favorite bookstore back in Tulsa (the 41st Street Barnes & Noble), and the manager (who looked amazingly like Pierce Brosnan) was telling me that I could have as many books as I wanted, free, on him, please, just choose to my little heart's content. The wonderful chef, played by Sean Connery, was personally preparing an exquisite meal for me (which I could smell cooking—lots of garlic), and a bare-chested pool boy who looked like Brad Pitt (who knows?) was pouring me a large glass of glistening Merlot…

…And I was sucked out of DreamLand to hover grumpily over the middle of the river.

I started to whine, and then I remembered the voice in my head that had saved ClanFintan—not once, but twice—and I kept my silly mouth shut.

"Okay, I'm ready for whatever you need me to see," I said.

No answer—except to feel myself drift upstream, retracing the path we had just traveled. I sighed and mentally prepared myself for Goddess only knows what.

The marsh glistened to my left like an open sore on the face of the land. It stretched as far inland as I could see. I shivered at the thought that we very easily could have been trapped in there forever. Lights began flickering ahead of me, turning my attention away from the depression of the marsh to the rocky area between it and the river. My body slowed as I came within view of several large campfires. They were spread up and down along the western bank of the Geal. My spirit body kept drifting upstream, until I came to an enormous circle of blazing firelight. I could see the winged creatures crouched around the fires. My body descended. It was obvious that they were all watching something that was in the middle of the ring of campfires. I saw movement within the circle, but blowing smoke from the fire obscured my view. Then the smoke cleared and my eyes widened in horror.

Within the circle, Terpsichore danced. She was naked. Her body was slick with the fevered sweat of the early stages of smallpox, which, ironically, made her skin glisten with an inviting luster. She spun and twisted, mesmerizing the creatures with her incredible grace and sexuality. Her hair clung to her wet body like an erotic veil. She writhed seductively from creature to creature. She was touching each Fomorian, leaving a trail of sweat and arousal in her wake. And, I prayed silently, disease. I watched as she danced toward the creatures who were crouching just outside the circle, being sure she touched as many of them as possible. Wings would twitch and begin to become erect, then she would spin teasingly away—and start the dancing game all over with another creature. It was like she was a lovely automaton. Her face was an expressionless mask, and I saw that her lips were cracked and dry. As I looked closer, I noticed the beginnings of the rash on her beautifully rounded arms.

Then one of the creatures unfurled itself from the ground and stepped into the circle, grabbing Terpsichore by the waist and pulling her against his engorged body. And I realized why none of the other creatures had allowed themselves to take her. Nuada had claimed her.

"Enough play, *Goddess*." He reached out and let one claw travel down the side of her full breast, leaving a thin line of blood in its path, which he licked from her wet skin with his pale tongue. "I am ready for you now."

He began dragging her from the circle; then he froze and glared directly up at me.

"Female!" I heard his scream as Epona wrenched me away and back into my body.

I jerked upright.

"Nuada has Terpsichore."

"May her Goddess protect her," his deep voice echoed in the night.

"She stayed behind on purpose," I explained. "She wanted to carry the pox to the Fomorians."

His head jerked back in surprise. "Will it work?"

"I wish I knew." Frustration was clear in my voice. "I know it's contagious, and I know how it's spread. What Terpsichore was doing would spread the disease to humans. I just don't know if the creatures are human enough to catch it."

"When will we know?"

"I've been trying to figure that out." I sighed. "I think I remember that it took about a week from exposure to the appearance of symptoms. But I have no idea if the Fomorian physiology will be effected like that. My guess is that they will either get very sick, very soon, or it won't hurt them at all."

"Then what we need is time," he said thoughtfully.

"And a lot of luck," I added. Silently, I sent a prayer up to Epona that the Muse's sacrifice had not been in vain. Exhaustion tugged at me.

"Rest, we should be near the temple by daybreak."

With his reassuring words ringing in my ears I closed my eyes and fell into a deep, uneventful sleep.

Sometime between my dream vision and dawn, a line of low-hanging clouds drifted in from the north, bringing with them drizzle that hung like fog in the moist air. It must have been several hours past dawn, although the sun remained hidden and the morning was gloomy, when we heard a shout, and one of my warriors burst from his post near the riverbank.

"Epona be praised! You live!" He saluted me and I was touched to see tears in his eyes.

I smiled at him, but ClanFintan didn't hesitate in his pace.

"Almost there," I breathed into his ear.

He grunted and nodded his head, concentrating on keeping up his pace.

We followed a familiar turn in the bank, and I can honestly say I was pleased beyond words to see the bridge stretching in all its scary length high over the water.

As we jumped onto the bridge, another sentry caught sight of us and sent up a yell that was taken up by another, then another.

"I guess some of my warriors got away from the creatures," I said as more and more voices were raised in excited welcome.

We crossed the bridge and made the sharp turn to the temple. Even in the gray of the foggy morning, its marble walls gleamed invitingly. People were pouring out of the temple and running toward us. From inside the walls burst a group of centaurs, led by a shimmering blonde who was followed closely by a young palomino.

"Victoria! Dougal!" I yelled as they galloped to us.

"I told her you would make it," Dougal said gleefully.

"This one time I will allow him to be right." Vic laughed happily and hugged me so hard I almost fell off ClanFintan's back.

Soon we were enfolded in a wave of jubilant people and centaurs. As we went through the rear entrance, Epi trumpeted a joyous welcome. Then I heard a familiar voice, and I looked into the courtyard to see Alanna and Carolan running to join us. ClanFintan wearily helped me down. Carolan gave me a quick inspection.

"I'm fine—I'm fine. Take care of him," I brushed him off and, after giving me one more look over, he began examining ClanFintan's many wounds.

"Come with me," he ordered the centaur in a grim-sounding voice.

ClanFintan kissed me quickly, whispering, "I will join you in your chambers as soon as he is finished with me." Then he did as the doctor ordered, much to my relief.

I stepped into Alanna's arms, returning her embrace.

"I believed you would return." Her voice shook with tears.

"Get me out of here," I said softly.

She slipped her arm around my waist, and began guiding me quickly through my adoring welcomers. I waved and thanked them, saying I would be fine and I just needed rest.

Still, it seemed to take forever to cross the courtyard and make our way down the hall to my bathing chamber. Before following me into the room, I heard her give orders to the smiling guard.

"Bring wine, water and fresh fruit. Then have a full meal sent to her chambers."

She closed the door and we clung to each other like school-girls. I was the first to pull away.

"Oh, I've gotten you filthy," I said as I sniffed and wiped the tears from my face.

"I do not care, but here, let me get you out of those things."

For once I didn't mind her nurturing ministrations.

"I can't seem to stop shaking," I said, laughing. Detachedly, I realized this must be what hysteria felt like.

Alanna took my hand and led me to the warm pool. Two knocks sounded at the door and an exuberant nymph entered carrying a loaded tray.

"Oh, my Lady," she bubbled. "We are all so happy you have returned safely to us!"

"Thank you." I tried to smile around my chattering teeth, "I am pleased beyond words to be home."

She curtsied and scampered out the door. I let myself lie back in the water with a deep sigh.

"Here—" Alanna handed me a goblet "—drink."

I did as I was told, gulping down the cool water.

"Easy, not all of it at once."

I came up for air, waited, then took another long drink.

"Thanks." I handed the empty cup back to her. I suddenly realized how filthy my hair was, and I wanted nothing more than to get it clean. I put my head back in the warm water, shaking it from side to side.

"Help me, I have to get clean."

Alanna didn't ask any questions, she simply poured a bottle of soap on my hair and set about helping me scrub. When that was done, she handed me a sponge and I lathered up my entire body. Then I dived into the middle of the pool, rinsing the filth from me. I returned to my ledge, and Alanna handed me another cup of cool water. As I drank it, I noticed my hands had quit shaking.

"Better?" she asked.

"Yes, girlfriend, thank you."

She sat cross-legged near me on the side of the pool, exchanging my cup of water for a goblet of wine. She slid the platter filled with sliced fresh fruit within my reach. I smiled gratefully, and popped a cube of melon into my mouth, chewing slowly, letting its sweet juice cover my tongue.

"It's so incredibly good to be home." I breathed a relieved sigh.

"Is there not some way we could stay?"

Her words reminded me that Dougal had been ordered by ClanFintan to begin evacuating the people across the river.

"ClanFintan doesn't think so." I remembered the scene of devastation at the Muses' temple. "And I think he's right. Did any other people from the Temple make it here?"

"Yes, a large group came in just before dawn this morning, escorted by centaur warriors and five Huntresses. Carolan has tended the wounded, and they are all resting quietly now. Victoria and Dougal arrived shortly after, with word that we must leave the temple. We should be ready to begin crossing the river at dawn."

"Was Thalia with them?"

"Yes, she is well."

"Sila?" I held my breath.

"No," Alanna said sadly. "No one saw her cross the river."

"Have no more centaurs come back?"

"Yes, another group arrived this morning shortly after Victoria and Dougal. They were escorting humans who are very ill with the pox."

"So, how many centaurs have made it here?" I held my breath.

"At last count a little over three hundred," Alanna said softly.

Out of one thousand, only a third survived? It was unimaginable. I closed my eyes, praying that more centaurs had lived, and that they were making their way back to their homelands.

"My warriors?" I asked.

"Two barges left, each with fifty warriors. One barge returned. The warriors said the creatures were waiting for them as they disembarked." Her voice sounded hollow.

"Woulff and McNamara?"

"Their arrival was too late. Connor sent word that they were forced to retreat. They lost many men."

I breathed deeply. "It's a living nightmare."

"There must be a way to stop them," Alanna said in desperation.

"Yes, and we will find it." But my words sounded empty, even to my own ears.

21

Dressed in clean clothes, with my hair combed through, two glasses of wine and a lot of fruit inside of me, I felt a little less gloomy. Alanna placed the coronet around my head, and we walked arm in arm to my room. We were almost there when a little handmaid rushed up, curtsying apologetically.

"Forgive me, my Lady, but there is a problem in the laundry room. Some sheets caught afire, and they were extinguished, but now there is a huge mess and much confusion about what should be done. And Una is arguing with Nora about who was responsible," she added to Alanna under her breath.

Before I could respond, Alanna smiled sweetly at the girl and said, "I will come." She turned to me and gave me a quick hug. "I will take care of this. Carolan will probably release your husband shortly. Dinner is waiting within for both of you. I will return later this evening." She followed the girl down the hall.

My guard opened the door for me, and as it closed securely behind me I realized that I could use some alone time. My room looked welcoming and familiar. The frame of my bed had been removed, and in its place the "marshmallow" was neatly made up. The drapes were partially drawn, allowing the rainy nonlight of day to give the room a cozy, curl-up-with-a-good-book-and-a-glass-of-wine ambience. The table was laden with food; delicious smells wafted to me enticingly. My stomach gave a loud roar, prompting me to walk quickly over to the waiting smorgasbord and to commence chowing down.

Just as I was lifting a delectable leg of some small, fat bird, a sound from the library room drew my attention.

"Hello," I called, wondering what nymphet was in there dusting or something. No one answered. I shrugged my shoulders and decided it must have been my overworked imagination.

The bird was melting in my mouth when I heard the sound again. This time it was louder—a thud like something heavy and hollow had been dropped.

Great. Some timid little girl had probably broken something, and now she was too scared to come out here and face Rhiannon the Bitch. That's what it probably was—but something brushed at the back of my mind. An uncomfortable feeling that was hard to define.

I sighed and wiped my mouth on the gold linen napkin and, giving the laden table a desirous glance, walked reluctantly to the library.

I knew it was ridiculous, but the closer I got to the arched doorway, the more uncomfortable I felt. I stopped, suddenly fearful that a Fomorian had somehow slipped into the temple.

No, the feeling wasn't one that portended evil. It was simply uncomfortable. And it was a familiar discomfort—I just couldn't place it. As I stepped into the room, I realized my stomach had started to hurt and I was gritting my teeth.

The library was lit by many flickering candles, all in the sconce skull decor. The room looked like it had the last time I'd been in it, only the map had been rolled back up. Books lined the shelves, giving the room a comfortable appearance that was in direct contradiction to the sick feeling in my stomach. I was beginning to think maybe I was just overtired and some of the fruit hadn't agreed with me, when something about the center table caught my attention.

And the breath rushed out of my body as if I'd been hit in the gut.

It was sitting in the middle of the table. The same pot I'd bought at the auction. The same pot that had caused my car wreck and my exchange of worlds. I tried to catch my breath, suddenly overwhelmed with dizziness. The room began to waver, like I was standing in a giant fishbowl looking out. I tried to step backward, but my body wouldn't obey me. I felt like I was being sucked into a giant whirlpool; I couldn't breathe; I was drowning. Then the pot began to glow, and I knew it had been sent there to pull me back to my old world.

I felt my sense of what was real dissolving. As the pot glowed brighter, I thought I could see an image of myself standing naked in an unfamiliar room. Plate-glass picture windows reflected the lights of a modern skyline behind the mirror image of me. My arms were spread and I was walking forward.

Suddenly I was flung backward and ClanFintan hurled past me, knocking the pot off the table so that it shattered against the tiled floor. Then he repeatedly reared up and came down with all his weight on the pieces of pottery, until it was nothing but rubble under his hooves. Slowly, the glow disappeared.

I realized I was still not breathing, and my legs gave way beneath me as everything faded to black.

"Rhea…Rhea," I heard someone calling, as if from far away. "Rhea…wake up," the voice continued calling. I couldn't answer it—I couldn't find my way out of the blackness.

"Shannon Parker! Open your eyes and return!"

My eyes flew open. I was lying on our mattress in Clan-Fintan's arms. His face was white with worry.

"What happened?" I asked, trying to remember. Then I remembered, and I struggled to sit up. "The pot! It tried to take me back!" A wave of dizziness passed over me.

"Lie still. I destroyed it." ClanFintan pressed a kiss against my clammy forehead. "I have sent for Carolan."

"I think I'm fine," I said, but I didn't try to sit up again.

"You look like a ghost."

"You don't look so great yourself." I touched his face gently.

Before he could answer, Carolan burst into the room, with Alanna close behind.

"What happened?" he asked as he knelt next to me. He touched my face and felt my wrist, checking my pulse.

"The pot appeared. Rhiannon tried to exchange places with her again," ClanFintan said.

"Oh, Goddess, no!" Alanna's hand flew to her mouth.

"I was outside in the hall,"ClanFinton said, "and I heard her scream inside my mind. I ran in here. She was in the library. The pot was glowing and the room seemed to be wavering, like a rippled pool of water. I pulled her out of the room and destroyed the pot. Then she fainted."

"I feel better now."

"Can you stand?" Carolan asked.

"Yes." They helped me get slowly to my feet. The room stayed put. "Help me walk over to the table, I'm starving and I seriously need a drink."

"She is better." ClanFintan sounded relieved, but he kept his arm around me as he guided me to the table.

ClanFintan took his normal place on the chaise, pulling me securely against him. Alanna handed me a goblet of wine, then she and Carolan sat across from us.

I took a long drink, focusing on getting the trembling inside me under control.

"She's trying to come back." I was surprised at how calm I

sounded. "I should have realized this would happen. She left here a Goddess Incarnate whose every whim was anticipated and fulfilled, to become an Oklahoma English teacher. Fifty out of fifty on the national pay scale. Please—who wouldn't want to return?" I knew they didn't understand everything I was saying, but they let me babble. "She somehow eavesdropped on my world. She saw cars and planes, huge skyscrapers and superhighways, the 'magic' of TV and computers." I giggled, feeling light-headed. "She thought she would be Goddess queen over it all. Hardly. Teachers are underpaid and overworked. We have to put up with absentee parents blaming us for the problems their poor choices have caused. I mean, really, some of us are even thinking about wearing bulletproof vests to school."

"Love…" ClanFintan's voice of sanity stopped my tirade. "I will not let her take you away from me."

"How are you going to stop her?" I was shaking again.

"Did I not stop her today?" He put his arms around me and I clung to his warmth and security.

"We will make sure everyone knows what the urn looks like." Alanna smiled reassurance. "We will say it is being used by the forces of evil. If another appears, it will be destroyed before it can harm you."

"Not if, *when*. I know she'll try again."

"Let her," Carolan said. "She will not be allowed to succeed."

ClanFintan's strong hands kneaded the tension out of my shoulders as I allowed myself to believe I was safe.

"Eat, love," he whispered into my ear. "It will make you feel better."

"It always does," I muttered and plunked a piece of delicious whitefish in my mouth. I was just beginning to relax, listening to Carolan and ClanFintan discuss the dynamics of the morning evacuation, when there was a quick knock and the door to my chamber flew open.

A sweat-covered guard saluted hastily and said, "Fomorians have been sighted outside the temple grounds."

ClanFintan surged off the chaise and lunged to the door.

22

"Get Dougal. Have him assemble the centaurs and the rest of the Temple Guard at the entryway to the top of the northeast wall," ClanFintan ordered, and the guard nodded and rushed off. The four of us moved resolutely down the hall in the direction of the entrance to the courtyard.

"How could they be here so soon?" My voice was incredulous.

We entered the courtyard, which was a scene of milling people.

"The rain," Carolan said grimly. "It has kept the sun shrouded, and they have used it to their advantage."

"I should have anticipated how quickly they can travel," Clan-Fintan said, turning to face us. "Carolan, get all of the centaurs and warriors to the top of the temple wall. I do not care how badly wounded or how ill they are—tell them we have no choice."

Carolan nodded, kissed Alanna briefly and rushed away.

"Alanna," ClanFintan said. "Have the women gather all the cooking cauldrons in the temple and bring them here to the center courtyard. Then have the barrels that hold the oil for the lamps carried out of storage and brought to the courtyard, too."

"Yes, ClanFintan." She rushed off.

"Don't even think about sending me on some friggin errand, I stay with you."

"I never thought otherwise," he said as we jogged across the courtyard.

We went in the direction that would take us out through the wide walls to the rear of the temple, but instead of passing through the exit, ClanFintan followed the wall around to the left. Soon we came to a ragtag-looking group of centaurs and humans assembled at the bottom of a narrow staircase that was built into the wall itself. It led up.

Dougal stepped out of the group. Victoria was at his side. "Fomorians."

Dougal nodded. "We heard. What now?"

"Where is the sentry who notified the guard?" ClanFintan asked.

A young man stepped forward and saluted crisply.

"Report," ClanFintan ordered.

"My Lord, I was stationed at the northernmost watch point this side of the river. I heard a series of unexplained noises, so I climbed an old grandfather oak near my station. To the north, as far as I could see spread creatures with wings. I ran back with the news."

"Victoria, get your Huntresses to the top of the wall. We have need of your crossbows."

Vic and her Huntresses moved immediately to the steep stairs and began climbing to the top of the battlements. Clan-Fintan addressed the rest of the group, which was made up of members of my battered-looking guard and a third of his original legion, who were exhausted but determined.

"The women are collecting cauldrons and oil in the central courtyard. Get them up to the top of the wall. Bring torches and firewood. It may be the only way we can keep them from gaining the temple."

The warriors sprinted away, leaving us alone with Dougal.

"Let us join the Huntresses," ClanFintan said and led the way up the stairs.

It was steep going, and I had a sudden, uncomfortable flash-back to just a couple of days before when I had followed Victoria up similarly steep steps, and into disaster.

The walkway that ran the length of the wall was smooth and wider than the roof battlements at the Muses' temple had been. Epona's balustrades were thick and well placed. We went up, and the Huntresses spread out, notching their crossbows at the ready. I stood between ClanFintan and Dougal, peering with them out into the murky evening light, trying to distinguish shapes from fog and mist. Nothing moved except the rain.

Noises from our side of the wall drew our attention as the warriors clambered up the stairs, straining under the weight of the heavy cauldrons and oil barrels. We concentrated on helping the warriors while the Huntresses and centaurs kept watch for the creatures.

Between every third or fourth balustrade, smoothed-out holes had been carved into the floor of the walkway. Hanging over the holes were iron hooks that were screwed securely into the side of the marble teethlike balustrades. The warriors began filling the holes up with hot coals and firewood. Then they suspended the cauldrons from the hooks, filled the cauldrons with oil and lit the fires.

I remembered ClanFintan's words that had praised Epona's Temple as a fortress, and Carolan explaining that, unlike the Muses, Epona was a warrior goddess. So the temple itself was ready for a fight—I just hoped we had enough warriors to man her.

Soon wounded centaurs and human warriors joined us. Their faces were set in grim lines and they followed orders without comment as ClanFintan stationed them around the length of the temple wall.

I heard him ask the sentry who had originally brought word of the Fomorians to us, "What is your name, warrior?"

"Patrick," he answered.

"Does the temple have a storeroom supply of longbows and arrows?"

"Yes, my Lord."

"Get them," was ClanFintan's sober response.

Carolan joined us briefly, checking on his patients.

ClanFintan pulled him aside to give him instructions. "Have Alanna gather all of the women within the temple. Tell them to bring one pack apiece—they should each be carrying a blanket, a bladder of wine and a weapon." He paused. "Any weapon. A kitchen knife or a pair of scissors is better than nothing."

"I will tell them." Carolan hurried back down the stairs.

"ClanFintan!" Victoria's voice snapped across the battlements. "There!"

We followed her pointing finger and saw that a line of creatures was approaching the temple wall. They came from all sides, like a tightening noose. I could hear their predatory hissing in the still evening air.

"Wait until the Huntress gives the word." My husband's voice was strong and sure. "Aim for their heads or necks. As most of you know, they are difficult to kill."

The line drew closer.

I saw Victoria take aim with her crossbow. The Huntresses and the other warriors followed suit.

The line drew closer.

I could see the individual creatures. Their eyes shone with an unnatural reddish glow, and even in the low light their claws and teeth gleamed wetly.

"Now!" Victoria cried. There was a great whooshing of arrows, and the sickening sound of flesh being pierced by the deadly shafts. Many of the first line of creatures fell, but their comrades stepped over them and kept coming, oblivious to their death throes.

"Again!" Vic shouted. And the arrows thunked home.

On and on the arrows rained, but it didn't stop the Fomorian mass. Too soon, they were at the foot of the slick temple walls.

"Spill the oil!" ClanFintan gave the order, and the cauldrons were dumped onto the creatures. Those nearest the wall screeched and writhed in agony as the boiling oil scalded flesh to the bone. The others hissed and paused, not sure they should continue climbing over the bodies of the dying.

"Drop the torches!" At ClanFintan's order, warriors dropped lighted torches down onto the oil-soaked creatures, who instantly became flaming effigies of pain, blundering blindly into their living comrades, causing them, too, to catch afire. The flames spread down the temple grounds, and soon the creatures were running frantically, clawing over the top of each other to get away from the temple walls.

I looked away, unable to watch their agony.

A victorious shout went up from the warriors of the temple and their centaur allies.

"More oil." ClanFintan took no time for celebration. "Rearm your supple of arrows. They will be back."

The scent of roasting flesh wafted up from the still-flaming creatures, and I pressed my hand over my mouth and hurried down the battlement stairs. I ran, following the wall a few steps, then folded at the waist and puked what little my stomach held all over the inside of the temple wall.

When I was finished, I wiped my mouth with the back of

my hand and stepped shakily away from the mess. My insides felt as if they had been knotted together with wire, and my mouth tasted terrible.

All kidding aside, I seriously hate puking. Really.

I had come to the realization that English teachers weren't made for all-out warfare. Gang wannabes yelling obscenities at each other—yes. Girl fights outside the lockers of ex-friends started by the words "You stole my boyfriend, you ho!"—yes. Semi-innocent ninth-graders who mix clear laxative into your water bottle while you're in the hall explaining to another ninth grader why throwing balls of chewed gum up on the ceiling is going to cost him time in detention—yes.

But real war—no. I wasn't made for it. I wasn't prepared for it. I couldn't handle it. I couldn't lead people out of it. I—

You have the strength, Beloved. I tried to catch my breath and let the comfort of my Goddess's words wash over me, but I still felt inadequate. And I had puke breath.

"Rhea?" ClanFintan stepped out of the shadows. "Where did you go?"

"I was puking." I sounded like a little girl, and I didn't care.

"Come here, love." He put his arms around me and I rested against his warmth.

"Just don't kiss me—I'm sure I taste like puke."

A laugh vibrated his chest. "Perhaps we can find some wine to wash the taste from your mouth." He kissed me on the top of the head, and his arm enfolded me. We began walking across the courtyard.

"Female!" The hiss surrounded us. *"Where are you, female?"*

The sound was carrying over the wall of the temple; it was as if the words were looking for me. I stepped out of Clan-Fintan's arm and sprinted up the stairs to take my place on the battlement. Nuada was pacing back and forth at the edge of the mound of smoldering corpses. His wings were fully erect. His colorless hair flew wildly around him, and his naked body was fully visible in the oily glow of the fire.

At the sight of him, the sickness in my stomach left me, and I was filled with a goddess's vengeful anger.

"What do you want, you pathetic creature?" I spoke the words softly, but somehow Epona magically picked them up, lifted and magnified them so that they carried easily across the temple grounds.

"You, female. I want you."

"Too damn bad. You will never have me." I knew what I said was true. No matter what happened, I felt my Goddess's promise that Nuada would never possess me.

"I will!" he shrieked. I noticed his normally pale face was flushed and covered with a film of sweat. "I will have you—soon! The rest of my army joins me on the morrow." Taunting laughter followed his words. "I let them amuse themselves with the women from the other temple, but that amusement did not last long. I have higher expectations for you!" He cackled more taunting laughter at me. "Tonight make peace with your weakling Goddess, and say goodbye to that mutation you call a mate. Tomorrow you belong to me!"

I felt ClanFintan gesture to Victoria, and she tossed him her crossbow. With a motion that blurred with speed, my husband sighted the bow. The twang of the shot was followed by a shriek from Nuada as the arrow sliced the side of his head, severing his ear from his body.

Nuada's hand tried to stem the flow of blood as he whirled around and disappeared into the fading light.

"That guy needs some serious therapy," I muttered.

"Sleep in shifts." ClanFintan's voice was flat and cold as he spoke to the warriors on the battlement. "Victoria, Dougal, Patrick, find Carolan and Alanna, then meet us in Rhea's chambers. Follow me," he said bluntly to me as he went down the stairs.

We did as we were told.

I had to scramble to keep up with him, and in no time we were rushing through the door to my room. Before I could catch my breath, ClanFintan pulled me roughly into his arms and covered his mouth with mine.

I wanted to struggle and remind him I had puked not too long ago, but his heat was overpowering and I felt myself enthusiastically returning the kiss. His mouth broke away from mine, and he pressed me against his hard body.

"That creature will never possess you. I will not let it happen."

"I know, love," I murmured against his skin as his hands roamed familiarly over my body. My knees had just begun to feel weak, when two quick knocks sounded at the door.

ClanFintan reluctantly let loose my body and yelled, "Come!" as I poured myself a large glass of wine and had a seat on the chaise.

Dougal, Victoria, Carolan, Alanna and Patrick poured into the room. Without any preamble, ClanFintan faced them and announced, "We leave at dawn."

To their credit, the assembled mix of people and centaurs didn't comment. Alanna moved quickly to the side of the room. With one of her Alanna miracles, she produced six goblets and began distributing them and pouring wine. I helped.

"How?" Carolan asked the only question.

"We form a phalanx. Part of the centaurs with claymores drawn and shields at ready will form the outside of the formation." He caught Patrick's eye. "Intermingled with human warriors holding their spears at the ready." He turned to Vic. "And Huntresses firing their deadly crossbows. Within the phalanx will be the women and children. The rest of the centaurs and human warriors will form a line between the creatures and the phalanx. We will move out as the sun rises, heading into the east to greet it, and to cross the river. We will hold off the Fomorians until the women make it to the river, then we will follow them."

The room was silent.

"It is the only way. If we stay here, we are all dead."

"Many will not make it across the river." Carolan's voice was not accusatory—he was stating a fact.

"But some will make it," I spoke up. "If the creatures get into the temple, the women will face something worse than death."

"There is no way we can hold them off?" Alanna asked ClanFintan.

"No." His answer was firm. "Not indefinitely. Nuada said more creatures were joining them. We cannot chance that their numbers will swell so large that they can trap us and overrun the temple."

"Where do we go after we get to the other side of the river?" Patrick's voice sounded young and afraid.

"To safety." ClanFintan grasped the young man's shoulder. "To the Centaur Plains. There we will rebuild and return."

Patrick swallowed hard and nodded.

Terpsichore's sacrifice flashed through my mind, and I considered asking for just a couple more days to see if smallpox could affect the creatures. Then I looked closely at the people and centaurs surrounding me. What if I was wrong and a few days of waiting would cause the Fomorian trap to snap shut? I simply was not willing to risk them for a maybe.

"To a new beginning!" I said and raised my goblet.

"A new beginning!" the group repeated solemnly and we raised our glasses together.

And then we got busy.

23

"Moving has never been any friggin fun," I mumbled to myself as I plodded down the hall to my bathroom. I needed to use the facilities, and I didn't want to use the public ones (even if I knew where the hell they were). I noticed there weren't any guards stationed outside the door to my bathing chamber, which made sense. The temple was alive with activity. Everyone had a job—there was no free time to stand in front of a door and look muscular (which was, in its own way, tragic).

The misty warmth of the room enfolded me, and I tried not to think about the fact that I may never see this room after this morning. I looked around at the steaming water and the skull candleholders—I'd miss this place.

After I'd finished my private business, I wandered over to the vanity, taking a moment to uncork a fancy bottle and breathe deeply of the soapy fragrance…and it brought back an evening under a fat moon when I'd bathed in a cold pool with a centaur who was rapidly becoming my lover. And my friend.

Please, Goddess… I closed my eyes and breathed a silent prayer. Please let him live through tomorrow. The door opened, and before I turned I recognized the click of hooves on stone.

"Alanna said she saw you sneaking in this direction." I could hear his smile.

"I wasn't sneaking. I just wanted some privacy."

"Shall I leave?" he asked.

"Not privacy from you." I grinned up at him and stepped into his arms. "How do your wounds feel?"

"Better—I told you centaurs have amazing powers of recovery."

"So I have already noticed." I nipped the spot just below the middle of his breastbone, enjoying the way his muscles twitched in response. "Too bad we don't have more time." I nipped him again.

"We will—" he hugged me to him "—tomorrow and tomorrow and many tomorrows after that."

"I hope so," I said, feeling safe in the circle of his arms.

"I know so." I felt his warm lips against the top of my head. "Morale seems to be good."

"They're really brave. I'm proud of them."

The women had been working since they had been notified hours before of the new evacuation plan. Told they could only carry a wineskin, a weapon and an extra change of clothing, they had set about preparing themselves for the move with an admirable lack of whining. Now, as dawn approached, families were assembling in the courtyard, quietly readying themselves for what was to come.

No one talked about the fact that there were obviously more Fomorians than humans and centaurs, and that many members of our group were hurt or ill. Or the fact that the sun was rising into another misty, rainy day—which was good for the Fomorians but bad for us. Unfortunately, we didn't have the luxury of waiting for a sunny day. And then there was the river itself, which was several hundred yards away from the temple walls, and was wide and treacherous. Many of the women could not swim. No one talked about it. Instead, the women sat with their husbands and fathers as the men quietly hefted the lances the warriors had distributed to them, trying to get a feel for weapons most of them had never before used. There were no tears—no hysteria. No talk of death.

"I'm still worried about Epi." We had decided that she and the other mares would have the best chance at making it out of the temple and to the river if they were let loose to run at the same time the warriors departed. The creatures shouldn't be interested in horses—so, they would probably leave them alone.

Unsaid was the thought that they might serve as a distraction, allowing the phalanx time to get closer to the river.

"She is fast and smart. She will make it to the river."

I nodded against his chest and sent up another plea to the Goddess for her to watch after the mare.

"I want you to know something." I pulled back so that I could look into his eyes. "You've made me very happy. You are everything I ever wanted in a husband."

He tapped the tip of my nose with his finger. "As I have already told you, I was born to love you."

"I think that's amazing." My eyes widened as I realized, "Hey! It's magic."

He laughed and bent to claim my lips, kissing me thoroughly.

Two knocks sounded on the door to the bathing chamber, and Alanna breezed in.

"ClanFintan, Victoria is asking for you. She wants to know exactly where you want her Huntresses stationed." She glanced at me. "And I need to get my Lady ready for our trip."

I could see Alanna was putting on a brave face, and I smiled in response.

"It's always the appropriate time for proper accessorizing," I said.

"Do not take long," he said as I pulled him down to kiss his cheek before he left.

The door clicked shut and I took Alanna's hand as a sudden idea sprang into my head.

"Dress me in something that shines!"

She looked confused. "Rhea, I do not think that is very wise. Nuada will be looking for you, you should not be easily seen."

"There are more important things than Nuada."

"Yes, keeping you from him is more important," she said simply.

"Listen, you have been telling me since I got to this world that Epona's Chosen is the leader of her people, spiritual and otherwise. Right?"

She looked a little trapped, but nodded.

"Well, how can a leader hide and expect her people to be brave and confident?"

"But you cannot be taken. That would devastate your people." She sounded shaky.

"I have no intention of being taken."

She looked doubtful.

"Alanna, do you truly believe I am Epona's Chosen? And I mean me, Shannon Parker, not someone who is only pretending to be Rhiannon." I watched her closely as she answered.

"Yes, I truly believe it." She didn't hesitate.

"So do I," I said slowly, realizing once and for all that I did believe it. "I need to be there for the people, and I believe Epona will protect me."

She still had a scared-rabbit look, so I added, "How about this—dress me in something that shines, but give me a dark cloak. I'll cover myself unless I'm needed."

A look of relief passed across her pretty face as she nodded in agreement and quickly began rummaging through the nearest wardrobe, discarding one silky outfit after another. I busied myself taking off the clothes I wore already.

"Yes!" Alanna squealed in delight. "Here it is."

She turned to me, holding a spectacular piece of material in her hands. I gasped with delight, and I couldn't stop my hands from reaching out and stroking it. The silk was unusually heavy and thick—it felt like cloth that had been made from a waterfall of copper gilded with gold. Within the fabric were sewn tiny crystal jewels, which caught the candlelight and flickered back a rainbow of fiery color.

"It's amazing," I breathed delightedly, holding out my arms so Alanna could begin her magic.

The dress wrapped around my torso in an attractive crisscross pattern. The skirt part of the outfit was long, and fell gracefully to the floor. I sat obediently and let Alanna comb out my hair. When she began the French knot of steel, I stopped her.

"Just pull it back with a tie."

"It may come loose and get in your way." She was confused by my request.

I shrugged my shoulders in a nonchalant way. "When *isn't* it in my way?"

Before she could answer, a knock sounded at the door.

"Come in!" I yelled.

"My Lady." One of my warriors stepped into the room. "ClanFintan asked me to tell you the time is now."

"Thank you. Tell him I am coming."

He hurried away and Alanna tied my hair loosely back. I set my coronet snugly on my head while she turned back to another wardrobe, from which she emerged carrying a long, drab, gray poncho-like cloak, complete with cowled hood.

"Oh, please. Rhiannon wore *that?*" Didn't seem her style; definitely wasn't mine, either.

"Only when she was going somewhere she didn't want to be recognized." Alanna helped me on with the mousy cloak. Then she stood back and surveyed her work. "You look covered." She sounded satisfied.

"Good, let's go." We walked to the door and headed out to the front courtyard. I took her hand. "No matter what happens, get to the river."

Her frightened gaze flitted to me, but before she could respond we stepped out into a mass of people.

The phalanx had been formed in the courtyard and stretched through the grassy area between the outside wall and the temple. The outermost ring was made up of centaur warriors interspersed with my human guard. Each of them carried wicked-looking long swords in one hand, and shields in the other. The next ring was made up of men who looked determined but out of place holding various weapons—everything from claymores to daggers. They were obviously the grandfathers, fathers, brothers and sons of the women in the inner ring. My heart squeezed as I watched the women standing quietly. Between comforting babies and watching toddlers, they sent encouraging looks and confident smiles to the men surrounding them.

"Hail Epona!" ClanFintan's strong voice greeted me, and the phalanx turned, echoing his words.

"Hail Epona!"

My husband reached my side and raised my palm to his lips. I felt very calm as I said, "I would like to bless the people before we go."

"Of course, Beloved of Epona." He bowed his head and graciously stepped aside. The temple grew still.

"We each have one life to live, one little gleam of time between two eternities, no second chances, no 'I'll go back and relive tomorrows.'" My voice carried like I was speaking into a microphone as it was enhanced by the tangible presence of my Goddess. "Life isn't about pain or pleasure—it is about the serious business of living authentically, and the magic that can happen between moments—" I glanced at my husband and smiled "—and between souls. Today let us walk boldly and bravely into the light, because just as surely as there are beasts and demons out there, so there is goodness and love in here." I swept my arm around me in an arch, including all of them. "Epona will be close to us on our journey. Darkness cannot cover a flame, so let us be flames!"

The people answered in a roar that was a single voice. Then ClanFintan stepped forward.

"The phalanx will move out when the Huntress gives word that we have taken our position between you and the Fomorians." He nodded and Victoria moved to the entrance to the top of the wall, disappearing briefly, then reappearing atop the battlement. "When we are in position, the outer ring of the phalanx will lead you through the temple gates. Do not hesitate. Do not stop. Your single goal is to make it to the river. When you cross it you will be safe. Then we will follow you. May Epona go with you."

The people nodded and turned quietly to face the temple gates.

"You must put yourself in the middle of them." He spoke softly to me.

"I thought you were going to lead us." I knew I had to be brave for my people, but the thought of him being surrounded by the entire Fomorian army was making my chest hurt.

"Victoria will lead you; I must stay with the other centaurs." He pulled me into his arms and whispered, "I will join you across the river."

"Please stay safe." My voice shook.

His kiss was hard and fast. Then he whirled and was gone.

Alanna took my hand in hers.

"Come," she said.

The phalanx parted, allowing us to move to the exact center where, I was pleased to see, Tarah and Kristianna stood bravely beside Carolan. He kissed his wife and greeted me.

"ClanFintan insisted I stay in the center. He said I must remain safe so that I can save him from Victoria's needlework."

I tried to come up with a pithy reply, but in actuality I was relieved when Victoria's voice cut through the need for any further words.

"The centaurs have left the rear of the temple and are moving out across the grounds." She was looking intently to the north. "The mares have been loosed." She paused. "They are in position—ClanFintan has signaled. Begin moving out!" The ring of warriors started forward as Victoria left the wall and galloped to the front of their ranks.

The pace increased steadily as the front of the phalanx passed through the safety of the temple walls. By the time those of us in the center of the phalanx departed the temple, we were jogging.

What had started out as a foggy, rainy dawn was rapidly becoming a clear, warm morning. I was pleased to see the distinct outline of the sun above and in front of us. Please, Goddess, I prayed, let it burn off all of this fog and be a serious hot pain in the ass (or wherever) to the Fomorians. I craned my head around to the left, trying to get a glimpse of the battlefield, but between the last vestiges of the fog and the tight ring of warriors, I couldn't see anything.

But soon I realized that didn't matter, because I could hear. Sounds of shrieks and snarls drifted eerily over the treeless temple grounds.

"Keep moving!" Victoria shouted when the women reacted to the noise by faltering in their steady jog.

"Come on." I took up Vic's encouragement and called to the women surrounding me. "We'll be fine—just keep up with the warriors."

Then the sound of hooves thundered through the dissipating mist, and as the last of the fog lifted, the herd of terrified mares galloped into view. They milled around, white-eyed and uncertain, when they saw us.

"Do you see Epi?" I yelled above the din, trying to pick her out from the sea of moving horses.

"No!" Carolan answered.

Then my eyes widened in horror as a dark, winged shape came into view. Then another, and another. They mowed through the terrified horses, slashing and clawing. Somewhere behind me one of the girls screamed, and that piercing cry carried across the field. I could see Fomorian heads swivel in our direction, and they left off the slaughter of the horses and began their gliding run toward us.

"Forward! Move!" I shouted in my best teacher voice, and our group surged forward. Another screech drew my attention back to the battlefield, and I looked over my shoulder in time to see a centaur warrior chase down and hack the head from one of the creatures pursuing us.

"They've broken through the centaur ranks, but the warriors are in pursuit." Carolan's voice was grim.

I tried to move forward while keeping part of my attention focused on what was happening behind us. The mares were still panicked, and they milled around haphazardly. More Fomorians were coming after us, but now I could plainly see the line of centaur warriors. They were still battling the Fomorian army, and attempting to pursue single creatures as they broke through. But they couldn't catch them all. And the dark winged shapes were gaining on us.

"Where is the damn river?" I yelled to Alanna.

"We are not yet halfway there." Her face was white.

"Huntresses, fall out and arm your bows!" Victoria's calm voice ordered, and five magnificent Huntresses stepped fluidly out of the phalanx, notching their crossbows as they moved. "Sight and fire at will." The ping of loosed arrows, and the shrieks of wounded Fomorians followed her words.

"Warriors, shields up!" The ring of men and centaurs around us responded instantly, temporarily blocking our view of the converging creatures.

The first creatures reached the phalanx, and our ranks responded with a violence that rippled through our group. Through breaks in the shielding men, I was able to catch glimpses of single creatures as they struck at our warriors. When a Fomorian fell, another stepped over him and assumed his place.

We kept moving forward.

I saw the familiar figure of Victoria firing off arrows quickly, each finding its deadly mark. Between loading and shooting, her attention suddenly wavered, and she met my gaze.

"Get them to the river or we will be overrun!" she shouted at me. Her face was set in stone and she was already spattered with gore. She was a silver goddess of death.

My attention was wrenched from her as a creature clawed his way through the men in front of us. Carolan pushed me aside and met it with a borrowed claymore. It seemed as if it happened in slow motion. Carolan parried the creature's razorlike talons, and the thing grabbed the Healer's sword arm. Ramming himself forward into the creature, Carolan shoved it off balance, and with a sweeping motion brought his sword up, then back and down, slicing through the Fomorian's exposed neck.

Alanna covered her face with her hands, sobbing, and Tarah

and Kristianna clung to each of my hands. I couldn't take my eyes from the decapitated creature. Neither could Carolan. We stood there, paralyzed in the center of a world of chaos.

Look, Beloved. Understand what you are seeing whispered through my mind, and I blinked in shock.

"There are sores on its body!" My excited exclamation made Alanna uncover her face.

"That is it!" Carolan yelled. "That is why it was so much weaker than I expected. They have the pox."

And then the suspended moment in time came to an end, and our group was stumbling forward again. More and more dark shapes joined fallen comrades as the warriors struggled to keep their women safe. I could see that the Fomorians were easier to kill—that the disease had obviously weakened them. But there were still simply too many of them.

With a detached sense of calm, I realized that we would not make it to the river, that we were actually still closer to the temple than to the water. Logic said we should return to the safety of Epona's walls. But we couldn't, at least not without more help.

Then you shall have more help. The Goddess's words sounded clearly inside my head.

Through the confused haze of battle, I caught a flash of silver. Not the silver of Vic's sleek hair, or the pale, dead silver of the Fomorians, but the otherworldly silver of an ethereal mare.

"Epi!" I cried as I saw her circling around our phalanx as she tried to catch a glimpse of me.

Call her, Beloved. Without conscious thought, I obeyed by lifting my fingers to my lips and splitting the air with a sharp Okie whistle.

Epi's head jerked up in response and she galloped purposefully toward me.

I started shoving my way to her, yelling, "Let her through!" to the warriors in front of me. The phalanx parted and my mare slid to a stop in front of me, blowing hard.

Mount her, Beloved, and see how the Chosen of a Goddess triumphs.

I looked around hastily and found—not to my surprise—Alanna running to join me.

"Alanna! Help me to get up on Epi." I turned and grabbed a fistful of shining mane.

"What are you doing?" she asked as she took my bent knee in her hands and boosted me up.

"Getting help," I replied, finding my seat easily. "I want you to get the women and children back inside the temple grounds."

She started to interrupt and I stopped her.

"No. Trust me—and trust my Goddess. Lead them home."

She closed her mouth and nodded solemnly. "I trust you. Both of you." Then she began calling the women and children to her, shouting that Epona wanted us to return to the temple. Soon she had the attention of the warriors. From the corner of my vision, I saw Alanna run to Victoria, grabbing her arm and earnestly motioning back toward the temple walls. I met Victoria's gaze long enough to nod my agreement, then the Huntress's voice joined Alanna's and the phalanx began shifting direction.

I pulled my attention from Alanna and what was happening around me. Instead, I listened to my heart, or maybe, more accurately, my soul.

Look, Beloved.

My eyes scanned the horizon, squinting over the heads of bloody creatures and warriors, turning Epi in a tight circle. As the western horizon came into view, my eyes widened and my breath caught.

Woulff and McNamara come.

The human warriors! A thick line of them stretched across the western edge of the temple grounds. Still far away, the sun bounced off their shields, glinting with a teasing distant beauty. But even as my heart raced with joy, I understood that they were too far away, that they would not make it to us in time. Our group would be overrun. We were trapped between the solid safety of the temple and the liquid safety of the river.

Call them, Beloved. Only you can.

And I knew why I was there. As unbelievable and miraculous as it seemed, I was in that world at the behest of a Goddess, chosen to take the place of a selfish, spoiled woman. Ten years of leading young people had readied me for this job—the people who surrounded me belonged to me. And I to them.

And I needed no further prompting from my Goddess.

Quickly, I drew the drab robe over my head, pulling the tie from my hair with it. Burying my fingers in my wild curls, I shook them until they were electrified, framing my face like a lion's mane.

Looking around me, I noticed a young farm boy who bravely clutched a claymore.

"Boy!" His eyes were large and round as he looked at me. "Give me your sword."

Without hesitation he rushed to me, offering the handle of the long sword. It felt heavy and solid in my hand, and with a surprising rush of pleasure I lifted it over my head, squeezed Epi's sides with my knees and leaned forward over her slick neck. The men around us parted in surprise as the mare sprang forward. As we broke free of the battling group I felt a sliver of hot morning sunlight touch first the shaft of the sword, and then my body, sending an electrified field of energy through me. I glanced down to see the molten fabric of my dress sparkling in the sunlight as if it had been cut from a jewel and faceted by angels for a fairy queen. I glowed with the same magic that had placed the stars in my footprints.

The ground in front of me came to a soft rise, and Epi galloped atop the small hill. Facing the distant line of human warriors, with my back to the battle, I pulled the mare to a halt. With the sword still held high above me, I pulled back hard on Epi's mane, gripping her sides with my thighs. The mare obeyed my thoughts and reared gracefully up, trumpeting a challenge across the field.

"*TO ME!*" I yelled, and my voice swelled with the same Goddess-enhanced quality it had had when I called ClanFintan from the edge of the marsh. "*WOULFF AND McNAMARA, COME TO ME!*" I pulled on Epi again, and she responded with another amazing trumpet as she reared in the air.

Even from there, I heard the voices of the distant warriors rise as one.

"Epona! To Epona!"

Their line sprinted forward with redoubled speed. I swung my sword in a glittering arch as Epi pranced from side to side.

"*TO ME, WOULFF!*" The passion in my voice vibrated across the field.

Woulff's warriors growled their battle cry in reply as their line rushed forward.

"*TO ME, McNAMARA!*" I could feel my hair crackling in the air around me as the cry shot from my lips.

McNamara's battle cry joined Woulff's, and they narrowed the distance between us in a charge that would have made the Duke proud.

Then the warriors behind me took up the cry, and I felt the renewed strength of their drive to the temple. Glancing over my shoulder, I was just in time to see a snarling Fomorian descending upon me.

"Epi!" I screamed. The mare spun around, lashing out and

catching the sensitive edge of the creature's right wing in her teeth. She jerked her head back, ripping the membrane from the thing's back. The creature shrieked in agony, and was off balance long enough for me to swing the heavy sword down with both hands, slicing him from the top of his shoulder to midway down his chest. Then the weight of its body tore the sword from my hands as the creature fell to the ground.

Almost instantly another creature scrambled atop his fallen companion's body. All I could do was hold on as Epi's teeth and hooves flashed in the morning light.

It seemed the mare battled on that small hill for time unending, but my mind knew logically that only minutes had passed before dark, winged shapes completely surrounded us.

"Leave them to me!" a familiar voice hissed. The creatures parted, allowing the blood-drenched figure of Nuada to cautiously approach our hill. "Female," he sneered, "how *kind* of you to set yourself apart from the others and to wait so patiently for me."

Epi stirred restlessly under me. As Nuada glided closer, she squealed a warning at him.

"It seems your friend is not as eager to see me." He laughed horribly.

"Rhea!" my husband's voice roared, and I looked up to see him in a flat run toward our hill.

Nuada saw him, too.

"Kill the mare," he ordered as he turned to meet ClanFintan's charge. "Quickly."

The circle of creatures around us hissed in pleasure and began to tighten, like a closing noose. Eyes flashing, Epi spun around, keeping the creatures wary of her hooves and teeth. But our hill had become slick with blood, and I felt a sickening lurch as Epi missed her footing and fell suddenly to her knees. The movement was unexpected, and I could not stop my body's momentum from the spin. I flew over the mare's neck, landing hard on the wet ground. A bolt of white pain blinded me as my head snapped against the cold hilt of a sword. Blackness as suffocating as an avalanche washed over me.

There was no pleasurable DreamLand interlude. Unconsciousness was complete and overwhelming as my conscious mind retreated deep within me, where only the voice of a Goddess could awaken it.

Come, Beloved, you cannot rest yet. He needs you.

My soul responded to the insistent call and I felt my spirit body lift with a sickening wave of vertigo from my crumpled body. At first I was unable to focus clearly. The battle below me was just a mass of unrecognizable red-tinged characters.

Concentrate, the Goddess whispered. I breathed slowly and tried to blink away the blurring of my vision. And abruptly the scene beneath me swam into focus.

Several members of my personal guard had joined Epi, and they were successfully battling the group of Fomorians. Relieved, my attention shifted to a scene being played out several yards away from any of the other warriors or creatures. ClanFintan and Nuada were circling each other warily. My spirit body floated over to where they fought. Both males were covered in blood and sweat. New blood was pouring from the arrow wound on the side of Nuada's head, and several angry-looking slashes made his wings look frayed and raw. I floated closer and noticed that what I assumed at first to be blood was really a scarlet rash that covered his torso. But as he lashed out at ClanFintan, and his deadly talons raked across the centaur's left shoulder, I realized that the disease had not yet affected his strength.

ClanFintan had lost his claymore, and he was fighting off

Nuada's increasingly wild advances with only a dagger and his hooves.

"Get out of my way, mutant horse, I wish to claim the body of your bride," Nuada hissed.

"Never." Instead of angering him, Nuada's words seemed to have a strangely calming effect on ClanFintan. He fought on methodically, not giving ground but also not finding any new openings in the creature's defenses.

"You know, horse man, she will welcome me." Nuada's voice lashed out with his claws. Neither found their mark.

"Never," ClanFintan's deep voice repeated.

"*If* she still lives," Nuada continued.

The new words did have an effect on the centaur. He lunged forward suddenly, and Nuada leaped to meet him. The two males locked together, Nuada's razor-edged teeth inches from ClanFintan's neck, while the centaur's dagger hovered just above the Fomorian's prominent jugular vein.

My body sank lower until it was floating just above and to the side of my husband. I wasn't going to watch another man I loved be killed by those things.

In the middle of my thought I felt the tremor that passed through my body as it became semivisible. I mentally crossed my fingers that I was doing the right thing.

"*Hey, Nuada. Am I what you're looking for, big boy?*" I called seductively to the Fomorian.

At the sound of my voice Nuada's head snapped up, his concentration wavering from ClanFintan for an instant. I watched as my husband's hand broke from the creature's grasp and the dagger sliced neatly through the pulsing vein on the side of Nuada's neck. I could clearly see the look of disbelief pass over Nuada's twisted features as he slipped on his own blood and fell to the ground. ClanFintan reared up, his wet hooves glistening above the creature's body.

"Never," my husband's voice rasped harshly as he came down again and again, smashing Nuada's evil into nothingness.

A shout below me caused me to look from the gory scene in time to see the armies of Woulff and McNamara joining our warriors. The centaurs and humans merged into a single force, and with a shared mind they began decimating the weakened Fomorian army.

A wave of dizziness passed over me, and I suddenly found it hard to breathe.

"Rhea!" ClanFintan's voice sounded a long way off.

"I can't…" I felt myself inexorably pulled back to my fallen body. As I was sucked down, my eyes fluttered open long enough to see ClanFintan rushing to me and gathering me in his arms.

"Hold on," he said as my vision darkened. "I am taking you home."

And then I knew nothing more.

24

As evening fell the wind shifted, and I gave thanks to my Goddess. For three days the stench of burning bodies had permeated the temple, which hadn't helped to soothe the enormous pain in my head. Carolan had assured me the lump on my left temple was only the size of a cockerel's stone (translation: a rooster's testicle—who knew?), but I was pretty sure it was the size of a mutated grapefruit, and it sported a veritable rainbow of bruised colors. Anyway, the consensus was that I would recover with all of my wits. Well, thank God(dess).

The Fomorians had been killed by the thousands. Our combined armies had rallied and the creatures, already weakened by smallpox, could not stand before their power.

Carolan hypothesized that because the Fomorians were humanoid, but not actually *human,* their bodies were exceptionally susceptible to the disease. Their incubation time was less than ours, and the disease progressed more rapidly with them. By the evening of the battle the scene outside the temple was something straight out of the old horror flick *Night of the Living Dead.* At least, that's how Victoria described it to me (not that she'd actually seen the movie). I had still been drifting in and out of the Concussion Land of Puke and See Double, so I only got a secondhand description. Vic said the creatures literally began rending the flesh from their bones with their own claws. They quit fighting. Each appeared to be in a world of his own, locked in some kind of agony with his own skin as his claws raked across already battle-bloodied flesh to gouge and tear mercilessly. She explained that the battle had been reduced to our warriors raining arrows down upon the agonized Fomorians as the Huntresses ended their misery.

"If we had allowed them to suffer," Victoria had said afterward, "we would be no better than them." So the battle had ended with the sounds of mercy.

There was still the question of what could be done to help the women who were carrying Fomorian fetuses, but Carolan was working diligently on that problem. By the time the women from Guardian Castle arrived, he assured us he would be ready for them.

"Jeesh, I'm tired of staying in bed," I muttered to myself. And it wasn't even a good kind of romantic interlude in bed with my handsome husband. It was a rest-my-big-head-and-take-lots-of-boring-naps kind of interlude.

Gingerly, I sat up, hoping the puking and spinning had stopped. Other than the ever-present splitting headache, I seemed fine.

So I stood up.

Well, maybe semi-fine would be a better description. I don't normally feel each beat of my heart in my head. Carefully, I walked to my floor-to-ceiling windows and opened one of the doorlike glass panes. The evening was beautiful and warm. Still being careful, I stepped out into my private garden and took a deep breath of the fresh scent of the honeysuckle bushes that were blooming all around its perimeter. (Note to self: ask one of my nymphs to cut a bouquet of these for my bedroom.)

"Lady Rhiannon!" a little voice chirped.

Thinking of nymphs had obviously conjured one, and I watched as the girl walked shyly across the garden to curtsy deeply before me.

"Tarah!" I reached out and gave her a hug that made her lovely face flush with pleasure.

"My Lady!" She returned my embrace enthusiastically before continuing, "The stable maidens sent me to inquire if you were well enough to come to the stable." Her smile widened. "The child, Kristianna, is ready for her ride on Epona."

"That sounds wonderful. Tell them I'm on my way."

"I'm pleased to see you have recovered, my Lady," she said, seeming reluctant to leave my side.

"And I'm glad to see you're better, too." Most of the scabs had already dropped off her face and arms, and I could see that she had been lucky. Except for a few marks that would fade over time, she would recover fully from her illness.

"Thank you, my Lady. I am anxious to return to my duties." She shyly turned her head to the side, and I was entranced by the unexpected view of her profile. The girl suddenly reminded me so strongly of Terpsichore that I felt my eyes fill with tears.

"Honey, have you ever considered a future in dance?"

Color flooded her face as she answered, barely holding in check her youthful enthusiasm, "Oh, my Lady, dance is all that I dream about!"

With an intuitive feeling I knew the martyred Muse would approve of this young replica.

"Don't rush it—but when you're feeling strong again, come see me. And we will talk more about your dreams."

I let her chatter gaily as we walked across the garden to the exit that would lead her in the direction of the stables.

"Remember," I called after her as she scampered ahead of me to announce that "Epona's Chosen comes," "see me when you are strong again."

"Oh, I will, my Lady!"

"Thinking of helping Thalia rebuild the Muses?" ClanFintan's velvet voice came from the shadows.

"Actually, I was thinking more about Terpsichore and what she would want," I said thoughtfully.

I tilted my head and watched him walk out of the shadows toward me. The gentle light of evening was kind to a face and form that had no need of the favor. His powerful muscles rippled smoothly, and his recent wounds gave him a decidedly bad-boy appearance.

He brushed an errant curl back from my face.

"Please don't ask me how I'm feeling, or order me back to bed." I realized I might have been sounding a little grumpy.

"You seem to be standing and walking straight." He leaned a little closer and sniffed at my face. "And it does not appear you have been throwing up."

"No, damnit, I haven't puked for an entire day." Now I knew I sounded grumpy.

But my mood didn't seem to put ClanFintan off.

"So, what *have* you been doing?" He sounded mischievous.

"I've been thinking about sending for Mariad so that Alanna can start training an assistant."

He gave me a quizzical look.

"So she's not so dang busy. Then she and Carolan can have more time *together*." I held up my hands like I was framing a picture. "I see…three little girls in their future."

He stepped closer and wrapped his arms around my waist, lifting my feet off the ground and pulling me firmly against him.

"And what do you see for our future?" His voice had

deepened to the erotic tone I knew so well, and had been missing the past several nights.

"I see—" I nibbled on his earlobe, thinking that maybe a romp with my husband would be the cure for my headache "—a Change coming on tonight."

He chuckled and kissed me quickly, slipping his arm under my butt and shifting my position in his arms so that I wasn't dangling haphazardly. "I meant about *our* future children."

"Children!" I squeaked through the pounding in my head.

"Of course," his chest rumbled. "We certainly have not been celibate."

"But—" I sputtered.

"In that old world of yours did they not teach how babies are made?" He peered in mock seriousness into my face.

"But—" I repeated. "What will it be?"

"Boy or girl?" he asked, suddenly all innocence.

I thumped him soundly on his hard chest. "Horse or human?"

"Well…" He smiled down at me and kissed me on the forehead. "Whatever it is, it will certainly have the makings of an excellent equestrian."

I let my hand slide between us so that it rested on my (relatively) flat stomach. I thought I felt a fluttering beneath my palm, and my hand jerked away like I'd received an electrical charge.

"A baby?" My voice was more than a little shaky.

"Perhaps you are feeling the promise of what is to come." He hugged me against him; I loved the way his warmth engulfed me.

"The promise of the future," I said.

"*Our* future," he corrected me.

"*Our* future," I repeated. "I like that."

"As do I, Shannon," he whispered against my lips. "As do I."

★ ★ ★ ★ ★